PRAISE FOR **LES ROBERTS** AND
THE MILAN JACOVICH MYSTERY SERIES:

"A clever plot, a vibrant Cleveland and rural Ohio setting, and a realistically drawn hero make this series one to watch. It exudes much the same sort of charm as the early Spenser novels did."
—Booklist (on Pepper Pike)

"Roberts handles the private-eye format with aplomb and takes full advantage of his Cleveland scene . . . Best of all is his Slovenian sleuth, vulnerable and fallible, whom we are likely (and would like) to see more of."
—San Diego Union (Pepper Pike)

"Fast-paced and smoothly narrated."
—Washington Post Book World (Full Cleveland)

"Another smooth page-turner from Roberts, who keeps the action moving and still fits in some wry observations on parenthood, teenagers, and marriage."
—Kirkus Reviews (Deep Shaker)

"Roberts combines a strong character and a clever plot with the ethnic diversity that Cleveland provides. He proves that Midwest private eyes can hold their own with the best ones from either coast."
—Des Moines Register (Deep Shaker)

"There's an affection for Cleveland and an insistence on its ethnic, working-class life that gives vividness to the detection. Roberts writes with sharp wit, creates action scenes that are drawn with flair, and puts emotional life into a range of people."
—Washington Post Book World (The Cleveland Connection)

"Roberts is one of the best crime writers around, and *The Cleveland Connection* is his best effort yet. The plot has all the right ingredients—danger, suspense, intrigue, action—in all the right amounts; Milan Jacovich is the kind of guy we want on our side when the chips are down; and Roberts even makes Cleveland sound like a swell place to live. Don't miss this one."
—Booklist

"Packed with unusual heroes, villains, and political twists and turns . . . a mystery that defies predictability."
—Midwest Book Review (The Lake Effect)

"A real treat . . . If you've somehow missed this series, definitely give it a try . . . If you're already a fan, this book will delight you even further.
—Mystery News (The Lake Effect)

"A corker of a whodunit . . . Gritty, grim, humorous, sentimental—a perfect 10."
                                   —Chicago Sun-Times (The Duke of Cleveland)

"Roberts affectionately weaves in the history and rich ethnic mix of Milan Jacovich's Cleveland turf."
                                   —Publishers Weekly (Collision Bend)

"Roberts is a wordsmith of high order, and *Collision Bend* is a terrific novel of the mean streets."
                                   —Meritorious Mysteries

"Roberts certainly creates a sense of place. Cleveland rings true—and he's especially skillful in creating real moral and ethical choices for his characters."
                                   —The Plain Dealer (The Cleveland Local)

"Jacovich [is] one of the most fully realized characters in modern crime fiction . . . Roberts is a confident writer who knows his character well and who has made him complex enough to be interesting."
                                   —Mostly Murder (The Cleveland Local)

"A series that gets better and better . . . strongly recommended for those who like their detectives cut from the classic mold."
                                   —Booklist (A Shoot in Cleveland)

"[Milan Jacovich] is a hero one can't help but like. Roberts's polished prose, inventive plots, and pleasantly low-key style add extra appeal to his long-running series."
                                   —Booklist (The Best-Kept Secret)

"Page turner of the week . . . narrative comfort food . . . a nifty spin on a classic P.I. formula."
                                   —People magazine (The Indian Sign)

"Brilliantly plotted, with a powerhouse climax."
                                   —Booklist (The Dutch)

"[A] roller coaster ride of a mystery . . . Roberts speeds the reader through an investigation offering plenty of delicious twists and turns without ever compromising credibility."
                                   —Publishers Weekly (The Irish Sports Pages)

"An enjoyable whodunit with a deep realistic look at Cleveland now and a nostalgic surreal look at the city in the 1960s though the distorted lens of memories."
                                   —Midwest Book Review (King of the Holly Hop)

"Solid prose and a consistent hard edge."
                                   —Publishers Weekly (The Cleveland Creep)

"A fast paced and riveting read of fiction . . . a much recommended addition to mystery and thriller collections."
                                   —Midwest Book Review (Whiskey Island)

WIN, PLACE,
OR DIE

For Cary Ann —
from Cleveland with love,

WIN, PLACE, OR DIE

A MILAN JACOVICH/ KEVIN O'BANNION MYSTERY

LES ROBERTS

WITH DAN S. KENNEDY

Les Roberts

— 2013 —

GRAY & COMPANY, PUBLISHERS
CLEVELAND

Gray & Company, Publishers
www.grayco.com

Library of Congress Cataloging-in-Publication Data
Roberts, Les,
Win, place, or die : a Milan Jacovich/Kevin O'Bannion mystery / Les Roberts, with Dan S. Kennedy.
pages cm
1. Jacovich, Milan (Fictitious character)—Fiction. 2. Private
investigators—Ohio—Cleveland—Fiction. 3. Sports stories.
I. Kennedy, Dan S. II. Title.
PS3568.O23894W55 2013
813'.54—dc23
2013018576
ISBN: 978-1-938441-37-0

Printed in the United States of America
First printing

For Ann Elder, with thanks—
a long-time West Coast pal and radio and
Internet film review partner, though we
never go to the movies together.

WIN, PLACE, OR DIE

PROLOGUE

MILAN

A nd they're off and racing!"

That's how the track announcer always begins the race at Northcoast Downs in a suburb south of Cleveland. I'd never heard it before that particular evening, but this was the beginning of the fifth race, and I was getting used to his call. It was my first time watching a harness race—unique, different from a horse race like the Kentucky Derby. I was as oblivious to this sport as I was about curling or croquet, but I was having a good time anyway. Leaning forward in my chair, watching horses and racing bikes pound around the track, I rooted for number six; I couldn't even remember the horse's name, nor the driver's, but I'd bet five bucks on number six to win and that's what interested me most.

I'd been to horse races before. I'm no gambler, except on pro football games—which is usually *not* a winning proposition here in Cleveland. I'd visited a thoroughbred track, Thistledown, in Cleveland's eastern suburbs. But I don't get out of Northeast Ohio much, not counting my Vietnam tour in the 1970s, so I haven't been to any other tracks.

Northcoast Downs was all about harness racing, though. It opened in 1957, and has gone from featuring races only a few months per year to more than two hundred events all year long. I can't imagine horses running races in Cleveland's January snow, but they do.

I've learned that Northcoast isn't just a place to watch races; it's a family-oriented entertainment venue—much more so than

Cleveland Browns Stadium, which was built for the enlighten-
ment of macho football fans—with a supervised facility in which
younger kids can hang out and play while mommy and daddy
watch and wager. Gigantic television sets all over the place show
racing at many other tracks outside Ohio—a perq for dedicated
gamblers—as well as other sports like basketball, even though
one can't legally bet on a basketball game at a racetrack. Several
bars and snack counters are scattered around, and before the
races began we ate dinner up in the white-collar clubhouse. Not
much diversity on the menu, but most of the diners, who have
their own TV sets at their tables, look a little bit dressed up for
the occasion.

On this brisk October evening, I'd been invited to join a former
client of mine, Glenn Gallagher. He owned an investment banking firm in the Key Tower, Cleveland's tallest and most impos-
ing skyscraper. Months earlier he'd engaged my company, Milan
Security, to run exhaustive investigations on all his top-level employees because one of them—he didn't know who—was ripping
off his wealthier investors to the tune of seven figures. I'd discovered, contrary to Gallagher's hopes, it wasn't true; one of his
rainmakers was the crook. The thief was fired, then indicted. My
company earned a handsome bonus, and Gallagher and I began
one of those relationships uneasily situated between friend and
acquaintance. He urged me to bring my assistant to an evening
at Northcoast Downs to toast our good fortunes.

In addition to the high-money, high-risk business that had
made him a multimillionaire, Glenn owned a large stable of
horses, both at Northcoast Downs and at several other tracks
around the country, and went to a great deal of trouble and effort
to secure his professional racing license so he could drive them in
races himself. On this particular evening he wasn't driving, so he
joined us in the clubhouse to enjoy food and drinks and to excite
us all about the sport of harness racing.

The "us" includes my young, eager private-eye-in-training,
who'd worked with me for several months, Kevin O'Bannion. He
prefers being called K.O., and not just because they were his initials. K.O.'s addition to Milan Securities in early summer marked

the first time in my entire life I'd ever had an actual employee, one who gets a paycheck and deductions and medical insurance every week. It was also K.O.'s first job, other than several years he'd spent in the United States Army, including three combat tours in Iraq and Afghanistan. His military job description: kill people before they kill you.

When Glenn Gallagher had dropped by my office to invite us to Northcoast, K.O. was his usual surly self. His late teens had been spent in juvenile detention because he'd attacked and nearly killed two neighbor kids who'd caught a stray dog on the street and cooked him alive in their backyard Weber Kettle for the fun of it. As a result, K.O.'s hot-button temper boiled over about anything remotely resembling animal abuse.

"Why would I watch horses getting beaten with a whip?" he asked when Gallagher extended the invitation. "Who in his right mind would like that and not get pissed off?"

I winced. One doesn't fly in the face of one's well-paying client and question his ethics. But Gallagher took the query seriously.

"A better question, K.O.," he said, "is why anyone in his right mind wanting to make money with winning horses would abuse them? Like in any sport, these horses are well-trained athletes, and are groomed, fed, and treated very well indeed."

"Nobody ever whips a football player," K.O. pointed out. "I hate those goddamn horsewhips."

"Well, a driver mostly uses that whip to hit the saddle pad or the wheel disk to get the horse's attention and make him focus. Sure, horses are hit sometimes, but if he's running slow and a whip doesn't make him speed up, there's no point in hitting him again. And if a driver or trainer uses the whip too often, or too hard, we do something to stop it. There *are* sadists who enjoy hurting animals; enjoy hurting people, too. But they're rare in horse racing, and when they're caught, they're reported."

"Sickos!"

"Sure they are, but you can't tell everybody they can't own a dog or a horse because a tiny group of them enjoy cruelty."

"Or a cat," I added; K.O. lived with a gray cat named Rodney and would gladly lay down his life for him.

"Most of us in this business love horses," Glenn said. "Why would we be here otherwise? Caring about horses is what got us into racing in the first place."

"Yeah," K.O. argued, "but some of those harnesses and bits and stuff hurt them."

"It doesn't hurt them, exactly," Glenn said. "Sometimes it's a little uncomfortable—to remind them they should run where they're supposed to and not take off over the fence somewhere."

"Uncomfortable! Man, that's barbaric!"

"K.O., football players are uncomfortable, too—all that padding along with helmets and mouthpieces. And every one of them is uncomfortable after the first play because the object of the game is to crash into other athletes wearing different uniforms."

"Yeah," K.O. said, "but what happens when horses get too old to race or just aren't good enough? Do they wind up in a dog food can?"

"We try to make sure that doesn't happen. I re-train my horses to gait so they can become riding horses, and then I sell them or donate them to a non-profit agency, New Vocations, which finds good homes for them." Glenn smiled broadly. "They aren't wild mustangs, they're domesticated animals, but most of them live good, long lives."

"Racehorses at tracks die every day," K.O. said. "I read that on the Internet."

"Mostly thoroughbreds. I don't think there've been more than three horses die at Northcoast Downs in the last thirty years."

"Yeah, okay," K.O. muttered, "but they're still prisoners. They have to live in those little stalls, and they only get to go outside for like an hour a day—if that!—to be trained or exercised so they can win some goddamn race. They're beautiful animals; they need to be free."

Part of me agreed with K.O., but I was at least mollified by the fact that trotters and pacers aren't really abused or mistreated. Besides, both of us had worked with Glenn Gallagher over the summer, and we liked him. "Chill out, K.O.," I said.

K.O. didn't answer. Silent and sullen is his way of life, especially when he's pissed off, but Gallagher had made sense, and K.O. wasn't mad enough to continue the argument.

"I've never seen a harness race, either," I said. "Bring Carli, too—I'll bet she'll enjoy it."

Glenn Gallagher walked over to K.O.'s desk and stuck out his hand. "I'm delighted you'll be joining us, K.O. I look forward to meeting, uh, Carli, is it? My guess is you've got pretty good taste."

"Damn right I do." K.O. rose for the handshake. He's five-nine or so, and the difference between his size and Glenn Gallagher's made him look like lunch bait. "Sorry about bitching. Animals are one of my big things."

"Mine, too," Gallagher said.

Shortly after Glenn Gallagher had left the office, K.O. called his girlfriend Carli and told her to save the date for the big outing. Carli, by the way, is Carli Wysocki, whom K.O. met while on his first assignment with Milan Security. She is around K.O.'s age, mid-twenties; she's astonishingly pretty and she smiles all the time. She's been front and center in K.O.'s mind every second since he first laid eyes on her. I knew my suggestion to bring Carli to the races would mollify K.O. enough to convince him to accept Glenn's invitation.

I waited until that evening to invite my own significant other, Tobe Blaine, with whom I was having dinner at the Lockkeeper's Inn in Valley View. That's Tobe, as in Detective Sergeant Tobe Blaine of the Homicide Division of the Cleveland Police Department, and she pronounces her name "Toby," even though she doesn't spell it that way. She and I met months earlier while working on different levels of the same case—and our relationship just sort of happened.

I'd never dated a cop before, even when I was a policeman myself. I'm not sure why, because all cops look at life—at least the life in which we function, that of law and order—in the same way. Tobe had never been to a horse race before, either, and now that we were here she seemed to be having fun. For whatever reason, she bets better than I do. I'd won one race bet and she'd aced three of them.

In case you're interested, this is my very first interracial relationship; Tobe is in her late forties and African American. If anyone has a problem with that, deal with it, because I don't have a problem with it at all.

This story, however, is not much about romance. It's not much about having a good time at the racetrack, either. This one is all about murder.

CHAPTER ONE

MILAN

Tobe Blaine had come to work in Cleveland P.D.'s homicide division three months earlier, after long stints in Raleigh and Cincinnati, and although she'd immersed herself in learning who's who in Cleveland—who's rich, who's important, who's artistic, and who is a pushy, obnoxious pain in the ass—she'd never heard of Glenn Gallagher until he invited us to the track.

"So you saved Glenn Gallagher's ass—and a lot of money," Tobe observed over dinner at Lockkeeper's. "I hope he paid you a bundle for it."

"The difference between you and me is that I only get money when I work. You get a paycheck whether somebody gets murdered or not."

"If nobody ever got murdered, I wouldn't *have* a job." She delicately placed a piece of salmon between her lips. They were kissable lips; I knew that for a fact. "I did a little research on Glenn Gallagher while you were working for him."

"And you discovered he's wanted by Interpol in seventeen different countries."

"I didn't find anything on him at all. He's rich, which means he's cheesed off a few people along the way, but for all intents and purposes, he's clean. Divorced, with a grown son—Cullen Gallagher—whose regular day job is teaching political science at Hiram College. You know where that is?"

"Naturally I know where Hiram is," I said. "I've lived here all my life. Liberal arts college with a nice little campus out in rural

Ohio between here and Youngstown, less than an hour from where we're sitting right now."

"Sorry, I'm still new here," Tobe reminded me. "Anyway, Gallagher's a registered Republican, a member of the Union Club, and the Chagrin Valley Gun Club. As one of Greater Cleveland's often-seen, he seems to show up most often for dinner at Johnny's, Lola, and Mallorca—that's a fancy-shmancy Spanish-Portuguese restaurant downtown."

"I know where downtown is, too," I said.

"Then you know where he goes on Sundays every fall, because he has season tickets to Browns games. His favorite after-dinner drink is Armagnac—but if he can't get that, he'll settle for Cognac."

I laughed. "How did you find out about all this stuff?"

"Umm—because I'm a detective?"

"You must be a damn good one. I researched Gallagher, too, before I took his job, but I never found out where he eats and what he drinks."

Tobe checked out the room. "I guess he doesn't know about Lockkeeper's Inn, because he's not here."

"Good," I said. "This is *our* night."

"We have quite a few of those, don't we?"

"*Our* nights? Yes, we do. Is that okay?"

"If it weren't okay," Tobe said, "I wouldn't be here."

"Will you come to Northcoast Downs with us? We can bet on every race if we want to—study the program and see who's good and who's not."

"Too complicated. I'll just bet on each jockey who's wearing yellow pants."

I laughed. "Actually, Glenn told me most women seem to bet on a gray horse—and gray horses don't wear yellow pants. By the way, they don't call them jockeys in harness racing. They refer to them as drivers. And their outfits aren't silks like at thoroughbred tracks; they're called 'colors'. K.O. is coming, too—with Carli."

Tobe smiled. "They've been dating as long as we have. He's a lucky man. Carli is terminally adorable."

"You aren't terminal, and probably too old to be adorable, but you're pretty hot, Tobe."

"I'm too old but I'm hot, huh?"

"Not old, mature," I said, too quickly. I've spent my life getting into trouble with women because I frequently say the wrong thing. "And sexy. Desirable. Great-looking."

"That's flattering, coming from a big swinger like you."

"I'm hardly a swinger."

"I've read those private eye novels—a gat in your pocket, a bottle of booze in the bottom drawer, and a blond client so gorgeous that you fall into her silver eyes."

"Silver eyes? You need to read better books," I said. "I don't have a 'gat' in my pocket; they haven't called a gun a 'gat' since *The Maltese Falcon*. There's no booze in my desk because I drink beer. And I can't remember my last blonde client, silver eyes or no. And that was a compliment, by the way."

"Which one?"

"That you're pretty hot. And you're welcome."

She shook her head. "You're a tough guy, Jacovich."

"Not nearly as tough as you."

"How so?"

"I'm not carrying a 'gat,' and you've got two of them—one on your hip, and one strapped inside your ankle."

"Good guess," she said. "Hurry and finish dinner because you can't wait to take them off me."

"That's erotic. Removing a woman's bra as prelude is sexy. Removing a woman's weapons as foreplay is *erotic*. There's a difference."

"Thanks for reminding me, Mr. English major. Have you removed firearms from lots of women before you went to bed with them?"

"Never slept with a woman who carried a gun until I met you."

"Lots of women have concealed-carry licenses in this state."

"True," I said, "but not many—men *or* women—actually know what to do with one."

"They get in the way of cops who get trained and paid to do their jobs—and what's to stop a cop from shooting an unknown civilian waving a gun around?" Tobe blew an angry breath out from between her lips. "I shot a guy once, several years ago. Thank God I didn't kill him, but he was standing in the middle of the street in front of his house waving a Smith and Wesson at all of his neighbors, who'd come out to see what was going on because the guy *thought* a robber was trying to bust into his house. Of course, I didn't know that until later."

"Where'd you shoot him?"

"In Cincinnati," she said, and didn't reveal anything else. "So tell me—besides my being hot, sexy, and desirable—and too old to be adorable—what should I learn about harness racing?"

She did study the sport before we went to Northcoast, even getting a copy of *The New Care and Training of the Trotter and Pacer*, and one of the first things she realized was that the drivers hardly ever wore yellow pants. The book was big and heavy enough to kill someone with, but her interest kept her going. She loves learning about all sorts of things, and if you mention something she's never heard of or knows little of, she'll make it her business to find out about it. Besides carrying two weapons even when off-duty, Tobe goes nowhere without her iPad, even though she bought it for herself only six weeks before Apple came out with a brand new edition of the damn thing. Anything you want to learn about—*anything*—she'll look it up on the spot. She tried laying all she'd learned about racing on me in my living room one Sunday afternoon while I was watching a Browns game on TV. It was too much. I lost focus, I guess; I wasn't interested in getting deeply involved in the harness racing business.

At least I *thought* I wasn't.

So the five of us—K.O., Carli, Tobe, Glenn Gallagher, and me—were up in the second-floor clubhouse, finishing our so-so dinners and watching the end of the fifth race. Glenn smirked as he rose, heading for the payoff window where he was about to collect a bundle. "How's everyone doing on drinks?" he said, winning ticket in hand. We all said we were fine. Then he leaned his head close to mine, his shoulders hunched nervously.

"Milan, we should get together next week," he said softly. "I've got something to tell you."

"Okay."

"I mean, I want to hire you again."

"More stuff at your office?"

He shook his head. "I'll explain it all when we meet."

"I'll call you on Monday, then," I said.

That relaxed him a bit. "If I were you guys," he said to all of us, smiling happily, "I'd carefully check the horses in the seventh race."

"Why?" Tobe asked.

"Read the program. You'll find out." Then he disappeared into the crowd.

"What's so special about the seventh race?" Carli wanted to know.

"I'll look it up," K.O. said. For a guy who never moved a little finger to help anyone, he took very good care of Carli, probably hoping she wouldn't have to open the program herself and risk a paper cut. I thought she wasn't so fragile, but K.O. didn't know that.

He thumbed through the pages, got to the seventh race, ran his finger down the list of horses, and said, "Holy shit!" He showed Carli first and then handed the program over to me, pointing to Number two in the seventh race. I couldn't believe my eyes.

"*Proud Milan,*" was the horse's name. I squinted at the small print. The horse owner was someone else, not Glenn Gallagher. I'd have to check the tote board on the track's infield before the seventh to see what the odds were.

"Oh, great! Now we all have to bet on Proud Milan to win," K.O. said.

"Is that because *I'm* a winner?"

"I'd never say *that!* I want to watch this race down by the rail and root for whoever I bet on, and it'll be easy for me to remember his name."

Carli hugged K.O.'s arm tight and put her face against his shoulder for a moment, closing her eyes and looking deliriously happy. I sighed. The last time I was around a very young couple that much in love, I was one of them—many decades ago.

I said to Tobe, "Shall we go downstairs and watch the race close-up? Although, knowing your super-sensitive nose, the smell of horse shit close up might bother you." Tobe had confessed to me early in our relationship that she suffered from a physical problem called hyperosmia, an over-active sense of smell that made some odors intolerable to her and caused violent headaches, which is why I'd started using shampoo, shaving cream, deodorant and soap that was fragrance-free.

"I don't *like* ca-ca, horse or otherwise," she said, "but it won't give me migraines the way some perfumes do. So by all means, let's watch the Milan race from the rail."

"The Milan race. Will that hound me for the rest of my life? The *Milan* race?"

"Lucky you," Tobe said. "At least you'll be a celebrity for a minute."

By the way, my last name, Jacovich, is even harder to pronounce than my first name, which is Americanized to MY-lan. For the surname, just pretend the *J* is a *Y.* YOCK-o-vitch. I was born and raised in Cleveland, but my parents were from Slovenia. There are more Slovenians in Cleveland than anyplace else in the world besides Ljubljana, but that never seemed strange to me. Most of the kids I grew up with in the St. Clair-Superior corridor east of downtown were Slovenian or Croatian and toted around hard-to-spell, hard-to-pronounce monikers. None of them had changed their surname to Wilson or Johnson, either.

Glenn Gallagher returned, carrying a brandy snifter in one hand and some tickets in the other, grinning as he sat down. He'd barely eaten any dinner—all he'd ordered was a plate of deep-fried zucchini sticks, and he shared them with the rest of us. "Who're you betting in the seventh?"

"Are you kidding? I'm in it to win," I said. "Who named their horse after me, anyway?"

"He's not named after you—he's named after the owner's father-in-law—who's Serbian, by the way."

"Serbian, huh?" Tobe nudged me in the ribs with one elbow. "Fame is fleeting."

"I mentioned you'd be here tonight—and if Mee-LAHN wins, they'll probably want to shake your hand anyway." Glenn raised his snifter. "Cheers." He swirled the drink around, inhaled it, and then took a sip.

Carli said, "What's that you're drinking, Mr. Gallagher?"

"Glenn," he corrected her. "You're too pretty to call me mister. It's Armagnac."

"Armagnac? What's that?"

Tobe said, "You've heard of Cognac. It's a brandy from a province in France, in the Gascony region. About a hundred miles south of there is another province where they make Armagnac. Both are brandies, but they're very different in taste."

Glenn Gallagher raised an eyebrow. "Where did you learn all that?"

Tobe didn't want to admit she'd Googled Glenn and discovered what he liked to drink. "Oh—I research lots of things. I like a brandy myself now and then."

"Want to try one of these, Tobe?"

"I started with vodka at dinner," she said. "I'd better stick with it. But I'm surprised a racetrack like Northcoast Downs actually keeps Armagnac behind the bar."

Glenn shrugged. "Not many bars sell it in Cleveland. They keep it at the clubhouse bar just because I drink it. I'm here three or four nights a week—of course, I don't drink on the nights I'm driving—so the bar won't go broke."

We watched the next race; Glenn had a big bet down but the rest of us hadn't wagered at all. Apparently Glenn had picked a loser because when all the horses and sulkies crossed the finish line, he crumpled up his ticket and tossed it onto the table. He'd bet a hundred bucks. To him, though, losing that much money was like me dropping a quarter on the street and watching it roll into a sewer opening.

"All of you go bet on Proud Milan," he said, "and I'll take you down to the grandstand so you can mingle with *real* gamblers." Then he wandered away, and we trooped to the betting window. Carli bet two bucks, K.O. bet five, Tobe slipped a ten dollar bill through the window, and I put down a twenty—a big bet for me, but after all, the horse and I shared the name. According to the tote board, Proud Milan was going at 5-to-1.

Gallagher eventually found us and as he led us toward the stairs to the outdoor grandstand area, he stopped. Another couple was coming up toward us.

"Oh, Jesus," Glenn muttered under his breath. Then, almost too loudly: "Evening, Chloe."

The woman looked startled, then annoyed. In her early forties, she was overdressed in Saks Fifth Avenue elegance and overly made-up with too much eye shadow and a slash of bright red vampire-like lipstick. Her loaded-on blush made her look orange, or "tangerine," as the cosmetics marketers called it. Her straight, dyed blonde hair hung loosely to her mid-back, with bangs. Most women that mature don't wear bangs anymore. She was attractive enough, in an ice-cold way. Her male companion was at least twenty years younger than her, wearing light blue slacks, a linen jacket over a blue dress shirt, white loafers with no socks, and with an ascot tied at his neck.

An ascot! Nobody's worn an ascot since charming actor David Niven died. It was hard to believe anyone wearing an ascot to a harness race, let alone wearing one in Cleveland—ever! If this guy walked around a neighborhood like Parma dolled up in an ascot, he'd never even make it to the corner.

The unsmiling woman bobbed her head once. "Glenn."

"Please say hello to my guests," he said. "Milan Jacovich, Kevin O'Bannion, Tobe Blaine, Carli Wysocki—this is Chloe Markham, the owner of Northcoast Downs."

Chloe Markham lifted her head to look a bit more like royalty, perhaps put out that no one bowed or curtsied. She deliberately ignored the two women but studied K.O. and me like zoology specimens. Finally she said, "*You're* Milan Jacovich."

"Present."

"You're the private detective."

"Investigator," I corrected her. "Only police officers of a certain rank are detectives." I was about to explain that Tobe was indeed a detective, but Chloe didn't care enough to shut up and listen.

"I read about you. Your name gets in the papers a lot, doesn't it?"

"More than I'd like it to."

Sneer. "Get off on being famous, do you?"

I was getting annoyed, even if I'd only been talking to her for ten seconds. Maybe it was her tone—or her wintry personality. I said, "If I ever do get famous, you'll be the first to know."

When Chloe spoke again, it sounded as if her jaw was wired shut. "What are you 'investigating' around here? Wanting to find out something bad and tell your newspaper buddies about it? I don't like snoops."

"Every once in a great while, I take an evening off from work and have fun. I hope my 'fun' tonight doesn't bother you *too* much."

I couldn't imagine even the Queen of England stiffening her neck that way, but Chloe Markham did so, staring off into a fantasy future inside her own head and ignoring me as if I hadn't spoken at all. "Come on, Skip," she ordered her companion, and they stalked off toward the clubhouse level.

"Skip," I mumbled. "Skip—with an ascot. Jesus!"

"What a personality that woman needs!" Tobe said loud enough for Chloe to hear. "She looked right through me like I was invisible. Is that a racial thing?"

Glenn said, "She ignores all women—and everyone else, too. It's probably a good thing she doesn't drink like her little friend there, or she'd *really* be a pain in the ass. We've had our problems in the past, mostly because I'm almost as rich as she is, and that gets her dander up. So she doesn't like me. Frankly, I can't stand her, either."

"If she hates everybody," K.O. said, "why own a racetrack that caters to people?"

"She inherited it from her uncle six years ago," Glenn said as we proceeded down the steps. "She tells anyone who'll listen to her that she cares about this park to honor her uncle's legacy." He snorted. "That's a load of horse puckey. Her younger brother Manley *didn't* get a piece of it, even though he thinks he should have."

"Manley?"

"That's his name. Chloe's already turning this place into what they call a racino—a racetrack with slot machines, but what she really wants is to own a genuine casino, just like the one downtown, so she can make more money than even she can piss away. She's already been handed a ton of money and a minority interest by a nationally known food chain to do just that. The restaurant company will be in charge, but I doubt Chloe gives a damn—and she won't have to pay people to shovel up horse shit every day, either."

"Skip!" Tobe said. "Who over the age of eight calls himself 'Skip'?"

"His name is Skip Swain," Glenn explained, "Chloe's boy-toy-of-the-moment. His father's one of the richest guys in Ohio. He already owns half the state legislature, and whenever he wants something to happen around here, it does. So Chloe's doing Skip—and if that doesn't work, she'll do Skip's daddy, too."

"Wearing an ascot is bad enough," Tobe said, shaking her head. "But *Skip?*"

We made our way down to the first floor, which was almost an alternate universe. While the upstairs clubhouse and restaurant were staid and relatively comfortable, the downstairs hosted a different species of sports fans.

Stretching almost the entire length of Northcoast Downs was a series of tiny carrels, like the soulless cubicles in which one might find the office employees of some huge corporation. There were probably six hundred carrels, each with its own personal TV set. Hunkering behind them in chairs much less comfortable than the ones upstairs were hardcore, dedicated gamblers—Glenn Gallagher had called them "degenerate gamblers." They were intent on what they were doing, which was betting not only on the races that went on approximately two hundred feet away from them but also on those taking place at many other race venues all over the country and the world. If they were real race bettors, Glenn had said, they knew how to handicap a race, which could take up to an hour or more. Their best work, however, was only about eighty percent successful—which happened to be much better than a baseball player's batting average.

A small crowd was gathered around a man well known in our town; Glenn pointed him out to me as a big race fan and bettor. Mike Trivisonno is a much-listened-to sports guy on Cleveland radio, mostly because he tells listeners exactly what he thinks, and if they don't like it, it's their problem. Trivisonno waved at Glenn, but was too busy chatting up his fans to come over and talk. That was fine with me; I hear him talk enough on his radio show.

I actually saw two men I knew, dressed differently from everyone else at the carrels. Their clothes were more expensive; loud suits with open-necked sports shirts. One wore sunglasses—at nine fifteen in the evening. I thought I'd seen him around in Little Italy, that colorful neighborhood on the east side of Cleveland where the Italian mob hangs out. The other I knew by name. John Terranova had for years been the designated driver of the local godfather, Giancarlo D'Allessandro. When the old man passed away a few years back, his nephew, Victor Gaimari, took over things. At one time Gaimari and I had been friends—but that came *after* I had punched him in the nose and he'd sent some punks to my home to get even.

John Terranova had been one of those punks.

The sunglasses man leaned over and whispered. Terranova glanced at me and nodded, the barest of smiles at the corners of his mouth. Then they returned to figuring out their bet in the next race.

We were all suitably amazed by the multitude of huge TV screens on every wall, side by side—more than fifty in that one carrel area, most tuned to racing at different tracks all over the country, but others showing a Major League Baseball playoff game, a soccer match somewhere, ESPN, and even a tired old sitcom.

K.O. shook his head in wonder. "How many TVs *are* there? They've got just about everything playing on one set or another, except maybe porn."

I said, "That's because no one ever bets on porn."

We went out into the crisp fall air to the grandstand, watching the horses warming up at a relaxed jog, stretching their muscles. The maintenance people raked the track with a grater, as they do between each race to smooth the ground and lay down deeper grooves. As we approached the rail, the horse smell was even stronger. I glanced over at Tobe and sniffed discreetly. "Okay?"

She flicked the end of her nose with a finger. "So far."

Glenn stood close behind me. "This isn't turning out to be one of my better nights," he mumbled. Another couple approached us; the guy didn't look any too pleased.

"You shouldn't be down here with us peasants," the man snarled as he got close to Glenn. "You should be upstairs with other people like you who think their shit don't smell." Mid-forties, grizzled, whipcord thin and needing a shave, his hands were curled into fists at his side, as if he were ready to fight.

The woman with him was a few years younger and several inches shorter, with one of those hard, slut-pretty faces looking as if she'd begun stripping for money when she was thirteen. Her dirty-blonde hair needed combing and her vivid scarlet lipstick smeared on her mouth was a red come-fuck-me flag visible for miles. Her breasts were too big for the rest of her, undulating with every step, struggling to burst free from her low-cut blouse. She ignored both Tobe and Carli, and her eye-batting, lip-licking flirtation with K.O. was subtle as a hurricane.

She finally tore her eyes from him and nodded to our host. "Hiya, Glenn."

"Wanda," he said without cheer, "you're looking great tonight, as usual."

She moved closer to him—by extension closer to me, too, and barely whispered, "*Still* just looking?"

The man with her grabbed her arm and almost jerked her away from us, throwing a looks-could-kill glare back at Gallagher.

Carli glared after Wanda as she was being taken away. "I love it when some bimbo hits on my boyfriend while I'm standing right next to him!"

Glenn said, "That was Del Fiddler—a trainer. He used to train my horses but we had—words."

"Words about the lady?" I looked after them as they moved away, or more specifically at her butt as it swayed and twitched beneath her flimsy peasant skirt.

"Wanda Fiddler flirts with everyone, sometimes ending with a payoff. I wasn't interested, but almost everyone else around here was. Del won't believe I turned her down, which is why he and I don't hang together anymore."

"He looked ready to punch you."

"He'd love to, but I'm twice his size."

"You're twice *everybody's* size," K.O. observed.

"Del gets into fights a lot around here. Now not many people want to work with him. Too bad—he was a damn good trainer."

"All this time," I said, "I've only thought of you as an investment banker with a hobby. But you live a pretty interesting life at this track."

"If I ever write a book about this business, nobody'll believe it." He searched the crowd then nudged me and pointed to a strange-looking man in tattered blue jeans and a stained pink hoodie. His hands were deep in his pockets and his jaw worked manfully on a chunk of chewing tobacco. He was middle-aged and obese, his gut and spare tire drooping over his too-tight Levis, and his face looked as if the entire Turkish army had marched over it. "Take Gecko over there," Gallagher said.

"Gecko? Like a lizard?"

"We call him that because he looks like one. Nobody seems to know his real name. He's a groom—takes care of things in the barn when he's of a mind to. An honest-to-God redneck. Whatever money he earns, he spends. His math starts and stops with how many packs of cigarettes can buy a blow job from one of the low-rent hookers living at his motel."

I stole a peek at Tobe and Carli, but they were talking together and laughing. K.O. paid no attention to either of them, leaning over the rail and studying the track as if he knew what he was doing.

"Otherwise, all Gecko cares about is his dog, a weird-looking thing. He's almost as fat as Gecko himself. He's got the body of a too-old English bulldog and the head of a wolf. That'll give you nightmares, believe me."

Gecko came over and said hello to Glenn Gallagher, head bowed respectfully, and then said "hi" to me in his hillbilly voice, wiggling his fingers in an almost feminine wave, his grin gap-toothed in both upper and lower jaw. He probably hadn't shaved for a week and didn't smell very good, but he seemed pleasant enough as long as he didn't get too close. When he merged back into the crowd, Gallagher said, "He's really a funny guy when you talk to him. He's kind and caring and so simple-minded that, except for his steady diet of creepy skanks he can buy cheap, he's almost childlike. And he's a damn good groom, too."

"Does he work for you?"

"Sometimes. Once he was actually late getting one of my

horses ready for a race because he got distracted; his excuse was his hooker friend was running a special that evening: a bubble bath, a back rub, and a BJ, all for fifteen bucks."

I rubbed my eyes. "I'm trying to lose the mental image of Gecko in a bubble bath."

"You'll never forget it," Glenn laughed. "It'll be with you always."

Horses and drivers filed onto the track. I squinted to get a good look at Number two, Proud Milan, carrying his chestnut head high, living up to his name. His driver wore black and gold colors, and looked every bit as menacing as the Pittsburgh Steelers on one of their good days. Unlike thoroughbred racing, where jockeys always wore the colors of the stable that owned the horse, in harness racing the drivers all had their own colors registered. I fingered the betting slip in my pocket, and while I haven't actually prayed since I was eight years old, I *thought* good vibes for Proud Milan and hoped they'd reach whomever was in omnipotent charge of horse races.

I moved over to stand with my group, Tobe, K.O., and Carli. The women had a lot to say about "our" horse.

"He's really pretty," Carli observed, pointing at the horse, except whenever K.O. heard the word "pretty," he looked at Carli.

"D'you suppose," Tobe murmured, "Proud Milan realizes how important this is?"

"I should've spoken to him personally," I said.

Gallagher joined us again at the rail. "He's in Number two position, you'll notice. That means he'll be able to drop right in behind the Number one horse, who leaves out of there like a rocket. He should carry Proud Milan right with him all the way around, twice, to the head of the stretch where the inside lane opens up. If Proud Milan has it in him, he can shoot inside, just past Number one, to win."

Hard-bitten gamblers—Glenn had called them "railbirds"—leaned as far out as they could, as if they wanted to *be* on the track, clutching betting tickets. They were probably at the track every day or evening—not to enjoy the sport, but to watch, trembling, as two dollars, ten dollars, or however much they'd wagered, galloped around the track pulling a driver and sulky. Within two minutes, they'd be smiling more broadly than usual or looking as if the weight of the world had just collapsed on their shoulders.

"Are you excited to watch your horse run?" Carli asked me.

"He's not my horse. And he only shares my name if you read it, not when you pronounce it. But I bet on him anyway."

Glenn lifted his snifter in a toast. "Here's to Proud Milan," he said, "all the way."

The crowd at the track got quiet for a few seconds, fortifying themselves for the race and the result, whatever it might be. Tobe quietly took my hand in hers and squeezed. That fortified *me*.

Then, the track announcer: "And they're off and racing!"

CHAPTER TWO

MILAN

We were back inside on the first floor where all the gambling addicts hung out, sitting around one of those large round tables, counting our winnings. Yes, Proud Milan won by three lengths, and we all collected five times what we'd bet. K.O. was jazzed about what he considered a big score, twenty-five bucks on a five-dollar bet. He'd probably never even been near a horse before, but he'd studied the program all evening as if there'd be a pop quiz on it, making scratches in the margins with his pencil.

"Are you turning into a big gambler now, K.O.?" I said.

"What should I bet *with*? My fourteen year-old Honda? My twenty-buck watch from Target?"

Carli Wysocki was draped over K.O.'s shoulder, studying the line-up for the next race, pointing out horse's names that interested her, that she thought were "cute." She said, "This is the first time I've been to a racetrack in my life."

"I hope you're having fun, then."

"Kevin and I always have fun."

Tobe Blaine rolled her eyes. She was more than twenty years older than Carli, and observing breathless young love probably drove her up a wall.

We'd all bet on Proud Milan because his name was close to my own. Glenn Gallagher had said that first-time gamblers often got lucky betting on a horse that was pretty, or their favorite color, or had an interesting name. We'd probably never get that lucky again, but it was a race to remember.

"Sometimes," Glenn told us, "gambler virgins will bet on dead money. That's a horse everybody knows doesn't have a chance in hell of finishing in the money. A useless bet, unless some weird thing happens during the race, like the favorite getting boxed in behind another horse, or the stone-cold front-runner that has great early speed runs out of gas in the stretch. People don't use that expression, 'dead money,' so much anymore, unless they've been around a long time, like me."

K.O. happily waved his money around, as if he'd just collected five grand instead of twenty-five bucks. "I'm not bitching because I won," he said, "but are these races ever fixed?"

Glenn said, "It's hard to do because the racetrack management watches for odd results. They'll investigate a shady-looking race, and there's a state racing commission watch-dogging things, too. Every winner is drug-tested after the race, and randomly chosen horses are drug-tested each night. They even make sure the right horse is in the right place."

"How do you know," Carli asked, "whether it's the right horse?"

"Tattoos. They used to tattoo the inside of the horses' lips, but now mostly they do it on the side of their necks, under the mane. Right before the race they test all the drivers to find out if they'd been drinking or doping. If they have, they don't race. It's pretty strict here. Screw up enough and you get suspended—or even banned for life."

"All over the country?" I said.

"Generally not. If you're banned at this track, you *might* be able to drive somewhere else. But if it's a serious enough offense, every track in America might cast a jaundiced eye on your work-ing there. A veterinarian comes around every morning to check the horses and take care of whatever's wrong with them—and there's an ambulance parked down near the far end of the track every evening in case, God forbid, anyone gets hurt—horses *or* people."

K.O. looked at his own winnings with new respect, then at me. We saw each other at least five days a week, if not more often, and I was feeling the stirrings of liking him, or at least getting more comfortable working with him. The good news, I guess, is that he's not always so pissed off about *everything*.

Glenn went off to get another drink. He knew practically everyone around the track and he kept disappearing to talk to them. K.O. and Carli headed toward the refreshment stand. After our recent dinner I couldn't imagine them being hungry again, but they were young, so what did I know? I wished I'd waited and ordered a couple of hot dogs down here, because the stand offers Stadium Mustard for its hot dogs—one of my favorite Cleveland foods. Stadium Mustard, pierogi, thin-crust pizza, klobasa (I know, everyone else calls it "kielbasa," but that's the way Slovenians pronounce it), and Buffalo wings are foods that keep Cleveland alive, healthy, and happily diverse.

Tobe and I studied the eighth race to decide how to lose all the money we'd just won. Tobe considered backing whatever horse was in the first position on the inside track; I looked for another interesting name. The only one I found, however, was a 30-to-1 underdog on the tote board, so I decided to skip the race altogether.

Then I saw Glenn Gallagher approaching again, another Armagnac snifter in his hand. He stopped at the table, licking his lips more than seemed necessary. His eyes were glassy. He bent down to speak to me.

"Milan, are you hung up on staying here for the rest of the races?"

"We planned to, but I don't think anyone is hung up about it. Why?"

"All of a sudden I feel odd—dizzy, feverish. I can't seem to keep my eyes focused. Blurred vision—and I'm having trouble breathing."

I looked at him more closely. I'm no doctor but something was obviously wrong. His skin and clothes were sweat-drenched, his face ashen, and he held onto the back of Tobe's chair to keep from falling on his face. I took the snifter from his hand and helped him sit down. "Relax, Glenn—take deep breaths."

He all but collapsed in the chair, his long legs sticking out into the main aisle. I took off my jacket. "Here—use this as a pillow."

He didn't move, though, just sat there with his hand on his chest.

"Is it your heart?"

Glenn shrugged with great effort. "I've had heart problems," he said through clenched teeth. "A-fib." I knew nothing about cardiac medicine, but I was aware that a-fib was shorthand for atrial fibrillation: too-fast, irregular beating in the upper chambers of the heart.

Glenn didn't want to discuss his health. "Nothing to worry about."

Not until now, I thought. "Are you in pain?"

He closed his eyes, not answering me.

"Can I do anything?" K.O. said.

I wondered whether he *could*. K.O. doesn't talk about it much, but he was in combat action; perhaps he knew a smidgen of medical training. But Glenn shook his head violently. "Milan." Speaking seemed like a superhuman effort. "Could you—drive me home?"

"Sure, Glenn. We'll go now."

Tobe stood quickly. "You drive his car, Milan; I'll follow in yours."

"He only lives a few minutes from here," I said.

K.O. was standing as well, looking worried and concerned. "We'll follow you, too."

I shook my head. "You and Carli stay as long as you want; you've got your car."

"We were probably heading home pretty soon, anyway. Call me at Carli's later, let me know what's going on."

It took a while, but the four of us managed to get Glenn on his feet. A big man, with little strength left in him. We all stumbled through a little-used corridor and finally out into the parking lot. Glenn had parked his Jeep Grand Cherokee very close to the door—being a horse owner, he had that privilege—and we helped him into the passenger seat. When I closed the door he leaned his face against the window, as if the coolness of the glass soothed him.

I handed Tobe my car keys and told her to follow me.

"How many drinks did you have tonight, Glenn?" I said as I started the car—but he was more than half out of it and just mumbled an answer I couldn't understand.

I'd only been to Gallagher's house once before, during the daytime. Now, at night, I wasn't sure where I was going. Once we cleared the parking lot, Glenn seemed incapable of giving directions, so I tried to re-create the neighborhood in my mind as I made a left turn on what I hoped was the correct street. In the rearview mirror, I saw Tobe following at a respectful distance.

I drove around looking for the street on which Glenn lived. Finally I recognized the street sign and turned left again to see his large, impressive home on a slight hill at the end of a cul-de-sac. There were lights on downstairs and floodlights illuminated the driveway. "We're almost there, Glenn," I said.

He opened his eyes, clutched his chest with both hands, and violently vomited all over his own lap.

I pulled the Jeep around to his front door, got out and ran around to the passenger side. When I opened the door, he raised his head slightly, staring directly into my eyes with what I imagined was terror. He reached out one hand to me, and then it fell into his lap as if he'd been shot. His head dropped onto his chest, and the entire upper half of his body lurched forward, hitting the dashboard. His other arm hung loosely at his side and the final breath of air escaped quietly from his lungs.

Tobe pulled up behind me, leaving the car running, and quickly joined me at Glenn's Jeep.

"Is he all right?" she asked.

I put my hand on his neck, feeling for a pulse that wasn't there. "I'm not sure," I said, "but I think he's dead."

It's one thing for a friend to die; it will make you sad for a little while. It happens often, especially when you get older. But you learn to live with it, to spend the appropriate time grieving, and then move on.

It's quite another thing when a person dies while looking into your eyes. It's happened to me before. My best friend, a guy I grew up with and the only man I could ever really talk to honestly and without bullshit, Cleveland Police Detective Marko Meglich, died in my arms under the arches of the Detroit-Superior Bridge in the dark shadows of a nightmare—shot to death off-duty but out there covering my ass nonetheless. I'll never really recover from that one.

Glenn Gallagher hadn't exactly been a friend. We'd grown to like each other; he was wealthy, powerful, and consumed with harness racing and the love of horses. I'm a lower middle-class working stiff, long divorced and living in a rented apartment for the last quarter of a century, a guy whose friends are almost all cops. Glenn and I had little in common.

But slumped over in his Jeep Cherokee, his heart fluttering and eventually failing, he had looked straight in my eyes, reached out to me, and died. And I couldn't do a damn thing about it.

CHAPTER THREE

MILAN

It was a well-attended funeral—not as grand as the standing-room-only crowd that gathers to grieve and mourn in Cleveland when a mob boss dies, as it did some years back when Don Giancarlo D'Allessandro, the Cleveland godfather, passed away quietly when he was almost ninety. The Cleveland bishop himself had performed that Mass—and three other Ohio bishops, five monsignors and an archbishop were seated up front inside Holy Name Cathedral, which quickly ran out of seats; half the mourners had to stand out in the street, weeping, blocking traffic on Mayfield Road in Murray Hill as the Mass was broadcast on loudspeakers.

Glenn Gallagher's services were held at Trinity Cathedral downtown. Both K.O. and I attended the event. K.O. put on his only suit—dark gray—and I'd loaned him one of my more sub-dued ties. Glenn wasn't very religious and probably had no connections at any of the local churches—so someone, probably his son Cullen, had to pull some strings. Trinity was beautiful, but it more resembled a tourist destination than a place for sacred worship.

I had little interest in what the minister was saying—his comments were rote for the funeral of a man he had never met—so I glanced around instead to see who was in attendance. I recognized many. I'd met some, worked for a few, worked against a few more, and knew the rest of them from newspaper photos—lawyers, judges, bankers, and a few mid-level politicians Glenn Gallagher had known personally.

One of the better-dressed attendees was someone I'd known for most of my life. Rudy Dolsak had never played football with me—he'd been portly, non-athletic, and far too short. He went on to Kent State University, as I did, except that he majored in business and worked his way up to being executive vice president of one of our larger local banks. In my early P.I. career, I'd often pumped him for confidential financial information about some of the people I'd dealt with—but since the World Trade Center incident, security in the banking world had grown so tight that you couldn't even tell anyone what color your underwear was, so I'd stopped asking him for help. He saw me and waved discreetly, and I waved back, making a mental note to call him and arrange a lunch. It had been too long.

"Who's that guy?" K.O. whispered.

"High school and college chum," I said.

"Tell me he never played football."

"He kept trying out, but he never made the team—so he volunteered to be water boy and errand runner. He's still a huge football fan; he has a box at Browns Stadium."

"When's he going to invite us to see a game?"

"It could happen. We'll meet him later."

I was surprised to see another old friend of mine sitting on the other side of the cathedral—or I should say a *former* friend. Victor Gaimari was an investment banker with offices in the Terminal Tower, Cleveland's most familiar building, overlooking Public Square, the Cuyahoga River, and Lake Erie. For years he'd been one of Cleveland's most eligible bachelors, almost always seen with a different but very attractive woman. Now, like me, he'd grown older and acquired silver hair sprinkled through his wavy locks. I thought it made him extra handsome, but we live in a youth culture, and the gray hair had probably slowed down his romantic pursuits.

Not much, though.

Because Victor was the nephew and only heir of the aforementioned Don D'Allessandro. Since the old man's death about four years ago, he was now the titular head of the Cleveland mob.

I wondered whether Victor and Glenn had been true friends or just business acquaintances. I also wondered if John Terranova had driven Victor to the funeral and was waiting outside in a limousine for the services to be over.

Victor and I made eye contact—a jolt, considering we hadn't spoken in several months after he'd informed me in no uncertain terms that our friendship was over. Nonetheless, we both nodded. Victor didn't smile; he used to smile a lot more. I guess he was still pissed off at me.

Sitting in most of the back rows were people who didn't own clothes proper for the occasion. Many men hadn't shaved; several sported visible tattoos, as did some skin-decorated women, and I surmised they all worked at Northcoast Downs on the backside— the barns, exercise yards and blacksmith shops the paying customers and gamblers never see. I recognized Gecko immediately; how could anyone miss Gecko? He'd tried to spruce up and look decent, wearing a white shirt and a pair of slacks that appeared relatively clean, albeit wrinkled, and he'd slicked his hair back neatly like basketball coach Pat Riley used to with the kind of "greasy kid-stuff" gunk they stopped selling to men sometime in the 1970s.

I didn't see Del or Wanda Fiddler—it would have been awkward for Del to attend the last goodbye to a man whose guts he hated, and Wanda probably chose not to cause marital trouble coming by herself to honor Glenn Gallagher's memory. I did see Chloe Markham, the track owner—obviously she *had* to be at the funeral of a horse owner and driver, but she'd chosen to sit with the more elitist attendees rather than with the backsiders. She hadn't brought her boy-toy, Skip Swain, either; he'd look more dorky than ever wearing his ascot to a funeral.

K.O. said very quietly, "This seems like two different funerals. Half the people look like they spend their time knee-deep in horse shit, and the rest in their thousand-dollar suits probably never looked at a horse unless John Wayne was sitting on it."

"Glenn got around," I said.

When the minister finally finished, most of the crowd lined up to file by the casket for one last look. I was reluctant, though, and K.O. wanted to know why.

"Because Glenn looked at *me*, right in the eye in the last mo-

ment of his life. It was like seeing into another man's soul. That
bothers me."

"I've looked into a dying man's eyes, too," he said. "In Iraq—
when the truck we were riding in hit a land mine and blew up.
I was lucky—I was in the back seat. He was driving—he lost the
whole bottom part of his body." K.O. rotated his head around on
his neck until something audibly popped inside. I think something was popping inside his head, too, a memory he wished he
could erase. "Are we going to the cemetery?"

"No cemetery. According to Glenn's request, he's to be cremated."

"Where will they sprinkle him?"

"I didn't ask. Maybe his son will keep him in an urn in the
living room."

"Like a souvenir from Atlantic City?"

I shook my head sadly. "You're a twisted little bastard, aren't
you, K.O.?"

"I'm just not sentimental, like you."

"I'm not sentimental."

"Oh, bullshit. Whenever someone mentions *The Cleveland
Press*—a newspaper that folded before I was born—or Browns
football players I never heard of, or somebody named Mister
Ding-a-Ling . . . "

"*Jing*-e-ling," I corrected him. "Mister Jingeling. He originally
worked for Halle Brothers Department Store—he was Santa's official Keeper of the Keys."

"I'm supposed to give a damn what his name was? But when
there's any mention of something that happened in Cleveland
more than three days ago, you get all misty about it."

"Maybe—but Glenn Gallagher died two feet away from me.
I'm not all choked up about it, K.O., but it wasn't a good moment.
You have a problem with that?"

He didn't answer. K.O. didn't know Glenn as well as I had, but
he stood in line and looked down at Glenn before he found his
way back up the church aisle. When we got to the door, the minister was there, shaking everyone's hand and thanking them for
coming. Next to him was Cullen Gallagher—not as tall as his fa-

ther had been and lacking Glenn's specific DNA that would have given him a full head of hair. Instead, he was completely bald. The facial features, though, made him a younger version of his late father.

"Cullen, I'm Milan Jacovich—this is my assistant, Kevin O'Bannion. We're sorry for your loss."

"Thank you," he said, shaking both my hand and K.O.'s. "You worked with my dad a few months back."

I nodded. "We'd been to the track with him on his final night, and I was driving him home. I'm the last person to see him alive. Again, my sincerest sympathy."

Cullen moved a few steps from the minister and lowered his voice. "Do you have a business card? Is there some way I can call you?"

"We're in the phone book or on the Internet—Milan Security. Call us any time."

"Will tomorrow morning be okay?"

K.O. and I looked at each other. I said, "We usually get there by about nine-thirty."

"It'd be better if I just came by and talked to you. How about ten o'clock?"

As we walked down the church steps, K.O. said, "He looks worried."

"His father just died. How do you expect him to look?"

"Just an instinct, Milan. He's got something on his mind."

We got to my car and I unlocked it. "Why," I said, "would any-one want to come see us early tomorrow morning if they *didn't* have something on their mind?"

Aladdin's Restaurant, which features extra-healthy Lebanese-type food, is within walking distance of my apartment in Cleveland Heights, so I picked up take-out that evening for Tobe and me. We sat on big poofy cushions on the floor in my living room on either side of the coffee table, enjoying our dinners.

I'd spent most of my life eating meat—so it even surprised me that I was eating mujadara—lentils and rice topped with salata (salad, for those of you who don't know much about Lebanese food) and toasted onions. I wasn't even jealous of Tobe's Mediterranean lamb plate. Lamb had never been on my list of favorites, but I knew with every bite that mujadara was good for my health—and a tickling feeling deep inside me made me glad no animal had died so I could eat dinner.

One of the only reasons I wish I were still young is that I could eat whatever I wanted to. No more.

"Standing room only at the Trinity this afternoon," I said, sipping my bottled iced tea. "Glenn knew everyone in town, and they all showed up for a last goodbye."

"I only met him once, Milan—the evening he died—so I thought it better to skip the funeral. Besides, I was busy yesterday with a neighborhood shooting. An old lady was watching a religious channel on TV when there was a gang shoot-out on the street, and a random bullet blasted through her living room window and right into her skull."

"Some choice," I said. "A gang shooting or a funeral."

Tobe clinked her iced tea bottle against mine. "Happy days."

"Glenn's son, Cullen, is coming to the office tomorrow to talk to me."

"What about?"

"Mourners were lined up to express their sympathies, so he didn't elaborate."

"He's a teacher, right?"

"College professor, yeah."

"Why do you suppose a college teacher wants to hire a private investigator? How could he afford to do that?"

"Don't forget, Glenn was a rich guy."

"A one percenter?"

"Not *that* rich, but well-off—and I imagine he left a big chunk of it to his son. Cullen was his only family."

"Hmm," Tobe said.

"Translate, please. What does 'hmm' mean in English?"

"It could mean all sorts of things—including his ex-wife wanting a piece of that bequest."

"Would she try screwing her son out of all that money?"

"How would I know?" Tobe speared a piece of lamb with her fork and held it out to me. "Want a taste?"

"You know I don't like lamb."

"Good—more for me." She pointed at my half-finished dinner. "You don't like fresh tomatoes, either, but you're eating them."

"I'm not eating them," I said. "I'm picking them out and avoiding them."

"You're a careful guy. So before he got sick, Glenn wanted to talk to you about something."

"He didn't say what."

She shrugged. "Now you'll never know."

"Unless Cullen wants to discuss the same thing."

"You said his son has nothing to do with harness racing *or* investment banking."

"Then," I said, "tomorrow morning, his visit will be a surprise."

"I prefer surprises at night."

My heart did a one-and-a-half inside my chest. I knew we'd end up making love later that evening, but even after several months together, the thought still excited me. There was a special something about Tobe Blaine I hadn't really felt about any other woman in my life—including my ex-wife Lila, who used several years of our marriage to whine and complain, challenging me every time I opened my mouth about anything except possibly the weather, and the last year and a half cheating on me with the man she now lives with, Joe Bradac. When we divorced, it was more of a relief than a tragedy.

Tobe was different—attractive, extremely intelligent, and quick-witted. I loved the verbal sparring between us. She was a police officer, too—strong and resilient, not taking crap from anybody.

"Just what kind of surprises at night do you like?"

"Want to find out? Eat your mujadara," Tobe said, and wiggled her eyebrows like Groucho Marx.

We'd awakened early and made morning love—surprises in the morning are just as good as the ones at night. Naturally Tobe had to go home and change her outfit before going to work; I couldn't imagine the crap she'd hear if she showed up in the same clothes she'd worn the day before.

Morning traffic down Cedar Hill was as heavy as rush hour traffic usually gets in Cleveland. When I arrived at the office, K.O. had beaten me to the punch and already made a pot of coffee. I was glad I didn't have to drink it anymore; K.O. is a bright, talented young man, but he couldn't make coffee to save his life.

Cullen Gallagher was prompt, showing up a few minutes before ten. He'd worn a dark-blue suit to his father's funeral; in my office he dressed like what he was, a college professor. About thirty-five, he wore a subtle blue plaid shirt with a loosely knotted, dull-colored knit tie, and pressed Dockers. His scuffed and battered brown loafers looked like they might have recently run a marathon. He must have been right at home in his academic/rural setting at Hiram College.

He and K.O. both drank coffee; he loaded his with sugar and powdered coffee creamer. I'd had two cups of green tea before leaving my apartment, so I occupied myself playing with a ballpoint pen, missing as I did each day the coffee I'd enjoyed for most of my life. I don't eat burgers anymore, either—the "pink slime" news report was a major turn-off—which often makes it hard to go out for lunch. Perhaps in my advanced age I was turning vegan without even being aware of it.

While Cullen spoke, I took notes on a yellow legal pad while doodling what I've doodled since I was in high school—a gallows with an empty noose dangling from it. My father, who was Ljubljana-born and who never really mastered English, would tease me about the gallows by telling me I had some sort of weird death wish, but I never stopped my doodling.

"You probably didn't know, Mr. Jacovich, but I met your son once when he was still at Kent State."

"Milan Junior?"

Cullen nodded. "While he studied at Kent, he had some Hiram friends, too—and some of them were in my classes. So we all went out and had a few beers one evening."

"Milan Junior is a pretty serious guy," I said.

"I noticed that—especially when he talked football. After three beers, though, he loosened up a lot. So for two reasons—first, that you worked for my father, and second, I used to know your son—I thought it'd be a good idea for me to run something by you."

"Fire away," I said.

Cullen got right to the point. "I've never known a private investigator before, Mr. Jacovich, so I'm not sure how to begin."

"You can start by calling me Milan," I said, "and my assistant here, K.O. Your dad and I worked together, but we were starting to become friends, too."

"Milan. K.O. It's my time to mourn, but I'm too upset for that—too worried."

"Why?"

"Dad's autopsy reads that he died of cardiac arrest. I know he had a-fib, but he saw his cardiologist every four months, he was on medication, and he took good care of his health."

"He was drinking a lot," I observed, "which isn't that great for the heart."

"He was nowhere near being an alcoholic. He just drank socially or at the track. He watched races a few times a week—and drove in plenty of them. Those days, he couldn't drink before a race or they wouldn't let him on the track."

"What about nights he wasn't driving?"

"Maybe making up for his dry nights? I hardly ever went with him."

"Not a racing fan?"

"Not a horse fan at all, and I don't gamble—except sometimes on the lottery."

"Horses are nicer."

"Yeah, but they're big enough to hurt you badly; I don't make friends with grizzly bears or mountain lions, either. Look, Dad enjoyed social drinking—I've seen him do it almost everywhere besides the track. But from what you're saying, well—he must've been upset about something."

"Maybe," I said. "He mentioned wanting to hire me again but didn't say why."

Cullen mulled that over. "Well, now *I* want to hire you."

"To do what?"

He hesitated. "I'm not exactly sure."

K.O. rolled his eyes, but I ignored him. "Can you be more specific?"

It took him a while, struggling for an answer. "I don't think my father died the way they say he did." He nervously clasped his hands together in his lap. "The autopsy said heart failure, which is believable—up to a point. I can't explain it—but it just doesn't *feel* right to me."

Alarm bells were ringing in my brain. When I was a badge-toting cop, I wasn't allowed to operate on hunches, but since turning private, I've dealt with many situations that didn't feel right to me, either.

K.O. said, "Did your dad have other physical problems?"

Cullen shook his head. "He was strong enough to sit in a sulky and control a thousand pound animal pulling him a mile around the track at thirty-some miles per hour. Hell, there was nothing wrong with him, except maybe a broken toe."

"How'd he get the broken toe?" K.O. said.

"A horse stepped on his foot."

"Deliberately?"

"You'll have to ask the horse," I said, and then turned back to Cullen. "We know nothing about heart disease. If you think it wasn't cardiac arrest, then what are you implying?"

He rubbed his fingers against his forehead as if he were getting a headache. I've been there, too—done that. It happens when you get hit in the head a lot; in my life, that's just part of the job. Finally he said, "I think somebody might've killed him."

"Whoa!" K.O. said.

Whoa indeed! I said, "Who'd want to do that?"

"If I knew, I wouldn't be hiring you."

"Don't you think you should contact the police?"

"For what? As far as they're concerned, there *is* no suspicion of murder."

"My friend Tobe Blaine is a detective sergeant with the homicide division. She was with us the night your dad passed. Maybe if you talked to her . . ."

"Dad lived in a suburb, raced in a suburb, and died in a suburb. The Cleveland P.D. has problems of its own. They won't talk to me, either."

"Have you tried?"

Cullen shook his head. "What the hell would I say to them?"

"Your father was very well off," I said, "and sometimes that makes enemies. But where would we look? In the financial business or at the racetrack?"

"Both places." He took an envelope from his inside pocket and tossed it onto my desk. "I made these lists up last night—two of them. One has the names of anybody he did business with in the last year, moneywise or otherwise, at his investment banking and hedge fund management firm. The other is a list of almost everyone at the track."

"Friends or enemies?" K.O. said.

"Don't ask me. We never talked harness racing, but I do have an owner's license—which gives me unlimited access to any harness track in Ohio. It's always bored me, so I know nothing about Northcoast or the people there. That'd be your job—finding out that kind of information."

"We'll have to sign a contract," I said.

"Fine."

"We're not cheap."

"I have money," Cullen said, "or will have, soon."

"Oh?"

"They'll read my dad's last will and testament within the next two weeks."

"And you want to spend some of that cash investigating a murder that might not have happened?"

Cullen Gallagher looked sad all of a sudden. "He was my *father*." He tugged on his shirt collar. "He actually gave me a copy of that will right after he wrote it."

"You've read it?"

He shook his head. "He asked me not to."

"OK," I said, "but he's gone. Why don't you read it now?"

"I don't know," Cullen said. "It would be creepy. And—well, you're not supposed to read a parent's will until the lawyer tells you to."

"Is that what your dad's lawyer told you?"

"Well—yes, I guess so."

Different strokes, etc., I thought. I picked up the envelope he'd given me; five or six pages were folded up inside. "Glenn owned several horses and the investment firm was his, too. What happens to all that now that he's gone?"

"I haven't met with his lawyer yet. That will be next week sometime. But unless Dad made changes to that will and didn't mention it," Cullen said, "I think I'm his only heir."

CHAPTER FOUR

MILAN

I made two more copies of the contract Cullen had signed before he left, checking the two lists he'd written for us. One was headed TRACK, the other FINANCIAL$$$.

"We ought to split this case evenly, K.O.," I suggested. "You want to take the racetrack people or the bankers?"

"I don't know a damn thing about harness racing," he said, "but I know even less about banking. I'll take the track list."

"Here you go. And there's a track pass for you; Cullen says you'll need it to get to backside where everyone works when no race is going on."

"Backside?" He grinned. "I think there's a different definition for that one, too."

"The good news is you won't have to wear a suit to walk around in the barns; I doubt anyone there even owns a suit." I put one signed contract in my own folder and another in the one I'd just created, marked "Cullen Gallagher."

K.O. scanned the names on Cullen's lists. "I don't think we met a lot of these people at the track the other night. Hmm—isn't Turtle on here somewhere?"

"It's Gecko," I laughed.

He found it. "Yeah, there he is. It just says Gecko. What's his last name? Gecko Reptile? Gecko Lizard?"

"Glenn said nobody knows what his real name is. Ask Gecko when you see him. But don't take notes about people right under their noses; it makes them clam up."

"This isn't my first investigation, remember?"

"Just trying to be helpful."

"Next you'll tell me to wear clean underwear in case I get into an accident."

"Let's not talk about your underwear." I rose and went to my closet, pulling out one of the spare neckties I keep in there in case I have to wear one. I slipped it around my neck and under my collar.

"A tie?" K.O. said.

"Sure, I'll be talking to finance people and bankers today, and they all wear ties."

"Are you really going to wear *that* one?"

"What's the matter with it?"

"A bright red tie? You look like a Hollywood pimp."

"Have you ever *seen* a Hollywood pimp?"

He held up a hand. "It's your neck, Milan. I'm just sayin'."

I stepped in front of the small mirror on the inside of the closet door. I didn't have to—I'm one of the few men who doesn't look at himself tying a tie in the mirror. Considering the bright red tie, though, it was hard to ignore K.O.'s shot across the bow. "The first guy I'll talk to today, one of the names on this list, I waved to at the funeral. You asked about him—my high school and college buddy, Rudy Dolsak. He's helped me on a few cases, giving me bank info I needed. We've drifted apart the last few years—but I still consider him a friend."

K.O. frowned. "Will talking to him about Gallagher be awkward?"

"If it is, I'll let you know." I started for the door. "Lock up when you leave."

"Hey, Milan," he said when I had my hand on the doorknob. "Remember—don't take any notes about him right under his nose."

Kevin O'Bannion is a world-class smart-ass—and it's good he's going to spend time at the track rather than in the sacrosanct confines of the alpha financial wizards Glenn Gallagher was a part of. I got the idea that K.O. isn't all that enthralled with those who are obscenely rich and obscenely arrogant about it.

Come to think about it, I'm not so crazy about them, either.

*   *   *

For many years, I ran my investigative and security firm from my
rented apartment on Cedar Hill in Cleveland Heights—but my
Tetka Branka, the only close relative I had left, passed away when
she was almost ninety, willing me a chunk of her savings I never
knew she had, allowing me to buy my own office building on the
west bank of the Flats. It's right next to a firehouse on the peculiar twist called Collision Bend, an impossible hairpin turn in an
already crooked river. It's a great location, only five minutes from
downtown—five minutes from Rudy Dolsak's fancy executive office in the main office of Ohio Mercantile Bank.

Rudy, overstuffed in a pinstriped gray suit with matching vest,
was sitting at a desk big enough on which to land a fighter plane.
At one time we'd been close friends, but times change without
our even realizing it. He seemed surprised by my visit, but tried
gallantly to act delighted.

"I don't see you for two, maybe three years," he said, hustling to
pump my hand with both of his, "and now it's twice in three days.
I'm glad you're here, Milan—assuming you don't want to open a
new account or hit me up for a humongo loan. You look a little
thinner than when last we met."

"A few pounds—cutting down on beer and pasta."

"I wish *I* were." He patted his comfortably round belly. "Too
busy to exercise—and now I eat out three or four times a week.
It's getting to me." He grinned. "But I'm loving it."

"You look pretty good."

"You *lie* pretty good. Sit, Milan. Talk with me. Want coffee? Or
tea? Somebody told me you're drinking tea these days."

"I'm good, thanks," I said, wondering who'd told him about my
tea-drinking habit. I settled into a chair opposite him. "You were
at Glenn Gallagher's funeral." He nodded. "Were you friends with
him or just business acquaintances?"

"A little of both. His investment company has a major account
here." Rudy looked down at his lap, embarrassed. "I can't give you
exact amounts of people's bank accounts anymore, Milan. You
know how it is these days . . . "

"I know how it is."

"You worked with Glenn this summer."

"It's no secret. I helped him solve some of his business problems."

"You must've done pretty well; his account still looks very healthy."

"His account is healthy, and so is mine. Nowhere near *his*, naturally . . . "

"I haven't checked your balance in a long while, Milan, but I guess you're in good financial shape—or I would have heard."

"Rudy, you seem to know everything."

"I know everything to do with money—especially the money in my bank. Glenn had other checking accounts at Key Bank, Dollar Bank, maybe even First Third."

I nodded. I've always wondered why a financial institution would choose to call itself First Third Bank. Why did the Second Bank get completely ignored—and why couldn't they make up their minds whether it was a First or a Third? "Did Glenn have any outstanding loans he wasn't paying off? Was anyone in the money business mad at him?"

Rudy was beginning to show his irritation with me. "You don't work for him anymore. He's dead."

"I'm working for someone else—his son Cullen."

"Cullen Gallagher hired you to find out about his dad's debts? They're all public record—unless he lost a lot of money gambling off-track." Rudy shrugged. "And when you invest big money for others, you don't make stupid gambling mistakes. At least I don't think Glenn did, and I've known him for fifteen years or so—longer than you've known him. So his son wants you to do—what?"

"It's confidential."

"Sounds mysterious."

"You keep confidential many things about *your* clients, but I wouldn't call that mysterious."

Rudy Dolsak said, "Well, Glenn was an open book. Most successful businessmen have secrets, but I don't think Glenn did. I'm just curious. You're curious, too, Milan—but don't forget that curiosity killed the cat."

If that remark had come from anyone other than the man

who'd grown up as water boy for the Kent State football team, it might have sounded threatening. "Cats have nine lives, Rudy. I'm part cat—I've got a few lives left. Tell me about Glenn Gallagher's partners and high-level associates—in his investment company."

"You probably know more about them than I do," Rudy said. "You investigated."

"At the time, I found most of them squeaky clean."

"Nobody's squeaky clean."

"I am."

Rudy Dolsak laughed. "You weren't squeaky clean when you played football."

"Nose guards rarely get nailed for a penalty. In seven years of high school and college football, I got called for off-sides *once*. So I *am* squeaky clean; the statute of limitations has run out on off-sides penalties from forty years ago."

"I didn't mean to sound insulting."

Sure he meant it, but I chose to ignore it. "I need to meet some other business people Glenn knew."

"And that's why you showed up here for the first time in years?"

"Well—we should have lunch some time, too."

"I'm flattered to hear that." Cold words rolled from between his lips like dried peas. Now that Rudy was one of the biggest big shots in the hallowed halls of Cleveland banking, wealth and authority had obviously rendered him stuffy—and a bit snotty, too. "Glenn had no partner. It used to be Jonathan Singer—but he screwed almost every one of the investors out of a hell of a lot of money. Which means, Milan, that he screwed this bank out of a lot of money, too, because most of those investors are our clients. But Singer's been convicted and is on his way to jail for fraud and embezzlement."

"I'm the one who put him there," I said.

Rudy looked smug. "I knew that. Is some other crime involved—some new crime?"

I sighed. "I can't really talk about that."

"Screw it, then," Rudy said, all business now. "I can't waste any more time with you. You want to find out more about Glenn's investment firm, go talk to Jen Taylor."

"And who's Jen Taylor?"

"Office manager. Executive assistant. The go-to gal when any-body wants anything done. Her name is also on Glenn's bank ac-count here. And no surprise—she's damn good-looking, too."

"Interesting, Rudy. Do bank executives always rate women by their looks?"

"Not me, Milan," Rudy said. "I'm a happily married man. But if anyone asked me, I'd rate Jen Taylor maybe an eight—with a bullet."

Gallagher Investment Management Inc. took up half a floor in a newish downtown building on Superior Avenue. On the glass door was a large icon, two artistically designed capital G's indi-cating the firm's late owner. I'd been there often during my in-volvement with Glenn Gallagher and recognized his not-so-sub-tle touch in the lobby. Glenn had been many things; subtle was not one of them.

A nearly life-size bronze statue of a horse, driver and sulky greeted visitors as they walked in the door, and the walls were filled with framed photos of Gallagher—in the Winner's Circle at Northcoast Downs and other tracks around the country or stand-ing, grinning next to local sports celebrities from the Browns, Cavs, and Indians, and top golfers from the Firestone Golf Tour-nament near Akron. There was a blank frame on the wall nearest the elevator. Glenn had explained the frame was waiting for the photo of the next win—there was *always* a "next win." The empty frame was an idea he'd gotten from Arnold Palmer. Now, sadly, it will remain forever empty.

On a table next to one of the waiting room chairs was a copy of a magazine called *Hoof Beats*, featuring a photo on the cover of Glenn Gallagher proudly wearing his colors. I glanced at it more closely; the date on the magazine was July 2007.

Ushered in by the receptionist, I realized I'd never been in Jen Taylor's office before. Glenn hadn't mentioned her to me, prob-ably because she wasn't in a position from which she could em-bezzle—and that was what my investigation had been all about.

Her office was a far cry from Glenn's bigger suite, one with a view of Lake Erie. Taylor's was smaller—just one window, facing the river, but it was pleasant enough. Maybe more disorganized; she dealt with paperwork and everyday problems, so files were spread out over her desk, along with a picture of her hugging a little boy about six years old. There were no photographs of the boy's father—Jen Taylor wore no wedding ring—but on the wall was an enlarged photo of her in a player's jersey and cap at the baseball stadium back when it was called Jacobs Field.

Most longtime Clevelanders—like me—still call it by that name, or more familiarly, "The Jake." Similarly, everyone refers to Quicken Loans Arena where the Cavs play basketball as "the Q." Cleveland is a nickname kind of town.

In this photograph, Taylor was heartbreakingly young, maybe even a high schooler. She stood in front of the first base dugout, smiling happily between Jim Thome and Omar Vizquel—so it must have been taken in the mid-nineties before both of them moved on to other teams. I wondered what she'd done to earn the right to be on the field with superstars.

She was stunning in person, although I didn't find her overly sexy or alluring. Her dark hair was pulled back into a no-non-sense bun, and she wore stylish glasses that made her gray-green eyes look bigger. Her figure was slim and svelte in a blue business suit with a dark blue blouse. She smiled when I introduced my-self, but she looked tired, her mouth turned down at the corners like the "tragedy" mask of drama. I'd seen her at Glenn's funeral, sitting in the second row behind Cullen Gallagher; at the time I hadn't known her name.

"Naturally I know who you are, Mr. Jacovich," she said. "You spearheaded Glenn's security a few months ago. He talked about you a lot. I'm surprised we never met before this."

"I'm glad that's been remedied—and I don't want to take up too much of your time now. I only have a few questions."

Her brows knit. "Questions? You don't work for us anymore, do you?"

"I'm working for Cullen. He wants to clear up a few things."

"Cullen," she said, barely above a whisper.

"Glenn's death is difficult for him."

"It's hard for all of us."

"I'm wondering, though—could anyone this company does business with have been angry with Glenn?"

"Angry?"

"Nobody in the hedge fund business sails through life without rubbing people the wrong way."

"Nobody anywhere sails through life," she said. "And your investigation put Jon Singer in prison—so I'd guess he's madder than hell. But I can't recall anyone still walking around who is truly angry. Annoyed, maybe."

She folded her hands primly on the desk top. "May I know why you're asking these questions?"

"I'm doing so for Cullen."

"I *know* that. The question is why?"

I couldn't tell Jen Taylor what I'd told Rudy Dolsak—that it's *confidential*—because to her it wasn't. "Cullen is worried about his father's death, although the coroner ruled it a heart attack."

She nodded.

"How long have you worked here?"

"Eight years or so."

"You probably knew Glenn even better than Cullen did."

A blush flamed her cheeks and she looked away.

"Was he having heart problems?" I said.

"Yes, atrial fibrillation. It only happened on occasion."

"He saw a cardiologist?"

"Several times a year. His heart was in great shape—that's what the doctor said."

"Cullen isn't so sure—so I'm wondering if *you're* sure."

"How would I know?"

I tried to frame my question carefully. "Weren't you and Glenn in a personal relationship as well as a business one?"

"You have no right to ask me that!" Jen Taylor's voice, previously mellow and soothing, turned into a whip crack that took me aback.

"If there's a question about Glenn's death, I have every right to ask it."

"No, you don't! You're not a police officer."

I knew that. Still, I persevered.

"I'm making inquiries at the request of the son of the deceased. If I understand your relationship with Glenn, I can ask you questions that will help Cullen. Okay?"

She neither agreed nor disagreed, but a slight nod told me it was all right to move on. "So, Jen—you and Glenn were—dating?"

"Jesus, that is *so* sixteen-years-old-and-never-been-kissed! All right, if you put it that way, Glenn and I were 'dating.'"

"For how long?"

"Almost since I started working here."

"Committed?"

She heaved her shoulders up around her ears. "We didn't label it—but I didn't see anyone else, and I don't think Glenn did, either."

I had to stop and think about that. She'd been Glenn's squeeze for eight years, but the child in the photograph with her looked to be six years old. "Handsome young man," I said, gesturing toward the framed photo.

"My son, Aaron," she said and couldn't help smiling as she spoke about him. "He's ten now—just in case you're wondering if it's Glenn's son. Glenn treated him as if he *were* his own, though."

"That's good," I said. "So you were knowledgeable about his health?"

"His health was pretty good for a man his age. Have you ever sat in a sulky and driven a horse?"

"Can't say I have."

"Well, you're no passenger back there. It takes strength and ability and balance, as well as knowing what to do and when to do it. Glenn was good at it and finished in the money about thirty percent of the time. He only drove his own horses, though. Most other drivers are freelancers—they're what they call 'catch drivers' and sometimes get their pick of three or four horses in each race."

"Okay, I get that. But what about Glenn's physical ability?"

"His hands, legs, shoulders—they were all very strong."

"And his heart?"

Jen took a moment too long before answering, compressing her lips and swallowing hard, apparently trying not to cry. I'm not so sure she was on the verge of tears; I think when she wanted to be, she was every bit as strong as Glenn had been. "He watched his diet—not as well as he should have, but he rarely ate red meat or sweets or fattening things. And he took Coumadin and other stuff for his heart."

"The night he died, he seemed to be drinking a lot."

"Maybe he *was* worried. He drinks—" She stopped, gasping as she used the present tense in reference to a man she'd loved who no longer *had* a present tense. "He *drank* more when things upset him."

"Do you know what might have been upsetting him?"

"Unless he's upset with *me,* he keeps things like that to himself."

I tried not to frown. "Was he upset with you often?"

"No more than any other couple. We were very happy together."

"When things got awkward at his firm this summer, did it affect his heart?"

She shook her head. "Healthy—and wealthy and wise." She allowed herself a small smile. "Before you ask, and you *will*—yes, we were in love."

"But no marriage?"

"It's a piece of paper, no matter what many of those congressional clowns think. Half the marriages end in divorce, despite that silly Defense of Marriage Act—but Glenn and I were nowhere *near* a breakup." She sighed.

"What now, Jen?"

"For me, you mean? Nothing. I own twenty-five percent of Gallagher Enterprises, so I imagine things will go on as they are."

"Glenn owned the other three quarters?"

"Fifty-one percent. Cullen owns the remaining twenty-four— or I *think* he does. I haven't seen the will, but I imagine Glenn left just about everything to him—the house, the cars, the company, the whole horse business. Glenn's attorney is tracking down all the heirs to get them together at one time for the reading of the will."

"Who's his attorney?"

"David Weaver—Schoenburg and Weaver."

I jotted Weaver's name in my notebook. "I might want to talk to him."

"Call him," she said, "but he doesn't know much about Glenn's health."

"Attorneys know things wives or lovers don't know."

"And dry cleaners know things attorneys don't know. Or lovers, either."

"Or ex-wives."

"Glenn's ex? Brenda? They've been divorced for almost twenty years," Jen said, "way before I came along. She re-married an oncologist and lives, I think, in Charleston, South Carolina, the last I heard. There's no post-divorce animosity there that I know of; if there is, Glenn never mentioned it to me."

"Under the circumstances, you're holding up pretty well."

"I have to. Sure, at night I cry myself to sleep. But that's home; this is work. Glenn wouldn't want me sobbing all over his office when I'm investing money for other people or managing their hedge funds."

"So—no clients were furious with him?"

"No—he rarely lost their money. When you nailed Jon Singer for stealing here, Glenn made up the difference to all his clients—out of his own pocket."

"What about other investment bankers in Cleveland? They're Glenn's competitors—and your competitor, too."

"I wouldn't call it a competition," Jen said. "It's like golf or tennis—people play to win. But if they lose, they usually shake it off and move on."

"Who's the one who *usually* went after a lot of the same deals Glenn did?"

Jen had to think for a while. Then: "All of them, at one time or another—that's our business. I'd imagine there are Cleveland private investigators who compete with you, too. Everybody smiles, though, because it's nothing personal. I'd guess our biggest competitor is a stockbroker and hedge fund manager named Victor Gaimari. Are you familiar with that name, Milan?"

I closed my eyes for a moment too long. I couldn't help it.

"Yes," I said. "I'm familiar with it."

Damn.

CHAPTER FIVE

K.O.

K.O. made the one-hour drive from his apartment in Mentor to Northcoast Downs—too early for him to even stop for coffee at Panera. He had a visitor's pass in his pocket to allow him free rein in the backside, and he'd heeded Cullen Gallagher's warning to wear his oldest shoes, as he'd be walking around a large area in which horses sometimes ignored the polite etiquette of pooping.

As he approached the park he checked the list of those he was supposed to talk to. He didn't know any harness racing people. As far as that goes, he knew few names of *anyone*.

He turned into Northcoast's huge parking lot, driving all the way to the rear where two security guards huddled in a tiny booth at the entrance. They asked his name, wanted to know with whom he was supposed to meet this early in the morning, looked at his visitor's pass, and even demanded to see his drivers' license. K.O. wondered what exactly they were guarding; he wasn't planning on stealing a horse. He knew from western movies that in the Old West they hung people for horse theft, but he didn't think that happened in Cleveland—not anymore, anyway.

Finally they lifted the gate and he drove through to look for Glenn Gallagher's barn. Some horses were already out, being worked by their trainers or grooms, ambling around a large exercise track. They weren't racing, just exercising, and none seemed in a hurry. K.O. felt easier because Glenn had sworn to him harness horses were rarely, if ever, abused.

He found the barn, parked as close to the doorway as he could, and walked inside. Seven or eight people wandered around doing things—K.O. couldn't ascertain what those things were. One young man, about K.O.'s age, but five inches taller and fifty pounds heavier, with small, dead eyes, was hooking a bay horse up to a jog cart.

"Hi," K.O. said, "I'm looking for Walt Holman."

The kid looked at K.O. with undisguised hostility, as though he'd been accosted at his quiet, barely sociable job by an alien from a far-away planet. "Who are *you?*"

The kid was obviously stoned. K.O. figured he was on some sort of recreational drug. Not that he was judgmental; while in the army, almost everyone was taking *something*, just to get through the endless days of boredom, interrupted occasionally by being shot at or running over a hidden bomb. Still, the kid's attitude got on K.O.'s nerves. "I'm a *person*," he said evenly, "looking for Walt Holman—if that's okay with *you.*"

The kid stood there, hand on the horse's bridle, clearly trying to decide whether he should make a big deal out of it and whether K.O. was small enough for him to hurt. Finally, with obvious reluctance, he jerked his other thumb at an older man near the middle of the barn.

"Thanks *so* much." K.O. took an extra beat before he moved—his reformatory years had told him never to turn his back on anyone who might surprise him—and headed for Walt Holman, who was leaning on a stall door and talking to a nearly black horse.

"Get with the program, Cyrus," Holman was saying around an unfiltered cigarette hanging from one corner of his mouth, softly stroking the black neck. "It's that attitude, boy—you're a pain in the ass to work with." He laid his head quickly against the horse's shoulder. "Always have been, you old crank." He pulled a peeled carrot from his pocket, holding it under the horse's nose. "Here you go, fella."

Cyrus ate it eagerly.

"Mr. Holman?"

"Hey—you must be Kevin O'Bannion. Cullen said either you or your boss would be dropping by here. Nice to meet you."

K.O. noticed that even this early in the morning, alcohol

hung on Walt Holman's breath. He was a big guy, almost as tall as Milan Jacovich, but the way he moved made K.O. believe he could be fast when he needed to be.

"Everyone calls me K.O. It's my initials."

Holman stepped aside so K.O. could better see the black horse. "This here's Cyrus. He only gets along with people about twenty percent of the time—otherwise he's a devil. Can't really help it, though; he's got a bad stifle joint and it's getting worse. Makes him irritable—like a bad hip would make *you* irritable. His racing days'll be over soon." He looked around. "There's no place in here to sit and talk. Let's take a walk."

The two of them headed outside. Holman said, "This is the horses' territory, so watch where you step."

They moved into the early morning. The sun wasn't completely visible; instead, waging war with the overhanging clouds. Holman said, "Cullen suggested we talk, K.O. But you gotta let me in on what it's all about."

"Just tidying up loose ends—that's the way Cullen wants it. You're Glenn Gallagher's trainer?"

"Trainer," he said, "driver, shit-shoveler, and the main tenant in this barn—and his partner, too. I co-own nine of Glenn's horses with him—along with many others both here and at other tracks." His eyes twinkled. "Should you write their names down in your notebook? The horses, I mean?"

"Not now—but I might want to talk to them later."

Walt whooped with laughter. "You're too sharp to mess with." Finishing his butt, he threw it on the ground and squished it with his work boot. "So, Cullen's trying to find out—what?"

"He's not sure his dad died of a heart attack."

Holman slowed down. "That's pretty heavy, young fella."

"You worked closely with Mr. Gallagher. Every time he drove a race, you were on the sidelines, right? Did you ever notice—even once—there might be anything wrong with him? Chest pains, trouble catching a breath, anything like that?"

Holman shook his head. "He was as healthy as any thirty-year-old. Strong, vigorous—and he took crap from nobody."

"He had a-fib. He took medicine for that."

"Coumadin, I think. But half the guys I know older than fifty have some sort of heart shit going on, and they take those meds, too."

"Mind if I ask how old *you* are?"

"Sixty-one," Holman said. "And I'm healthier than Glenn was. Remember, I said *half* the guys. I'm the other half. No heart problems."

"Okay," K.O. said. "Who in the harness racing business didn't like him?"

Walt Holman shoved his hands into the hip pockets of his denims. "I'm guessing you don't have a million bucks or more in the bank, right?"

"No—that's more money than I'll probably ever see in my lifetime!"

"Well, if you were rich enough to outbid other owners at auctions and to take good horses in claiming races, and to indulge yourself while others worked their asses off to make a living, would you think everyone loved you?"

"I can count on one hand everyone who loves me," K.O. said, and held up one index finger. "And I'm not that sure about her, either."

"Not to mention," Holman continued, "the idea of getting in the sulky and competing against guys who've been doing it for their entire lives. It might insult a few, especially when he beats 'em. No, Glenn didn't have that big a fan club back here. Some people hated his guts."

"Now we're getting somewhere. Who?"

"Not me. He was a good friend and an honest partner. Never dicked me out of a single dime. And when I got caught short once, maybe seven years ago, he didn't ask one damn question— he just sat down on a bale of hay and wrote me a check." Holman leaned sideways, putting his mouth close to K.O.'s ear. "And he never asked for it back. I repaid him, though—six months later."

"But not everyone thought he was a good friend."

"He was rich and had power—and if you didn't know him well, he sometimes came off like an asshole. Nobody ever shot at him or anything. I don't think anyone backside even *has* a gun on the premises. I sure as hell know I don't."

"Who do I talk to that didn't like him?"

"Start at the top. Chloe Markham. She owns this track."

K.O. nodded. "I met her here—the night Glenn died—or *sort of* met her. I got the idea they weren't crazy about each other."

"You can sing that in *G*. But she's pretty much of a witch to everybody."

"I'll talk with her. Meanwhile, where can I find Manley Markham?"

"Her baby brother? When Cleveland opened the Horseshoe Casino downtown, Manley-boy became a regular—so he doesn't come around here anymore. I don't know how to get in touch with him."

"I'll find out. Meantime, who else should I talk to?"

Holman waved a hand around at the whole place. "Everybody in our barn. We all worked for Glenn—some happily, some not."

Walking briskly, Holman gave K.O. a quick tour of the backside as they approached what looked like a carnival merry-go-round, except perhaps three times bigger. It was a wide, round wooden structure in which horses are led into individual compartments, approximately twenty feet long and ten feet wide, and allowed to work out at their own pace, usually at a slow trot, unencumbered by driver or sulky. The compartments were separated by metallic fencing walls that were about ten feet high—too tall for any horse to jump. At the bottom were sheets of rubber covering a wide space between the fencing walls and the ground; if a horse fell, it wouldn't be hurt as the rubber rolled over them. In the middle of the enclosure was a machine looking like an enormous metal octopus with its many legs stretching out to those compartments that made the wheel turn.

This particular morning, four horses moved in counter-clockwise circles at a brisk walk. In a small booth off to one side, a young man in overalls and a rally cap squinted over the smoke from his cigarette as he worked an electronic board.

K.O. stopped to watch. Holman said, "We call this here an exercise wheel. Keeps the horses healthy."

"They're going slow, though."

"At the moment. The kid in the booth—Carl Fulwood's his name, by the way—he controls how fast they move. It's early, so he's not putting pressure on the horses. The wheel *can* go as fast as race speed, but we rarely push it any faster than a brisk jog. Hang around here for a few more minutes and he'll speed 'em up a bit."

"Carl Fulwood—he works for Glenn?"

"I guess he works for me, now. Before we get the horses into this thing, he goes in there with a shovel and smooths everything down. The track's a mixture of dirt and chewed-up tires, so it's easier on the horses' feet." He leveled a finger at two large piles just outside the enclosure—a pyramid of dirt about four feet high and another of what once were black tires.

"What about the kid in the barn who pointed you out for me. Who's he?"

"That'd be Jobie Dash," Holman said. "Like Fulwood, one of the grooms."

"I guess he never went to etiquette school."

"Spend every day up to your ass in horse shit, and you wouldn't be polite, either."

"Wasn't he taking that horse out for exercise just now?"

"Nope—he's no driver—not even a trainer. He was hooking him up for Pike Sullivan."

"Who's Pike Sullivan?"

"A driver—actually one of the younger ones, because we got guys around here in their seventies who still drive in races. Pike's a bit of a celebrity, at least locally—popular and very successful. The trouble is, he knows it. He and Glenn butted heads a lot."

"I'll probably want to talk with him, too," K.O. said.

"Take your time. We're here all day."

Holman left K.O. by the exercise wheel and hustled off to do other things; working backside at a racetrack is no easy job. K.O. watched the horses. Some seemed happy to be jogging in circles, almost as if they were showing off. Finally he strolled over to stick his head into the small booth.

"Hi," he said. "Carl Fulwood? Can I talk to you for a minute?"

Carl Fulwood looked up from his control panel. His eyes were listless, his facial features presented no expression whatsoever, and he was mostly breathing through his mouth. His response to K.O.'s greeting: "Huh?"

"I'm collecting some background on your boss—your *late* boss. Glenn Gallagher."

"Yuh."

"Did you know him very well?"

Shrug. "Some."

"He a friend of yours, then?"

"Nah."

"How come? Didn't you like him?"

Fulwood shook his head. "He di'n pay shit."

"Don't all the grooms get paid the same?"

"Nah. He paid some more'n me."

"You feel bad that he died?"

Shrug. "I could care less."

K.O., remembering his military service in Iraq and Afghanistan, thought Fulwood might have been in the army for a time, which was the only place he knew where guys used the expression "I could care less" when what they actually meant was "I *couldn't* care less."

"Will you stay here now that Glenn Gallagher's gone?"

Carl had to consider that for too long a moment until he arrived at an answer: "Dunno. Long's I get paid."

"Who's paying you now, Carl?"

Carl Fulwood blinked his eyes several times in rapid succession, and answered the way he always did, with a shrug.

For a few minutes, K.O. watched the horses move in circles around the exercise wheel, and then strolled back toward Gallagher's barn. More horses were out, stretching their muscles while pulling a jog cart and driver behind them. Second only to equine residents on the backside were cats—many of them. None seemed receptive to K.O.'s patting them—they just ignored him, too busy solving the barns' mouse and rat problem. He was glad his cat, Rodney, was on the back of the sofa with the morning sun warming him as he snoozed instead of ducking out of the way of horses' hooves on a search for a delectable mouse.

He'd learned from Cullen Gallagher that many of the people who did Northcoast Downs' dirty jobs actually lived at the track in a building of tiny apartments that was probably once a cheap motel. The rent was $105 per month, and they generally ate in the backside kitchen, or on rare occasions walked off the property to a nearby coffee shop or pizzeria. Many of them didn't own cars, so if they couldn't cadge a ride from someone else who did, they were stuck at the track, 24/7.

Cullen also told him that grooms and trainers generally worked from six-thirty until about eleven, then went home for a few hours of shuteye before returning to the track at five in the afternoon on race days. Often they stayed until midnight, or even later. K.O. was beginning to realize they didn't mix well with civilians at all—most got along much better with horses than with people.

At Holman's barn, the working stiffs were still at their toil. One of them was leading a horse into a huge therapy pool near the middle of the barn. It was large and deep enough for a horse to wallow in and work out muscle kinks in their legs and shoulders. He watched this particular horse splash around, obviously having a good time like most human babies do in the bathtub.

He looked for Walt Holman, but didn't see him right away, although he did notice a man who hadn't been there earlier— mid-thirties, handsome in a rough way, dressed in a sports shirt and blue and red sweater over pressed jeans. *Pressed*, K.O. thought, to walk around in a horse barn.

"Hey," the man said pleasantly. "I haven't seen you before. New around here?"

"Just visiting," K.O. said, "getting the feel of harness racing from the inside."

"Nice." He stuck out his hand. "Pike Sullivan. I'm a driver—one of the top at this track, or even in all of Ohio. Glad to meet you." After the shake he reclaimed his hand and fumbled around in his jeans pockets. "Looking for a pen here . . . Ah, got one! Did you want my autograph?"

K.O. couldn't reply for a moment. He'd met General David Petraeus once—actually exchanged a few words with him in Baghdad—but the general hadn't assumed his autograph was wanted. If not a signature from General Petraeus, then why Pike Sullivan's? Finally he just shook his head and said "No."

Sullivan looked more shocked than hurt—he must have assumed *everyone* wanted his autograph.

K.O. gave Sullivan one of his business cards. "I work for an investigations firm. We're asking questions on behalf of Cullen Gallagher."

Sullivan raised one eyebrow. "Investigating? Like Sherlock Holmes."

"You knew Glenn Gallagher well, did you?"

Pike replaced the pen into his pocket. "Pretty well. Sometimes Glenn had me race one of his horses. But we both drive, so I wouldn't call us best buddies. Besides," and he primped his casually permed hair, "he was older than me."

"But you weren't enemies?"

He shook his head. "Not *enemies,* enemies. Just—friendly enemies."

"You got in each other's faces a lot."

"That's the cost of doing business, Ace. So what's with all these questions?" He was about to respond but stopped when Walt Holman appeared at the far end of the barn, waved, and came over.

"I see you two have met," Holman said.

"Sort of," K.O. said.

"Pike, maybe we can hook up one of Glenn's horses to a two-person jog cart and you can take K.O. around the track a time or two, just so he can see what we do."

Sullivan frowned, clearly not happy about the idea. "Taking a tourist on a buggy ride?"

Holman paid him no attention. "Jobie!" he bellowed. "Get out here!"

Jobie Dash came slouching out of one of the unused stalls near the far end of the barn, his back and jeans covered with hay; he'd obviously been asleep in there.

"Huh?" he said.

"Hook up Imperion onto a two-man jog cart for Pike."

It seemed to take Dash a second or two to remember which horse Imperion was. Then he slouched over to another stall and emerged leading a gray-almost-white horse.

"Well, hello there, Imperion," K.O. said, patting the horse's long neck. Imperion nickered softly and nuzzled him back; he'd quickly made a friend.

Jobie wheeled over a lightweight two-seater jog cart more easily than he would a bicycle. Positioning it behind Imperion, who was more interested in getting to know K.O. better, Jobie yanked the horse's bridle roughly to make him look forward.

"Hey! Take it easy." K.O.'s calm demeanor immediately morphed into an enraged sonofabitch. "Don't jerk a horse around like that! You wouldn't like it if somebody did it to *you*."

Jobie glowered. "I'd like to see somebody try."

"Chill out," Sullivan soothed, patting at his hair again. "We're all friends here, right?"

K.O. faced Pike. "As long as we treat animals right."

"Hook up Imperion and shut your mouth, Jobie," Holman warned. Then he gave K.O. a hard helmet and a large pair of goggles. "You'll look like a clown in this shit, K.O., but wearing it is mandatory—just in case you fall off."

"Nobody falls off. It's like riding a carousel," Pike said. When K.O. had donned both helmet and goggles, he moved easily into the driver's seat. "Jump in."

K.O. sat on the edge of the seat and swung his legs over the side.

Imperion stepped proud and alert out into the sunshine, and Pike guided him toward the main half-mile track. "This is just a warm-up jog for Imperion. It stretches out his kinks, gets him breathing pretty good. He jogs every morning; all the horses do."

The fall morning air was invigorating on K.O.'s face. On the track several other horses moved clockwise, even though the races were all staged counter-clockwise, and one or two of the drivers waved to Pike, who waved back.

"You know who Vivian Truscott is?" Pike said as he flicked the reins and Imperion picked up speed. "The TV news gal? Sexy blonde, not that young anymore, but pretty hot stuff."

"Sure."

"About a year and a half ago, I took her for a ride like this one, with her camera guy in another sulky alongside us. Channel Twelve wanted Vivian on the track for everyone to see." He laughed. "You'll never guess what happened."

"I stink at guessing."

"Well, the horse must've ate a little late that morning. So

we're going along at about this same speed, and all of a sudden, whammo! The horse let go of breakfast." He snickered—not a cheerful sound. "Vivian got herself a face full a horse shit!"

"That must have been some newscast to watch."

"They didn't show it at all," Pike said, sitting up tall as if there were cameras present—and beautiful women. "It was disappointing, because they scrapped an interview with me. I even got Vivian Truscott chuckling. I think she was coming on to me, too."

"Isn't she married?"

"Didn't ask, didn't tell. Isn't that what fags had to do in the army?"

"No, that's not what fags did in the army," K.O. said tightly. "Fags were too busy killing off al-Qaedas who wanted to come over here and blow up *your* ass."

Pike chose to ignore that as they moved around onto the backstretch. For Imperion, breathing easy and finding his own rocking rhythm, it was a lazy morning jog, moving just fast enough to get those endorphins popping—if, as K.O. wondered, horses even *had* endorphins.

Pike Sullivan said, "I don't understand why you're here, Ace. Was there something funny about Glenn Gallagher's dying?"

"I'm trying to find out if there *was* something funny."

"Some will take it badly if you're poking around asking questions."

"Are you taking it badly right now?"

"I got nothing to hide—nothing that's got to do with Glenn Gallagher. Either way, it's none of your business."

"Actually, it *is* my business—asking questions."

"You sound like a cop."

"I've got no badge. I just try finding out what my client wants to know."

Pike bobbed his head up and down; K.O. couldn't tell if he was agreeing, absorbing, or simply nodding his head in rhythm with Imperion's trot. Then he said, "Why would Cullen want to know something like that?"

"If it was your dad, wouldn't *you* want to know?"

"If *my* old man died, it'd be his kidneys giving up the ghost. He's alcoholic."

"Are you an alcoholic, too, Pike?"

"No, just a heavy hitter, booze-wise. I'm a kinda big star in this game, so I got a busy social life. Lotta pussy, lotta drinking. It's all part of the package, Ace."

They passed the clubhouse and the grandstand seating for those who wanted to watch the race close-up, and Pike Sullivan leaned slightly to his right, guiding Imperion easily into the next turn. Then he said, "You notice these turns are really banked, don't you? When you're up in the clubhouse watching a race, you'd think the track was completely flat—but it's not."

K.O. enjoyed the ride silently for a while. Then he said, "Is your first name really Pike, or is it a stage name?"

"It's my real name. Why?"

"I'm wondering if you made it up because your name was Elmer or something, and you wanted to be called something else—like you calling me 'Ace.'"

"I call everybody Ace."

"I'm not everybody. Not particularly pissed off about it. I'm just sayin'."

Finally K.O. was flying up Pike's nose like a mosquito. The driver's gritted teeth made the sides of his jaw jump. "I'll call you whatever you want." He guided them off the track and they turned into the barn, scattering three cats in the doorway who were basking in the sunshine that had battled through the clouds minutes before. They both got out of the jog cart, and K.O. gave Imperion an extra pat and hug before Jobie appeared to disengage him and walk him back toward his stall.

Walt Holman stuck his head out of his office door. "You survived the ride?"

"Exhilarating," K.O. said, meaning it. He took off his helmet and glasses. "It made me realize how hard it is to win."

"For me," Pike Sullivan boasted, "it's pretty easy. See you around—Ace."

"Pike Sullivan," Holman said as the driver walked off. "He's something else, though. The man's got three wives. Well, I don't know if he's really married to any of 'em, but that's what he calls 'em."

"Three wives! Most people can't even handle one."

Walt grinned. "There's one of 'em can't boil water to save her life, but she can fuck an entire football team in one night without pausing for breath and leave 'em all smiling. One of 'em cooks great—her meat loaf could make any man crazy—but she's lousy in the sack, or so Pike tells us."

"And the third one?"

"Pike thinks she's—pleasant to be around." He clasped his hands at the back of his neck—a luxurious stretch made him groan aloud. "So you got more people to talk to? If you ask enough questions, someone might come up with the right answer."

"Someone who thinks there might be something funny about Glenn's death?"

"You never know," Holman said. "It's too bad, really—and my sympathies to Cullen and to Glenn's girlfriend, whatever her name is. But there's work to do here, kid. Life doesn't stop just because someone has a fatal heart attack."

"Mine either, Walt," K.O. said. "If it *was* a heart attack."

CHAPTER SIX

MILAN

Schoenburg and Weaver, attorneys-at-law, were as big and powerful as any downtown law firm. For their own reasons they'd set their offices in a sprawling, remodeled old warehouse in Solon, a suburb southeast of Cleveland and right on the Summit County line. Most people working at the firm were dressed as casually as the warehouse itself, but I had no doubt they all had stashed sophisticated wear-to-court clothes in their closets and lockers, just in case.

David Weaver was close to my age. He wasn't dressed up, either; his pullover purple sweater covered a white dress shirt open at the neck. He had more hair than I did, though—blondish and matching his neatly trimmed mustache and his too-long sideburns. His commanding voice could carry from a stage to the back row of a big theater—a characteristic he'd obviously worked on for speaking in court so all the jurors and the media could hear every word he said. Since all the offices at Schoenburg and Weaver were cubicles, everyone could eavesdrop on conversations from all over the warehouse.

"I can't tell you much, Mr. Jacovich," he said heartily. "I don't know squat about horse racing."

"Mr. Weaver, having been Glenn's attorney for almost thirty years, you must know more about Glenn's life than just the names of his employees."

"Let's just say that I can't share anything with you that's—uncomfortable."

"Uncomfortable for whom?" I said. That unbalanced him; few people use the word "whom" in conversation, even if they know better.

"For me—for you," he sputtered. "Glenn liked getting where he was going before everyone else did. You don't lay your own company's secrets on the table so everyone and their uncle can take a good long look at it."

"I have my own business, too, Mr. Weaver. I was hired by Glenn this summer and saved his ass, as I'm sure you know."

Weaver nodded. "Don't take this wrong—but you don't work for him now."

"No. Now I work for Cullen Gallagher."

"Cullen. The son and heir."

"Really? I guess that means you've read the will before anyone elsc has."

He lowered his voicc; someone still could have heard him half a block away. "I used the expression sarcastically. I can't reveal the contents of the will to you, naturally."

"Naturally. But Cullen thinks Glenn's death might not have been a heart attack."

"That's not just jumping to a conclusion—it's a running leap. Cullen's no doctor. How would he know?"

"He doesn't know. That's why he's hired me to find out."

A shrug. "It's his money, then."

"Would this worry of Cullen's have anything to do with Glenn Gallagher's will?"

"I've already said I can't discuss Glenn's will with you," Weaver said, "until it's been formally read, with all those involved present."

"Then," I said, "invite me to that reading."

David Weaver laughed the way he might at a boringly unfunny remark at a dull cocktail party. "Don't be a fool. You're *not* involved in the will."

"Didn't think I was. So I imagine you won't tell me who *is* involved."

"Bingo!" He pointed a finger at me. "But good imagination there."

Bingo. I wanted to tie him to the roof of my car and drive to

Alaska. I chose not to. "Were you just Glenn's lawyer, Mr. Weaver, and not his friend?"

"Did we go to lunch or dinner together? Sure. Did we meet for drinks? Often. But friends? There are different definitions for that word. We didn't share our skeletons in the closet, or wishful dreams or sexual fantasies. Glenn moved money around expertly; my job was to ensure he did so legally. We were lawyer-client; that's *all* it was."

"I don't think anything in the world is 'all it was.' That's why we're talking."

"Talking?" Weaver laughed. "Flapping the breeze is more like it. As far as I know, you might be trying to throw a monkey wrench into Glenn's will—for Cullen's sake or maybe even your own."

"I don't even own a monkey wrench, Mr. Weaver, and I wouldn't cheat anyone—especially my client—out of what he might gain from his father's will."

"It's nice knowing what a wonderful human being you are, then."

"Must be nice for you to be sarcastic when you're not talking to a judge."

Weaver shrugged. "I'm sarcastic to judges sometimes, too."

"When you can get away with it. So you flat-out refuse to help Glenn's son find out the truth?"

"You *have* the truth. The autopsy said heart failure; why not leave it at that?"

"Because Cullen can't leave it at that."

"Then," David Weaver said, "go knock on Cullen's attorney's door and ask *him* questions. As for me—" and he looked pointedly at his Rolex, "I'm done."

I was done, too, as far as Weaver was concerned. I've never gotten on well with lawyers; each time I run into a new one, I seem to have trouble. It's my karma. At least Carli would call it that; she was into karma and many other hippie-like ideas from thirty years before she was born.

My next meeting would be even more difficult. I'd called earlier that morning and begged the receptionist, or executive assistant, or whoever she was, for an appointment for that afternoon and was granted one for two-thirty. I drove back downtown from Weaver's suburban office, and went into John Q's on Public Square. Eating lunch alone at the bar was not nearly as lonesome as sitting by myself at a table. At least I got to chat with the bartender.

I walked across the square to Terminal Tower and took the elevator up to Victor Gaimari's office. I wasn't ushered into his inner sanctum as usual, though; he came out into the waiting room instead.

We didn't shake hands.

"I'm surprised to see you," he said—chilly.

"Thanks for letting me come up, Victor. I'm looking for information, and since you and Glenn Gallagher knew each other, maybe you can help."

He glanced at his receptionist, who tried looking busy, and then he motioned me to step out into the hall with him. Evidently I was no longer welcome in his private office the way I once was.

"I thought it was clear you'll get no more inside information from me," he said in that high-pitched voice that didn't fit his macho appearance and size. "I can guess why you're here. You always came to me for the same reason. And if you're blaming the Italian community for something, you can push the DOWN button right now." He pointed toward the elevator door as if I wouldn't have known where to find it.

"I think you know me better than that," I said.

"I'm not sure I know you at all. What do you want?"

"I'm working for Cullen Gallagher."

"Who?"

"He's a college professor at Hiram. Glenn Gallagher's son. I worked for Glenn too this past summer for about three weeks."

"One of his employees was a murderer or something?"

"Nothing like that. It was an internal security problem."

"And," Victor Gaimari said, "you're telling me this—why?"

"I saw you at Glenn Gallagher's funeral."

His jaw was rigid; he looked over my shoulder at something that wasn't there. "Many people were at that funeral. It wasn't a formal gathering of the Five Families."

"I was friends with you for years, Victor, and why we aren't friends anymore is in your head, not mine. You know I loved your uncle, so knock the shit off about my being anti-Italian, whatever else you think."

He considered it. "What I think," he said, "is that I don't do your job and you shouldn't do mine. I can't tell you anything about Glenn. We were in the same business and sometimes ran into each other at dinners and benefits. That's it."

"You were competitors?"

"Everybody's a competitor. Ditch digger A wants to be thought of as a *better* ditch digger than ditch digger B. That's how the world works."

"Platitudes don't give me much. Who were Gallagher's competitors besides you? Ones he didn't get along with."

"That might be a long list."

"I saw John Terranova at the racetrack the night Gallagher died. Did he have something to do with him, too?"

Annoyance made him purse his lips before he said, "Ask John."

"Victor, must we stand out here in the hall?"

"I'm busy—and I'm all out of standing-in-the-hall time. I'm not spending an afternoon making you a list." Victor touched his well-trimmed mustache, clearly debating whether to tell me anything. Then: "Go see people at Aventura."

"Aventura? That's a rock group."

"It's also a city in Florida. But for your purposes, it's a venture capital firm right here in Cleveland. Talk to Carol Watterson. She's the CEO."

I took out my notebook. "Do you have Aventura's address?"

"I'm not the White Pages," he snapped. "Look it up." Almost spinning on his heel, he went back inside, leaving me standing like a schmuck in the middle of the hallway. Waiting for the elevator, I considered that I'd called Victor by his name three times during that short conversation, but he hadn't used my name once.

My assessment of him as being "chilly" dropped about fifteen degrees.

*   *   *

Aventura Investments was headquartered a short walk from the Terminal Tower, in what used to be called the BP Building back when British Petroleum had major offices in town. I think they stopped calling it the BP Building almost a decade ago; I don't know what it's known as now, nor do I care. Our new casino, The Horseshoe, is located in what used to be the Higbee Building—a classic old department store. Old-time Clevelanders will continue thinking of it as the Higbee Building, no matter what goes on in there, because when we were kids our parents took us downtown to see their Christmas windows. They've changed the names of our baseball field and basketball arena, too, and so many other buildings and places in our town that I've stopped keeping track. The old BP Building falls into that category.

Carol Watterson's CEO office was pleasant and spacious, in a two-window corner overlooking Public Square and Collision Bend, the bend in the river where I had *my* headquarters. She was fifty or so, perhaps ten pounds overweight, in a somber dark gray suit and one-inch heels, and her hairdo, at odds with the rest of her, was a short cut she couldn't have fussed over that morning for more than five seconds. I ascertained that her personality was Type-A—aggressive, alpha, in charge of everything in her life. I'd explained on the phone why I wanted to meet face-to-face. Her examination of documents, making iPad notes that had nothing to do with me, and the incessant drum of her fingers on the desktop shouted that she was a multi-tasker.

She looked at my business card and rubbed her thumb over the face of it to find whether it was embossed. Then she said brusquely, "I'm sorry, but I've never heard of you."

"Well, that levels the playing field," I said.

She didn't like *that*. Her eyebrows soared toward her hairline but she refused to react further. "What can I do for you, Mr. Jacovich?" Her correct pronunciation of my name indicated that she, at least, paid attention.

I asked her again, as I'd done on the phone, whether she'd known Glenn Gallagher, which brought a near-sneer. "We've met," she said.

"I didn't see you at the funeral."

"I had things to do that day. Besides, we weren't friends."

"Why is that?"

"I've met thousands of people, and I don't count all of them as friends. Why do you want to know?"

"Cullen Gallagher wants to put some pieces together now that his father is gone."

"Pieces? Glenn was an investment banker and a hedge fund manager. His hobby was big-time horse racing. How many more pieces do you want?"

"Just trying to figure out who liked him and who didn't."

"*I* didn't. He was a miserable shit. Who cares who liked him? *I'm* not one of his beneficiaries."

"Cullen's feeling is that Glenn's death was—complicated."

"What's so complicated about a drunk having a heart attack?"

"It might not have been a fatal heart attack."

If I'd believed in those corny vampire movies, I'd have sworn Carol Watterson's eyes turned momentarily red. She clenched both fists. "Are you saying it was murder?"

"I'm asking questions."

"Like asking me if *I* murdered Glenn Gallagher?" She pushed herself up from her chair to a standing crouch and leaned over her desk at me. "Don't lay that bullshit on me. Glenn screwed me out of clients, I screwed him out of clients, we all screwed each other in this town. Don't believe for one second that I'll put up with an accusation of murder*!*"

If I'd believed it for one second, she might've punched the crap out of me. "Not an accusation. But if it wasn't a heart attack—if it *was* murder—someone did it."

"Call the police, then."

"The police are barely aware of Glenn's death."

"Then you're making a big deal over nothing." Her words were insulting. "That's why you do what you do—scratch around for the next buck and make everything seem important so that people pay you."

"If it has to do with the death of Cullen's dad," I said, "it *is* a big deal."

She sat back down in her chair, crossing her arms defensively across her chest, and made a sound that might be written phonetically as "Hmphh!"

"You know who else makes it a big deal?" I said. "*You.* Perhaps you doth protest too much."

Carol Watterson' laugh was nasty. "Oh, I see. Well, go on, Jacovich. Go ahead, say what you're dying to call me—a bitch, right? Most men who talk to strong, successful women just *love* that word."

"It never crossed my mind to call you a bitch," I said. "I was considering calling you a dick."

She glared at me for an endless moment. Then she started to laugh; she didn't want to, but couldn't help it. I laughed, too.

"Good one," she admitted. "I'll take that as a compliment."

I gave her a half-hearted salute. "Knock yourself out."

She relaxed—just a bit, mind you, as she was still very much in charge of this office. "I *should* apologize, then—but don't get *too* excited; I don't believe in apologies. I'm defensive because Gallagher ticked me off on a regular basis. He constantly raided my client base, saying bad things about me, telling out-and-out lies to lure them away from me. It was legal—he always took competition one step too far. But thinking someone's a shit is a far cry from actually murdering them, Mr. Jacovich."

"If I killed everyone who I thought was a shit," I said, "we'd be living in a ghost town. And after the name-calling, just think of me as plain old Milan."

"Then there's no help to give you, plain old Milan. Nothing's wrong besides Cullen's gut feeling that something isn't kosher."

"Carol," I said, "empires have risen and crashed on a gut feeling that things are not kosher."

CHAPTER SEVEN

K.O.

Chloe Markham had a large office on the second floor of the racetrack, but it didn't look to K.O. that she had any work to do. Her door was wide open to frame her pose—standing there dressed not like a CEO or a business owner but a wealthy housewife shopping at Saks Fifth Avenue in white linen slacks and a silk blouse with a cashmere sweater's sleeves artfully tied around her shoulders. She was chatting socially about some Kardashian divorce with a few of the workers who moved papers around on their desks and answered phones when they had to. When K.O. re-introduced himself to her, she had no idea of who he was until he reminded her they'd met a week earlier at the races with Glenn Gallagher. Even then he had to mention his employer's name before the incident rang a memory bell for her.

"Oh, yes," she said. "Milan Jacovich. I remember *him*. The big-shot Cleveland private eye, right?"

"He's just my boss, Ms. Markham."

"You were with him at the track that night?"

"I was a member of his party," K.O. said.

"So how did *you* find your way up here this morning—and why?"

"To chat with you for a few minutes, if you have the time."

She hadn't moved from the doorway to her private office and showed no inclination of doing so. "I'm pretty busy."

Was there anyone in the world, K.O wondered, who'd never blown off someone else just by saying they were busy?

Chloe said, "Look, I'm being blunt—but you're too young for me."

"First of all, I'm not a kid. Secondly, I'm too young for *what*?"

"I'm already seeing someone," she said.

"Wait until you're asked, Ms. Markham." Chloe was so shocked that she let her jaw hang open for a moment too long. "I met your current—someone—that evening, too. Skippy."

"*Skip!*" she snapped, biting off the last consonant like the tip of a celery stalk. "It's not Skippy, it's Skip."

"If you say so. You met *my* girlfriend too, but I doubt you remember."

"Like I care." She looked pointedly at her watch. "Tick tock," she said, "you're wasting time."

"I'll get right to the point, then. My company is conducting a small security operation. For Cullen Gallagher."

"Who?"

"The late Glenn Gallagher's son."

"What does Cullen Gallagher want with me? I barely know him."

"He's tying up loose ends. He suggested I speak with several people, including you."

"About what?"

"Glenn Gallagher died the night you and I met."

"I know. I was at the funeral."

K.O. nodded. "I saw you there. I didn't see Skippy with you, though."

"*Skip!*"

"Oh, right. You knew Glenn Gallagher pretty well?"

"He's a horse owner and driver, so naturally I knew him. But we're not buddies, for Christ's sakes; he's thirty years older than me."

"You saw him at the track three nights a week. You must've talked with him a lot."

"Not so much."

"Were you aware of him having heart trouble?"

She frowned as much as she allowed herself, fearful of inviting wrinkles. "We don't share medical problems with each other.

Most people don't—in case you want to tell me about your deviated septum."

"That'll be my secret," K.O. said, not quite sure what a deviated septum *was*.

"All I know about Glenn is that we didn't get along. He was arrogant—full of himself, too damn demanding, too damn critical." Chloe tossed her hair out of her eyes and leaned her head back so she could look down on K.O. "I don't need criticism, not from *you*, and certainly not from someone like Glenn. His hobby with horse racing—and that's all it was, a hobby, not a business—got in my way and bugged the shit out of me. When I want opinions, I pay people to give them to me."

"Is that why you disliked him? Because he had opinions?"

"Because he had too much ego."

"You have a pretty big ego, too."

"I'm *entitled* to a big ego," Chloe said. "I'm rich. I own this whole damn place."

"Is there anyone in this whole damn place who disliked Gallagher as much as you did?"

"Lots of people." A thought struck her and her forehead crinkled as she gently touched the corner of her mouth with her forefinger. "What's going on here? Are you saying somebody *killed* him? Come on, that's a load of crap."

"I'm just asking questions."

"So go ask them someplace else." She turned away, retreating back into her office. "Sorry, kid, but I've got things to do. Tick tock, tick tock . . . "

Tick tock my *ass*, K.O. thought as he found his way back downstairs. Chloe didn't do any work at all except raking in the money and standing around looking pretty. He'd have to find out who *really* operated this racetrack.

He trudged back to the Gallagher barn, pulling from his pocket the list of names Cullen had given him. Jobie Dash, one of the grooms whose name was not on that list, was *almost* working, moving as slowly as he possibly could, but he paused long enough to send K.O. another one of those hateful glares. It didn't bother K.O. in the slightest. He'd also grown up angry, and his personality ground the guts of many besides Jobie—probably Milan's, too, sometimes. He was used to not being liked.

Walt Holman was in his tiny office to the left of the barn entrance, his head bent over his desk as he worked on his account books, listening to a very old table radio playing country music. K.O. knocked and poked his head in.

"Am I bothering you?"

Holman said. "Any excuse to avoid all this paperwork. How you doing? Everything okay?"

K.O. tipped his hand back and forth. "Par for the course."

"Did you enjoy your ride?"

"It was fun—and the horse was extra-polite."

"Wanna learn how to drive? It's not just sitting there flicking the reins, y' know."

"Maybe tomorrow. I just talked to Chloe Markham—not my most pleasant morning, but I guess in my racket there aren't many pleasant ones."

"Your racket?"

"Asking questions of people who don't want to answer them. Walt, who's the on-hands person around here who *really* keeps this place operating? I know it's not Chloe."

"His name's Everett Valmer—the CFO. He's not 'horse people.' He's a damn good businessman—otherwise this track would've closed a week ago Tuesday."

"Does he know what goes on backside?" K.O. said. "Does he ever come down out of his front office? Does he know personal stuff about all of you?"

Walt chuckled. "Not unless there's a spy who squeals on us. He doesn't give a shit about who likes who and who hates who and who screws who. He checks the bottom line every morning while the rest of us read the sports pages. But I don't think he's coming in today. You can swing back here tomorrow. Everett, though, he doesn't show up until around nine thirty or ten."

K.O. nodded. "Good enough." He checked Cullen's list again. "Where can I find Del Fiddler?"

Walt's face darkened along with his frown. "Aw, crap, not Del Fiddler!"

"Why not?"

"He's a big sour bite of trouble, that's why not. Del Fiddler and Glenn almost came to blows about six months ago. Come to think of it, they *did* swap punches a while before that."

"I didn't know this. Why?"

Walt lifted both eyebrows. "You never saw Del's wife Wanda, huh?"

"Yeah, I did. That's what the fight was about? From what I saw of Wanda, which wasn't much longer than ninety seconds, she's a flirt."

"Some people might say flirt, some might say she's just friendly—and her husband thinks she's a slut."

"What do *you* think, Walt?"

"I think I should keep my trap shut. Anyways, this last time there weren't any punches actually thrown, just pushing and shoving in the barn. If I didn't break it up—and I got an elbow in the mouth for my trouble, by the by—who knows what might of happened."

"Did Del train Glenn's horses?"

"Not after that argument. Glenn wouldn't of hired him and Del wouldn't of worked for him. Like I say, everything backside is related in one way or another. It's a big family." Walt cocked his head to one side. "You noticed I never said 'one big *happy* family,' did I?"

"Nobody's happy?"

"Well—" Walt drew the word out the way Ronald Reagan used to. "We're *all* happy when we're around horses. We push 'em too hard sometimes. There's not the money in harness racing there used to be, so everybody wants to win real bad. But we love our horses. When we're around other people—civilians like you and Milan Jacovich—that's a whole different kettle of fish."

"I'll have to be more polite, then," K.O. said, and Walt didn't recognize the sarcasm. "Where do I find Del Fiddler?"

Walt Holman glanced up at the old wall clock. "He's probably over in Barn Four right about now—if he's not exercising a horse on the track."

"Thanks."

"Hey—watch yourself with him, son. He's feisty."

"So am I," K.O. said.

The sun was out in full force, but the October weather would never really get warm again, and a healthy wind was blowing from the lake up north. K.O. zipped his jacket as he made his way to Barn Number Four. With the possible exception of Carl Fulwood and Jobie Dash, most of the workers involved in everyday cleanups actually looked happy, as if they were having a good time. He didn't imagine himself working with horses, though, as much as he loved animals. Horses were five times his size, those huge teeth could easily bite off his finger while he lovingly held a carrot, and one flick of a hoof could crush his chest and kill him. Despite occasional dangers and fisticuffs, he'd stick with private investigations—for now.

There was little difference between Barn Four and Gallagher's, except Wanda Fiddler was improving the scenery, crooning quietly to one of the horses. Her jeans were two-hundred-and-fifty-buck designer types, and as snug as they were on her it was unlikely she'd get any real work done wearing them. Her blouse was royal blue, open to the third button to display her lighter-blue bra, and her cleavage was deep enough to hide a Mini Cooper.

Her smile at K.O. was dazzling—outdoor sunlight sparkling off brilliantly whitened teeth. It was as phony as a three-dollar bill. She left the horse and sashayed over to where he was standing. "Sashay" isn't a word people use much anymore—but it's precisely what Wanda Fiddler did. Every muscle in her body moved in rhythm to her walk.

"Hey," she breathed, perfume emanating from her like an invisible force field.

"Mrs. Fiddler?"

"Wanda." She dimpled prettily. "I know you from somewhere."

"I'm Kevin O'Bannion. I was friends with Glenn Gallagher. I was with him on his last night, which is when you and I saw each other."

"Aw. Poor Glenn. May he rest in peace." She crossed herself awkwardly. Then she chose a Shirley Temple sad, lower-lip-extended look—wasted, because K.O.'d never heard of Shirley Temple.

"You and he were friends?"

"Mm-hmm," she hummed.

"Did you talk with him a lot?"

"Sure. Don't friends talk to friends?"

"Sometimes. Did he ever talk about his health—physical problems?"

She fluttered her eyelashes, throwing her shoulders back. Her breasts struggled valiantly to blast through her blouse. "I wasn't aware of his—um—physical problems."

"How about alcohol?"

"Ooh—I'd *love* some!" she teased.

"That's very amusing in the middle of the morning," K.O. said. "But I meant Glenn's drinking."

She was disappointed he didn't laugh, clearly unaware that "amusing" is almost always a put-down. "I only saw him during the day, and he was too busy to booze it up. On race nights—well, nobody'd dare drink alcohol before they drove or they'd get kicked out of here—suspended, or even told they can't ever work here again."

"Tough regulations," K.O. said.

"Yeah. But guys like what they do. They like horses. Me, I like 'em okay, but I like people better."

"Good for you."

"Hey," she said. "You're staring at my tits, aren't you?"

"It's hard not to."

A coquette, sparkling merrily. "I don't mind, really. I had them done about two years ago," she said, "and now everybody wants to see 'em." She opened her eyes wide, and her hand moved to the fourth button of her blouse, one of the few still buttoned. "Do *you* wanna see 'em?"

"Sorry," K.O. said, "but I'm trying to quit."

Wanda looked surprised; few men said no to her. "Hon, are you queer?"

"Not that I've noticed."

"It's all right if you are."

"Now I have something to think about. Is your husband here?"

She wrinkled her nose as if smelling something worse than a resident horse barn. "Oh, hell, Del's *always* here. You don't wanna talk to him anyway. He's a prick."

"Oh."

"Del hated Glenn's guts. He was so jealous of him . . . "

"Because of you?"

"That's the shitty part. Nothing happened between me and Glenn. It could of, y' know, but it didn't. He had a girlfriend of his own."

"I have a girlfriend, too."

"Oh."

"And you have a husband, Wanda."

She grimaced. "Tell me about it."

"Was that the only reason Del didn't like Glenn?"

She shook her head. "Del don't like many people. With Glenn, even before I was in the picture—or Del *thought* I was in the picture—it was all about money stuff."

"What kind of money stuff?"

"I don't know nothing about money. Del makes it—and he don't think Glenn and the other owners give him enough—and I spend it. But they fought over a horse, too."

"As to who owns it?"

"Nuh-uh. Glenn owned it. Gallagher's Sugarbush, his name was—a pretty bay. Glenn hired Del to train him, mostly because Walt Holman was too busy with other horses to do it. Sugarbush was a pretty good pacer, he'd won lots a races. But this one night, for one reason or another he was off his speed a little. Del doesn't have much patience with horses, and I guess he was pushing Sugarbush way too hard."

"Doesn't Del love horses?"

"Only if they make him money."

"And if they don't?"

She shrugged. "Then he'd just as leave sell 'em for dog food."

K.O.'s guts twisted—that feeling that tied him up inside every time an animal was cruelly abused, that ice-cold rage. But he wouldn't pursue this subject now; he was on assignment—strictly business. "What happened with Gallagher's Sugarbush?"

"Del thought Sugar could go a lot faster than he'd been running. He demands a lot from horses."

"What did he do?"

"Well, they lost a race that night, even though Del really put the whip on him for the last half mile. And when they finished out of the money, Del was humiliated, you know what I mean? And he—well, after they got back to the barn, he kinda took it out on Sugar in his stall. When Del loses his temper he goes out of control—so he laid open a couple of bad cuts on Sugar's neck whacking away at him with a pitchfork! Remember, now, this was Glenn's horse, not Del's. And when Glenn saw that, Sugar in his stall with his head hanging almost down to the ground, and the blood and all—well, that's when him and Del had the *real* fight."

"In the barn?"

She shook her head. "Glenn made him go outside with him— and Del woulda been too embarrassed not to. It was almost midnight, but everybody followed them out so they could stand around and watch. Some of 'em even cheered. Nobody was on Del's side, y' know?"

"Because of what he did to the horse?"

"Partly—but nobody liked him anyway."

"How did the fight turn out?"

Wanda closed her eyes and shook her head, not wanting to remember. "Glenn was bigger and meaner than Del ever thought about being. Glenn busted two of Del's ribs and knocked out three teeth. I don't even think Del landed one punch. And then Glenn fired him on the spot—even before Del could get up off the ground."

"And the horse?" K.O. said, his rage almost toxic in the back of his throat. "Did he race again?"

"I don't think so. That beating injured a tendon so bad that Glenn decided to retire him. Then he and Walt trained him for a saddle horse and sold him to someone on a farm out in Burton—y' know, in Geauga County where they make maple syrup?" Her look for a moment was far, far away, possibly remembering a kinder, quieter time when she wasn't married to Del Fiddler. "A farm with a little girl living on it, I hope. Little girls on farms all love horses."

"That fistfight was over a year ago," K.O. reminded her. "Did Del stay mad enough all this time to—do something to Glenn? Something bad?"

"Del stays mad every minute he's awake."

"I don't want to embarrass you, Wanda—but does he ever do anything bad to you?"

She laughed, but there was no mirth behind it. "If he ever did, I'd cut his nuts off with garden shears." She glanced out the door of the barn and jammed her hands into her pockets. "Here he comes. Ask him yourself."

Del Fiddler guided his horse back into the barn, then slid off the seat of his jog cart as one of the grooms—a young kid about eighty pounds too heavy who seemed to be suffering with terminal acne—took the reins, unhitched the horse and led it back to its stall. Fiddler removed his helmet and goggles and tossed them into a corner. Still holding the whip, he looked at K.O. suspiciously, and glared after his wife's undulating ass as she headed toward the rear of the barn. "Who're you?" he demanded gruffly. "What're you doing in this barn?"

K.O. introduced himself and explained to Fiddler why he was there.

"You don't work for Gallagher. He's dead," Fiddler said.

"I work for his son, Cullen. You know him?"

"Don't have much use for him—nerdy little pussy. As for *Glenn* Gallagher—fuck 'im! I don't wanna talk about him."

"He's been dead for a week and your reaction is 'fuck him'?"

The trainer flicked the whip at a buzzing insect only he could see. "I don't cry no tears over him."

"Is there anyone else not crying tears over him?"

"Give me one good reason why I should tell you."

"Because I'm asking nicely?"

"I'll give you a good reason why *not*. I just don't give a shit."

"You're glad he's dead?"

"Not glad. Not sad. Not *interested*." Del Fiddler hiked up his trousers and jutted his chin toward K.O. Wanda had been right— Del really *didn't* like many people. "This is my barn. Don't come back here and get in our way."

K.O. stifled his urge to dismember Del Fiddler piece by piece. "Nice meeting you," he said and started for the door.

"And you better stay the fuck away from my wife," Del called after him, "or you'll be sorry."

K.O. stopped walking. If this moment had occurred a year or

more earlier, he would either have had a knockdown drag-out with Del, or he would have made it his business to have sex with Wanda Fiddler—even though he wasn't attracted to her. Just so he could tell her husband afterward that he'd done it. However he had Carli in his life now and better things to do with his time. Still, he had no intention of giving Fiddler the last word. He turned slowly, hands loose at his sides.

"I'm sorry *now*," he said.

CHAPTER EIGHT

MILAN

When I was a kid, if you needed a doctor and it wasn't a big emergency, you'd phone, he'd enter your home wearing a suit and tie, carrying his little black bag, and when he left you'd pay him directly—if not with cash, then with a live chicken, or a basket of tomatoes or green peppers grown in your backyard. If you needed to visit *his* office, chances were it was only a few blocks walking distance from where you lived, and you'd take the chicken with you—who unfortunately didn't have a choice in the matter.

Not today! On the unlikely assumption that the doctor comes to your home nowadays, it's usually for dinner, he doesn't bring his black bag with him (if indeed he owns one anymore), and your time together is all social and no medical business. The conversation is never about what hurts or itches or makes you worry that you might never wake up again, but about *his* golf score, *his* membership in the Chagrin Valley Gun Club, *his* multi-million dollar vacation home on Florida's Sanibel Island. Things have changed. The world has changed. America sure as hell has changed.

So Dr. Howard Lichtig didn't make house calls, and his office was nowhere near where I could walk to it. A cardiologist, he held court in Lake County's Willoughby Hills, a half-hour's freeway drive from where I lived. Cullen Gallagher hadn't even known who his late father's heart specialist was until he discovered Dr. Lichtig by rummaging through Glenn's papers and eventually checking his iPhone. When I called, the doctor was reluctant to talk to me; many doctors don't encourage conversations in the office with strangers who actually keep their clothes on. After I begged the nurse, she finally put me on hold for too damn long until Lichtig came on the line. I explained I was working for Cullen and that Glenn had been a client of mine earlier that summer, which apparently pressured him to "give in" and grant me a visit to his office.

At the appointed hour, he made me cool my heels in his reception room for almost thirty minutes, where the only magazines available were all about health. Doctors are never on time for appointments. I wondered: if I clutched my chest, gasped for breath, and collapsed on the floor, would they pay immediate attention to me? Frankly, I was doubtful.

Finally a nurse emerged from the inner workings of the cardio department, loudly called my name so that all other waiting patients would know it, and bade me follow her. Marching behind her down the corridor, we made several right and left turns before she eventually stopped in front of a scale and gestured for me to mount it. "We need to get your weight," she said.

"Why?"

"Doctor won't examine you unless we get your weight."

Doctor won't. Why do nurses invariably use only the title when referring to their employer? Why not *the* doctor or Doctor Jones? No one refers to others by profession as "Lawyer" or "Plumber" or "Hooker." I said, "*Doctor* isn't going to examine me. We're just going to talk."

That seemed to trouble her—patients never just came in to chat, and she wasn't prepared to vary from the routine. Finally practicality topped annoyance. She made her lips into a slash and choked out, "Very well." That's another usage you rarely hear spoken anymore. *Very well.*

She plopped me into a chair in an examination room, clearly confused because she had no chart of mine to slip into its nest outside the door. Then she told me *Doctor* would be with me shortly and disappeared.

Another ten-minute wait. Nothing to read while biding time in an examination room, either.

When Dr. Howard Lichtig entered, he looked annoyed already by my presence, which attested to his not offering a handshake. About fifty, he had a round face covered by whiskers—not a beard, mind you, but a look announcing he hadn't shaved in several weeks. It was the *current* movie star look. In my day, the only film actor who looked like that was George "Gabby" Hayes.

"This is very unusual, Mr. Jacovich," he said, mispronouncing my name as he read my business card. "This is a medical office. I never chat in the office about anything except medical concerns—specifically about hearts."

"This *is* about a heart, Dr. Lichtig—just not *my* heart."

"You have no heart problems?"

"Nobody's even broken it recently."

That didn't amuse him. "Cullen Gallagher phoned you wanted to see me. I can't imagine why. I've never laid eyes on Cullen Gallagher. I don't meet patients' relatives all that often—especially deceased patients' relatives."

"According to the post mortem, Glenn died of a heart attack."

"I read the coroner's report. Yes?"

I tread carefully. "Could something else have killed him, Dr. Lichtig? Besides a heart attack?"

"He could've been hit by a bus."

"Pretty flippant."

He sat back and folded his hands across his belly like a pissed-off Buddha. "I deal with living patients—and I try keeping them that way. If they unfortunately pass on, I move along to the next patient. That's how I keep my sanity."

"You're moving along now without another thought about Glenn Gallagher?"

"I don't have time. Hearts are like car engines; they break down more frequently the older they get. I do my best to keep them alive—and I have a pretty good record of doing that. But sometimes . . . " His grimace made him look like the character on the cover of *Mad Magazine* who always asked, "*What, me worry?*"

"How long were you—caring for Glenn?"

"Six, maybe seven years. I don't have his chart in front of me."

"When he started seeing you he was in his early fifties."

"That sounds right."

"For his atrial."

"Actually a form of atrial arrhythmia."

"Explain that to me, please."

He looked at his wristwatch. I've observed that most people look at their watches during a conversation and never mentally record what time it is. "Let's say his heart rhythm was off—faster than usual, without real provocation. It wasn't a severe case—but we kept an eye on it nonetheless."

"And you prescribed medication—Coumadin."

Lichtig nodded. "Lots of people take Coumadin. Before he began seeing me, Glenn Gallagher had a mini-stroke—and his CAT scan revealed he'd had another stroke sometime earlier than that. No damage was done—no physical damage, anyway, and no mental impairment because he was rushed to the hospital early enough. He was one lucky sonofabitch!"

"Who rushed him to the hospital?"

"A woman who works in his office. Jen Taylor. In the past few years, I prescribed digitalis for him also."

"Digitalis—I've heard of it, but I can't remember exactly what it does."

Dr. Lichtig sighed. "Digitalis treats congestive heart failure and rhythm problems. Again, not an uncommon medicine."

"Pills or liquid?"

"It can be either. Gallagher preferred liquid. He had a specially marked dropper to measure his doses."

"Everyone gets the same dose?"

"Of *course not!*" Lichtig's pissy mood was growing by leaps and bounds. "Everyone has different doses of *any* medication!"

"Would taking too much Coumadin or digitalis be dangerous?"

"Any overdose of any prescribed pharmaceutical—or even aspirin—could be dangerous."

"Glenn Gallagher was taking the same dose from the beginning."

"That's my recollection, yes."

"Can one just go into a drugstore and buy Coumadin or digitalis over the counter?"

"Certainly not. They're both prescription medications."

"Is there any other place where they can be purchased?"

"Not legally," he said. "Who knows what one might do over the Internet? But in America, prescription meds are carefully guarded in pharmacies and hospitals."

"And if someone stole a medication from the hospital?"

Lichtig went into full high-dudgeon haughty! "Only licensed people are allowed anywhere near where medicines are kept in the hospital—and the drugs are checked and counted twice a day. If even a thimbleful of anything were missing, we'd know it!"

"But a drug addict—someone on the street—wouldn't want to steal digitalis or Coumadin anyway, right?"

"No addict would. That would be a dumb way to get high. And *this* is a dumb way for me to piss away a valuable hour, so I suggest you leave quickly and quietly. And don't call me again." Then a thought struck Dr. Howard Lichtig, and he almost smiled. "Unless you yourself are noticing heart problems or palpitations. You're not a young man anymore—things happen. In that case, I'd be more than happy to take care of you."

The arrogant son of a bitch! I thought as I motored onto the westbound I-90 freeway and headed back downtown. He'd be "happy" if I actually had heart difficulties. I'd rather beg K.O. for the name of the vet who prescribes medicine for Rodney vomiting hairballs before I'd ask Howard Lichtig for anything.

"I can't touch this, you know," Tobe Blaine said much later that evening, watching me get dressed, "this so-called investigation into whether Gallagher was murdered. Cleveland P.D. can't butt into suburban police situations unless they're asked—and as far as I know, it's on the books that Gallagher had a fatal heart attack."

"You're probably right, Tobe." I buttoned my shirt. "But he died in my arms."

"People die all the time, Milan—from sudden heart failure, brain aneurysms exploding, all sorts of things. Younger than Glenn, too; sometimes we can't bring ourselves to accept it."

"I know."

"One of the men on my squad in Raleigh—a health and fitness nut—ran every morning. Five miles, six, it all depended on the weather. He bragged about his running, talking about 'getting into the zone,' which, by the way, bored the crap out of most of us. So one morning after his run, he comes home, steps into the shower, and drops dead on the spot from a massive heart attack. Forty-six years old, a wife, two kids, went to church on Sundays, loved watching the Durham Bulls, and voted straight Republican."

"Voting Republican causes heart attacks?"

"My point being," she said, pulling the hem of her robe down over her beautiful smooth cocoa-colored legs, "that you're wasting your time, you and K.O. The only one who thinks this was a murder is Glenn's son—and he doesn't know a damn thing about his father's life. He's guessing."

"Going on instinct."

"If *I* went on instinct, I'd arrest half the people I know, including you."

"What did I do?"

"Nothing—it would've been instinct."

"We're getting paid, Tobe."

"You have other projects on your books. Why a wild goose chase like this one?"

"It's hard to explain," I said. "It was that scintilla of connection, that last moment of eye contact with Glenn before he stopped breathing. That flicker of a second where he was trying to tell me something—with his eyes."

"Telling you goodbye?"

"No, it was more than that. It bothered me—kept me up at night."

"You weren't awake *that* night," Tobe said. "Half the time you snored."

"While we're on the subject," I said, "I'm not the only one who snores."

"I never snore," she said. "It's not ladylike."

"It's cop-like, though."

"Really? Slept with a lot of cops, have you?"

"I choose not to discuss it."

"It's a damn good thing you made that choice. And really, Milan—drop this Gallagher thing before it makes you completely crazy."

"Can't drop it. He had racetrack friends he could have asked to drive him home. He could've called a taxi. But he asked me, and I did, and he died while I watched."

"And because you're getting paid."

"It's worth it to Cullen to hire me to find out the truth." She started to say something but I put up a hand. "And it's worth it to me. That's just how it goes, Tobe."

She smiled ruefully. "Then do it. I know you by now—you'll do it well." She stood up, waited until I put on my windbreaker, and then threw her arms around my neck, pressing her whole body against me. "I'll get my next-week work schedule tomorrow," she said, "and we can decide when we get to spend the whole night together again, and the next day, too, instead of this screw-and-split business."

"Screw-and-split. You *do* have a way with words."

"A way with words? You think?"

"You have many ways, all of them terrific."

She gently squeezed the back of my neck. "You haven't seen all my ways."

"Then I'll keep hanging around until I do."

"One of my ways," Tobe said, "is to get a halfway decent sleep instead of boffing all night long before I show up for work first thing in the morning."

"Screw-and-split and then boffing. A too-wordy way of saying goodnight?"

"Way with words again! Go home, Milan, and drive carefully."

The kiss was equal to all our others, which was pretty amazing, and in mid-kiss I slipped my hand down and cupped her buttock through the lightweight robe.

"Mmm," I said. "Goodnight, then, *ljubimec*."

She pulled back and looked up at me. "Did you just call me a dirty name?"

"No—it's a Slovenian word."

"I might be the first black policewoman in history to be spoken to in Slovenian while somebody gropes my ass."

"*Ljubimec*," I said. "It means 'lover.'"

That took her off guard. She gulped and took a few steps backward, looking up at me, her palm flat against my chest. "Well, *that's* pretty heavy—the dreaded L-word."

"It's one of the L-words, yeah."

"You sure you want to say that?"

"I *did* say it."

"Didn't you mean some other word? How do you say 'main squeeze' in Slovenian?"

"I'll have to look that up. But you aren't my main squeeze, you're my *only* squeeze."

She moved away from me. "We're going to have to talk about this."

"Main squeeze in Slovenian?"

"Milan—"

"Tobe, I didn't say 'I love you,' did I? Not in any language."

"That's a meaningless expression anyway. 'I love chick flick movies.' 'I love football.' 'I love pizza with anchovies.' Too many people say 'I love' all the time."

"So?"

"So saying 'lover' is different. More—intimate."

"Need I remind you," I said, "that we just spent several hours in bed being intimate?"

"How many women you've been intimate with have said they were your lover?"

"This is becoming a fascinating evening. We start out talking about whether anyone deliberately killed Glenn Gallagher and wind up discussing intimate love."

"For me, Gallagher's death isn't personal."

"And this is?"

She turned away from me, looking at something on the other side of the room no one else could see, and considered her answer for too long. Then she said, "And this is."

"If it bothers you, just forget I said it."

"It doesn't bother me."

"I'm glad it doesn't bother you." I put my arms around her and buried my face in the wispy hair at the back of her neck. "And I'm hoping you won't forget it." Then I turned her around for one last kiss. "Goodnight, honey."

Before I got to the door, she said "Milan—you never answered my question."

"What question was that?"

"How many other women have you called 'lover'?"

"Oh. Well, let's see," I said, silently counting on my fingers, frowning in sarcastic concentration. When I got up to twenty-three I said, "None."

"Not one?"

"No," I said.

"Not even your wife?"

I plumbed my memory. "I must've said 'I love you' to Lila many times—that's what husbands do. But I don't think I called her 'lover,' Tobe. You're the only one."

We stared at each other in silence for at least half a minute. Then she sighed, and twiddled her invisible necktie in front of her like Oliver Hardy used to. "Well," she said, "this is another fine mess you've gotten us into."

CHAPTER NINE

K.O.

K.O. arrived at the track about an hour later than the previous day to talk to General Manager Everett Valmer. It was a *very* fall morning, cool and snappy, with the sun just up. The distant trees behind the track were autumnal yellows and reds and browns, and even the smell of horses and hay made him think that Cleveland, beautiful in its own way, was nothing like the rural "feel" at the park this morning. K.O. had never lived in a small town. He wondered what it would be like to make his home closer to nature, to horses, to a place where everyone knew their neighbors' names and their business.

And what would he do in such a setting, he wondered? Plant corn and tomatoes and lettuce? Set up a workshop and become a one-of-a-kind carpenter? Wake up before sunrise to take care of his horses? No—that wouldn't work for him. Law enforcement, setting to right things that were wrong, had driven him since he was a teenager. There might not be that much to do in, say, Lakeside, Ohio, right on Lake Erie.

Still, he enjoyed the feel of backside at Northcoast Downs.

He'd sent Milan Jacovich a detailed email of his interviews and experiences at the track and had eagerly read Milan's report on his own adventures in the banking and investment business. Interesting, K.O. figured, but he was happier sidestepping piles of horse poop and, for the most part, talking to real working people than dealing with bankers and doctors and lawyers. Other than his mandatory army medical checkups, he hadn't visited a doctor for at least two decades—four-fifths of his life.

The night before, Carli had hinted that she'd love to come with him to the track so she could visit with the horses herself. Fine, he'd thought—but not until this Cullen investigation was finished and no one was antagonistic toward him anymore. Besides, although Carli might love the horses, she'd be scared to death of the backside crew; spitting, crotch-scratching, dirty nails and dirty necks were not exactly Carli's crowd.

K.O. slowed a step as the phrase that had crossed his mind unbidden stuck around to bite him. What *was* Carli's crowd? In three months, she had never exposed her group of friends to him. She'd mentioned a few of her gal pals, but no intros, no let's-all-meet-for-a-drink suggestions, no parties. He was the quiet one, the secretive one, the one who never talked about himself. Yet she knew much more about him than he knew about her.

He'd have to explore that more fully, ask her about her family, her friends, her "gang"—when he had the time, when this Gallagher business was done once and for all.

He walked into Walt Holman's barn past a longhaired tabby cat stretched out in the doorway, who bestowed upon him one of those crushingly uninterested looks that told him he wasn't really welcome. There seemed to be no one around, so he walked up to a few of the horse stalls nearest the door. Some horses seemed genuinely glad to see him, putting their heads out over the half-doors for petting. K.O. could have kicked himself for not bringing carrots or apples.

One of them, dark brown with a black mane, actually laid his head on K.O.'s shoulder as he stroked his neck, breathing gently, almost sensuously, into his ear. Then, realizing there were no carrots in the immediate offing, the horse moved back into his stall, flopped down on his side, and began rolling around in the hay, back and forth, legs waving in the air, making a satisfied sound. Only for a second did K.O. worry something was the matter with him; then he knew it was the big guy's way of showing off and getting attention.

He went to the middle of the barn and scanned the entire length, noticing one man down at the far end, pitching hay into one of the stalls. When he got closer he saw it was Gecko, the strange-looking guy he'd seen talking to Gallagher the night he died, the one good with horses but gross about his sex life. Gecko hummed quietly to himself, the smoking stub of a bad cigar stuck in the middle of his mouth like a binkie at which he relentlessly sucked. Apparently everyone backside was a smoker; why barns don't burn down all the time was anyone's guess.

"Hello," Gecko said pleasantly around his cigar.

"Gecko, isn't it?"

Gecko broke into a smile, moving his cigar to the right side of his lips, flattered that a perfect stranger knew who he was.

K.O. told him his name. "I'm a friend—or I *was* a friend—of Glenn Gallagher."

Gecko's features, such as they were, crumpled in on themselves, and for a moment K.O. thought he was crying. "Aw, damn!" He sniffled. "So fuckin' *sad!* I don't like it that he's gone. He was a nice man; he treated me real good. He got respect for me—as a human being."

K.O. nodded. Evidently buying blow jobs from skanky hookers with a carton of cigarettes didn't make Gecko a bad person. "Glenn *was* a nice man. So I'm here to find out a little more about him." He surrendered one of his business cards to Gecko, who just stared at it. It appeared that reading was not one of Gecko's strong points.

"You're like honoring his memory then, huh?"

"Exactly."

"What should I tell you? I don't know nothing. I come in, do my job, and he was good to me."

"He paid you well?"

"Guys like me don't get paid much 'cuz we're not big shots. We're the little people. We do all the work and shovel up the shit, and there's no money in that. Mr. Gallagher, he paid me okay, though."

"Did he pay everybody good?"

"Dunno. You don't ask what somebody else gets paid or they'd chew off your face. Man, this is a funny place—everybody gets mad sometimes." He heaved his broad shoulders in a magnificent, eloquent shrug—if anything Gecko did could be considered eloquent. "People get mad at me alla time."

"Why's that?"

Another shrug. "'Cuz I'm—slow. Or sometimes I'm late, or I get a little hammered when I shouldn't of. Sometimes I fuck up. Everybody fucks up sometimes."

"Me, too," K.O. said. "Did Glenn ever get mad at you?"

"Sure, lotsa times. But he treated me good. Sometimes he'd bring in a big bag of kibble food for my dog—for free, y' know? *That* was treating me good, right?"

K.O. looked around. "Where is your dog?"

"That's Booger. I gotta leave him home, poor li'l bastard, 'cuz there's no dogs allowed backside—they spook all the cats that hang out in the barns to eat the mice and rats. My dog, he's old—and fat, just like me."

"Do you live around here?" K.O. jerked a thumb in the direction of the "apartment building" where many of the backside workers rented.

"I can't live here with no dog. I'm about half a mile away, in a motel, just like this one here, only I gotta pay a lot more. It's okay, though—a couple hookers live next door on either side of me, too." He grinned. "Which is good for me. But," and here he shook his head sadly, "I wouldn't wanna live without my dog. He's my best friend."

"And Glenn Gallagher was your best friend, too."

"One of 'em, sure."

"Even though he pushed you around?"

"He pushed everybody around—an' they let him, 'cuz he was one big sumbitch. Everybody was a-scared of him, not just me."

"Everybody?"

"Well . . . " Gecko thought it over. "Not Walt, y' know, 'cuz they were partners on a couple a horses. And not the lady doctor."

"What lady doctor?"

"She comes around every day to make sure the horses are okay. She's got a big truck with lotsa medicines and stuff. I don't think she's scared of nobody. The rest of 'em, well, yeah, they were kinda scared of Mr. Gallagher."

"Scared of him enough to want to do something bad to him?"

Gecko started to answer then backed away from K.O. as Walt Holman came in through the barn door.

"Gecko, goddammit, we don't have all day!" he barked as he

made his way down the long aisle. "These animals are starving to death and you're wasting your time jibber-jabbering!" He shook his fist. "Get to it, boy, 'fore I take a horse whip to you and kick your ass from here to Pittsburgh!"

Gecko jumped as though an electric shock had gone through him and scurried back to the rear of the barn to do his chores. Holman obviously noticed K.O.'s disapproving scowl. "Don't make a big deal out of it, K.O. Some you gotta yell at or they won't get nothing done. It's no good being nice to people all the time." He cocked his head to one side. "I wouldn't a hit him with the whip, though."

"He was just filling me in about life backside—from his point of view. Different from yours."

"What'd he tell you?"

"I've forgotten most of it," K.O. lied; he'd remember everything. That was one of his strengths—he absorbed everything and never let it drift out of his brain.

He looked toward the door of the barn again; a woman was silhouetted against the outdoor light. Her hair was tied back in a casual pony tail, and there was a large leather bag, about three times the size of a book bag, draped over one shoulder.

"Hey, Bunny," Holman called and motioned K.O. to follow him outside. She was dark-haired, brown-eyed, wearing Wrangler jeans and a gray sweatshirt.

"My favorite sawbones," Holman announced. "Mr. K.O. O'Bannion, say hello to Sheila McHale. *Doctor* Sheila McHale." They shook hands. She was somewhere around thirty—very young, K.O. thought, to be a veterinarian.

"Oh boy," she said, smiling. "O'Bannion! Not another Irishman!"

"*You* have an Irish name," K.O. said.

"What can I do about it? I was born Irish and married Irish. We met in vet school and discovered we both liked horses. So we opened a practice near Canton—mostly large farm livestock—and of course the racetrack. But we're out and about more than dog-and-cat doctors."

"Nobody brings a horse to your office, then."

She smiled. "Usually not. No cows or hogs, either. Maybe a

piglet now and then—or even a chicken." She turned and pointed at a white panel truck parked near the door. K.O. had never seen one like it before and figured it must have been custom-built. "My office-away-from-my-office carries all sorts of things—medicines and liniments and whatever else we might need."

"Are you here this morning because a horse is sick?"

"I hope not," she said. "I come here at least five days a week, usually checking small complaints—and hopefully not big ones."

"Do you have many big complaints?"

She shook her head. "Very rarely, knock on wood. Just little ones. "

"I'm glad you take good care of them," K.O. said. "I like all animals—I have a cat."

McHale grinned. "I'm no cat expert—but if you need a vet in a pinch, I'm here for you."

Walt Holman said, "Doctor Bunny, whyn't you show K.O. your truck—he'll be impressed."

"Bunny?" K.O. said.

The doctor smiled shyly. "That's what my family and my friends call me. It's a nickname I had since I was a child. Come on."

K.O. followed her to the truck parked in the chilly sunshine; a breeze off the lake made it feel colder than it had been earlier. Halloween couldn't be that far away. It was a holiday he couldn't ever remember celebrating—not even trick-or-treating for candy corn or mini chocolate bars.

When the vet opened the side panels of the truck, K.O. felt as if he'd stumbled behind the counter at a pharmacy. There were hundreds—perhaps thousands—of little bottles and boxes, carefully labeled, and Bunny McHale explained all of them were for helping and healing a horse.

"I've got everything here, short of surgery," she said. "Bandages, pills, salves, disinfectants." She held up what looked like a barrel stave, only it was made of plastic. "These are splints, in case a horse injures a leg that needs to be adjusted and then rested for a while." She waved a hand at vast numbers of medications and began naming them for K.O., who tried taking notes. Alfalfa pellets for worming. Aloe heal. Cosopt, for equine eye problems. Digitalis for the heart. Cimetidine and Metronidazole for minor intestinal upsets. Isoxuprine for lameness. EquioPathics for respiratory difficulty. Even Dormosedan, used as a sedative. There were many others, and K.O. couldn't write in his notepad nearly as fast as the vet spoke. He wished he'd brought his recorder. At least he'd heard of alfalfa and aloe and digitalis, but he couldn't have known what they were used for if his life had depended on it.

"We have more stuff in our office all the time, actually in a storage room set up like a prison cell. You couldn't get in there with a blowtorch. Drug addicts won't want anything in a horse pharmacy that'd get them high, anyway. Sick as a dog, maybe. But it's a rule—all doctors and hospitals, even veterinarians, have to keep all their meds locked up like the Crown Jewels of England."

"So you only put medications in the truck that you'd likely use on any given day."

"Usually. We only stock the meds for stuff we run into all the time. For instance, I took care of a horse in Barn Number Three just now—he needed to be wormed." Dr. McHale made a face. "Trust me, you won't want to go into that stall for a while. Yuck-o!"

K.O. leaned against the side of the truck. "You were acquainted with the late Glenn Gallagher?"

"Sure. Horse owner *and* driver? I saw him at least three times a week, usually right in here."

"Were you two friendly?"

"No reason not to be. He took good care of his animals—and he always paid me right on time." She frowned. "Why do you ask?"

"I'm a private investigator," K.O. said. "An apprentice, really. I'm working for Glenn's son, Cullen."

"What is it you're—investigating, then?"

"Clearing up a few details. I wasn't even aware of you until ten minutes ago."

"That's okay," McHale said. "It was nice talking with you. And if you ever wind up with a sick horse—I'll make him feel better for you."

"I appreciate that, Dr. McHale."

"Dr. Bunny—that's what most people call me."

"Okay, Dr. Bunny," K.O. said, feeling ridiculous. He shook her outstretched hand. "But I plan on keeping my horse healthy—if I ever have a horse."

K.O. watched as McHale's truck moved off toward another of the barns. Then he went inside and searched for Walt Holman again.

"Nippy kind of morning," he said, rubbing his hands together. "Where can I get a cup of something hot?"

"This ain't the Ritz," Walt said, "but there's coffee." He pointed, giving K.O. directions to what everyone referred to as "the kitchen."

It was a ninety-second walk from the Gallagher-Holman barn to the only place backside in which anyone could buy something to eat or drink. It wasn't elegant nor was it supposed to be. It looked like a school cafeteria; long tables, utilitarian chairs, a vintage TV playing some endless morning network news show, and nobody else eating or drinking anything. One employee lurked behind the counter; he snatched up K.O.'s dollar and directed him to pour himself a cardboard cup of coffee.

K.O. sipped what tasted like motor oil—but it was hot and strong, which made drinking it less of an inhumane punishment—and thought about his morning so far. Gecko—a sweet, simple, fat guy with what must have been a sweet, simple, fat dog, was scared to death of his own shadow—scared to death of Holman, and he'd been scared to death of Glenn Gallagher, too. His only friends, apparently, were his dog and a couple of hooker neighbors, whose companionship he bought, cheaply, with a carton of cigarettes.

Sheila McHale—Doctor Bunny. He could recall army doctors—majors and light colonels—who probably weren't half the physician she was, having to take care of men and women who were blown half to pieces by hidden bombs on a desert road. But they'd been born rich and gone to Harvard or Princeton, entering the service with oak leaves on their collars. He screwed up his face trying to read his scrawled notes: Aloe. Digitalis. EquioPathics. He'd have a tough time putting all that stuff in his report.

Just then another man came through the front door of the kitchen: late middle-aged, wearing a brownish-bronze suit, baggy and wrinkled, that had seen better days, and bottom-line cheap when it was new. The hat he wore was probably stylish for only a few weeks, back in the early 1970s, and his black-rimmed glasses teetered low on his fleshy nose. Physically, no one would forget his circular scraggly Amish-type beard—no mustache. He got himself a cup of coffee, emptied a great deal of sugar into it along with some powdered creamer, looked around and then zeroed in on K.O.'s table as if the chair across from him was the only one in the place that wasn't occupied.

"Join you?" he said, pulling out the chair and collapsing into it. "You must be new here—haven't seen you before." He grasped K.O.'s hand and pumped it. "Jerry Nemo. I'm around a lot."

"Just call me K.O."

Nemo sipped the coffee and smacked his lips as though judging a fine Burgundy. "You're a young guy—that's good. Harness racing needs young, energetic guys. In the horse business, are you?"

"Around the edges," K.O. said. Well, it was only a *small* lie.

"Ah. Own horses?"

"No."

"Too bad. You should, it's a great experience—and a great way to make some money. I got a great horse I could sell you."

"Not in the market."

"Don't be hasty." Nemo shifted in his chair so he could lean closer and put a hand on K.O.'s arm. "He's a beauty. Big—seventeen hands high. A nice bay—good eyes, good teeth. Listen, he raced down in West Virginia, Tennessee, places like that. Around Cincinnati, too. He's fast and strong, and I got him for a song. His stupid-shit owner didn't know what the horse was worth, almost gave it to me."

Nemo shrugged. "I'm not exactly *giving* it away. I gotta make a *little* profit. Profit's what makes the world go round, isn't it?"

"That's America," K.O. said. "You sell lots of horses?"

"Enough. At some other tracks, too—like the Meadows." He looked up as a woman came into the kitchen to pour herself some coffee, affixing a cover to the cardboard cup. Her graying hair was bound up in a bandana, her overalls loose and a bit dirty from her grooming work. Nemo's mouth twisted into a sort of kiss and he sucked cold air through his lips. "Ooh," he said, loud enough for the woman to hear. "Nice titties."

The woman turned and leveled a glare of disgust. "Go fuck

yourself, Nemo," she said, tossed a dollar on the counter, and walked out.

K.O. tried not to laugh. "Friend of yours?"

"Naw, but I wish," Jerry Nemo said, cupping his crotch with his free hand to better make his point. "Bet you have a girlfriend, right? Nice rack on her?"

K.O. looked at the other man for at least half a minute without speaking. Then he said quietly, "Don't even go there."

It didn't slow Nemo down. "So—we have a deal on the horse or what?"

"How the hell could we have a deal?"

"You wanna see the horse? Come with me—he's over in Barn Number Four."

Barn Number Four—Del Fiddler's barn. "I don't think so," K.O. said.

"Come on, kiddo, be smart. You'll go crazy over this horse. I bet your girlfriend loves horses—girls just *cream* over horses. What's her name again?"

"Nunya."

"Nunya?"

"Nunya fucking business," K.O. said.

"You're a hard man to do business with, kiddo."

"That's my reputation. Did you ever sell a horse to Glenn Gallagher?"

"Gallagher? He's dead."

"No shit. Did you sell him horses?"

Big, innocent eyes. "Sure—a long time ago."

"How many?"

"Huh?"

"How many horses did you sell Glenn Gallagher?"

Nemo stroked his beard wisely, deep in thought. "Uh—one."

"One horse? A long time ago?"

A nod.

"How'd that work out for you?"

Nemo looked as though he smelled something bad. He stood and picked up his cardboard cup. "I can't do business with you, kiddo. I'm outta here."

"So soon?"

"Time is money. You ain't got money, I ain't got time."

"You didn't answer my question, Mr. Nemo."

"What question was that?"

"How did your business deal go with Glenn Gallagher?"

Nemo turned the cup around in his hands slowly. "NSG," he said. "Not So Good. He was pretty pissed off with me." He screwed his mouth into a pout, resembling a stubbornly angry three-year-old—with an Amish beard—but he was no more Amish than the Pope. "He went around telling everybody I was a thief," he said. "I'm no thief, I'm a businessman, same as him. The difference is he was a real prick!"

"Speaking ill of the dead, are you?"

"You're goddamn right," Jerry Nemo said.

Everett Valmer wore a charcoal gray suit and conservative tie. Unusual. You wouldn't expect *anyone* at Northcoast Downs dressed up like that, especially at eleven in the morning. But Everett Valmer was the Chief Financial Officer, and despite rarely seeing outsiders in his own office, he obviously believed in dressing the part. When K.O. shook his hand, he wondered whether Valmer wore the suit jacket in the middle of summer, too.

"Glenn was quite a character around here," Valmer said. His desk was stacked high with manila files and account ledgers. "Northcoast Downs will miss him—mainly because he was so damn big."

"Will *you* miss him, Mr. Valmer?"

He carefully considered his answer. "I wouldn't say that, exactly."

"What *would* you say exactly?"

Valmer took a moment. "Why are you here, anyway? What's the point? To find out whether everybody loved him?"

"That's part of it," K.O. replied. "So you didn't love him, then?"

Valmer touched one of the account books on his desk lightly with his fingertips—almost a caress. Now, K.O. thought, *there* is a real businessman—one who paid attention to something *only* if it turned a profit.

"I deal with figures," Valmer said, endorsing K.O.'s unspoken surmise. "'Figures' meaning *money*. Glenn spent a good bit of money here—barn rentals, facilities for his horses—like any other owner. He also ran up a healthy bar tab every month."

"I heard that."

"But here's what you've got to remember, at least when you're talking to me. Gallagher died, which is too bad, but someone else will move up to take his place. They always do. That's the way life is—the way nature is."

"Nature?"

"Certainly. When the alpha male wolf dies—or lion, or baboon, for that matter—another alpha male steps in to assume leadership."

"And who," K.O. asked, "is the alpha male around here?"

Valmer didn't try disguising his sneer. "That would be me," he said. "CFO. But I have no desire to walk in Gallagher's shoes because I don't know a damn thing about horses or care about them, either, unless they make money for us." He ostentatiously shot his cuffs. "Pretty soon it won't matter. This park will eventually be a casino; the deal's in place and the finer points are being negotiated as we speak."

"So will you still have harness racing here—or just slots and cards?"

Valmer rolled his eyes ceilingward. "This *is* a racetrack, Mr. O'Bannion."

"But you, Mr. Valmer—you're the CFO, as you pointed out, so you'll be getting a hell of a lot more money when all this happens. Right?"

"No comment."

"I'm not a reporter."

"*Still* no comment."

"Then again," K.O. said, "you *do* work for Chloe Markham. You're an employee."

That flustered the older man. "I own stock here."

"Sure. Five percent?"

"That's none of your affair!"

"My affair," K.O. said evenly, "is to determine whether or not Glenn died of an ordinary heart attack."

"That's ridiculous. This is family entertainment. The parents bet, the kiddies like watching the horses. Nothing terrible ever happens around here." Valmer touched the knot of his tie. "People come here for fun and so do those who work here. As far as that goes, the horses enjoy themselves, too." His voice dropped half an octave. "Most of the time," he added.

"Getting hooked up to a sulky with a bit in their mouth and running faster than they want to or else they get hit with a whip? That's fun?"

"They're athletes!" Valmer thundered, losing his temper for the first time. "Athletes get hurt—scratched, bruised, banged up. It doesn't mean athletes don't love their game, whatever it is."

K.O. pointed to the account books at Valmer's elbow. "Your game is counting money."

"Right!" Valmer took a deep breath; when he spoke again, he'd attained some measure of calm. "Starting rumors, Mr.—uh— Bannion . . . "

"*O*-Bannion."

"Yes, sorry, Mr. *O*'Bannion. Spreading rumors—lies—about this place can cost us a lot of money. We can't have that."

"You mean if it got out, even into the newspaper or TV that Glenn Gallagher didn't die of natural causes, it might screw up your pending casino deal?"

Valmer shouted again, leveling an accusing index finger at K.O. "*Nobody* talks about any deal before *we* talk about it."

K.O. gently took his own deep breath. Then: "Is that a threat, Mr. Valmer?"

Fluster, fluster went Everett Valmer. "I didn't threaten you. I don't threaten. My lawyers do the threatening. Listen—without proof, it isn't right to spread rumors and seriously impact our business, don't you think? I mean, we *are* here to make money."

"Obviously your lawyer wants to make money, too," K.O. said.

"All right, be that way. But we make a profit, and we'll make even more profit when the business proposition is finalized. So for you to blackmail me . . . "

"*Blackmail* you? What are you, paranoid?"

"Sorry," Valmer amended quickly, struggling to calm down. "I don't mean to go off the deep end. But to spread rumors about an actual crime committed at Northcoast Downs when you don't even know there *was* a crime? I don't think it's fair."

K.O. smiled. "Life is *never* fair. Is it, Mr. Valmer?"

CHAPTER TEN

MILAN

Cleveland has very few restaurants that boast a view of Lake Erie. East 4th Street, West 6th Street, and Detroit Road all have great places to eat—but there's no way to look north out the window at the lake. When I become emperor, I'll tear down all the on-shore crap and build great hotels and restaurants to take advantage of one of the great bodies of fresh water in America.

There is one upscale lakeside eatery on the west side that enjoys its own kind of royalty, located on the lower floors of one of a cluster of high-rise apartment buildings on the Gold Coast. Pier W had been remodeled into a modern/elegant/*au courant* restaurant, boasting a three-quarters circular bar with lights from beneath that change colors every few minutes. The view of the water and of the beautiful downtown Cleveland skyline is worth the trip; the excellent food is another. Beginning at about four o'clock in the afternoon, the bar stools fill up quickly with Happy Hour boozers. It's the kind of place in which one enjoys seeing and being seen.

That's where Manley Markham was part of the scenery.

I spotted Manley as soon as I entered, sitting so the afternoon sun illuminated him. At first glance, he was extremely handsome, with almost feminine big brown eyes, too-long lashes, and a sensual mouth. Only in his late thirties, he'd now become used-looking and tired, desiccated like a beautiful garden zinnia drying up and turning brown as soon as the weather cooled off. An attractive middle-aged woman sat next to him, but they obviously weren't together; there was too much space between their bodies, and they neither looked at each other nor spoke. It wasn't yet five o'clock and an empty martini glass was in front of him, right beside a fresh one—lemon twist, no olive—and he was well on the way to becoming totally besotted.

When I told him who I was, my name didn't register with him, nor did my business card; he stared at it quizzically as if it were printed in a language he'd never heard of. It wasn't until I mentioned his sister that I got his attention.

"Chloe?" He struggled to focus. "You're kinda old to be her current—uh—*stud*, aren't you?"

"I hardly know her. I'm looking into what happened at the track."

He made a circular motion, counterclockwise, with his index finger. "Horses run around—*that's* what happens at the track. They just run around—and it's none of my business, buddy. It all belongs to my cunt sister—everybody's li'l princess."

"It's not nice to talk that way about your sister."

"Why the hell not?" He took a slug of his new martini; the lemon peel got stuck on his lower lip and he flicked it away with his finger. It sailed off behind the bar, and the woman next to him watched it go like an Indian home run at Progressive Field. "She got everything. I got nothing but a trust fund."

A trust fund is hardly "nothing," but it's not the norm in ethnic Cleveland. I got to the point. "Did you know Glenn Gallagher?"

His forehead wrinkled as he tried to remember. "The big tall guy? Rich? Yeah, I know him."

"*Knew* him. He died."

"Died?" His brain tried valiantly to rise up from swimming the backstroke in gin martinis with a twist to parse that sentence. Then: "Oh yeah, I heard about that."

"Did you know him well?"

"He was a horse guy. He di'n give a shit about me."

"Why not?"

"'Cuz I'm *not* a horse guy—or a business guy, either. I tried lots of times to make some kinda deal with him, but he blew me off every time. What I am is—a drunk! To him—Gallagher—I was just some goddamn nobody!" He drank with predatory gulps. I'm no martini-drinker, but I'd assumed people *sipped* their martinis, not slammed them down like Manley Markham did.

He'd obviously entertained the hell out of himself over what he'd just said, and he cackled a laugh through his nose. "I *am* a goddamn nobody. I'm nothing! I'm rich, but I'm nothing. No career, no job, no place to go every day except here or some other bar. So fuck Glenn Gallagher, wherever he is. Fuck my sister, too." And that made him giggle again. "Everybody else has."

The woman next to Manley Markham turned her head to look at him with more disdain than I'd ever witnessed before—from anybody. Then she glanced at me, raised her eyebrows, shrugged, and went back to staring at her own drink—a grasshopper, creamy and sickly green.

"You never spent enough time with Gallagher to talk about his health?"

"He never spent enough time with *me!*" He waved at the bartender and pointed to his two empty martini glasses. "Want a drink?"

"No, thanks."

"Shit!" he mumbled. "You don't wanna spend time with me, either!" And he turned away.

It wasn't yet Thanksgiving—we still hadn't experienced Halloween—but I'm thankful for many things: my health, my work, my kids, my lover. I am especially grateful, though, that I was *not* rich, bitter, lonely, and totally spiffed or trust-funded like Manley Markham. What a rotten way to spend a life!

K.O. was back at the office when I arrived. Having never worked with a partner or an associate before, it was unusual for me to investigate a case with someone but yet not spend a lot of face-to-face time with them. It was like that with my long-time best friend Marko Meglich. He'd been a homicide lieutenant, so we didn't have much opportunity to work together, although each of us would include the other in a particularly baffling case. He'd never really forgiven me for quitting the police force to go private, and when he was killed it saddened me that we *hadn't* turned out to be the Butch (me) and Sundance (him) he thought we should've been.

K.O. typed up his notes from his day's meetings at the track, and after he emailed them to me, I suggested we discuss the case.

"Thanks for letting me check out Northcoast Downs," K.O. said, "and the backside workers who really deal with the livestock. They're—strange folk, living in a strange world."

"Do they spend too much time with horses?"

"They spend too much time with each other. And most of them didn't like Glenn Gallagher."

"Why?"

"Because he was rich. The ones who run the place—Everett Valmer and Chloe Markham—they had no use for him, either. He was too rich to take crap from anyone. He danced to his own tune, not theirs."

"When they're rich and powerful," I observed, "it generally offends them if everyone doesn't bow down and kiss their asses."

"If you're sitting around waiting for me to bow down and kiss *your* ass, Milan, you ought to fire me now."

"I'm not rich and powerful—and if you come anywhere near kissing my ass, I'll break both your legs. I'm not too old to do that, either."

"Time will tell," K.O. said.

"I pretty much let you do your own thing, right?"

"True."

"Good. So shut up."

K.O. mimed locking his lips and throwing the key away. Then he said, "Del Fiddler, the trainer. You met him and his wife at the track the night Glenn died. You *must* remember her. She looked like she could eat both of us with a spoon."

"Oh, yes—her."

"She was hanging out of her blouse yesterday, too—which is peculiar because usually the only ones to see her like that have four legs and twitched their tails."

"Maybe her cleavage gets warm in that barn and she likes being cool," I said.

"She didn't say anything bad about Gallagher—but she's not head over heels about her husband. He and Gallagher had *some* history—fistfights and near fist-fights. Fiddler must be one of those guys who picks fights with any guy twice his size, like Glenn Gallagher." He leered at me. "Or like you. Oh—another thing: Fiddler warned me to stay away from his wife."

"Did he need to?"

"Be serious, she's old enough to be—well, she's way too old for me. I was standing there chatting with Wanda, mostly about Gallagher, and Del Fiddler went batshit crazy when he saw me. He's one jealous sonofabitch, Milan!"

I covered my smile with my hand at his use of my name; almost any other guy K.O.'s age would probably have said "dude."

I *hate* "dude."

"Did he threaten you, K.O.?"

"Not exactly. He told me I'd be sorry. Maybe it was all talk, maybe not. Hey, I'll be happier than hell if he feels brave enough to come after me. The bastard beats horses, too, with whatever is handy, like a pitchfork. Wanda told me about that."

"We agreed you wouldn't kick the crap out of other people, didn't we?"

"We agreed I'll *try* not to. Glenn Gallagher already knocked out a few of Fiddler's teeth; if I punch out the rest of them, he'll need dental implants—which might just make him look halfway decent, too."

"Only hit others in self-defense, K.O."

He nodded. "In the kiddie slammer, I had to hit in self-defense every day." A dimple appeared in his right cheek. "That was until I developed a reputation with my fellow inmates, and for the last year or so, nobody came near me to fight."

"You're not a big man," I said. "How did you learn to fight? Somebody teach you boxing?"

"Boxing? That went out with Muhammad Ali. When someone's bigger than me, I fight dirty. I don't punch much—I maim."

I winced. "Maim? That's a hell of a word. Would you hit a man if he's down?"

"Hitting a man when he's down is the best way to make sure he won't get back up and hurt you again." K.O. cocked his head. "If *you'd* learned that, Milan, you wouldn't have so damn many concussions."

"Right," I said. "Then I wouldn't have had to hire you."

"Next time somebody wants to cave in your skull, tell 'em to wait and then give me a call. I'll run right over."

I waved a hand in front of my face to get back to business. "So everybody backside at the track might be a suspect?"

"We still don't know if it *was* a murder. But everybody dissed Gallagher—except Gecko. Remember him?"

"Sure. How would one forget him?"

"He seemed like a sweet guy, cut-rate hookers notwithstanding. He respected our dearly departed, and he's sorry Glenn won't be signing his paychecks anymore."

"That's pretty cynical."

"I *am* pretty cynical." He snapped his fingers. "Hey, remember the guy on the Bert Loftus case this past summer? The Russian guy?"

"His name escapes me, but yes, sure I remember."

"He said he hangs out at a Russian monastery right on the campus of Hiram College."

"So?"

"So—Cullen Gallagher teaches at Hiram," K.O. said. "One of us ought to go out and talk to Cullen again."

"Why would we want to do that?"

"We had one short meeting with him when he hired us. Maybe another chat will remind him of something he forgot in the first place."

"Good idea," I said. "You do it."

"Me?"

"No," I said, "it's the other six guys in the room I'm talking to."

K.O. shook his head. "I've never been to Hiram; I'm not sure how to get there."

"A zillion techno-gadgets can tell you how; MapQuest on the Internet, for example."

"If I walk around on campus, everyone'll think I'm a college boy."

"Then don't wear a pullover sweater or a sweatshirt with the school logo on it. Get one of those leather jackets with all the zippers like Fonzie used to wear."

"Who's Fonzie?"

"Look it up," I said. I pulled out the Cullen Gallagher file and copied his home phone number and the one at Hiram College, then handed it to my lone employee. "Enjoy your trip tomorrow."

K.O. regarded the piece of paper with trepidation. "Are there any restaurants out there?"

"Just a tiny pizza joint. It's in the country, K.O."

He put the note in his shirt pocket, closed the lid of his computer, neatly cleared off the top of his desk, and stood up, heading for the door. "Just hope I don't starve to death. While I'm talking to Cullen tomorrow, what will you be doing with your day?"

"Poke around some more—and find out something I didn't know before about those business people who don't have a clue about harness racing."

"Poke around?" K. O. shook his head. He hadn't been with Milan Security—or hung out with *me*—long enough to understand how I work. "That's your elaborate plan? Poke around?"

"That's what I do," I said.

I spent most of the morning in the Department of Records in the courthouse, looking up as much as I could find on people I'd already talked to, hoping to discover something that might cast suspicion on them. But what I studied were all dry, boring documents. I knew approximately how much money these people were worth now—but I wanted to know things that aren't in public records.

I checked my watch—twelve-thirty and time for a lunch appointment.

The Flat Iron Café seems as if it's been there since several years before the signing of the Magna Carta. That's only a slight exaggeration—it opened its doors in the Flats, just steps from the swing bridge, as restaurant and bar in 1910. Before that it was a hotel until the top two floors were destroyed by fire in the 1880s, and then it became a blacksmith shop. Its menu is Irish in origin, promoting comfort food, and it's always crowded—at lunchtime with workers from nearby businesses and in the evening mostly with young people who enjoyed the stinging cold beer and the entertainment.

It hasn't changed much in the course of a century. Most of the brick walls are *still* brick, and what little plaster covers the other walls are painted a vivid Kelly green. Giant TV sets are scattered around in case one might want to watch an Indians game—the restaurant provides shuttle service to Progressive Field on evenings when the Tribe plays.

Ed Stahl, with whom I have been friendly since I ankled the police force and went on my own as a private investigator and security specialist, keeps a now-dusty Pulitzer Prize in his bottom desk drawer along with a few half-finished rolls of Life Savers, an eraser of the type we used when we went to school in the 1960s, and an odd collection of rubber bands and paper clips he never bothered throwing away. He writes a daily column for the *Plain Dealer*, and if there's anything in Greater Cleveland he does *not* know about, the chances are excellent that it's not worth knowing.

Ed has a roaring ulcer, so he's careful about what he eats; on this particular day he'd ordered a vegan pasta dish that wouldn't kick up his discomfort, but the ulcer apparently ignores the copious amounts of Jim Beam bourbon he drinks every day. The pain in his gut can stoop him over, which doesn't wrinkle one of two tired tweed sports jackets he alternates. His perpetual grimace, with his outdated black horn-rimmed glasses, makes one think of how Clark Kent, Superman's alter ego, might look had he lived to be sixty-five and never considered stopping his booze intake or his smoking addiction.

"I'm having trouble understanding," Ed Stahl said as he deftly twirled his pasta onto a fork with the aid of a spoon. "You're still working for Glenn Gallagher even though he's dead?"

"I work for his son, now. Cullen Gallagher seems to think his father didn't die of a heart attack—that somebody helped him along." I was enjoying my corned beef sandwich and trying not to feel guilty for eating it in front of Ed.

Ed patted his chest pocket where he keeps his pipe and, not finding it, looked even more down in the dumps. Nobody smokes a pipe anymore—I mean *nobody!* And even if they did, it's illegal to smoke in a public place, so Ed grumbles while he follows rules—any rules—although he generally smokes in bars that don't serve food, and *always* in his *Plain Dealer* cubbyhole, whether anyone complains or not.

"Sounds far-fetched," he said. "Gallagher wasn't shot or stabbed or poisoned—and then he was cremated, so there's nothing left to investigate. Has Gallagher's son gone off the deep end of paranoia?"

"Possibly. But Gallagher told me he wanted to discuss something very important that was worrying him. Then he died. It *could* have been some other kind of murder."

"And you and your associate are busting your asses over a could-have-been?"

"We're being paid," I said, "and my 'associate's' name is K.O."

"Right. Jesus, Milan, I've known you for thirty years. I keep forgetting someone else works for you now. How's that going?"

"He's good," I said. "We've split this case between us. I check Gallagher's high-stakes business dealings, and K.O.'s dealing with the racetrack."

"I don't know much about horse racing—so I gather you're buying lunch to ask about financial stuff."

"You know about everything, Ed—including horse racing."

"Bull. I haven't watched the Kentucky Derby for the last ten years—especially now that racehorses get hurt all the time and they put them away right in front of a big crowd. Besides, I'd always bet on the horse that came in last. I might as well flush a fifty dollar bill down the john."

"Dead money," I said. "That's what racing people call a no-chance horse. Dead money."

"Creepy."

I pulled out my notebook. "Let's talk about Carol Watterson."

"Carol—I think I've heard about her."

"Boss person at Aventura—venture capital outfit."

"I know Aventura," Ed said and waved his nearly empty glass at the waitress.

"You're bathing your ulcer in *another* drink? Easy, Ed, that stuff'll kill you."

"Good idea. Quit drinking for the rest of my life, do all the twelve steps—and while I'm crossing the street on my way to an

AA meeting, I'll get hit by a truck." He reached into his pocket and pulled out a small tin of Tums, washing down two of them with what was left of his Jim Beam. "Aventura," he said, "is a relatively interesting company. There was a knock-down-drag-out between this Carol person and her preceding CEO—Merriford Wane."

"Merriford? CEOs have peculiar names."

"Peculiar names of white people means their parents were rich. Otherwise they'd all be named Ed—like me. Okay," Ed said, "this is coming back to me. Watterson became a partner about two years ago, and she wanted that job something awful—so she romanced a bunch of her stockholders and clients and other important people in investment banking and old Merriford got booted out on his ass."

"I got the idea she was difficult," I said, "until I made her laugh."

"Tell her a joke?"

"No. I called her a dick."

Ed Stahl threw back his head and laughed—loudly. Everyone in the Flat Iron turned to look at him, even the hardcore drinkers at the bar. I'd never heard Ed laugh aloud before.

"Well, that sums it up nicely," he said when he finally caught a breath. "Merriford Wane and Glenn Gallagher were friends, so Gallagher must have been one of his allies."

"That explains why Carol didn't like him—and why she kicks and scratches to steal his clients away." I considered that. "And why Gallagher always tried kidnapping *her* clients."

Ed accepted his new bourbon from the waitress and handed her his now-empty glass. "Doesn't sound like a motive for murder."

"Killing someone just for their smart phone could be a motive," I said, and the waitress's head snapped around to stare at me in minor shock.

"Sorry, hon," Ed said, "my friend here is a big kidder."

She rolled her eyes. "I hope so," she said, moving away, "and I don't even *own* a smart phone."

"So since Merriford Wane got shut out of Aventura, what is he doing now?"

"Trolling. He's telling everybody in town about *this* great investment deal or *that* great investment deal, hoping they'll give him money."

"Are these investment deals for real or is he blowing smoke?"

Ed shook his head. "I stay away from guys wanting me to invest my money, Milan. I don't have that much to begin with, and I'm not about to give it to some cornflake like Merriford Wane."

"That makes sense to me," I said. "Do you know Glenn Gallagher's attorney, David Weaver?"

"The Weaver of Schoenburg and Weaver? Uh-huh . . . " He sipped. "That firm—and Weaver specifically—make fortunes representing the one percent—very rich people. I'm certain they've taken a few cases *pro bono,* but I can't think of a single one. I don't know how good their lawyering is, but they're pretty skillful at milking money out of everybody."

"Their own clients?"

Ed nodded. "Why not? Money doesn't have anyone's name on it—except dead presidents."

"Benjamin Franklin was never president."

"No kidding, Milan. Jeez, I never knew that!" Ed Stahl, with a German ancestry not known for their senses of humor, can be more sarcastic than any Irishman I ever met.

"So everybody's game is to try getting money out of somebody else."

"*Everybody* else. That's the American way."

"Was Weaver screwing over Glenn Gallagher, too?"

"I'm not the friggin' encyclopedia."

"I wonder how I can find out for sure."

"Tarot cards," Ed said.

"You think Weaver skimmed money from his own client?"

Ed laughed without mirth. "A shocker, huh? Milan—money keeps the world spinning. I write my column because they pay me money. If they stop doing it, I'll spend my life in bars like this one—anyplace where they'll let me drink quietly and won't bitch if I smoke my pipe. You're on this so-called maybe-murder-maybe-not case because the Gallagher kid is giving you money. You think that cute little waitress comes in to the Flat Iron every day and carts food and booze around for old farts like us because she *likes* it? She does it to make money! So you better know David Weaver, or any other lawyer for that matter, will contort himself into a yoga master for a few extra bucks."

"But you're not certain—about Weaver, I mean."

"I'm not certain about *anything*. But we believe what we believe or else we wouldn't get out of bed in the morning." He gulped down more Jim Beam. "Or *you* wouldn't get out of bed because now you have good reason to stay there. I couldn't blame Detective Blaine for *that*."

I felt myself blushing. "Not *every* morning."

"At your age?" Ed said. "Of course not *every* morning."

I stopped talking to eat my lunch; the Flat Iron Café has terrific French fries I salt too heavily. Tobe scolds me whenever I use too much salt—but she wasn't here. Finally I said, "One more name, Ed?"

"That depends. It'll cost you another Jim Beam." He grinned. "But then you can put it on Gallagher Junior's tab."

"It's my tab," I said, waving once more at the waitress, "like it always is. When's the last time I took you to lunch and made you pay?"

"Beats me," he said. "But once again—it's all about money."

I waited until he got his final drink. "What do you know about Jen Taylor?"

He sipped, deep in thought. "Do I get a hint?"

"She runs Gallagher Investment Management—as office manager or executive assistant."

Ed ran through possibilities in his mind—not as quick as a computer but fast enough. "She was Glenn Gallagher's lady of the moment?"

"I think it was quite a long moment."

"I seem to recall seeing her at a few benefits, always with Glenn Gallagher. Good looking woman, right? Not exactly my type, but . . ."

I chuckled. "What exactly *is* your type, anyway?"

He shook his head in sadness. "The rare type who knows how to say yes. Let's stick with Taylor. She's worked for Gallagher a long time? Then she's gotta be good at what she does and not just sexy. She's how old?"

LES ROBERTS

"Not sure," I said. "Late thirties, maybe—but she wears those years well."

"Did he bequeath her his venture capital business?"

"Bequeath? Nice word."

"Of course it's a nice word, dumb ass; I write words for a living."

"Hooray for you," I said. "Jen Taylor seems to think Glenn 'bequeathed' his business to his son."

"I'd imagine he left her *something*. If he didn't, he was a bigger shit than anyone thought."

"A lot of people thought he was a shit in the first place."

Ed stirred the ice cubes with his index finger. "If that's really the case, Milan—well, maybe you've got a murder investigation going great guns after all."

CHAPTER ELEVEN

K.O.

Hiram College came to being in 1850, thanks to the Disciples of Christ Church—a liberal church back then, if anyone alive today even remembers those two words were sometimes used in the same sentence. So it quickly changed from a church college into a liberal arts college and has remained so for the better part of a century and a half.

Around the campus one might be overwhelmed by red brick, as almost all the buildings were constructed in more or less the same style. On the side streets the mandatory white clapboard houses are owned by the school and are used either as classrooms or dormitories, or are rented as residences to the staff and faculty who don't even have to drive to get to work.

K.O. wandered for a time, taking in the sights. He'd never been on a college campus before—and Hiram, Ohio, was indeed a small town. Everyone he saw on the street seemed small-town, too; many, especially the older ones, smiled or waved hello.

The political science building wasn't hard to find. It's located in a remodeled church that once stood in the nearby town of Mecca, fairly close to Youngstown. It was carefully taken from its original location and moved, piece by piece, to Hiram. It was rumored that former Ohio governor, Hiram College president, and eventually President of the United States, James A. Garfield, often stopped in Mecca on a Sunday to worship, so when the church was restored in Hiram it was christened Garfield Hall. Its dedication in 2009 featured an impressive statue of Garfield set out front, near the doorway—but in the morning it had been beheaded! Someone had stolen the president's head and disappeared, finally confessing the theft several months later to a neighbor, who turned him over to the local police.

President Garfield's head is back on now. The real president was assassinated in Buffalo a century before his statue's head was pilfered. The building was re-named Koritansky Hall in honor of Professor John Koritansky, who still teaches political science at Hiram after forty-two years. K.O. thought it strange that someone still living would have a building named after him, and an office in it where he could quietly work. At least no one had tried to steal Dr. Koritansky's head.

The main room of the hall, once the church sanctuary, had been converted to a classroom with cathedral ceilings and exposed oak beams that have held up the roof for more than a hundred years. K.O. thought it might be nice to study something as serious as political science in a room that looked nothing like a classroom. The acoustics were perfect; he could hear his footsteps as if they'd been added for effect to a scary movie.

Cullen Gallagher's office was in the basement, and K.O. found him behind a desk that was one of a kind, handmade by a master carpenter. Cullen, however, didn't look all that comfortable. He was perspiring, despite it only being mid-October, and his bald head gleamed under the overhead fluorescent light.

"I thought we covered everything at our meeting," he said. "When I hired you."

"Two people working full-time on your problem deserve updates and fill-ins every so often."

"Well . . . " He checked the wall clock. "Would you mind coming outside with me while we talk?" He lowered his voice. "I'd prefer nobody in this department overhears us."

Gallagher pulled on a cardigan sweater and a driving cap, then led K.O. upstairs.

They strolled along, the October morning wind crisp, the sun playing peek-a-boo with the fluffy clouds. Many students, staff and faculty were also out walking, and there were benches outside the Hiram library on which several serious-looking scholars studied their texts or worked on their laptops. The aura was academic, but felt rural as well, as did the drive from Route 44 to the campus. K.O. inhaled deeply, smelling rain that might not arrive for another ten hours or so.

"This is nice," K.O. said. "Never been here before."

"It *is* pleasant, isn't it? Where did you go to college?"

K.O. hesitated only a moment. "Iraq," he said. "Then I got my master's degree in Afghanistan. I majored in ducking-in-case-a-bomb-blew-up-under-my-ass."

"I'm sorry. I didn't know."

"How could you know? I left my Medal of Honor in my other pants." That made Cullen's head whip around to look at him, so K.O. added, "Joke."

"You could almost pass as an undergraduate rushing around between classes. You look young—you *are* young. But there's something—mature, I guess—around the eyes. You don't look like daddy paid your tuition."

"*Daddy* is only vaguely aware I'm still alive. It's more comfortable that way."

"Fathers and sons always have interesting relationships."

"Did you and your father?"

Cullen shrugged. "Dad's driving force was making money. His hobby was horses. I don't share either passion, so sometimes our conversations were awkward."

A pretty young woman came toward them on the sidewalk, carrying a book bag bearing a picture of a panda and wearing tight blue jeans and a light blue Hiram hoodie. "Hi, Professor Gallagher," she said as she passed by. It wasn't flirtatious—but it wasn't *not* flirtatious, either. Cullen returned her greeting.

"Great scenery to look at every day," K.O. observed.

"I try to act like everybody on campus is a fifty-year-old guy, even ones as cute as she. I don't want my nuts caught in a wringer for just looking at a student."

"I sympathize with you."

As they emerged onto a large square known as Oliver Park, K.O. said, "About your father . . . "

Cullen slowed his walk half a step.

"You must have certain suspicions about his death or you wouldn't have hired us in the first place."

"I do. He was a healthy man, as far as I know. The massive cardiac arrest that killed him just—doesn't feel right to me. Too sudden."

"It happens, though. Perfectly healthy people drop dead from heart attacks all the time. We understand your concern, but why your—suspicions?"

"Because those healthy people aren't worth millions of dollars. They don't have high-profile businesses and a stable of horses and their photograph hanging on the wall at Northcoast Downs. So my dad might've been worth more dead than alive to somebody."

"You haven't heard the will read, yet. That somebody could be you."

"It could be, sure. But then why would I hire you to investigate *me?*"

"Bad guys do that all the time," K.O. said, "so they'll *look* innocent."

"Bad guys?"

"Yep—but it rarely works."

"No such thing as a perfect murder?"

"Close—but if they get away with it, it's because the police give traffic citations and sell tickets to the policeman's ball and don't do much else. *We* haven't discovered a murder so cops aren't looking."

"That's why I came to your company," Cullen said.

"Who else stands to inherit your father's money, if not you?"

"Could be lots of people—at the track, in his venture capital dealings, maybe even his girlfriend."

"Jenny Taylor?"

"*Jen* Taylor."

"You don't think she'll be in the will?"

"I'm sure she will be. Her name's on the bank account. She can draw checks whenever she wants."

"His business account? That's not such a big deal. If Glenn were out of town, why wouldn't his office manager sign checks for him?"

"I don't know." Cullen's head was down as if he were watching every step he took. He sounded miserable. "Really rich guys always have people hanging around, doing major things for them. They could take control away—if they wanted to."

"I've got a vision," K.O. said, "of Warren Buffet personally balancing his checkbook."

They walked by the Renner Theater of the Performing Arts, and K.O. slowed to look at a huge sculpture just outside the door—also all red brick, but constructed in swooping, abstract lines—and glanced quickly at the plaque identifying the work as "Place of Origins." He shook his head. It was a pretty sculpture but he just didn't get it. "So," he said, "your interest is making sure nobody squeezes you out of your inheritance."

Cullen Gallagher's back stiffened. "That's cold."

"I didn't mean it to be cold," K.O. assured him, "but if you're looking for yes-men, you've hired the wrong guy and the wrong company."

"The only 'yes' I want to hear is that my father died of natural causes. The rest, Mr. O'Bannion, is bullshit."

K.O. considered this, his third major case with Milan Security. In all three, he'd looked askance at the motives and truthfulness of his clients. He should probably discuss this with Milan when he reported this current meeting. Is it possible, he wondered, that I've actually chosen the wrong profession?

"You never discussed anything with your dad about his will?"

"Would you ask *your* father who'd get all his money when *he* dies?"

K.O. couldn't help his mirthless laugh. "You mean the eight dollars and sixty-three cents in his pocket when he kicks off? No, we've never talked about it."

"Sorry. That was insensitive of me." Cullen stopped beside a stone bench with the heads of Roman gods carved into each front support and sat down quietly. "A few years ago he gave me a copy of his will—sealed. I didn't look at it. Didn't think it was right. Still don't think so. I'll wait for the reading of it."

K.O. sat beside him. "When *is* the big reading of the will?"

"Soon, I hope. It's up to the lawyer; he runs everything."

"David Weaver?"

"Yes—as far as my dad's venture capital firm is concerned.

Weaver's the only one who gets to open every single bank statement, so I guess he does run everything. Jen Taylor is more of an administrator than a business tycoon."

"You don't have anything to do with that business?"

"No."

"And you're totally out of the horse racing business, too?"

"I teach political science," Cullen said. "I'm 'out of' everything else."

"What would happen, then, if you *did* get control of all your father's businesses?"

He looked almost frightened. "I haven't given that much thought."

"Sell everything?"

"Who'd buy it?"

"I asked *you*," K.O. said.

K.O. found nowhere to eat anywhere near Hiram College, with the exception of a McDonald's about five miles away from the campus. He was okay with McDonald's coffee, but even when broke and between jobs, it never occurred to him to order a Big Mac or chicken tenders—he always wondered just where on a chicken's body *were* the tenders and why anybody would want to eat them. So he drove the I-80 toll road west toward Stow, switching over to I-8 that took him within a few miles of the quaint, upscale town of Hudson, and picked a Mexican restaurant, Luchita's, in which to have lunch. It was past lunchtime and the place was empty. He chose a table in the far corner, nowhere near anyone else, and after ordering a wet burrito and an iced tea, he called Milan Jacovich to tell him about his conversation with Cullen Gallagher.

"You got to talk with him one-on-one," Milan said. "Do you have an overall impression of him?"

"It's hard to say. He isn't dancing for joy because he's an orphan—but he's not exactly shattered by grief, either."

"Then why is he suspicious it might have been foul play?"

K.O. laughed. "Foul play? You've seen too many lousy movies."

"You get my drift."

"Cullen acts—uneasy. He's worried that when they finally read the will, he won't hear his name mentioned."

"It could happen, but that doesn't make him a murderer," Milan said. "Why kill a parent when you think they've cut you out of the will?"

"If it were me, I'd bust my ass instead to make sure that if I'd been ignored in the will, my father would love the hell out of me and put me back in it." He took a sip of his iced tea and cut into his wet burrito.

"What else transpired between you and Cullen?"

"I found out Hiram College is a nice place." K.O. took a bite.

"It sounds as if you've started eating. Don't give me your report with your mouth full."

"Not even full of wet burrito?" He looked over what he'd written in his notebook. His handwriting was chicken scratches, but at least he could read it.

K.O. got halfway through his report, alternating incidents with chewing and swallowing, when Milan said, "Hold on a minute. Glenn's attorney, David Weaver, was the only person allowed to open and examine his bank statements?"

"That's what Cullen said. You talked to Weaver. What was your take on him?"

"Difficult question," Milan said. "For me, lawyers are problematic."

"I guess I don't know what that word means."

"It means they're a pain in the ass."

K.O. grinned. He had his own personal list of pains in the ass; would he eventually add lawyers? It was a distinct probability. "Weaver didn't tell you he opened all of Gallagher's bank statements first?"

"I never thought to ask him," Milan said.

"Maybe you should," K.O. said.

There was a pause as Milan took a deep breath and let it sizzle over the phone line. "Maybe I *will*," he said.

CHAPTER TWELVE

MILAN

I t's none of your goddamn business!" David Weaver said.

This probably won't surprise you—but I'd heard *that* before.

I'd tracked Gallagher's attorney to an upper floor of the Justice Center Complex. Much of its twenty-six stories are either cop shop or part of the "corrections facility," a polite way of saying "city jail." Higher up there are courtrooms, the natural habitat of lawyers, even big-deal lawyers like David Weaver. The hallways outside the courts are always crowded, usually with those related to the poor bastards about to be tried, and cops, bailiffs, clerks, and city and county prosecutors standing around, laughing and joking as if they were not about to seriously fuck up somebody's life.

Weaver was battling his way through the hangers-around like someone trying to exit a toy store first thing in the morning on Black Friday when everyone else was fighting to get in. He was hurrying from Courtroom 12 when I intercepted him in the corridor. Dozens of people rushed past us and around us carrying stuffed briefcases. Weaver's was clutched tightly against his chest like a flotation device.

"Since I'm getting paid," I said, "I think it *is* my goddamn business."

"You're not getting paid by my client."

"Your client is deceased, counselor."

Weaver refused to meet my eye, he was so intent in trying to get away from me. "I don't have to talk to you. You're not a cop."

"I know a dozen cops right downstairs," I said. "Maybe I should get hold of one so you could tell *him* you don't have to talk to him."

"There's nothing to talk about. It's all legal." He waved his free hand at me and started off, walking as fast as he could without actually running. My longer stride easily kept pace with his.

"Who says opening other people's bank statements is legal?"

"Glenn said so."

"I'd think," I said, "that would be the accountant's job."

"The job," he snapped, "is anybody's job that I say it is because I'm the late Mr. Gallagher's attorney of record! The attorney trumps the accountant, along with everybody else, including the office manager, the partners, and even the boss's *son*. And *all* of them, Mr. Jacovich, trump *you!*"

"Thanks for the reminder. What happens after you open the bank statements?"

"What do you mean, what happens?"

"Do you file them someplace, make copies, throw them away?"

We had arrived at the row of elevators. He was obviously frustrated, although the crowd made it difficult for him to get into the car and head downstairs, leaving me with my finger on the button. He sighed loudly. "Of course I don't throw them away. Don't be ridiculous."

"Answer me straight out, and I won't be ridiculous anymore."

The door slid open, and Weaver rushed into the elevator before some passengers were able to get out. I slipped in beside him and said loudly into his ear, "What happens to the bank statements?"

He looked around nervously but no one paid attention to him except me. He stood on tiptoe and craned his neck to whisper at me. "I check them over to make sure there's no hanky-panky going on."

Hanky-panky? I cupped my ear with my hand, although I'd heard him perfectly the first time. "Excuse me—what?" I said. Too loud. "Hanky-panky?"

"I check them over for mistakes," he said again, even faster than before, "and *then* I send them to the accountant."

"And what does he do with them?"

I guess I hit a nerve because Weaver stopped whispering. "How in shit do *I* know what he does with them? Maybe he feeds them to his dog!" A few fellow passengers snickered but most looked at him with contempt. One doesn't shout in a crowded elevator; it isn't done.

Embarrassed, his next sentence became a low rasp. "My job is over after I've checked them."

"Your job? I thought you were his attorney."

Now his voice soared into a higher register, and everyone in the crowded space heard him. "My job is to take care of him! To take care of his goddamn company!"

More snickers. The elevator reached the first floor, the door slid open, and Weaver elbowed a woman ahead of him and rushed past her toward the door to the street. I was right behind him.

"Who is this accountant?" I said.

Weaver zoomed through the revolving door. "I can't talk right now, I have a meeting," he said over his shoulder. It was mid-fall, temperatures in the low sixties this close to Lake Erie, but Weaver's forehead and upper lip glowed with sweat. He lowered his head and plowed forward, as determined as any running back.

"The accountant's name!" I shouted. Several passers-by looked at me curiously. Weaver almost stumbled, then stopped, turned around and glared at me.

"Darrie! Paul Darrie!" His voice was laden with frustration.

"Where's his office?"

"Goddammit, look it up!" he howled, then spun around and barreled on toward whatever he was aiming at—probably his car parked nearby, although all I could see in his direction was the bulky Medical Mart Center blocking out the lakefront sky, built so recently that I haven't yet grown accustomed to it.

I didn't have an iPad or a smart phone with me; I'm a techno-phobe, and those damn things would drive me nuts anyway—so I couldn't look up Paul Darrie's address right there on the street. I stepped back into the lobby of the Justice Center, but not too far; I'd had to go through an electronic device earlier, just to make sure I didn't have a weapon of any sort, which meant I had to empty my pockets of change, just like one must now do at the airport. I took out my cell phone. The Information operator sounded much like Lily Tomlin did during the old *Laugh-In* days, but through whatever magic she had at her disposal, we found Paul Darrie—a CPA in Beachwood, clear out in the Heights area.

My fingers hovered over the cell phone keypad. Should I call Darrie and make an appointment? Probably not; I'm sure he'd prefer not to talk with a private investigator. I didn't want to lie that I was someone else and then spring my real job on him when I arrived. What the hell—Beachwood isn't that far from my apartment in Cleveland Heights, only about fifteen minutes. It was a decent enough excuse to go home early.

Before I could ransom my car from an overpriced garage across the street, I saw Tobe Blaine getting off the elevator, looking terrific in her slim black slacks and cinnamon-colored leather jacket—but then, she always looked terrific. She noticed me immediately; her wave was subtle, as was her smile. I waited for her near the door.

"Are you stalking me?" she asked.

"If I were stalking you, I'd hang around the Third District where you work."

"Hey, I'm still the new kid on the block in Cleveburg. I had to drop by and fill out paperwork and stuff. The more pressing question: What are *you* doing here?"

"Something only slightly better than conversing with a fence," I said. "I was talking with an attorney who hoped I'd disappear into the mist like Amelia Earhart."

"I hope you aggravated him, at least." She checked her wristwatch. "You can buy me a coffee if you want."

"Love to, but I have to go to Beachwood and find a CPA who won't want to talk to me, either."

She zipped up her leather jacket. "Lawyers and accountants! Some day you're having!"

"You could improve my day by spending the evening with me."

She cocked her head to one side—a particularly appealing gesture I was now getting accustomed to. "You mean spending the night."

"That suggestion was tacit—but true."

"Not a bad idea—but I won't get loose from work until at least nine o'clock, maybe even later. I have four murder cases on my desk. No homicide cop works eight-hour days."

"Can I help?"

She laughed. "Bring in my private eye boyfriend to volunteer? The commissioner will love that."

"I hate that word!" I said.

"What word?"

"'Boyfriend.' It makes us sound like we're fifteen years old."

"If I said 'lover,' it'd raise some eyebrows. What was that word you called me in Swedish—the word for 'lover?'"

"You know damn well it was in Slovenian. *Ljubimec.*"

"I'd never be able to pronounce that unless I wrote it down on the back of my hand," she said. "Besides, a black woman speaking Slovenian? That'll raise even more eyebrows." She squeezed my arm subtly so no one would notice. "Let's try for day after tomorrow, okay?"

"What if I can't wait that long?"

Her eyebrows climbed toward her hairline as she started for the revolving door. "Then don't forget about that fence," she said.

The stretch of Chagrin Boulevard between Green and Richmond roads is one long reiteration of ugly, squat office buildings, probably designed in the mid-1960s by architects who were high on LSD. The building in which Paul Darrie's CPA firm occupied a small suite was depressing from the parking lot through the lobby to the stuffy, hushed corridors on the second and third floors. I shared the short elevator ride with a woman who cringed in the far corner and stared straight ahead like a passenger on a crowded New York subway train; I think she might have been afraid of me. The building, for all its occupied offices, felt lonely and almost abandoned.

Darrie's office was indeed lonely. There was no receptionist or secretary or assistant present, and no visitors filled up the four uncomfortable-looking seats in the outer office. My guess was that customers rarely walked through the door, but did most of their business via telephone or email.

In an inside office, a short, slightly chunky man in rolled-up white shirtsleeves and a dull tie bent over some account books, his fingers working furiously on an old-fashioned adding machine. He didn't look up until I tapped politely on the open door.

"Mr. Darrie?"

"Yes?"

"My name is Milan Jacovich. Milan Security. I did some work for Glenn Gallagher this past summer."

I watched him struggle to remember who I was; Gallagher's accountant had certainly heard my name before. Finally his eyes brightened. "I recall hearing about that. I'm surprised you didn't come around here to poke at me and ask me a lot of questions."

"That's because I didn't need to," I said, and then added, "*did* I?"

He pushed his adding machine a foot further away from himself and pursed his lips—not a kissy kind of pursing but one of barely contained irritation. "You need help *now*? Or are you looking for your own CPA?"

"No—I'm working for *Cullen* Gallagher."

Darrie's forehead crinkled, but he looked more like an actor copping a phony frown-pose than someone who was mildly disturbed. "Isn't he a professor at Kenyon College or something?"

I corrected him. "Hiram College."

"Hiram—right. What would *he* hire Milan Security for? Did some student cheat on their final exam?" He allowed himself to gloat over his own bad joke.

"He has a few questions. Maybe you can answer some of them."

Darrie put his opened palms together like a four-year-old readying to recite, "*Now I lay me down to sleep.*" "I don't like questions when I'm not expecting them." He pointed at the account book in front of him. "As you can see, I'm busy."

Everybody was busy. I wondered if everybody lied. "This won't take long."

He sighed. "I'm trying to get rid of you. Politely."

It wasn't all that polite, but I let it go. "When Glenn was alive, you received the bank statements for Gallagher Investments Management. Isn't that so?"

"Of course it's so. I'm an accountant; I'd *naturally* get the bank statements."

"Did you get the bank statements regarding Gallagher's horse business, too?"

"I was his—total accountant. I got statements for all his businesses—and his personal account. A guy'd be crazy to have several businesses *and* a personal account and spread them all out between four or five CPAs."

"Are you a harness racing fan, Mr. Darrie?"

"Whenever Glenn invited me," he said. "Otherwise, I don't pay much attention to races."

"Did he make a lot of money on his horse business?"

Darrie shook his head. "He won lots of races—ran in the money about twenty to thirty percent of the time when he drove. Now, that's pretty damn good. But it takes more money to feed a horse than to feed your poodle—so, no, he didn't make a profit. He lost money, just on horse upkeep. His gambling wasn't my job, so I didn't ask."

"A lot of money?"

"Define 'a lot of money.'"

"I don't know, Mr. Darrie. Take a guess for me."

"Maybe thirty or forty grand a year."

"I'd call that a lot of money," I said.

"Glenn Gallagher wouldn't."

"Did you bet on the races, Mr. Darrie?"

Condescendingly he said, "CPAs don't gamble."

"Were you social with Gallagher otherwise?"

"We weren't friends," Darrie said. "We didn't run in the same uber-wealthy circles. He's a client—he *was* a client. That's all."

"When you received the bank statements—was that every month?"

He nodded. "He had five different accounts in five different banks—not counting stocks and bonds, which was another situation altogether."

"You didn't handle that part of it?"

"Hell no; ask his stockbroker. I had nothing to do with it."

"The statements you received—had they been opened before they got to you?"

Darrie's shoulders slumped. "Yeah."

"By David Weaver?"

"That sonofabitch thinks he's in charge of everything." Darrie shook his head angrily like a St. Bernard clearing his slobbering jowls. "Lawyers!" he snarled.

"You made copies for your files?" I nodded at several large filing cabinets lined up against one wall of his office.

"Of course."

"And when you entered all that stuff in Glenn's account books, you sent the statements to him?"

"Actually I sent them to Jen Taylor."

"Then did she look them over? Or did Glenn himself?"

"How the hell would I know? Maybe they used them to wipe their butts!"

"You don't check up on them?"

"He wasn't my only client!" Darrie actually picked up the account book from his desk and shook it at me. "I have twenty-two clients. I'm too damn busy to run over to Gallagher's offices every day and hold hands. I keep charge of their accounts, I do it damn well, and I get paid for it!"

"Do you get paid for it damn well?" I said.

"That's none of your concern. So if you'll excuse me . . . "

"One more question."

Sigh. "*What?*"

"How come," I said, "you and everybody my assistant and I have talked to ever since we started working for Cullen Gallagher have been rude, abusive, dismissive, secretive, highly reluctant or resistant to answering questions, and almost impossible to talk to? Why is that, Mr. Darrie?"

That gave Paul Darrie the opportunity to act some more, turning into a drama queen this time to impress me with a shrug of pure adolescent innocence. "I don't have the foggiest notion."

"Maybe," I replied, "it's because everybody seems to have something to hide."

CHAPTER THIRTEEN

K.O.

Finishing his Mexican lunch, K.O. wandered through Hudson, investigating some of the shops in the First and Main Shopping Center, which was half-crowded with extremely well-dressed middle-aged women who'd parked their Mercedes and BMWs as close to the shop doors as possible. There wasn't much in the way of fashions for men that he could cruise, so he spent some time in the Learned Owl Bookstore, and bought a copy of John Steinbeck's *The Grapes of Wrath,* a book he'd heard about all his life but had never read.

Afterwards, he strolled a few feet north to a shop called Main Street Cupcakes on the corner and took his elaborate to-hell-with-calories dessert outside, eating it while he walked back to where he'd parked his car.

Driving home, he replayed the conversation with Cullen Gallagher. Was this whole case undertaken simply to ensure that Cullen wasn't given short shrift in his father's will? The brief, pointed exchange with him about K.O. and his own father caused an ache somewhere behind K.O.'s eyes, but he preferred not to think about it. You can choose your friends and lovers, it's been said, but you can't choose your family. If he could have, K.O.'s choice of fathers would have been different.

What would he have done, he wondered, if Atticus Finch, from *To Kill A Mockingbird,* had been *his* father? He'd read *that* book—and seen the movie three times. Atticus Finch was nowhere near like his father.

There was no reason for any father-son hatred between K.O.

and his dad, but no reason for caring, either. His father had never paid attention to him in the first place, hardly ever visited him in juvie, and after K.O. was released—"sprung," as he used to think of it—and joined the army—whatever was left of the O'Bannion family had simply shriveled up and blown away.

Damn few people meant much to K.O., one way or the other. There was Jake Foote, the cop who'd originally arrested him for assault when he was fifteen, but who also cared for K.O. and let him know he'd always have his back, the one man who'd welcomed him home from the Middle East. Suzanne Davis, the Lake County private investigator (and Jake Foote's one-time girlfriend, K.O. guessed, but wasn't sure) who'd introduced him to his current boss and encouraged them to try working together. And Milan Jacovich, naturally—although they still searched for the right pitch to their relationship—less than friends, less than partners, but more than employer-employee, even in such a short time.

Then there was Carli. *No* question about Carli. He'd known from the very first time he'd seen her, the very first time he'd kissed her, the very first time they'd made love together, that he was completely silly over her—the closest approximation of love he'd ever known. The mistakes and failures and victories most adolescents go through as learning moments had been overwhelmed by his struggles of just trying to survive adolescence and very young manhood.

But Carli was, for him, the lonely years of imagining and romantic fantasy come alive—and K.O. desperately needed to spend time with her, to look at her and touch her and hope she'd make him laugh. In the three short months since they'd met, she had become his main reason to wake up in the morning—she, and his new-found employment, and the possibility of one day getting his own P.I.'s license.

He forced his mind back to his present job, the Gallagher case—if indeed there was a case. Had he asked the right questions during his walk through Hiram College campus? Had Cullen Gallagher and his father stayed in close touch, or had they drifted into alternate universes without even realizing? Was Cullen really spending his money to find out who, if anyone, was screwing him out of his inheritance?

He had a plan—but he feared Milan would prefer doing it himself, and K.O. didn't want the smallest scrap of accomplishment taken away from him. He'd do what he needed to do the next morning and then include it in his report.

Besides, he had plans of his own for that evening.

Pizza—pepperoni, sausage, black olives, green peppers, and extra cheese, delivered by one of many pizza chains in Carli's neighborhood in which all the pizza looked and tasted pretty much the same as the other guy's, and washed down with Great Lakes Brewing Company beer, Dortmunder Gold. Like so many men in their twenties, K.O. had been a Bud guy until he'd discovered this local brewery. Milan's beer of choice was Stroh's, but younger guys had more modern tastes. Now Carli made sure she always had a supply of Dortmunder Gold in her refrigerator.

Sustenance was augmented by watching an old movie on DVD: *The Way We Were.* Carli's choice—a favorite she thought the saddest and most romantic film ever—except that they didn't quite get to the last third of the movie because they went to bed.

There was lovemaking—on and off with cuddling and intimate conversation until nearly one o'clock in the morning, when they both finally fell asleep at the same time.

Radio alarm—jarring at 7 a.m. K.O. had started listening to the early morning Lanigan and Malone craziness on WMJI-FM, as Milan did. Since the two lovers had gotten together, Carli had gotten into that habit too. Both awakened, groggy. Then, more lazy kisses and more cuddling. K.O. outwaited Carli until she reluctantly got out of bed, went into her kitchenette, and started a pot of coffee.

"I've got to get to work early," she said, "in case some hot guy comes in to question me about perverts who hang out in my shop. Besides, we're doing inventory."

"I have to start early, too. Places to go." K.O. had changed clothes the previous evening before he'd arrived at Carli's apartment, so he wouldn't have to go back home at all. "Can I use your razor?"

"*I'm* using the razor," she said. "But I have a couple of disposable ones."

"Just in case one of your other boyfriends wants to shave?"

"That's no problem. All nine of them wear beards."

"All *nine* of them? Imagine that!"

"You're the only one without a beard," Carli assured him, "so I don't worry about razor burn."

"I knew there was a good reason you kept me around," K.O. said.

They showered together, a tight fit for two of them in the tiny stall. Carli's dark hair was short and semi-curly, so she was used to shampooing it every morning, and K.O. gently massaged the liquid into her scalp. He loved the smell of her shampoo almost as much as her natural scent. They shared a bottle of body wash, and Carli turned her back to him, leaning against him as he soaped up her breasts.

"Your skin is like silk," he murmured into her ear.

"Does the feel of silk turn you on, then?" She pressed against him harder. "Hmm, I think *something* is."

His lathered hands gently explored the front of her body, running them over her stomach and hips as he moved lower. At his first touch between her legs, she turned around, wrapped both arms around his neck, and lifted one leg to rest upon his hip as he entered her easily, leaning her against the glass door of the shower stall. Soft whimpers became gasps as his thrusts grew more aggressive. She took a fistful of his hair in one hand—he'd let it grow longer than at any time in his life when she'd said she liked having enough of it to grab—and met his intensity with her own.

The pressure built inside K.O., hovering between fervid pleasure and exquisite agony—not just in his groin, but in his gut and his chest and inside his head, yet he didn't allow himself release until she quivered all over, crying out before taking his lower lip between her teeth and he felt her body relax against his own. Then, pulling her so close that it seemed he could feel every inch of her body against his wet skin, he willed his energy and passion to burst inside her.

They stayed close without speaking or even moving, just

catching their breath, until she lowered her leg, putting her foot on the tile floor and pressing her face against his chest. Finally he moved away, gently disengaging.

He stepped backward, his hand groping for the wall, and he slid down into a sitting position, the water still beating on his legs and abdomen, his eyes closed and a dreamy smile playing about his lips.

Carli watched him for a moment. Then she said, "Are you awake?"

"Just re-living."

"Is that why you're smiling?"

"You betcha."

Carli stepped back under the spray to wash off whatever soap was left. "Are you going to sit there all day, Kevin?"

He opened one eye. "I'm considering it."

"The hot water will run out in approximately ninety seconds and you'll freeze."

"It's worth it to me."

She smiled down at him. "You probably should have taken that cold shower in the first place."

"If I had, then *you* wouldn't be smiling."

She reached up and adjusted the shower head so the spray hit K.O. full in the face. "And on top of everything else, you made me late."

K.O. spit out the excess water, looking horrified. "Don't say *late!*" he begged.

Dried, combed and dressed, they sat at the counter separating her kitchenette from her living room, drinking coffee; he watched while she slipped two slices of bread into the toaster. Maybe, he thought, he should buy her a new toaster for Christmas—but then he shook his head, appalled. What kind of a romantic, loving gift for their first Christmas is a toaster? As good as their time together had been—he considered it as sort of a non-legal honeymoon—he realized he'd never had this kind of relationship before and he had much to learn.

"Where are you off to this morning?" Carli asked as she retrieved two toasted slices from the silver toaster and replaced them with two more.

"You won't want to hear," K.O. replied.

"Why? Are you going to dig up a grave?"

"Almost. I'm going to talk to the Summit County Medical Examiner. The coroner."

"OMG," she said, pronouncing each letter that was used a zillion times a day on emails and Facebook and Twitter. "Will you actually get to watch an autopsy?"

"I hope not." He spread whipped butter on his toast, wishing he understood *why* anyone whips butter. "But if I do, I won't faint."

"You *won't?*"

He tried not to think of when the truck he'd ridden in during his second tour in Iraq had exploded and blown the driver into several pieces. He was only burned a bit on one leg, but he'd never forget that day, that moment.

"I won't," he said in that crusty tone that clearly conveyed he didn't want to—and would *not*—discuss it further.

She steered the subject in a different direction. "Does this involve Glenn Gallagher's dying?"

"I hope not, but it might."

"Why do you hope not?"

He rubbed his eyes with a thumb and middle finger, trying to erase that horrific Iraqi memory. Focus, he said to himself more than once. Focus, goddammit! "We're asking what might have killed Gallagher besides heart failure—except we don't *know* that something happened to him. It might have been a natural death. We're guessing."

"And the coroner will know for sure?"

He shrugged. "When anyone dies from something other than old age or cancer or some other disease, it's the law that a post-mortem must be done. Whoever did that post found indications of cardiac arrest and signed the paper that says so. No further investigation was done—there wasn't any need."

"But," Carli said, "wasn't Mr. Gallagher cremated?"

He nodded. "That was the scientific finish. We can't examine ashes."

"Then why interview the coroner?"

"Because I can't stay in bed or in the shower with you all day. Seeing the coroner is my second choice."

*   *   *

It was a strange place for K.O. to be. He'd been to cemeteries before; just after returning from Afghanistan, he'd visited one near Mansfield where one of his Army buddies was buried—but cemeteries are sad and peaceful, where you can bow your head, whether you're religious or not.

The Medical Examiner's office in downtown Akron? Not peaceful. As he cooled his heels in the waiting room, it struck him that below his feet were recently deceased people. He imagined the odor of the autopsy room, and it made his skin crawl. The so-called customers—they weren't "patients" because they were dead and no one could help them, but he didn't know what else to call them—might not have had a funeral or memorial service, or might have died from murder, a drunk driver plowing into them at eighty miles an hour, a drug overdose, starvation, or neglect. Cancer, diabetes, and heart failure might have done the job, too; those sicknesses were more or less normal.

He'd called his one-time mentor, Jake Foote, in Lake County, and Jake had leaned politely on the Summit County Medical Examiner's office to determine which physician had performed the Gallagher autopsy and whether K.O. could get an appointment. Few people demanded an audience with a medical examiner who had examined the entrails of someone they'd known in life.

The air conditioner was running merrily, as though it were mid-July and not almost November, and he rubbed his hands together so they wouldn't be cold when he finally shook hands with the coroner.

Finally summoned, he found himself across the desk from a white-haired woman. Dr. Maura Keeling, an assistant coroner, smiled pleasantly at him. When he shook her hand, he tried not to think that hand had within the last hour been poking around in someone's organs.

"You're a private investigator," she said. "You're young for that kind of career."

"You learn better when you're young," K.O. said.

"When I heard from Sergeant Foote, I pulled out Mr. Gallagher's file and gave it a quick once-over, Mr. O'Bannion."

"K.O.," he said. "I go by my initials."

"K.O. How did that happen?"

"It makes me sound like a tough guy."

"Are you? A tough guy?"

"I hope you never find out."

"Me, too," she smiled. "Anyway, regarding Mr. Gallagher's PM report—you're probably not familiar with technicalities, so I'll make this as simple as I can."

"Good, because I won't finish medical school for another fifty years or so."

Her eyes twinkled. She pushed a slim folder across the desk. "It's in here, what little there is."

He opened the folder, scanned it quickly. "How come there isn't more?"

"Not much more to put in a report. Glenn Gallagher was late middle-age—and he had a-fib," she said. "Atrial fibrillation. So his myocardial infarction wasn't surprising."

"He was medicated?"

She pulled the file back and ran her finger down the lines. "He took Coumadin—once daily. Many people are prescribed Coumadin for one reason or another. He was also on digitalis. That's for heart problems, naturally—and arrhythmia." She brushed her very white hair off her forehead. "Sorry, I don't get to talk to non-doctors very often. That means irregular rhythm of the heartbeat."

"Could that be fatal?"

"So could digitalis—or too much booze. But there was no reason to think so. I don't usually look for something criminal or illegal unless it jumps up and bites me."

"And the cremation? Who decided that?"

"I have no clue," Maura Keeling said. "The body was released from here to a funeral home. I have no idea what they do after that. But the next-of-kin usually makes that decision."

"Even if the deceased wrote down he wanted to be buried somewhere like a veterans' cemetery or at Lake View?"

She put the autopsy report file into a drawer of her desk. "That might cause legal problems. Again, that happens after I've finished."

"Is it possible," K.O. asked, "that someone on those meds might take too much at one time that could be fatal?"

"Any medication that's abused and overused could kill—even aspirin. I wouldn't think Mr. Gallagher—a wealthy and successful man—would be dumb enough to overdose on digitalis."

"Could he have taken an extra dose by accident?"

"One extra dose wouldn't hurt him—or kill him."

"And during the post-mortem, were you able to tell whether he'd overdosed on digitalis?"

"I could have—if I'd tested for it in the first place."

K.O. nodded. "One more question, Dr. Keeling. Could he have collected enough prescribed digitalis that it might be fatal?"

The medical examiner thought about that for a bit, her forehead creased. "With everything on computers, I doubt anyone could 'collect' too much prescribed medication without someone in authority finding out. He might have gone to several different doctors for the same prescription, I suppose, if he had really wanted to take his own life."

K.O. shook his head. "He invited four of us to join him at the track that night, and he was entertaining and generous. When he got sick, he obviously wanted help. He asked my boss to drive him home. If he were suicidal, he wouldn't have killed himself in front of a whole crowd of people."

"Why not?"

"Ego. *Not* egomania, just plain everyday ego. Glenn Gallagher had a positive, healthy regard for himself." K.O. rose and once more shook the medical examiner's hand, this time not thinking of where it might have recently been. "I appreciate your talking with me, Dr. Keeling. You've helped a lot."

"I enjoyed this, too," she said. "I spend *most* of my work day with people who don't talk back."

K.O. walked outside to where he'd parked his car, and it wasn't until he had slid behind his steering wheel that he was struck with the creepy notion that one day, Dr. Maura Keeling, assistant Summit County medical examiner, might get to see him naked.

He shuddered. He didn't want to think about that.

CHAPTER FOURTEEN

MILAN

'm glad I hired K.O. He's good at what he does, he learns quickly, and he has no problem taking his own initiative. At first I was irritated that he went off on his own without checking with me first, but now it makes life easier for me.

There are other projects, other cases I have to handle besides the Gallagher situation. That morning I took care of them, doing research, checking with sources, knowing K.O. was busy doing whatever it was he does. When I was younger, Milan Security was strictly a one-man band. Now it's harder getting everything done in one day without some help. I guess I've slowed down a bit.

That makes me nervous.

I played football—a hard, full-body contact sport—in my youth. I became a military policeman in what used to be Saigon, a place where you never knew whether or not your next-door neighbor, or your grocer, or the bartender at your local hangout was on your side or was a Viet Cong sympathizer waiting for the right opportunity to slit your throat. I came back to Cleveland, joined the police force, carried a weapon and arrested people who sometimes carried weapons of their own. When I resigned and began my own company, I was shot, shot *at*, stabbed, and knocked unconscious many times—leaving concussions that have saddled me with recurring headaches—but it had never really occurred to me that I was going to die.

Now that I've matured, as they say—or gotten old, as they prefer *not* to say—the prospect of my unavoidable demise pops into my head every so often, having little to do with my job and everything to do with my age. I'm now older than both my parents were when they died. My right knee is sending surprise messages of pain to me on occasion, reminding me that my joints aren't as good as they were at twenty or thirty or even fifty. My heart still operates at full capacity, but now I take better care of it—herbal tea instead of coffee, being careful about red meat and carbs, and avoiding desserts. As for alcohol, most of my life I'd toss back at least ten beers every week. Now, three of them in a month is a big deal.

Business was good. *Life* was good. My ex-wife Lila, who left me a few decades ago for the man she's lived with ever since, had faded quietly from my life once our two sons were grown. My younger son, Stephen, always a smiling and pleasant kid, is a senior at Kent State—my alma mater. My older son, Milan Junior, lives in Chicago and prospers as a middle-management executive, despite inheriting his mother's Serbian sulkiness and an anger that simmers under his skin. I love them both, and keep in contact, but they aren't foursquare in the middle of my life anymore. That makes things easier.

And I'm kind of in love. I say "kind of" because Tobe Blaine wasn't ready to admit that, yet, either. Our racial difference didn't trouble us, but it was *there*. It made things difficult. Not impossible, obviously—but difficult.

I *have* slowed down, and time *does* tumble by more quickly as one ages. In any event, I was secretly delighted Kevin O'Bannion—K.O.—was on my side. In my office—*our* office—we reviewed our work so far. One of the best parts of our business now was our end-of-day meeting.

"I'm of two minds," K.O. said. He was sipping a Sprite and I was downing one of my many herbal teas of the day. When our clients weren't around, he was more affable and more relaxed.

"Let's hear both of them," I said.

"Cullen Gallagher might be more concerned over whether he's going to be the major beneficiary of Glenn's will than of the possibility that his dad was murdered."

"That may be," I said. "But he sure as hell wouldn't have killed his own father without knowing what's in that will."

"What if he did know, though?"

"He swears he never opened it, as his father had asked him not to. There's probably only one person who'd ever seen that will before Glenn died—the lawyer, David Weaver. For him to tell anyone about it while Glenn was still alive would have cost him his license."

"But if Weaver wound up owning Glenn's company—and his horses, too—well, that might not be such a bad thing, not practicing law anymore."

"Weaver would rewrite the will?" I mused. "Cullen would have his ass in court before the day was out."

"Hell, I would, too. You talked with Chloe Markham's brother? Manley?"

"He was so hammered, he won't remember he ever met me."

K.O. scratched the back of his head. "A drunk can't be a murderer? Don't kid yourself." He wriggled in the chair, staring at the wall or out the window or somewhere else. "In Iraq—one of my company got really plastered one night. Well—*all* of us got plastered. The day before, I was in a truck that blew up and the driver was killed. Everybody'd liked him. So we were pretty shook up and drinking. Don't ask me *what* we were drinking, or where we got it, because I don't remember."

I nodded. I'd been in a war, too—a different war, a long time ago, but a war nevertheless. But K.O. sometimes gets lost in a memory.

"So this guy—Buddy, everybody called him, and I can't even remember his real name—Buddy was either crying or crashing around the barracks throwing and breaking things. Finally he grabbed his weapon, screamed, 'Goddamn motherfuckers!' and went charging out into the night, wearing only camouflage pants, a T-shirt, and flip-flop sandals. No helmet, no boots, no nothing!" His voice grew quiet. "By the time we caught up with him, he'd murdered four Iraqi civilians—two men, a woman, and a teenaged girl. He might have shot more if we hadn't taken the gun away from him and decked him cold on the street."

"Jesus," I said.

"We weren't pissed off at him. We all felt like killing that night; he was the one who did it—for real." His head was down, studying

his own lap. "The thing was—two of those civilians were women."
His voice drifted off. I couldn't see his face, but I knew he wasn't
crying. I couldn't imagine K.O. ever crying. Then he shrugged,
meeting my gaze. "It was what it was."

"What happened to Buddy eventually?"

He wasn't lost in a real nightmare anymore, so his reply was
casual, as if I'd asked him what time it was. "The next day, the
three of us who chased him—shit, were we hung over!—anyway,
we went to the company commander to report it."

"And?"

"The captain listened until we got to the part about civilians
getting shot and then he jiggled his finger in his ear and said, 'I
can't hear you.' We started telling it again, and he said, 'I've got
work to do! I have no time to listen to all your shit!' So what could
we do? We saluted and started out and he called after us: 'And no
other officer has time to listen to your shit, either!'"

"They didn't do anything to Buddy?"

"Nope. They moved him out of our squad, put him in some
other company, and stuck him in an office for the rest of his tour.
They wouldn't let him on patrol or anywhere near a weapon. I
never saw him after that. His tour ended about eight weeks before mine, so he must've gone home."

"He didn't get any mental help?"

"We should *all* be on a shrink's couch. But it didn't happen
then, and it won't now. So I lost track of Buddy. It's a good thing—
he was fucked from the start."

"You didn't report it to somebody with more rank?"

"We were soldiers. We *were* stupid enough to slog around in
the desert in a hundred and twenty degree heat, lugging seventy
pounds of equipment wherever we went. But report it to some
bird colonel and spend the rest of our lives elbow-deep in shit?
We weren't *that* stupid!"

Then he waved a hand in front of his face as if erasing everything he'd just said, like cleaning off a teacher's blackboard.

"K.O.—I wouldn't share this story with Carli."

"Sure I will—on our fiftieth wedding anniversary." Now he sat
upright and leaned his elbows on my desk. I could almost hear

his brain clicking off one subject and on to a new one. "Okay, so what are we looking at here, Milan?"

"We've eliminated Manley Markham. I also had a brief conversation with Paul Darrie—Gallagher's accountant."

"How did that go?"

"He was loath to tell me a damn thing."

"Loath?"

"Look it up in your dictionary."

"I don't have a dictionary."

"Look it up on your computer, then. Darrie did make me sit up and take sustenance. David Weaver opened and looked at the bank statements before he did, and Darrie eventually sent them to Jen Taylor—Glenn Gallagher's office manager and girlfriend."

"You mean," K.O. said, "Glenn didn't even see them?"

"They're on file at his office. Whether he saw them, nobody knows."

"I'll bet Jen Taylor knows."

"I'll bet, too. Why don't you go ask her?"

"The deal was you take Gallagher's business acquaintances and I take the gang at the racetrack."

"Exactly!" I said. "I've already talked to Jen Taylor. She might have been careful about what she said to me; I don't know. Maybe you can get her to say something she chose not to tell me." K.O. didn't look happy. "She's closer to your age. She might be more relaxed."

"She might not *be* relaxed. She might have motives, too. She was Gallagher's gal pal."

That made me think of Tobe. "After eight years with Glenn, she was a lot more than his 'gal pal.'"

"So that means I gotta go talk to her?"

"You don't 'gotta' do anything. Call it a learning experience. The next case we get won't be about horses and racing—and you'll have to be ready."

"I'm ready for anything," K.O. said. He moved to his own desk and closed up his computer. "I'll go see Jen Taylor tomorrow. How about you? 'Poking around' again, is it?"

"Well—if you're going to get your feet wet with Glenn's business associates, I'll take a page out of your book and visit backside at the harness track tomorrow."

"Wear jeans or a pair of pants you can wash," K.O. advised. "And whatever you do—watch where you step!"

I arrived at Northcoast Downs at about nine o'clock the following morning. The wind, blowing from the northwest, was a quiet warning that autumn, with its colorful leaves and pumpkins and cider and little kids in costumes browbeating you for candy, is just the precursor to the oncoming winter. It was still too warm for a parka, but too chilly for a windbreaker, so I'd donned a sweater under my tweed sports jacket and hoped I wouldn't get too cold.

There was a shack at the far end of the parking lot, with a not-very-secure-looking wooden barrier that could be raised and lowered by two security guards, whose jobs were to guard the backside from unwelcome visitors. Both of them, first singly, and then together, examined my visitor pass closely, as if someone were trying to give them a twenty dollar bill with Rush Limbaugh's picture on it instead of Andrew Jackson's.

I waited too long and then said, "That pass isn't counterfeit, you know."

"Who's this Cullen Gallagher guy again?" the older of the two asked, holding the visitor pass up to the light and looking through it for whatever watermark should have been on it—or possibly should *not* have been on it.

"Cullen Gallagher is the son of Glenn Gallagher. You knew *him*, didn't you?"

The younger one grunted. "Are you a friend of this Cullen guy?"

"That's right."

"How are you friends with him?"

"What's the difference *how?* Do you want to see my passport, my social security card, and my federal tax returns for the last twelve years? I'm showing you a valid pass; will you let me in or not?"

Both of them glowered like members of the Eichmann jury. The older one said, "You park over there," and he pointed. "Back in. Don't park in any other spaces, especially the ones marked 'reserved,' or you'll be towed away and have to pay the towing charges." Before I could put my car in reverse to get to where I was supposed to park—and I recall K.O. was allowed to park *inside* that gate—the older one added, "And don't go nowhere else but that first barn back there or you'll get arrested." Apparently he wasn't going to raise that flimsy wooden barricade for *anyone* on this particular morning. Maybe he woke up with a bellyache.

I did as I'd been told, backing away from the shack and then craning over my shoulder to guide myself tail first into the spot he'd advised. No one feels quite as powerful and authoritarian as an unarmed security guard at a parking lot.

It was a long walk back to the barn. I'd hoped to talk to Walt Holman—or anyone else I might find there. I might get the same answers K.O. had elicited from them—or I might get different ones. I was curious to find out.

There were many horses out and about already. As K.O. had warned me, I watched my step, managing not to ruin a pair of shoes. When I went inside the barn, a large tabby was stretched across the entrance, guarding it like a stone lion in front of a Chinese temple. He looked at me only for a moment. Then, bored, he crossed his front paws in front of himself and closed his eyes. I stepped over him with utmost care.

It took me a while to adjust to the dimness. The sun hadn't been out this morning, but it was more gray and dingy inside than out. No windows. The several aromas in the barn didn't offend me; horses *do* smell, but they smell natural, even if no one has yet cleaned out their stalls. Fortunately, horses don't eat the same things we do.

Finally I located the only person moving around inside, near the other end of the barn, lifting heavy bales of hay and tossing them over the stable half-doors to the horses, grunting loudly with every lift and every toss. He was a large and ungainly young man with dead eyes and a slack mouth—Jobie Dash, from K.O.'s description. I called out a hello, but either he didn't hear me or chose to ignore me. I made my way back to where he wrestled the bales.

"Good morning," I said.

He looked at me and bobbed his head once, then continued

to ignore me. I think that was his way of saying "good morning" back.

"Is Walt Holman around?"

He glanced all around the barn as if he expected Holman to be there. Not finding him, he just shook his head no and continued his work.

"You expect him back soon?"

Shrug.

"Mind if I wait?"

Another shrug. It was like talking to a mime, who never answered back.

I returned to the front of the barn, stopping to see the horses in their stalls. Most of them greeted me eagerly but were disappointed to discover I had no snacks for them. One actually nuzzled me anyway. K.O. told me that if you show love to *any* animal, they're certain to love you back. Maybe this horse knew that, too.

Walt Holman's office door was open. I peeked in; it wasn't much bigger than bathrooms in most newer homes. Holman was no neat freak, but he wasn't sloppy, either. Papers and folders and account books were stacked on every level surface, along with copies of the daily *Racing Form*, *The Plain Dealer*, an old and well-thumbed copy of *Hustler*, and several magazines from the harness racing industry. On a battered metal file cabinet perched an ancient plastic table radio. Several color photos of racing horses hung crooked on the wall in inexpensive frames, and under the old desk—so scratched and discolored that no one could guess what color it was originally—were tucked a shredding machine and a portable safe. Against one wall was a miniature refrigerator, similar to the one I had in my own office, except mine was done up to look like a Wells Fargo safe.

At about nine-fifteen, I began to wonder whether Holman was actually on the premises. He might have been out exercising a horse, but that was usually the job of the trainers and not Glenn Gallagher's sometime partner who ran the barn. And then I heard Jobie Dash's voice for the first time, loudly taking the name of Jesus Christ in vain. His tone was terrified.

I hurried out of the office. He was about halfway down the barn, staring fixedly at something and shaking his head as if he refused to believe his own eyes. He backed up one step at a time, his hands out in front of him as if for protection, his head shaking an impotent "no" at whatever he could see.

He was staring into the therapy pool, where they let horses soak in warm water up to their withers to smooth out some of the tight muscles; he didn't notice me standing beside him.

There was no horse in the pool.

There was a body, though, floating face down, arms spread wide at either side as if he were flying. I moved closer for a better look. I couldn't see the corpse's face, but I recognized the clothes billowing around him from when I saw him alive—fat, grubby, more than half drunk, and wearing the same outrageous filthy pink hoodie and tattered jeans in which he probably lived.

And died.

Gecko.

Deputy Keith Johnson of the Summit County Sheriff's department—that's Keith *Barent* Johnson, according to his business card—wasn't a bit put off by investigating a murder. Akron is in Summit County, too—and *sometimes* not exactly Pleasantville. But gang-shootings and domestic violence culminating in a death were more familiar to him than a corpse floating around in a horse therapy pool at a racetrack, and he didn't know where to begin looking first.

I seemed to be his best bet. He wasn't impressed that I flashed both my P.I. license and my visitor's pass at him; I was the only one there who didn't belong at the track, and for all intents and purposes I became a "person of interest."

"Tell me again what you're doing back here in the barn," he said as he leaned against the stack of hay bales, "where you aren't supposed to be."

Again was the operative word; I'd already explained it to him. Twice. "The visitor's pass says I *am* supposed to be back here, Deputy. I work for a client who's marginally involved with racing—one who pays me to ask questions." Again I waved the pass at him. "A client whose signature is on this piece of paper."

"Questions about what?"

"That has to be confidential. Trust me, it has nothing to do with the deceased."

"*'Trust me'?* You actually just said that?" Johnson laughed.

"I don't even know the deceased's real name. Everyone called him Gecko."

The deputy pulled out his notebook and flipped it open to the most recent scribbles. "Gecko's real name was Royal Shadcoe." He shook his head. "Royal. How does a man wind up like this," and he pointed to the pool, "with a name like Royal, for Christ's sakes? Royal Shadcoe, fifty-seven years old, born in Brazil, Indiana. You ever hear of that town?"

"I've hardly ever heard of Indiana."

He didn't appreciate wit; that was obvious from the contemptuous glare he bestowed on me. "We'll check into it further, but as far as anyone knows, he has no family. Never married, no kids, lives in a fourth-rate motel within walking distance of here. No car, no driver's license, no nothing." He titled his cap sideways on his head. "Everyone says he was half smashed all the time. Maybe he staggered in here, fell into the therapy pool, and drowned."

"Maybe," I said. "But he worked here early mornings; I can't imagine why he'd come in here in the middle of the night."

"To sleep off the booze?"

"His motel at least had a bed, instead of him sleeping in the hay some horse pissed in."

He squinted at me. "Are you implying this wasn't an accident?"

"Not necessarily implying. Just saying."

"Everybody around here is 'just saying'! Nobody ever knew him to fall asleep in the barn before."

"Much less in the therapy pool," I said.

"You know a hell of a lot for someone who's never been in this barn before," he said, and actually poked me in the chest. If he hadn't been wearing a badge, I would have slapped his hand away. He wore a gun at his hip, though—and I hadn't thought to bring mine.

"It's a *barn*, Deputy. Horses. Stalls. Hay. Tack. Horse shit. And Royal Shadcoe is in the therapy pool and not the Olympic swimming pool at some elegant downtown hotel."

He sighed and blew his breath out through his lips. "Got you, Mr. Jacovich."

Several grooms and trainers of both genders milled around, shocked. Lab techs from the medical examiner's office huddled near the pool, speaking softly but not really doing anything. Nobody'd fished Gecko's lifeless body out of there yet. The regular veterinarian, Dr. Sheila McHale, had arrived for her morning check-ups and of course was asked to stick around for a while. Walt Holman had finally shown up, now sitting alone in his office looking stunned, staring at nothing, probably wishing the police would leave so he could open his desk drawer and take a long pull from the bottle he must have kept hidden in there.

The horses were restless with too many strange people invading the place where they lived. They moved nervously in their stalls, whinnying back and forth; I could swear they were talking among themselves.

Framed in the doorway to the barn now, clouded sunlight behind rendering her a silhouette, was Tobe Blaine. She spotted me at once—Johnson and I were several inches taller than anyone else in the room—and sauntered over, her hand cupping her badge and holding it high so everyone could see it. It was good having a friend there with me in hostile territory; I'd called to tell her what happened, even before I called the sheriff. I'd also phoned K.O.

"Milan," she said, making it sound casual. Then she addressed Johnson. "Detective Sergeant Blaine, Cleveland P.D."

If Deputy Sheriff Johnson had no use for me, it was immediately obvious he couldn't stand the sight of Tobe Blaine. Was it her badge? The color of her skin? Or just her attitude? "How did you get in here?"

"With a badge—just like yours, right? Of course those guys argued with me before they let me in, but eventually I persuaded them to cooperate."

"How'd you do that?" I said.

"I threatened to shoot them."

Johnson didn't find that funny. "You're out of your jurisdiction, Detective. This isn't Cleveland."

"It's *not?* Gee whillikers, I must've made a wrong turn on Buckeye Road."

The gee-whillikers line didn't amuse him, either—but it sure amused me. He said, "What are you doing here, then?"

"I came to be with Mr. Jacovich."

"He's not under arrest—not yet, anyway. Does he need police protection?"

"Nope. I'm just here for moral support." Tobe hooked her arm into mine and pressed her body against me. "He's my lover boy."

That slowed Keith Barent Johnson down considerably. Now I was certain: the interracial thing bothered the crap out of him. I didn't give a damn.

Tobe didn't, either. "Just for the record," she said, "I met Gecko personally, just like Mr. Jacovich did—only for a moment. But it's hard to forget somebody like him."

Johnson tucked his notebook back into his hip pocket. "Why hard to forget him? His charm? Wit? Brilliant intelligence?" Then his eyes squinted; he'd just thought of something nasty to say. "Or did he want to fuck you, just like your lover boy does?"

"I suggest, Deputy, that you watch your fucking mouth—gun or no gun. Summit County has laws against that kind of shit, too."

He clamped his mouth shut; he knew he'd stepped way over the line.

"It was his high fashion," Tobe said. "How many middle-aged men run around wearing pink hoodies?"

"You mean he was a fag?"

I asked, "Is *fag* politically correct here in Summit County?"

"Fag's just a shortcut word for homosexual," Johnson said. "Homosexual has five syllables. Fag only has one."

"So does *prick*," Tobe said.

Anger darkened Keith Barent Johnson's face like a black thunderhead just before a hurricane, and his chest filled up like a helium balloon about to soar off into space. Fearing a shit storm about to break, I jumped in fast. "Did you want to question me any further, Deputy? I have a business to run."

"So do I," Tobe said.

Johnson turned his wish-you-were-dead look directly on her. "Leave me your card, then, Detective Sergeant Blaine," he said, extending his hand, palm up. "Just in case I might desire your much-needed law experience to help me solve this crime."

"My pleasure." She gave him one of her newly minted business cards. He looked at it with contempt and then stuffed it into his shirt pocket.

He turned to me. "I want your business card, too," he said. Pause, as he allowed his upper lip to curl like a man-killing Doberman in a bad movie. "Lover boy."

As he pocketed it and walked away, I whispered to Tobe, "I could murder you for that."

We wound up in one of those little coffee shops a few blocks from the track. Not Starbucks—not *that* kind of coffee shop with the *venti*-sized five-buck half-regular and half-skimmed milk caramel latte with whipped cream. It was a place where they'd pour you endless cups of coffee, cook you pancakes or eggs for breakfast, and scrub down the grill only when anticipating an inspection from the county health department. Tobe ordered coffee and a muffin, and I got a strange look from the waitress when I asked for a bagel and some herbal tea. I guess I don't look like a tea-drinking type.

Why is it that, in most places like this, they'll refill your coffee at least ten times without a murmur; a tea drinker might get more hot water as often as he wants, but if he desires a fresh tea bag, he has to pay extra for it? That's one of those mysteries of life I've never been able to crack.

I did my own dunking. "Two people dying at the track within ten days sounds more than fishy to me," I said.

"I can't do a damn thing about it," Tobe told me. "Sheriff Andy Taylor there was right, as much as it grinds my guts. It's not my jurisdiction. I only showed up because I thought you might be in some difficulty."

"I won't be. Besides, Jobie Dash—one of the grooms—told the deputy he was there in the barn before I got there. So even though I'm a 'person of interest,' I doubt they'll bounce me around." I clinked my tea mug against her coffee mug. "But thanks for showing up."

"Don't mention it. I only drove twenty five miles from downtown because I wanted somebody to buy me breakfast."

"When the M.E. finally gives up the body, who will claim it?"

"Who knows? Gecko might wind up in a potter's field. Do they still have those? Potter's fields?"

"They do but they don't call them that anymore." An idea struck me—stunned me. "Damn, Tobe—Gecko has a dog. I don't know how long Gecko's been floating in that tank, but that dog must be locked up in his motel room. If somebody doesn't take him out for a walk and give him food and water, he'll die, too."

Tobe sighed. "Well, let's go walk him and feed him, then."

"How do we get into his apartment?"

Once more she took out her police badge, this time putting it on the table in front of me. "I have a magic key," she said.

The motel owner, who identified herself as Mrs. Jonas, was over sixty years old, wearing the type of housecoat my mother used to and which no one has seen since the fifties—and she might not have washed or combed her hair in at least that long. She wasn't distraught to learn Gecko was dead, but she was upset she'd have to *hire* someone to clean and repaint his room before she rented it out again. And she didn't want to let us into Gecko's dwelling.

"Who'd want to clean and paint that room when they find a starved-to-death dog lying in his own shit?" Tobe growled. That got Mrs. Jonas off her ass and moving quickly, jingling a huge key ring as she led us outside. It was a one-story motel, imaginatively named MOTEL on the dingy sign, and the room in question was almost in the middle of the horseshoe-shaped building. As we approached, we heard the dog whining, frantically scratching the bottom of the door.

"If that dog bites you," Mrs. Jonas said, "I won't be responsible."

"Does the dog bite other people?" Tobe asked. "Or just not white people?"

"Well—uh, no . . . "

She unlocked the door and the dog raced out, dancing around our feet, wagging what little tail he had. Gallagher's description had been accurate. His body was short, stout, once muscular but now running to overweight, his legs thick and bowed. His head looked more like a German shepherd's, with a tapering snout and upstanding ears. I doubt even a dog expert could figure out his ancestry and parentage.

"If he does his bidness on my proppity, it's your job to clean it up," Mrs. Jonas warned us. "Bidness" and "proppity" tattled on her rural origins, probably Kentucky or farther south.

"We'll take care of it," Tobe told her; the edge in her voice could have cleanly shaved a bearded face. Mrs. Jonas backed away, admonishing us to make sure the door was shut before we left.

Inside Tobe coughed, wrinkled her nose and waved her hand in front of her face. "He must've smoked three packs a day in here! They'll never get the cigarette stink out of this room."

"Even *I* can smell that."

"When I get home tonight I'll have to shampoo my hair three times—and burn these clothes." She looked around, finding the dog's leash hanging on a nail that had been driven into the wall next to the door. "I'll take him out. His food and water dishes are probably in the bathroom. Try finding him something to eat." She clipped the leash onto the dog's collar and ruffled his ears. "Come on, guy," she said, "it's potty time."

The room itself was half the size of most motel rooms, but if your needs are few, you could live in it. Gecko's bed looked hastily made, a thin, worn flowered spread tossed over untucked sheets. There was a microwave, a tiny refrigerator, a cabinet with half a bottle of cheap whiskey inside, and a small closet with no door— just a cheap, wrinkled drape and few clothes hanging in it. The bathroom was small as well; the shower probably hadn't been cleaned in more than a year, nor had the toilet. I found the dog's dishes next to the john, and after I rinsed them out, I took from the pantry a small can of the generic dog food and prepared his breakfast.

When I stood up straight again, a woman I didn't know was standing in the doorway. Probably in her forties, but looking a decade older, her dyed hair was Bozo-the-Clown red, and her heavy lipstick, also scarlet, was smudged around her mouth and all over the cigarette on which she puffed. Her Walmart clearance-rack pink rayon blouse and her black skirt, several inches too short for anyone older than eighteen, were wrinkled. There were tiny black burn marks on her clothes; she must smoke constantly and let the ashes fall where they may.

"Who the fuck are you?" Curiosity, but no animosity behind it.

"Do you know Gecko well?" I said.

"I'm next door." She jerked a thumb over her shoulder in the general direction of her own abode. "Whatcha doin' in his room?"

"I'm sorry to be the bearer of bad news," I said, "but Gecko—passed away this morning."

"Shit." She stepped into the room, looking more disappointed than sad.

"Are you a friend of his?"

"I s'pose you could call it that." She leaned against the door jamb, cigarette now dangling at her side, and I wondered if that was one of the cigarettes he traded to her in exchange for services rendered. "What happened to him, anyway?"

"He drowned."

Her penciled eyebrows jumped. "He went swimming?"

"He drowned in the therapy pool at the racetrack."

"Jesus. Drunk?"

"I don't know."

She crossed her arms over her breasts. "He's always drunk—maybe this time more than usual."

"Could be."

"So—I still don' know what *you're* doin' here."

I started to tell her when Tobe Blaine appeared in the door-way, Gecko's dog wrapping his leash around her legs. One more time, she flashed her badge.

"Police department," she said. Her voice and bearing have the kind of authority that gets everyone's attention. The woman didn't look too closely at the badge to realize Tobe was a Cleveland police detective and had no real rights in this suburb.

"Hey," the woman said, backing away, "I didn't do nothing. I just live next door." She looked down at the dog. "What're you doin' with Booger?"

"Is that his name? Booger? That's a lousy name for a dog." Tobe bent down and stroked the dog's ears, to his obvious delight. "We were taking a walk, weren't we, Booger?" She unclipped the leash. "And who might you be?"

"I *might* be Leanne." She seemed nervous but not really frightened; this was evidently not the first time she'd ever spoken to a police officer. "Leanne Sturgiss. I live next door. I saw this guy," and she pointed at me, "rummaging around in Gecko's stuff."

Tobe wrinkled her nose and fanned her hand in front of her face. "Where'd you get your perfume? Whipped it up in your own bathtub, did you? Whew!" She said to me, "I'll get a headache from that, sure as hell."

"I don't even *have* a bathtub!" Leanne protested. "All I got is a shower."

"I told her," I said, "Gecko was dead."

"Yeah. Bummer." Leanne's eyes flickered from Tobe's face to the bulge beneath her jacket. "Hey, I'm not doin' nothin'. You don' need to hassle me."

"Not hassling anybody," Tobe said. "But we do have a few questions."

Leanne looked sullen, but hadn't yet figured out she could just walk away. She nodded.

"How well did you know Gecko?" Tobe said.

"I live next door. So, sure, I knew him pretty good."

"He buy you that perfume?"

"I don't remember."

Tobe closed her eyes and shook her head. "Boy, *I'd* remember. So Gecko—he drank a lot?"

Leanne rolled her eyes. "Gimme a fuckin' break, excuse my langwitch, but we *all* drink, okay? Who do ya think we are in a joint like this? Brain surgeons?"

"That would've been my second guess," Tobe said. "Did he get falling-down drunk? Literally?"

"Naw, nothin' like that. I never saw him pass out or nothin'."

"Did he have enemies?" I said.

She lifted her shoulders then dropped them. "People probly got pissed off at him a lot. Wouldn't call 'em enemies."

"Anybody he was afraid of?"

"Don't know."

"He never mentioned names?"

"He said sometimes, 'Walt Holman's gonna kill me.' But lotsa people say that, right? I mean he worked for Walt Holman—but I don't think he thought Walt was really gonna kill him or anything."

"You know Walt Holman, too?" Tobe asked.

"Seen him in the restaurant across the street. We ain't friends or nothin'."

Tobe produced one of her own business cards. "Thanks for taking the time. Here's my number in case you want to tell me anything else."

Leanne Sturgiss handled Tobe's card by its edges. "I don't tell cops much."

"I'm not arresting you. I thought I was being polite."

"That's one for the books!" Leanne Sturgiss said. "A cop bein' polite to me! Holy shit!"

"Don't push your luck, Leanne."

Leanne sulked. "Who's gonna take care of Booger?"

"You are."

"Hell, no! First of all he ain't my dog! An'—an' I work outta my place. How'm I gonna have a stinky dog in that little apartment?"

"*Somebody* has to take care of him," I said.

Tobe Blaine turned her head and just looked at me.

CHAPTER FIFTEEN

K.O.

Kevin O'Bannion wasn't completely at ease in Jen Taylor's office—he wasn't an office-and-desk kind of guy, and this was his first conversation with anyone involved with Glenn who didn't work at the racetrack. Besides, he was having difficulty acknowledging she and Glenn Gallagher had been longtime lovers. The age difference was only part of what troubled him.

"I know Milan Jacovich talked to you before, so I hope you don't mind a few more questions," he said, consulting his notebook.

"Just a few more," she said. "I do have work to do this morning."

"Sure. Now, you own twenty-five percent of this firm—of Gallagher Investment Management. Is that right?"

"Yes, I own a quarter of the stock."

"You bought it yourself?"

Her cheeks colored slightly. "No. It was—a bonus."

"A gift?"

"*Not* a gift, Mr. O'Bannion."

"K.O."

"K.O., then. If you're asking if Glenn ever gave me gifts—of course he did. I gave him gifts, too. It was part of a personal relationship, not a business arrangement. The business arrangement was giving me stock in the company."

He sat up straighter. "Do you think you'll inherit anything more, then?"

"We never discussed his will. We never discussed mine, either."

"You're young to have a will."

"Young people die sometimes. Don't *you* have a will?"

"I have nothing to leave—and no one to leave it to."

Jen said, "Well, I have a mother, a sister, and a ten-year-old son. If anything happened to me, I'd want them to have what I have—and that includes the stock."

"Okay," he said. "Let's shift gears. As office manager, you were sent all the statements by your CPA—Paul Darrie, isn't it?"

"Yes—and he was Glenn's CPA, not mine."

"But he wasn't the first to see them?"

"It's my understanding that David Weaver saw them first, then passed them along to Darrie, who re-checked them and sent them to us."

"'Us,' meaning you and Glenn?"

"Right."

"But Glenn never looked at them."

Jen Taylor frowned, her lips disappearing. "I wouldn't say *never*. But he rarely saw them. He was too busy running the investments himself—and of course his horses."

"I'm not much of a businessman," K.O. said, "but I wouldn't ignore business statements and let other people take care of them."

"Maybe if you had a partner," Jen said, "you'd trust him to take care of everything."

"And Glenn Gallagher trusted you? Like checking his accountant's statements to be sure every penny is where it should be?"

"Well . . . " She chewed nervously on the inside of her cheek. "I looked them over when I had time—but I knew David Weaver always checked them first, and then Paul Darrie *re*-checked them. So I didn't give it a hell of a lot of thought."

"Pretty casual, considering you're the office manager."

She lowered her voice to an irritated whisper. "You have no goddamn idea how much work an office manager has to do."

"Right," K.O. said. "And that's why Glenn trusted you."

"Yes, he did."

"With everything?"

"Everything."

"Even with his life?"

She stood up angrily. "Bullshit. It has nothing to do with you, Mr. O'Bannion."

"K.O.," he corrected her again.

"Well then, fuck you, K.O.," Jen Taylor said.

K.O. pulled up in front of the veterinarian's office and parked near the door. It wasn't a hospital like the one to which he'd rushed Rodney shortly after he'd rescued him from a shelter, where the cat had been diagnosed with worms and then cured. New-looking and rather elegant, its classy sign identified it as The McHale Veterinary Clinic, located in Stark County, not too far from Canton. It had been a long drive for K.O., all the way from Mentor, four counties away. All he knew about Canton was that the Pro Football Hall of Fame was located there—he'd never visited, not being much of a sports fan—and something called the First Ladies Museum, in which he was uninterested; most of what he knew about national politics he didn't like. Heading south, he'd driven I-77 many times before, but noticed this time that just south of downtown Cleveland the freeway had been christened Vietnam Veterans Memorial Highway.

He was a veteran, too, and he wondered whether there would be a freeway named after *his* war in the future. But I-77 is called a "Memorial Highway" and that, he supposed, was in honor of the veterans who didn't come back from Vietnam, whereas he had returned from his three combat tours safe, if not necessarily sound.

His cell phone had rung before he left his apartment—Milan, telling him that he'd found Gecko floating dead in the therapy pool at the track.

Poor sad old guy, K.O. thought. Had he finally drunk himself silly and fallen in by accident, or had someone pushed him?

K.O. hadn't told Milan where he was going—there was too much going on at the site of Gecko's demise, although Tobe Blaine was there for support. Besides, he'd been toying with an idea for a few days, and perhaps this long drive might answer some of his questions.

Dr. Sheila "Bunny" McHale was surprised to see him, although she remembered their first meeting. She couldn't imagine why he'd walked into her office without an appointment, but she was warm and welcoming, even offering him coffee.

"Had two cups already," he said, a small lie; he'd had four cups of coffee and a cinnamon bun at Panera before he began his drive and had already stopped once at a McDonald's to use their facility on the way. "I know you're busy—but do you have a few minutes?"

She waved a hand at her cluttered desk. "Sure. You're a welcome distraction. Today's my day to do paperwork—a real pain in the butt. I love being with horses, but I hate sending out bills."

"I can believe that. Were you at the track this morning?"

"No, my husband went there, early. We usually alternate going to the track each day, so it never gets boring. Of course we take care of horses that aren't racing, too—farm horses, saddle horses, any horse that needs us."

So Bunny McHale had not yet heard about Gecko. "Any horse problems at the track lately?"

"The usual. Sore muscles, some breathing problems, an eye infection. Nothing really major."

"You must love your job."

"That's why I went to school forever, to learn how to *do* my job." She grinned. "My husband and I have finally paid off our college loans, thank God."

"How do you know when a horse *has* sore muscles? They don't tell you, do they?"

"Actually they do. You can spot a muscle pull when they jog in the morning. That's why we come after they've been exercised— the groom or trainer lets us know. Or we let *them* know."

"And then you sell them the medicine they need."

"Sure. I mean, that's how we make our money."

"So you're both a doctor and a drug store." That made Dr. Bunny flush, though K.O. couldn't tell whether it was from embarrassment or anger. "Okay. So what if the horses have heart problems?"

McHale shrugged. "It's not easy to see right off the bat, but eventually a good horse vet can."

"Meaning you."

"Meaning me—or my husband. People might have a heart condition, too, that nobody knows about. If they lack energy, if they run short of breath, if they seem exhausted all the time, that's a sign in both horses and people that something's wrong—and we examine further. A good trainer knows how to spot problems, too—and they tell us about it. The trainers know the horses better than the owners."

"A trainer's main job is to train the horses to win, right?"

"Sure."

"So sometimes your treatment is more about winning races than what's necessarily best for the horse?"

Doctor Bunny suddenly grew icy, her pleasant smile morphing into a straight line that might have been drawn with a ruler. "My job is to do what's best for the horse."

"Especially one with a heart condition?"

"With *any* condition."

"If a horse *does* have heart trouble, do you give him digitalis?"

"If the condition calls for it."

"What if you overdosed a horse with digitalis?"

"It'd take a hell of a lot to hurt a horse. They're pretty big."

K.O. persisted. "*If* they were given too much—by accident?"

"Only a dumb vet would overdose digitalis," she said. "Why? Did a horse have a heart attack?"

"Not that I know of. A horse heart attack might come from too much digitalis?"

She nodded.

"Is that the same with humans?"

"I don't treat humans."

"But a digitalis overdose would cause a heart attack in people, too? A fatal heart attack?"

That stopped the conversation. Sheila-Bunny frowned, folding her arms across her chest, the classic defensive gesture. "Did somebody die of a heart attack?"

"Glenn Gallagher did."

"But I never gave Mr. Gallagher any medicine at all." With emphasis: "I don't medicate human beings. I hardly ever saw him in the morning, just once in a while. He ran another business besides racing, which kept him pretty busy."

"Could anyone get hold of medicine from here, though? Steal some, I mean."

"I told you," she said, "our drugs are stored in a room you'd need a blowtorch to enter. And no one took a blowtorch to any door in here."

"What about your truck?"

"The truck's buttoned up tight in a locked garage when we're not using it."

"When you *are* using it? When you're at the track in the morning?"

"Well, nobody watches the truck every single second—if I'm in the barn with the horses, the truck's parked right outside . . . " McHale's voice faded to a whisper and her normally healthy flush paled. She was hardly breathing. "What are you suggesting?"

He filled his lungs with air. "Gallagher's only health problem— heart problem, actually—was a-fib. He was on a digitalis prescription for that—from his own doctor. If he'd overdosed, it might have killed him—and we'll never know now because his body was cremated. But he didn't commit suicide that way because I was with him the night he collapsed. Maybe someone dosed him with too much digitalis in order to kill him. Possible, yes?"

She closed her eyes for half a second too long. "Possible."

K.O. rolled right along. "Do you count your medicines every day, Dr. Bunny? Would you know if something was missing?"

Dr. McHale looked ready to cry. "We check once a month to figure out whether we need to add anything, because we order from the pharmaceutical companies—but we don't keep count every day."

"So somebody could've stolen medicine from your truck?"

"Nobody goes near the medicine except the two of us. We've never been stolen from before."

"Doctor Bunny—when was the last time you gave digitalis to a horse?"

"I don't know, exactly. A few weeks ago. I'd have to look it up."

"A few weeks ago. Okay, then. Which horse?"

"I think it was Cookie's Clipper."

"Does Cookie's Clipper have heart trouble?"

"Arrhythmia, yes."

"Is he all right now?"

She nodded. "They're not racing him for a while until he gets better."

"That's good to hear. Where do I find Cookie's Clipper?"

Bunny McHale massaged the back of her neck where K.O. guessed a headache had just started. "Cookie's in Barn Number Four."

Barn Number Four, K.O. thought—the barn rented to Del Fiddler.

The security guards at the gate hemmed and hawed, looked worriedly at one another, and said that no "visitors" were to be allowed backside. When K.O. wanted to know who *said* so, the older guard reluctantly told him that no one had given the order, but an employee had died and there were police all over the place.

"But the police didn't lock this place down, right?" K.O. insisted. "So I have every right to come in." He flashed his pass again. "I belong here. This paper says so."

The guards put their heads together, whispers hissing like a pair of rattlesnakes. The younger guy's hand hovered over the telephone as he wondered who to call who might ban K.O.'s entrance. Finally the harsh mumbling stopped—it wasn't as if K.O. hadn't overheard every word—and they raised the bar to allow him inside again.

He avoided going anywhere near Holman's barn where Gecko had been found. There was no point to K.O. wading into a sea of blue uniforms and flashing red-white-and-blue lights atop police cruisers to get a better look. *Why* their cruiser lights were flashing, he had no idea. There was no car traffic back there, although several horses pranced along heading to or from the race course, pulling jog carts behind them. Not even a human corpse in a therapy pool would slow down the *business* of harness racing.

When he arrived at Fiddler's barn, K.O.'s appearance scattered three cats who'd been napping in the hay near the door. There was no one in sight, but a few of the horses had poked their heads out over the stall doors and were looking at him, hoping he'd brought some carrots or apple snacks. It struck him that when he'd gone through Holman's barn for the first time, he'd talked to and petted almost all the horses, but in this barn he was a stranger to the residents, and they might not deign to nicker at him.

He called out a tentative "Hello," and Wanda Fiddler emerged from one of the stalls.

"You again," she said, hands on rounded hips.

"Me again."

"Back to give me more shit?"

"I wouldn't do that to you, Wanda. You know about Gecko? About what happened to him?"

"Yeah, I heard." She blew a puff of air between her lips. "Dirty old man, that's what he was—always wanting to fuck me."

"Some people might want to fuck me, too—but I wouldn't wish them dead."

That evinced a small gasp. "Jesus, I didn't mean *that*."

"I know," he said. "You were just kidding around."

She heaved a sigh of relief, not catching K.O.'s insult. She didn't smile, but didn't frown, either. "So whaddya want?" She brushed her hair from her forehead with the flat of her hand. "I told you before, I don't know nothing—and I haven't learned nothing since then, either."

"I figured that," K.O. said, zapping her again without her realizing it. "But these won't be tough questions for you, Wanda. We're BFFs, aren't we?"

A nervous look toward the door. "Don't let my husband hear you say that. He'll piss a fit."

"Okay—I won't let him hear me. Did he ever have a fight with Gecko?"

"I wouldn't call it a fight. I mean Gecko's old—*was* old and half smashed alla time. Del pushed him around sometimes, though. Once he shoved him so hard, Gecko fell down. But it wasn't no fight."

"Gecko was a lover, not a fighter, hmm?"

That made Wanda Fiddler laugh.

"Here's what I wonder," K.O. said. "Which horse here is Cookie's Clipper?"

Wrinkles at the corners of her eyes deepened as she frowned. "Cookie? Why? You wanna buy him?"

"I'd like to meet him first."

"Forget about it. We don't own him—I mean Del don' own him; he just trains him. The owner lives down in Florida somewhere. Besides, Cookie's pretty much all used up for anybody to race him."

"Used up?"

"Too old, too many races. Del pushed him hard, too. He's probly finished."

"What'll happen to him now?"

"Dunno. Not my horse."

"Maybe he'll make a good riding horse for some little kid," K.O. said, an unexpected pain in his gut when he realized Cookie's end might be in a Mexican slaughterhouse. "Can I have a look at him?"

"Whatever you think is right." She beckoned him to follow her. Halfway through the barn, she stopped and turned to her right. "Here's Cookie," she said.

Cookie's Clipper was about sixteen hands high, medium brown in color with big dark eyes and a shaggy black mane. Immediately he came to the stall door to check out his new visitor. K.O. petted his neck, running his hand over the horse's smooth side.

"He got a heart problem," Wanda volunteered.

"That's too bad. What kind of problem?"

She lifted her shoulders and then dropped them again. It was cooler than the last time she and K.O. had spoken together—temperatures in Northeast Ohio vary frighteningly from day to day. On this particular morning she wore a white V-necked sweater over a white T-shirt, both two sizes too small for her, and the shrug lifted her breasts. "I dunno. I don't understand those medical things."

"The veterinarian takes care of him?"

Wanda nodded. "Yeah, both Bunny and Sean McHale. They check him out every day or so—her especially. Doctor Bunny, she likes Cookie a lot."

"I like him too." K.O. put his cheek against the horse's head. "Nice fella. Is he good-tempered?"

"Pretty much. He's a-scared of most people."

"Why?"

"Del's not that nice to him. Of course Del's not nice to nobody. But he'd get frustrated when Cookie couldn't win no more."

"Did he hit him?"

Wanda pressed her lips together, deciding whether or not to answer. Finally: "Like I say, Del's not nice to nobody."

The heated branding iron began roiling in K.O.'s gut. He was pressing his face against an affectionate and loving horse that had been beaten—for no reason. There was no reason to ever hurt *any* animal, and the thought of Del Fiddler taking a whip to Cookie's Clipper was setting off that white-hot rage inside him. He sucked in the autumn air trying to calm down; otherwise he'd find Del Fiddler and beat him half to death when there were police officers just three barns away to see it.

Besides, he had other questions to ask, albeit through gritted teeth. "Wanda—when Doctor Sheila—Doctor *Bunny* or her husband were in the barn taking care of Cookie's Clipper or any of the other horses, did you notice anyone messing around outside near their truck?"

"Del?"

"Anybody."

"Huh. Well, whaddya mean, messing around?" She lowered her voice to an embarrassed whisper. "Like *doing* it?"

Wanda Fiddler could turn a hand of solitaire into something sexual. "I mean," K.O. said, "anybody hanging around their truck, touching or fooling with the medications or maybe stealing anything?"

"I dunno. I never watched. I never even thought about it; I was more interested in what the docs do inside with the horses."

"So no one watched the truck parked out there?"

"All I know is it wasn't me," she said. Her face was a mask of worry, and she gave another frightened look toward the doorway.

"There are lots of grooms and trainers back here in these barns. Did you ever notice *anybody* hanging around the veterinarian's truck?"

She brushed her hair back again and said, "I'm real busy back here, y' know."

"Maybe Gecko didn't fall in the pool by himself. Maybe he was drowned by someone else?"

Wanda pointed her chin at him. "Now, how'm I supposed to know that?"

"Just an opinion."

"Well, I dunno, then. Lotsa people didn't like Gecko 'cuz he was a scumbag. Del'd chase him out of here every time he came over."

"Lots of people didn't like Glenn Gallagher, either, did they?"

That caught her short. She put her chin in her cupped hand—awkward because she was standing up. "I guess. I thought Glenn was kinda cute for an old guy—but Del didn't like him much."

"Ever see Del hanging around the vet truck, Wanda?"

"He don't hang around nowhere. He's out jogging the horses or he's not even here at all."

"He's jogging the horses or he's beating them with a whip or a pitchfork, right?"

"Hey, don't get him all wrong," Wanda said.

"Why not?"

It was difficult for her to get her thoughts together. Finally she said, "He's—he used to be good at what he does. But he never got the breaks. Lots of the trainers and drivers, they got breaks, made big money, made—*something* of themselves. Like Pike Sullivan—one of the top guys in the whole racing business. And Glenn, too—living pretty high when you got lots of money."

"Pike Sullivan comes to this barn a lot?"

She shook her head. "No love lost here. Del don't like him." She paused for half a second and then added, "Either."

"Pike Sullivan and Glenn Gallagher were competitors, right?"

"All the drivers are competitors. It's a sport, love bug, not a corn-dog eating contest."

"So you never saw Pike hanging around the truck?"

"If he did," Wanda said, "it wasn't anywhere near this barn." She gave her head a "yes" jerk—just one—letting K.O. know the conversation here was just about over.

He thanked her and trudged out into the fresh air again, once more disrupting the three napping cats who had resumed their places. They scooted over to one side of the barn door and glared at him. He didn't blame them.

He walked in the general direction of Barn Number One. Most

police units had already pulled out; only a few cops remained, talking to each other and smoking cigarettes as if they'd just as soon stay there and do nothing else all day. The autumn wind was kicking up, its chill a nudge of warning that winter wasn't far off. K.O., thoughts racing through his head as he reviewed his interviews so far that morning, decided to stop in the "kitchen" for a cup of coffee to warm up before heading back to the Flats.

It wasn't until the horse and jog cart was right behind him that he heard and became aware of it. Turning around, he was practically looking up the horse's nostrils.

"Watch it, motherfucker!" the driver barked, neither slowing down nor guiding the jogging horse around K.O., who leaped quickly to one side before he was trampled. He almost fell over, but righted himself in time to see that the driver was Del Fiddler.

Anger burned. Bile rose. K.O. fought down the rage. After all, Del Fiddler had not actually injured him. Perhaps he was trying to, or maybe just throwing a scare, but K.O. chose to let it go.

This time.

He entered the kitchen and paid for his coffee. Jerry Nemo, who'd tried to sell him a horse, was there again—wearing the same outfit as before. In front of him were about fifteen packets of sugar. He waved K.O. over.

"Making this place your second home, kiddo?" he said.

"Sure. I like sleeping in the hay." He sipped; the coffee was too hot and he blew on it. "Heard about Gecko?"

Jerry thought for a beat too long. "You mean that fat, drunk guy—works for Walt Holman? Is he the one drownded?"

"That's him."

"How drunk could you *get* to fall into water and drownded?"

"How drunk could you get to wind up floating in a therapy pool that's only used by horses?"

Nemo shrugged. "I hardly knew the guy. I mean, *he* wouldn't buy no horse from me."

K.O. took another sip of coffee, wishing he'd left some room at the top for a big dollop of non-dairy creamer to smooth out the bitter taste.

"Did you come back today 'cuz you changed your mind about buying my horse?"

"Mr. Nemo," K.O. said, "I never owned a horse in my life. I must've ridden one sometime, but I'm damned if I remember it. I'm in no shape to lay out every cent I have for a horse—which I could only afford to keep if I let him live in my second-floor apartment. Give it up, okay?"

Nemo shook his head. "You wanna know the trouble with you? You got no spirit of adventure. Like everyone around here—they don't smile no more. Ever notice that? Nobody smiles—'cuz everybody's scared."

"Scared of what?"

"Everybody else." Nemo began stuffing the unopened sugar packets into the pocket of his jacket. "They're gonna turn this place into a casino—or a *racino*. And what happens if that makes a hell of a lot more money than the races? They'll cut out horses altogether, and hire more dealers who know how to cheat for the house, and hire more cops to make sure everybody loses their bankroll nice and quiet, and hire young snatch in Hooters-type outfits to peddle drinks. Then the horse people'll be running all over the country looking for a job at some other track. *Any* other job at any other track."

Now that he'd collected as much sugar as he could, Nemo looked around for something else he might legally steal. "That guy—Gecko—we don't know for sure, but he just mighta taken himself off the map. Sure as shootin' nobody else'd ever hire him—and he knew that."

"Sure as shootin'," K.O. said. "Was Gecko scared of everyone, too?"

"Gallagher was mostly okay to him. Everybody else treated him like he was funny in the head or something. Maybe he was—you shoulda seen some of those bimbos he was dipping his wick into—maybe 'cuz they charged him about what you might pay for a sangwich."

"He worked for Gallagher?"

"Everybody backside is free-lance," Nemo explained. "Gecko mostly worked for Gallagher and Holman. Holman rode his ass all the time. I'm glad I'm not him. He musta lived an—unhappy life."

"And died an unhappy death," K.O. said.

Nemo took off his hat and ran his fingers through his hair, his hand trembling slightly. He was aging badly, a low-rent chiseler who'd picked an unprofitable business trying to sell damaged or outdated merchandise and, like everyone else, he was scared, too. He said. "Maybe you're right, Mr.—um . . . "

"Just K.O."

"Sure, sure. Maybe Gecko didn't just fall into the therapy pool and drownded. Maybe somebody got cheesed off at him and dumped him in there."

"Cheesed off about what?"

Nemo said, "I dunno what somebody did or who he did it to. Gecko, Gallagher." He wiped his brow "I'm just talking to hear myself talk 'cuz you don't wanna buy a horse from me, which gets me nervous 'cuz my clock's running. But a guy floating in a pool in the middle of the night—that creeps me out."

"If somebody did him in, Mr. Nemo, the coroner's office will find out."

"All I know is *I* didn't do it. Must've been some other guy." He stood up, straightened his suit, waved a goodbye, and headed out the door, stopping only to grab a fistful of napkins from the holder and shove them into his pants pocket, since the sugar packets were already in his jacket. If he came to this kitchen every morning, ordered a cup of coffee, and filled his pockets with stuff he could get for free, he'd probably never have to go to a grocery store again.

K.O. also flashed on Nemo's last remark: "Must've been some other guy." That was becoming one of the most often-heard remarks in America.

He deposited his cardboard cup into the wastebasket, not helping himself to sugar, salt, ketchup, mayonnaise or napkins before he left, and walked out into the bracing October air. The local police and the Summit Count Sheriff's department had not all gone away from Gallagher's barn yet. Avoiding anyone with a badge, he circled around the kitchen building the other way and proceeded toward where he'd parked his car, anxious to get back to the office and exchange his morning's report with Milan's.

He was stopped by a voice just behind him—a raspy, snarling, angry voice.

"Hold it right there, motherfucker!"

"Hold it right there, motherfucker" sounded a lot like fabricated "cop talk" on bad television, so K.O. knew at once it wasn't a law enforcement officer. He turned slowly to see Del Fiddler, standing about five feet from him. His left fist was doubled up near his waist. In his right hand, held easily as if it always belonged there, was a harness driver's horsewhip.

CHAPTER SIXTEEN

MILAN

I sat at my desk as the afternoon sun shouldered its way through the clouds, slamming down spiced chai tea, as I do all day now instead of coffee, and thought over my morning. When I'd sent K.O. to the track, giving him that side of the case while I took the more stuffy big business area, I'd felt a bit jealous. Being backside playing with horses sounded fun, no matter what else might be going on. I guess I was wrong.

I was the one who called Tobe, even before I contacted the local police. I don't know why I did. Perhaps her proximity to me in bad times like these made me more secure. And how had that happened over the few months I'd known her? You've got me; if *you* ever figure it out, let me know.

If and when Gecko's autopsy report arrived, K.O. would have an easier job of getting to the Summit County medical examiner than I; he'd interviewed her already. I had no facts, just instincts. I'm not the smartest guy in the world, but my "gut feelings" often turn out to be right. This time, instinct told me Gecko *was* a murder victim and not an accident—and if that was true, I had no further doubt that Glenn Gallagher had been iced, as well.

By the same person? But *why?* A multi-millionaire and a minimum-wage horse groom both had been killed in the same place, within a few days of one another.

Cullen Gallagher had been right—dead right—in hiring me. Now it was my job to help find the killer or killers. I wished Tobe Blaine could help; I was impressed with how she does her job as a homicide detective. But her official jurisdiction is Cleveland, and that left the investigating up to me. I had little faith in Deputy Sheriff Johnson—but to be fair, he had no faith in me, either.

I sat there, doodling empty gallows on a sheet of lined yellow foolscap, running through all the possibilities: those I'd interviewed and the reports I had from K.O. With the possible exceptions of Carol Watterson, one of Gallagher's business competitors, and Manley Markham, who probably hasn't been sober enough in years to have killed anyone, *all* of them were "persons of interest." That included Cullen Gallagher. I didn't think he was guilty—unless he'd hired me to make himself *seem* innocent—but I wouldn't know for sure until the will was read.

As I ran everything over in my mind, a strong and exceptionally fragrant fart drifted past my face, and I was glad Tobe, with her relentless headache condition of hyperosmia, hadn't been there—even though I knew *I* hadn't done it.

I looked down as an elderly dog named Booger rolled over on my right foot and farted a second time, even worse than the first.

How did I wind up with a dead man's dog in my office and no idea what I'd do with him when the day ended? Sometimes it's just hard to say "no."

I like dogs. I never pass the chance to pat one on the head or scratch behind the ears. But I'd never owned a dog—not as a kid growing up, not when I was married and raising two boys who'd never had a pet, either, and certainly not in the decades I've been single and living in the same apartment at the top of Cedar Hill. I tried to think of people I knew who *did* have dogs but none came to mind, which got me worrying. Maybe I was drawn to dog-haters, or if not, to dog ignorers. I didn't like either option.

Is that a word? Ignorer? One who ignores? I didn't know.

But here I was, with Booger relentlessly cutting the cheese right underneath my desk. Who in their right mind would name a dog "Booger"? Although the dog had no idea his name was gross and disgusting, which made it not quite so bad.

I'd brought with me the few cans of generic dog food remaining in Gecko's pantry and found a few bowls in my own office that I use when I scarf down some cereal for a snack. I put his food and water against one wall, close enough to the bathroom so the bowls could be washed at the end of the day—and close to K.O.'s desk. I wondered what he'd say when he next walked in.

I had no idea where K.O. was or what he'd done all day. He had his own rhythms, his own methods, and while it sometimes irked me, I couldn't fault his results. He was a thinker.

Young people in their twenties aren't always "thinkers." They, like my younger son Stephen, are relentless tweeters and texters and cell phone addicts and iPad junkies, which doesn't give them much time to think about things. K.O., who never got a college degree, spent his detention years reading and learning and thinking, and probably knows more "stuff" about more subjects than people with a doctorate.

Maybe he'd walk in late that afternoon with evidence, a criminal, a motive, and a pat on the back from the local police for putting it all together and discovering someone had killed both Gecko and Glenn Gallagher without even getting his hair mussed.

And maybe the Browns, the Indians, and the Cavaliers will each win it all in their sports in the same year, too.

Booger awoke and decided to take a slow walk around the office to see if anything had changed since his first sniffing tour. He had a strange-looking walk, pretty agile considering his bandy legs that made him move like a guy who'd awakened one morning with a huge beer belly. He didn't find any interesting smells, though; I'd occupied this office for nearly two decades, and to my knowledge no animal had ever visited me—not counting some mice or rats this close to the river.

Nonetheless, Booger had installed himself at home, and when he returned to lie across my feet under the desk again, he did so with proprietary precision, firing off another loud, malodorous salute before going back to sleep. I found myself wishing for spring or summer again so I could open the windows. I had no room deodorizers handy, either—and they wouldn't have done much good anyway.

I made out a few invoices—that part of my business I dislike intensely—but my mind was still on Gecko face down in a pool. As a result, I didn't hear anyone come up the wood stairs outside my office. Everyone made noise as they ascended—unless they wore ballet slippers and happened to be extremely graceful.

So when Victor Gaimari walked through the door, his noiseless climb made it a *double* surprise.

He stopped there in the doorway, wearing a lightweight trench coat over a dark suit, gray-and-blue tie and thousand-dollar shoes—posing like an old-time leading man making his first stage entrance on Broadway and pausing for the applause. I stood up but didn't move from behind my desk.

"Milan," he said, that high voice of his matching neither his looks nor his personality. No emotion was behind it. The use of my name served as a hello.

"Victor."

"Is it all right if I come in?"

"It's all right."

He almost floated across the room to stand by one of my visitors' chairs and then waited. He didn't offer a handshake, nor did I.

"Have a seat."

"Thank you." He doffed the trench coat, laid it carefully on the other chair, and sat down, adjusting his pants legs, not speaking until I sat down, too.

"Thank you for coming, Victor. Tea—or a soft drink?"

He shook his head. "Thank you."

This was two baby-steps from being ridiculous; we seemed to be thanking each other for thanking each other.

"What brings you here?"

He cleared his throat and set his hands almost gently on his thighs. "Royal Shadcoe died this morning." Not a question but a statement.

"Yes, he did. Where did you hear about that?"

His look answered me—one of his looks that says, *"Don't you realize I have spies everywhere?"* Then his forehead crinkled and he looked around, then sniffed and curled up his nose. "Beans for lunch?"

"I'm afraid not." I reached under my desk and snapped my fingers, and Booger yawned, rolled himself out, touched my hand with his cold wet nose, and then pattered around to the other side of the desk to introduce himself to Victor Gaimari.

"All right, Milan," he said, pulling his hand away. I knew he liked dogs—but purebred ones like those he owned. He had no love for mutts like Booger. "You've finally surprised me again."

"He's not my dog. I rescued him until I can figure out what to do about him. He belonged to Gecko."

"Gecko?"

"Royal Shadcoe."

"Gecko." Victor rotated his head around on his neck, hoping for something inside to pop. "Gecko is a lizard. That's an ugly nickname for a man."

"If you think *that's* ugly, wait until you hear what he named this dog."

He waved his hand as if making smoke or fog disappear. "Let's talk about Glenn Gallagher, instead."

"All right."

"I have no information for you. He and I were business acquaintances and not much more. I went to his funeral out of courtesy. But—I do think there was something strange going on at the track."

"How would you know that?"

"I heard it from John Terranova. You remember him?"

Inadvertently I ran my hand over my ribs, which Terranova had badly bruised two decades earlier. "Vividly, Victor."

"The track is one of his hangouts; he goes there at least twice a week when he isn't on duty. He knows just about everyone there, including Glenn."

"Glenn was involved in something strange at the track?"

"As I've said—I hardly knew him."

"Maybe I should ask John. Maybe he can shed more light on it."

Victor closed his eyes for a moment. "I won't order him to talk to you."

"Is he downstairs? Did he drive you here?"

The answer took about thirty seconds before he offered it to me. "He's—in the car, yes."

"Good," I said. "I appreciate your coming here, Victor—under the circumstances." I stood up and once again snapped my fingers. Booger trotted after me and waited while I took down his leash and snapped in onto his collar.

"Jesus Christ," Victor said, "is that dog going to go *everywhere* with you?"

"I'm just going to the parking lot, Victor. I'm not having sex." I opened the door. "Coming?"

Victor rose, put his trench coat back on, and followed Booger and me down the stairs. His black Lincoln was parked half in the shade, with John Terranova, in a dark suit and black tie, waiting at the wheel. When I approached, he got out of the car and stood with one hand on the handle of the opened door. I noticed he was wearing leather gloves, too—surprising, because October is rarely cold enough for gloves in Cleveland.

"Hello, John," I said.

"Whaddya say, Milan?"

"Not much." I took a good look at him. Like Victor—like *me*—he'd aged since I'd last seen him up close. His hair, once the rich dark waves of many Italian men, had thinned out so his scalp was visible through the comb-out, and I think he used drugstore dye so his head looked as if he'd smeared black shoe polish all over it. His neck and jowls were now beefy, his complexion more yellow than tan. His teeth were yellow, too—a heavy smoker.

"John, you're a regular at the harness track, huh?"

His eyes flickered to Victor who nodded assent. Then he said, "Yeah, I go there a lot. Why?"

"You told Mr. Gaimari something funny was going on there."

Terranova got defensive, his eyes frightened. "Hey, I got nothing to do with it, okay?"

"Not saying you did, John. Maybe you could tell me a little more about what you saw."

His hand went to his pocket; I could see the pack of cigarettes making a bump in his jacket, but then he changed his mind. Victor didn't like people smoking in his vicinity; he never approved when I did it back in the day. "I know all those guys—drivers, trainers, guys who shovel up the horse shit."

"And?"

"Just a lotta talk, that's all."

"About what?"

John's gaze was everywhere except at me. "It's gotta be tough working at a track like that. Like, everybody hates everybody else."

"People hated Glenn Gallagher?"

"Hate is a strong word," Victor Gaimari added.

"Yes," I said, "like a belly ache. You can't see it, but it's still there."

Victor pursed his mouth, irritated, and took a few steps away, presumably wishing he had never come to my office, never trotted out John Terranova for me to question. Now it was too late.

"Okay, then, I'll find a better word. Why did they *dislike* Gallagher?"

"Because he was rich," Terranova said, "and when you're rich like him, you don't just go along to get along—you do what you goddamn please."

"In what way?"

He looked down at his shoes then up at Victor again. Finally he said, "I been goin' to that track since I was a teenager. I'm not as dumb as I look, Milan."

"I never thought you were dumb. And you don't *look* dumb, either."

I guess that made him feel better. "Those people that own the track—whatsername again, Chloe? Yeah, Chloe—and the guy right under her, the one who runs everything—well, they got certain ways to handle everything, and they expect the horse owners to do what they tell 'em. Gallagher was one of the ones who didn't. He wasn't as rich as them, but he was damn rich anyway, and told them and everybody else to kiss his ass. I don't think he wanted them to change the track into a casino, y' know?"

"Why not?"

"If it works, don't fix it. That's my motto, too."

"John, what about Gecko? Did you know him?"

Terranova tried not to laugh. "Everybody knew Gecko. A few aces short of a full deck—but I guess he was a nice enough guy."

"Do you think somebody drowned him? I'm not asking who—I'm asking if that's a possibility."

Victor said, "Everything's possible."

"Let's put it another way; did the big shots at the track like Gecko?"

"If they didn't," Terranova said, "it was because he couldn't keep his mouth shut."

"About what?"

"About everything—like when one of the horses pulls a muscle or comes down with the runs, or who was fucking who backside, or what he had for dinner, or whenever he got fifteen bucks together to buy head from his next-door hooker neighbor."

"You mean Leanne?"

Terranova drew himself up to his full height. "I don't know what her name is, Milan. Come on, will ya? I'm a married man!"

That slowed me down a step. I'd known Terranova for decades; I'd never had any idea that he was married. "So what you're saying, John, is that whatever went into Gecko's head came out of his mouth? Maybe he was talking about something he shouldn't have been talking about?"

"That's enough," Victor said tersely. He nodded at John Terranova who clamped his lips tighter together and got back into the car.

"I don't get it," I said.

"What?"

"Why you came here in the first place."

"Just to make sure," he said, "that if there *were* murders committed at Northcoast Downs, you won't try to blame them on Italians."

"I don't blame anything on Italians, Victor—you know that better than anyone."

He sighed. "Then let's just say I was trying to help you."

"I didn't ask for your help."

"Sure you did. You even came up to my office. If that wasn't asking for help, what was it?"

"I'm guessing, Victor—stop me if I'm wrong—I'm guessing you, or someone connected with you, is *very* involved in seeing this whole casino deal come true. Maybe that's why my interest upset you enough to actually come down here and talk to me. Yes or no?"

Victor thought about that for a long while.

"Or," I continued, "did you come all the way over here because you're not as mad at me as you used to be, and this was a tentative try at renewing a friendship?"

"Mind your business, Milan," he said.

At that moment Booger urinated on the right rear tire of Victor's car.

Victor almost leaped out of range; it was the most energetic exercise I'd ever seen him display. "God damn it anyway!" he snapped.

I tugged gently on the leash and reeled Booger in closer to me, then smiled at Victor Gaimari and gave him one of my patented shrugs. "Everyone's a critic," I said.

The long, black Lincoln Town Car drove out of my parking lot. I leaned down and scratched Booger's neck and behind his ears. "Well played," I told him.

Upstairs again, I gave Victor's visit serious thought. Apparently he'd decided several months earlier that he and I were once again enemies, a throwback to when I'd first run into him more than twenty years ago. I could live with that—especially when he'd all but thrown me out of his office when I'd tried to talk with him about Glenn Gallagher. But then he shows up to talk, bringing his driver/muscle punk John Terranova to tell *me* about Gecko.

I had to sift everything out in my head. What resonated for me is that the late lamented Royal Shadcoe probably blabbed too much about things he should have kept to himself. Did that cause his untimely death? If so, who was behind it? Chloe Markham and her second-in-command, Everett Valmer? I punched up my laptop and checked K.O.'s reports because I couldn't recall all the other people he'd met at the track. Pike Sullivan. Jobie Dash. Carl Fulwood. Del Fiddler and his lovely wife Wanda.

I chuckled. Who the hell ever *really* says "lovely wife"? Only on television.

I was almost finished with my paperwork and was addressing bills when K.O. walked in the door. Immediately Booger roused himself from his endless nap, trotted over to K.O. and presented himself to be petted. It didn't surprise me; K.O. has a way with animals—*all* animals.

"Do we have a mascot now?" he said, squatting down and looking Booger right in the eyes.

"Temporarily—until I find out what to do with him."

"Find him in a beauty contest, did you?"

He straightened up. I was startled to see a vivid welt, about four inches long, running across his left cheek. He held one arm in a strange way, too, supporting his elbow with his other hand.

"Jesus, what happened to you?" I said.

"I cut myself shaving."

With a machete, I thought. "Lie number one—but we'll let that pass for a minute. What's wrong with your arm? You're holding it funny."

"I had a slight accident."

"What kind of slight accident?"

"Somebody hit my elbow with his face—accidentally."

K.O. had kept his temper since someone had kidnapped him off the street during the late summer, with the intent of sailing out into the middle of Lake Erie and drowning him. I didn't want to hear he'd just killed somebody. And I sure as hell didn't want to hear that because K.O. was my employee, *I* might be sued for everything but the clothes on my back.

"Are you going to tell me you were attacked by aliens from outer space?"

"That's what happened, Milan—if you'll believe it."

"I don't believe it."

"Thought not."

I carefully evened out the stacks of papers on my desk. "Why don't you just tell me about it?"

He wandered to the window. "The river looks choppy. The wind's picking up some."

"Is that it, K.O.? A weather report?"

"Not quite." He made himself comfortable behind his own desk. Booger, delighted with a new friend, trotted over to him and flaked out across *his* shoes. This time the fart was actually loud.

"Well," K.O. said, "it's a long story."

CHAPTER SEVENTEEN

K.O.

Del Fiddler had just tried to trample K.O. with his horse and sulky. Now he stood there, on the far side of the kitchen building where hardly anyone would see him. A furious scowl clouded his face.

He was looking for a fight.

K.O. would just as soon not. He didn't like fighting—didn't like hurting other people. Except for the battle putting him in the clink for three years, he couldn't remember ever starting a fight—but he vividly recalled each time he'd had to finish one. He wasn't sure why the owner-trainer wanted to tangle with him, as he hadn't done anything wrong. His guess was that Fiddler was mad about something else and had decided to take it out on him.

He had a moment of awkward recognition: he, too, was angry all the time. However, he'd learned self-control—first in juvie and later in the army, where unbridled anger could have gotten him killed.

But a battle was brewing, and he hoped to talk Fiddler out of it. He squared his shoulders and quietly arranged his feet into a position from which he could move quickly. "What's your problem?"

"My problem is you, you little shit!" Del Fiddler growled. It wasn't much of a growl and K.O. tried not to smile. "Didn't I tell you to stay away from my wife?"

"Rest easy, cookie—I have no interest in your wife, okay?"

The "cookie" part enraged Fiddler even more. "Then what were you doing in my barn?"

"They found Gecko dead this morning."

"Fuck Gecko! Loudmouth goddamn drunk, he'd give anyone the key to Fort Knox and tell 'em how to get there, too—just for the price of a drink and getting his dick sucked."

"Nice."

"He don't work for me, so he's none of my business—and none a yours, either!"

"I'm asking questions. That *is* my business."

"I don't give a shit about your business."

"You didn't like Gecko?"

"*Nobody* liked him—except that whore lives next to him, and all she wanted outta him was a carton of cigarettes and a couple a bucks whenever he got horny." K.O. noticed Fiddler's hand squeezing and unsqueezing the horsewhip. "Gecko's a skeevy sonofabitch—now he's dead. So what?"

"Is there anybody around here who didn't like him enough that they pushed him into the therapy pool and held his head down?"

"How would I know?"

"I don't know how you'd know, Fiddler—that's why I'm asking questions."

"Well, I don't know whether he got drownded all on his own or somebody gave him a swimming lesson. Either way, I'm not crying."

"If you're not crying, what pissed you off enough to try running me over?"

Fiddler gave that extra thought. Then, "I told you to keep your ass out of my area."

"I remembered that," K.O. said, "when you tried to trample me down just now."

"You deserve worse than that!"

K.O. moved a few steps closer. "Is that a threat? Seriously?"

Fiddler's laugh was contemptuous, not amused. "Look at you, punk! Shaking in your boots!"

K.O.'s voice got quiet and calm so that Fiddler had to take a few steps closer just so he could hear him. "My whole life has been fighting, Fiddler. I'm not talking boxing or martial arts, and I'm not talking *rules*. And I didn't practice fighting by beating horses with whips—or pitchforks, like you do."

Fiddler's tense body jerked in anger.

"I've learned about hurting *people*," K.O. continued, "hurting them so bad that they'd never try to hurt me, or anyone else, ever again." His hands hung loosely at his sides. "I'm hoping you get my drift."

Apparently Fiddler did *not* get K.O.'s drift. His hands were surprisingly fast, and before K.O.'s instincts kicked in to move out of the way, Fiddler lashed him across the left side of his face with the horsewhip.

For half a second, K.O. was in shock. Cheek on fire, he tried blinking the pain away, but it only caused him to see red. Too many times in his life, crimson rage had bubbled up inside him like boiling water that quickly rises to the edge of the pot and pours over the side. But his uncontrolled fury was brief enough that when the second blow came he took the brunt of it on his raised forearm, covered by his shirt and jacket. That hurt, too, but not nearly as bad as the blow to the bare skin of his face.

Del Fiddler never got the chance for a third try. Before he could get his arm pulled back for another strike, one kick from K.O. sent his kneecap from the front to one side of his leg.

Fiddler screamed, teetered, about to fall, but he attempted one more whip slash. K.O., protecting his face and his eyes, turned away and jerked back violently with his crooked arm. Bone hit bone—K.O.'s elbow slamming into the point of Fiddler's chin.

The trainer went down, flat on his back, blood spewing from his mouth; his own teeth had pierced his tongue. K.O. whirled, ready to land on his chest with both knees to end the conflict once and for all and stave in Fiddler's ribs—but he stopped himself. Whatever had propelled Fiddler to start a kick-up in the first place had leached out of K.O. He bent down, picked up the horse whip, broke it over his thigh and then threw it away.

Del Fiddler's sounds were somewhere between a scream and a moan as he rolled from side to side in agony, his left leg at a peculiar angle. One glance was all K.O. needed to confirm that Fiddler's jaw was shattered and he couldn't seem to get his mouth closed.

Damn! he thought. *Now* what would he do? He couldn't just leave Fiddler lying there in the dust.

"Fiddler," he sighed, "you can't fight for shit." He bent, took Fiddler's left arm in his and pulled him slowly to his feet where he swayed and wavered. Repugnance polluting the air between them, K.O. looped Del Fiddler's arm around his own shoulders. "Lean on me. Don't try to talk anymore."

He wished he could just walk away and let Fiddler take care of Fiddler. "We'll get you—where somebody'll take care of you." Then he added, wisdom and sadness in equal numbers, "You sorry, stupid son of a bitch!"

Milan Jacovich didn't say anything for a while after K.O. finished telling his story. He stared vacantly out the window at the gray current of the Cuyahoga River passing his office building on Collision Bend, heading toward Lake Erie. He was thinking.

Finally K.O. broke into his reverie. "Am I in trouble for busting up a witness?"

"That welt across your cheek says something about you—but I'm not sure what it is. Are you in trouble with the law now?"

He shook his head. "Maybe, but I doubt it. When I finally got Fiddler back to Wanda in their barn and told her what had happened, she said she'd take him to the hospital about a mile away and tell them he got kicked by a horse."

"In the face and in the knee?"

K.O. shrugged. "Maybe the horse was in a bad mood."

"Why did he start the fight in the first place?"

"Pick a reason. I dared to talk to his wife when he wasn't around. I asked him about Gecko. Or maybe he doesn't like the color of my eyes. He's always looking to pick a fight with somebody; I just happened to be there at the right time."

"He actually hit your face with a whip?"

"It's not much of a whip. Drivers and trainers mostly use it to hit the side of the cart to get the horse's attention. It's lightweight and flexible. Only the handle is rigid."

"Fascinating," Milan said. "And you know all this because . . . ?"

"Because I took it away from him."

Milan rose, walked over to K.O.'s desk, and took his chin in his hand, moving his head around so he could see the welt more clearly in the fading afternoon light. "You should let a doctor look at that."

"It'll heal."

"It might leave a permanent scar."

"Then I'll tell everybody I got it at—what's the name of that college in Germany where they fight duels with swords all the time?"

"Heidelburg."

K.O. gave Milan a thumbs-up. "Sounds right to me. I got it at a duel in Heidelburg."

"I don't think they fight duels at Heidelburg anymore. Does it hurt?"

"Only when I laugh." K.O. fingered the welt, wincing.

"How about your elbow? You're holding your arm funny."

"He hit me in the elbow with his chin." K.O. flexed his arm. "Sore as hell but it's not busted."

"Let me call my personal doctor," Milan said. "He'll take care of you."

"He'll tell me to take two aspirin and call him in the morning. I'm not paying him to say that."

Milan chuckled. "He's told me the same thing—many times."

"Now, horse doctors, on the other hand . . . "

"Yes."

"They're on retainer to a lot of horse owners and horse trainers—but Doctor Bunny McHale, or should I say *Doctors* McHale, because they're married—make most of their money selling drugs to use on horses. I'm guessing they push meds on the trainers or owners that aren't really needed—to make a quick extra buck."

"That sounds shitty."

"It *is* shitty," K.O. said. "It's also shitty to package face tissues a hundred twenty in a box, instead of a hundred thirty like they used to, and then sell them at the same price. Same deal with cereal and candy bars. Cheating is what most manufacturers do these days."

"You sound like you've studied the subject."

"I read the paper, Milan—as you suggested. I also *shop*—otherwise I'd starve to death. The whole world is about profit."

"I still think you should see a doctor—and get that welt on your face taken care of."

"Forget it. All I need is for Carli to touch it gently with her fingertips and it won't hurt anymore."

Milan ran his hands through his thinning hair. "For someone who breaks jaws and dislocates kneecaps as all in a day's work, you're the most romantic sonofabitch I've ever met."

"See how much I'm learning from you?"

"I'm not all that romantic, K.O."

"Next time I see Tobe, I'll ask *her* if you are."

"And next time I see *you*, I better hear my doctor examined your various injuries." Milan jotted something on a piece of paper and gave it to K.O. "Dr. Ben Sorkin—I'll call and tell him you'll be there first thing in the morning. I'm paying for it, K.O. So—you got hit with a horse whip. Did you learn anything?"

"To duck quicker."

"I mean, did anybody answer your questions?"

K.O. gently touched the welt again, frowning with the pain. "I got the idea that Gecko's worst habit—and he had lots of them—was talking too much."

"Did he say something he shouldn't have to you?"

"I can't pinpoint anything specific—but somebody wanted to shut him up."

Milan leaned forward, interested. "Who?"

"Could have been anybody."

"That doesn't help, K.O."

"It helped me."

"How?"

"I'm almost sure Gecko wasn't drunk enough to fall in the therapy pool and drown."

"Why do you say that?"

"Everybody's seen him sloshed, but no one remembers him being falling-down drunk and out of control." K.O. shook his head. "If one of his neighbor skank hookers offered him a B.J. on the house and he was too drunk to do anything about it, he'd never forgive himself for the rest of his life."

"So you're saying somebody killed him?"

"And chances are good that he—or she—killed Glenn Gallagher, too."

"The same person."

"That would be my guess."

"Del Fiddler?"

"He's a fighter, Milan—and a shitty fighter at that—but he's no killer. If I could wipe up the floor with him, so could Gallagher. He did it before."

"So Gecko knew a secret, and it made somebody nervous that he might not keep his mouth shut."

"Nervous enough to dunk him in the pool until he drowned. Again, I'm guessing." Milan scratched notes on his yellow pad. "Does this mean we're both out of a job?"

"You have a job."

"I know, I meant—off this case for Cullen Gallagher."

"Private investigators—the good ones, anyway—never walk away from a case unless they're fired by their client."

Milan left the end of the sentence up in the air. K.O. said, "*Or?*"

"Or," Milan said, wondering about Cullen's interest, wondering about the Gallagher will, "unless the client is the dirty one."

"I hate it when you get hurt!" Carli Wysocki said.

K.O. sat at the dinette table in Carli's apartment in Beachwood, his head tilted back as she did something soothing to the side of his face, his elbow wrapped in an electric hot pad. "Just as long as you can heal me afterwards."

"I'm not a nurse, I'm a clerk in a cosmetics store. You should see a doctor."

"I don't know any doctors."

"You could go to Milan's doctor."

"Milan's doctor only takes care of old farts like him."

Carli's left hand held K.O.'s head while she ministered to him; now she yanked on his hair, hard. "Milan's not an old fart!"

"He's way old enough to be my father—and he's losing his hair, too."

"I think he's cute."

"Who cares how cute he is? You think I'll have a permanent scar on my face?"

"I don't think so. It didn't even bleed."

"Would you still like me if it did leave a scar?"

"It won't."

"But if it does."

"Well, sure I'll still like you. I think you're cute, too."

"Milan Jacovich and I are both *cute?*"

"In different ways," Carli said.

"You probably wish you were messing around with him instead of me."

She mulled that over. "Okay, when you put it that way—Milan *is* an old fart."

K.O. laughed, wrapped his arm around Carli's waist, pulled her down onto his lap and kissed her. "Ow," he said.

"Does it hurt to kiss?"

"I can live with it." He kissed her again. "I always like kissing pretend nurses."

She stopped messing with his face and stood up. "I wouldn't shave for a few days if I were you."

"I'll look like a homeless guy wandering the streets."

"You'll look sexy."

"-*Er?*"

"What?"

"I'll look sexi-*er* than I usually do?"

"You always look sexy, honey. I just wish you weren't getting involved in murders so often."

He sighed. "Murders aren't our business."

"I met you," Carli said, "when you were investigating a murder!"

"I was investigating a pervert."

"Yes, but that turned into a murder. And when you finished that case, the very next day you got involved with another one."

"Sometimes," K.O. said, "it works out that way. I had six weeks after the last murder just looking stuff up on the Internet or hanging around in libraries and city halls." He grinned. "You know that gigantic thing that looks like a rubber stamp that says 'FREE' on it backward—it's right next to City Hall?" She nodded. "I haven't figured out what that means or what it's doing there anyway."

She giggled. "It means 'free,' silly."

"Backward?"

"Why not? It's better than a statue of a Civil War general on a horse that pigeons poop on fifty times a day. Don't worry about it."

"Statues of generals don't worry me." He felt a frog forming in his throat and cleared it. "Were you nursey-nursey with all your old boyfriends?"

"They never fought with guys who had horse whips." She tried not to smile.

K.O. took too long before his next question. "How many serious boyfriends were there, Carli?"

"They're all gone, Kevin, and you're here."

"No, but—I mean, how many?"

She let her chin drop to her chest as she sighed. Then she said, "My father once warned me *never* to tell a guy how many men I'd been with."

"Your father knew?"

"I didn't tell him—and I'm not telling you." She touched his hand. "You're the only man in my life right now. So don't fret about it."

"I'm too busy fretting—Jesus, where did you learn *that* word?— fretting about who dumped an old, fat drunk into a horse therapy pool."

Carli shuddered. "How do you know he didn't fall in there by himself?"

"The same way I know Glenn Gallagher dying that night wasn't a run-of-the-mill heart attack."

"Fatal heart attacks are never run-of-the mill."

"See? You should have been a nurse! You know this stuff."

"That's why I worry about you."

"The guy I fought today is a bully—and jealous of hell that his old lady—sorry, *wife*—runs around all day with her boobs hanging out. So he starts fights—especially with a whip in his hand."

"Bastard!" Carli said with heat. "I'd like to kick him right in the balls for taking a whip to you."

"His balls are just about the only things I didn't bust up."

Carli got up and wandered into her tiny kitchen. "You want a beer or a Pepsi?"

"Just water."

She came back with a Deer Park and sat opposite him, her cheeks flushing.

"Kevin . . . "

"Cheers," he said, raising the bottle and then drinking from it.

"You live so far out to have to go into downtown Cleveland every day."

"I know. It's a drag."

"If this is a permanent job, have you thought about moving in a little closer?"

"Thought about it," K.O. said, "but I've been too busy to look."

She took the bottle from him and swallowed several gulps of water. Then: "How would you feel about moving in here?"

"You mean in this building?"

She rolled her eyes to the ceiling. "Oh God—*yes*, in this building. With *me*."

"Moving in together? In this apartment?"

Carli nodded.

"Gee. I never lived with anybody in my whole life."

"You lived in a barracks. You lived in a juvie dorm. That's living with people."

"Yeah—but they weren't women."

K.O. said nothing for a while, his brain racing. He'd never cohabited with a woman he loved and wasn't even sure how to do it. He had no idea how a husband or live-in lover might act.

Then again, when he'd started his job with Milan Security, he'd had no idea how a private investigator acted, either. He'd learned from Milan—perhaps he could learn from Carli as well. The idea of seeing her every night—and waking up to that beautiful face on the pillow beside him every morning—sounded to him like one hell of an idea.

Carli waited. K.O. stared down at his thighs, thinking. *Over*-thinking. The clock ticked.

Finally: "Well," he said, and the word swooped up to end on a high note indicating he wasn't finished talking.

CHAPTER EIGHTEEN

MILAN

Tobe Blaine couldn't recall ever visiting a Slovenian restaurant. Italian restaurants? Dozens of times. Mexican, Chinese, Greek restaurants? You can find them just about anywhere that calls itself a city. But you won't find a Slovenian restaurant on every corner.

That's why I took her to Sterle's.

Sterle's Slovenian Country House is big and sprawling, and at lunchtime one can see politicians, lawyers, sports celebrities and elite CEOs from nearby downtown having a ball with chicken paprikash or liver and onions, washed down with an ice-cold Union, a Slovenian beer. In the evening, though, Slovenians from all over Greater Cleveland come to rub elbows with families and friends. On the weekends a polka band takes the stage, and you'd be surprised how many people get up in mid-dinner to dance the polka without inhibitions. I'm no dancer—not at my age and size—but I'm told the Slovenian terpsichoreans don't bounce nearly as much as the Poles do when *they* polka.

On this particular evening I was enjoying one of my favorite Sterle's dishes, *klobase and zelje*. Translated, those are Slovenian words for kielbasa and local sausage. Tobe experimented with a new culinary adventure—for her, anyway—potato-and-cheese-stuffed pierogi.

"I never had a pierogi in my life before," she said.

"My mother made them every Friday. Once the Catholic church told us it was okay to eat meat on Friday, she got really creative in the kitchen."

"Did those pierogi make you tall?"

"Sure," I grinned, "but it takes more than one dinner. Besides, you're tall already."

"That's so I can go to a parade and not have to fight my way to the front of the crowd to see it."

"I'll have to take you to the St. Patrick's Day parade next March. It's the second-largest Paddy's Day parade in the country."

"I thought St. Patrick was Irish. Is he Slovenian, too?"

"In Cleveland," I said, "on March 17th, *everyone* is Irish."

"Then Kevin O'Bannion will fit in perfectly," she said. "Unless the scar he picked up today leaves him looking like that Leatherface guy in the movies got to him with a chainsaw."

"The whip didn't break the skin. When the welt heals, he'll be as pretty as ever."

"He'll kill you if he hears you call him 'pretty.'" Tobe carefully bisected a pierogi with the side of her fork. "Why was he at the track this afternoon, anyway?"

"Because Gecko drowned."

"You should both back away. You know damn well private investigators shouldn't stick their noses into murder investigations."

"I have a client—Cullen Gallagher."

"Who hired you," she said, finishing my sentence, "to find out who murdered his father."

"Not exactly correct, Tobe. He hired me to find out *if* his father was murdered."

"And if he wasn't?"

"*Then* I'll back away."

"Then what does Gecko have to do with you?"

"Maybe Gecko and Glenn Gallagher were killed by the same person."

She put down her fork, took a sip of wine, and got serious. "If they did—it's not your job to find the killer."

"Is it the job of that smartass deputy—what's his name again? Keith Johnson?"

"Keith *Barent* Johnson. How can anyone forget a middle name like that? But yes, it's Summit County's case—not yours."

"Why did *you* even show up, then?"

Tobe hesitated before answering me. "Because you told me on the phone the sheriff wanted to question you—and I thought I should arrive for moral support."

Touched, I reached across the table and squeezed her hand—the one she was *not* using to eat her pierogi. She returned only half a smile. "I have about as much clout in Summit County as I do in Katmandu. But if you butted in on a police murder investigation in Cleveland, I'd arrest you and lock your ass up."

"Ooh!" I said. "Handcuffs, too? That sounds sexy."

"I'm not joking. Investigating capital crimes or treason is illegal for a P.I."

"I didn't notice any treason in the horse barn."

"Milan, you're like a pit bull. Once you bite down on something, you won't let loose."

"Not until I finish the *klobase and zelje*. Nobody does it like Sterle's."

Tobe sighed. "What am I going to do with you?"

I took a healthy swallow of Slovenian beer. "Finish your pierogi," I said, "and I'll tell you."

"One-track mind."

"Do you always have clashes with your cop partners, too?"

"First of all," Tobe pointed out, "I've only been with the Cleveland P.D. for a few months. Secondly, I don't *have* a cop partner, and I didn't have one in Cincinnati, either. And most important, Milan, you are *not* my partner."

"What am I, then?"

"You're my lover boy," she said. "Just ask Deputy Johnson."

After dinner we drove downtown to East 9th Street, parked as close as we could to the lake, and took a stroll on the walkway for which hundreds of people had donated money to see their names inscribed on a brick that people step on.

"It's chilly tonight," Tobe said, hunching her shoulders against the lake breeze.

"Are you too cold?"

"Getting there."

"Didn't you have cold winters in Cincinnati?"

"Cincinnati," she said, "is right across the river from Kentucky—and Kentucky's a southern state. They wouldn't dare have cold winters in the south."

"This isn't winter. It's Cleveland."

"Yeah, but it's cold, anyway—almost Halloween."

"Have you picked your costume to go trick-or-treating?"

"Sure—and you're my inspiration."

"Me?"

"Well, you're a private eye—so I'm going as Sam Spade." She giggled. "Pun intended."

I put my arm around her, pulling her closer. "I like funny cops."

"I live to amuse you," she said.

We turned away from the lake and enjoyed the downtown lights winking in the night, stretching from the recently re-named First Energy Stadium to the Great Lakes Science Center to the Rock and Roll Hall of Fame to Burke Lakefront Airport. Skyscrapers like the Terminal Tower and the Key Building provided a dazzling background. "In the spring," I said, "we'll take a cruise on the *Nautica Queen* some evening—dinner, dancing, and a view even more incredible than this one, from out on Lake Erie."

Tobe looked up at me—not that *far* up because she was five-nine and her heels lifted her another two inches, but she was still a few inches below the top of my head. "You're proud of this town, aren't you, Milan?"

"It's *my* town."

"True—but it's my beat. I'm learning."

"Think you'll stay here forever?"

"Forever is a long time. But I have no plans to move to Bora Bora just yet."

"You don't like Bora Bora?"

"It's Bora Boring. Cleveland is many things—but nowhere near boring."

I kissed her quickly. "Do I get a little credit for that?"

She laughed. "You and your credit!"

"I get too much credit sometimes—they put my name in the paper so often."

"Think you'll be in the Cleveland paper if you solve two murders down in Summit County? Two murders you aren't even sure *are* murders?"

"Glenn was a one-time client—and becoming a friend. So I owe him—and Cullen—*that* much."

Tobe leaned on the railing and looked out over the water. On a starless night with clouds smothering the moon, there's nothing quite so dark as Lake Erie. "Like I said, my beat is Cleveland proper. I can't tell you what to do."

"Nobody tells me what to do, Tobe. That's why I left the army—and the police department. Good or bad, I run my own life. Completely."

"I don't like being told what to do, either." She turned to face me. "What if we butt heads?"

"We will—but not about business. So—what'd happen to Cullen if K.O. and I bail?"

"What happens to him isn't your concern."

"What if I make it my concern?"

"Then you're dancing on tippy-toes, investigating a murder illegally."

"Two murders."

"Maybe," she said. The wind kicked up—colder. She shivered, her hands in her coat pocket.

I said, "Shall we leave?"

"In a minute. Why would the same person kill a multi-millionaire and make it look like a heart attack, and then drown an overweight, smelly drunk who doesn't clear twenty grand a year?"

"If I knew," I said, "I'd tell everybody. Gallagher was cremated, but I'd sure like to see paperwork on Gecko's death."

"You don't have a chance in hell of the sheriff's department letting you see that."

"I know."

"However . . . " She left that hanging and took her police badge from her coat pocket, waving it in front of my nose. "They might let *me* see it."

"As you pointed out, that is *not* your beat. Why would they let you see the autopsy report?"

"Professional courtesy," she said.

"That'd be a great help to me, Tobe."

"*If.*"

"If what?"

Her eyes grew big and full of laughter. "If you come home with me tonight—and do every single thing I say. But of course you hate being told what to do, don't you?"

I wrapped my arms around her and pulled her close, my mouth on her mouth. "Just this one time," I said, "I'll make an exception."

CHAPTER NINETEEN

K.O.

Dr. Ben Sorkin was the same age as Milan Jacovich, although several inches shorter, and his silver hair was curly and plentiful. A general practitioner, his office was on Chagrin Boulevard in Beachwood, his nurse was his wife Dorothy, and his receptionist was his daughter. Just like a nearly vanished mom-and-pop grocery store, this was a mom-and-pop doctor's office. He and Milan had been friends for upward of four decades, and for the most part he'd overseen Milan's medical care. Like most of Milan's Kent State University pals, he'd longed to play football, but was too short and not very athletic. He'd lived through Milan's gridiron career just by watching.

Milan had insisted Kevin O'Bannion see Dr. Sorkin after his dust-up with Del Fiddler the day before, and K.O. figured he had to show up. Now he nervously fidgeted as Sorkin finished spreading some sort of oily salve over the welt on his cheek.

"That stinks," K.O. complained, screwing up his nose. "What is it anyway?"

Sorkin showed him the tube of ointment. "It'll make that welt heal faster—or at least feel better. Don't tell me it doesn't hurt. Try not to wipe it off the minute you walk out the door—but I'm sure you'll do it anyway. And don't shave for about four days to avoid aggravating the wound."

Sitting on the edge of Dr. Sorkin's examining table, the reluctant patient shook his head. "I'll look like a homeless bum."

"Homeless people aren't bums," Sorkin corrected him, "and

lots of them don't look that bad at all. Brad Pitt looks scruffy sometimes, too—and Angelina Jolie doesn't seem to mind." He screwed the top back on the tube and handed it to K.O. "Use this no more than four times a day—just a dot of it on the end of your finger." He stood up. "Take off your jacket and shirt."

"Why?"

"So I can look at your elbow."

"There's nothing wrong with my elbow."

"When you go to medical school for twelve years, then you can tell me there's nothing wrong with your elbow. In the meantime, I get to tell *you*. Off."

"Shit," K.O. muttered, removing his jacket and unbuttoning his shirt.

"Well-muscled. You must exercise."

"Not as much as I used to. I was in the army for a while—and in the middle of Afghanistan there isn't much more to do besides exercising—and playing Angry Birds."

"What are Angry Birds?"

"Are you kidding me, Doc?" K.O. waved a dismissive hand. "Ah, never mind. Milan probably wouldn't know what Angry Birds is either."

Ben Sorkin said, "Milan and I lived right across the hall from each other in our dorm at Kent for three years—which is what got you in here this morning instead of to an ER downtown that'd make you wait for half the day. Where did you go to college, anyway?"

"Knox," K.O. mumbled. "Hard Knox."

"I wasn't prying. I don't really care where or *if* you went to college. Just making conversation—that I hoped was pleasant."

"Sorry. I'm not used to doctors being pleasant."

"Most of us doctors," Sorkin said, "are pussycats." He observed K.O.'s elbow, fingering it as K.O. winced. "That's one hell of a bruise, isn't it?"

"I don't know—I can't see my own elbow."

"Trust me." He messed around with it some more. "Swollen, too. Does it hurt when you bend your arm like this?"

"A little."

"Well, don't do that." K.O. looked blank. "Old joke, sorry. Your elbow isn't broken; if it were, it'd hurt worse than 'a little.'" Sorkin opened a drawer and took out a stethoscope.

"What're you doing with that?"

"What do you think I'm doing with it? Listening to a ball game through this thing? I want to hear your heart."

"My heart is fine."

"Good. Let's make sure." Sorkin put the stethoscope against his back. "Deep breath."

"That thing is cold."

"I'll call in one of my slave girls to warm it up for you." He moved the stethoscope. "Inhale and exhale." K.O. breathed. "Good. Now again."

"I got hit in the face, Doc, and banged up my elbow. Why do you have to listen to my heart?"

"No extra charge. It's like the mechanic checking your air filter while he's changing your oil. Just enjoy it." He moved the stethoscope to K.O.'s chest. "Breathe normally. Don't talk—that's hard for you but force yourself."

K.O. didn't speak until Ben Sorkin moved away. Then he said, "Finished with my heart?"

"Let's just say you don't need a cardiologist right now. Put your shirt back on."

"Do you think I'll live?"

"I don't know. What time is it now?"

That got a smile from K.O. as he re-buttoned his shirt. It wasn't a big smile; in recent times nobody had seen him smile big except Carli. But it *was* a smile. "So I don't need heart medicine?"

"You're healthy as a horse."

He stopped buttoning. "A horse, huh?" K.O. ran his fingers through his hair. "Speaking of horses—I'm at the harness track a lot these days. I think somebody got killed there—by someone else."

"Wow."

"So—like if I was taking heart medicine—"

"Were," Ben Sorkin corrected him. "Not *was*. *Were*. I can't cure you because there's nothing wrong with you—so all I can do is correct your grammar."

"Okay, *were*. If somebody *were* taking heart medicine—and they took a real big overdose—could it kill them?"

Sorkin became more interested. "If anyone took too big a dose of *aspirin*, it might kill them. Same with any medicine. Meds work differently on different people."

"Like digitalis?"

"No one in their right mind would overdose themselves on digitalis."

"What if they overdosed without knowing it?"

"How would they do that?"

"Maybe mixed with alcohol by someone else? Mixed with a strong-tasting drink?"

"Who got to this person's booze?"

"*That*," K.O. said, putting on his jacket, "is what we're trying to find out."

Before heading back to his office, K.O. stopped into the Prosperity Social Club in Tremont for lunch. Since working for Milan for the past several months, he was learning more about local restaurants on the near west side and in the Flats, and the Prosperity Club was one of his favorites—*not* a "club" one must belong to, but a homey, neighborhood-scale joint featuring great ice-cold beers and an interesting menu—and owner-manager Bonnie Flinner was always good for a chuckle. Before she'd bought the place, she'd tended bar at Milan's Cleveland Heights hangout, Nighttown, and Milan had introduced K.O. to her new establishment.

Today K.O. ordered a vegetable curry, of all things—yellow curry, green beans, yams, multi-colored bell peppers, and coconut basmati rice. He'd always been a strictly meat-and-potatoes guy—there hadn't been much else to eat in Afghanistan—but Carli was more of a vegetable eater, and he was finding himself drifting over to her side of the culinary experience. He had two beers with lunch, too—something he didn't do often—but after his experience with Dr. Ben Sorkin, he figured he'd earned it.

Even more than his lunch, K.O. enjoyed the other customers. One couple in particular, both in their very green twenties, caught his eye—but then *anyone* might have stared at them, too. The woman was tall, almost gawky, dressed all in black—jacket, sweater, grayish-black scarf wrapped around her neck several times, black gloves with the fingers cut out, supposedly so she could eat, and what might best be described as a knit fishing hat. Her companion, his fierce black Vandyke and mustache making him resemble a villain in an old costume movie, sported flowered pants—big, boisterous red flowers on a black background—red shoes, and a heavyweight hoodie jacket, the hood up around his ears and revealing only his face. Both of them must have been very warm, as the autumn temperature outside was somewhere around sixty degrees. On his head was a floppy pink hat—*pink!*— also with flowers.

So much, K.O. thought, for Cleveland's reputation as a stodgy Rust Belt city.

When he got to the lot in front of the building Milan Jacovich owned on the west bank, K.O. noticed an unfamiliar car parked near the door. He knew Milan's car, naturally, and had grown used to the vehicles driven by the guys working in the iron shop on the first floor. The sleek Mercedes Benz—shiny black and freshly washed, stood out in the Collision Bend parking lot as "different."

When he got upstairs, he recognized the car's owner. "Hello, Professor Gallagher," he said.

Cullen Gallagher sat opposite Milan's desk, his look wavering between rage and total panic. He could only nod and grunt at K.O.'s greeting. Milan said, "Everything all right at the doctor's, K.O.?"

"Fine." K.O. hung his jacket on a hanger near the door. "What's happening?"

"Cullen heard the reading of his father's will this morning."

K.O. sat down in the other visitor's chair. "And?"

"I've been fucked," Cullen Gallagher said, and he waved a stack of papers at K.O.

"It's a copy of the will," Milan said. "Bottom line: Cullen's father left him the sum of two hundred thousand dollars."

"Impressive," K.O. said.

Cullen's face turned aubergine with anger. "My father was worth at least twenty million dollars. Two hundred K to him is like you buying a six-pack of Bud Lite!"

Milan consulted his own copy of Glenn Gallagher's will that Cullen had run off for him. "All his horses, including the ones he co-owned with Walt Holman, along with all the sulkies and bridles and other equipment used at the track and all the horses and equipment he owned at other tracks, are now Holman's exclusive property—along with fifty grand per year for the next five years so he can feed and care for the horses."

"I'm no math genius, Professor," K.O. said, "but the horses got more money than you."

"I don't give a shit about horses!" Cullen exploded. "What about Glenn's financial business—where he made all his *big* money? What about—what's her name again, his long-time girlfriend? Jen Taylor."

Milan said, "Gallagher Investment Management. Glenn gave her twenty-five per cent of that business several years ago—a minority partner. According to the will, that percentage still belongs to her, but she doesn't get anything else."

"Any large bequests to charities?"

"His biggest one was to a sanctuary for farm animals—Happy Trails, it's called. It takes in rescued and abused horses and pigs and goats and sheep."

"How much money did he leave them?" K.O. asked.

Milan held a hand up. "You don't even want to know."

"I'm glad to hear *that*. When we worked for him this summer, I wasn't sure he gave a damn about the treatment of horses. This part of his will makes me feel better about him." He looked over at Cullen. "Sorry—I'm sure you wanted that money, too. Did he leave you his house?"

"Hell, no. He specified it to be *sold!*" Cullen Gallagher almost spit it out. "He didn't own the house, anyway—his *company* owns it. Whatever the price is, that money goes into his power of attorney account!"

"Stocks?" K.O. asked. "Bonds? Investments? Ownerships of other businesses or real estate?"

"All that," Milan said, "along with whatever liquid cash he might have left, is completely under the control of Glenn's designated power of attorney—according to his will. And that will was concocted by the very same lawyer who's been given all the power. Can you guess who that might be?"

"If this is a game," K.O. said, "I think I win. David Weaver."

Milan pointed his finger at K.O. and pantomimed pulling the trigger.

Cullen actually shook his fist. "That means whenever I want to buy a movie ticket or a cheeseburger, I have to go *beg* that sonofabitch for the money." He moved from rage to sorrow within milliseconds. "How did this happen? What did I ever do to my father that made him screw me like this?"

"I don't know," K.O. said quietly. "I don't know what your relationship with your father was. Right now, though, I'm more interested in what Weaver will *do* with all of your father's money."

"Invest it if he wants to," Milan said. "Buy a new house with it."

"Or buy my father's house," Cullen sputtered, "for ten cents on the dollar. Weaver always loved that house—because he couldn't afford to buy a fancy one like that with his own money. Damn him!"

"Weaver can retire from his law practice, relax for the rest of his life, even take a round-the-world trip for the next two years," Milan said. "The money is his to spend as he sees fit."

"On himself?"

"He'll figure out a way for it to look like it was something Glenn wanted, Cullen. I imagine he's a good enough attorney to do that."

"It's my father's *will*. Can't you stop Weaver from pissing everything away that should've been *my* birthright?"

"Birthright?" Milan said softly. "That's very biblical."

"Like Jacob and Esau," K.O. said. "I read the Bible a lot when I was in the desert. There wasn't much else to do." Then to Cullen: "Can't you do anything about Weaver?"

"If I could, I would. I could sue him," Cullen said. "But by the time it came to court—three or four years from now—most of the money would be gone, anyway."

"Or," Milan offered, "*he'll* be gone. If *I* had control of twenty million bucks that didn't belong to me, I'd put it in a secret no-tax account in the Cayman Islands—it's been done before—and follow it down there myself. David Weaver could live like a king for the rest of his life, and nobody could do a damn thing about it."

"How could this happen, Milan?" Cullen whined. "How could my father let some lawyer completely control everything he owned—everything he worked for?"

"Gallagher always had control of his own money," Milan said.

"Maybe," K.O. wondered aloud, "that's why he's dead."

"What could David Weaver have to do with two killings at the track—if they really *are* killings?" Milan said.

"You can only get back there with a membership," K.O. said. "Or a visitor's pass like ours."

"Let's check who was issued a visitor's pass for the track—and for backside. And find out who authorized those passes."

"You can't do that, Milan," Cullen said. "The security guards don't have that list. They only have it in the front office."

"Everett Valmer?"

"Possibly. Or Chloe Markham herself."

"And why," K.O. asked, "wouldn't she give us that list?"

"Two reasons," Milan said. "The last thing Northcoast would want is for people to suspect something fishy was going on at the track and stop coming—and Chloe and Valmer know turning over that list to P.I.s like us just might wind up on the six o'clock news."

"What's the second reason, Milan?"

"I can answer that," Cullen volunteered. "Valmer and Chloe can go anywhere they want at Northcoast Downs. They own the fucking place. So if those two deaths are murder ... "

"That," Milan concluded, "makes them suspects."

CHAPTER TWENTY

MILAN

Manley Markham's condo was right downtown, a three-level home carved out of an old warehouse—after all, the Cleveland neighborhood *is* known as the Warehouse District. Markham lived in solitary splendor there with a sprawling and rarely used kitchen, dining room, and office on the lower floor, a living room—back in the 1980s they used to call it a "great room"—with a terrace that wrapped itself around the entire building on the second level, and bedrooms on the top floor. Every window boasted views of either Lake Erie and the waterfront venues of the Rock and Roll Hall of Fame, the Great Lakes Science Center, and the First Energy Stadium, or the twisting, bridge-dotted Cuyahoga River and across to the background of the west side with its many religious landmarks—minarets or domes or sky-reaching spires. Strolling around the room, I could actually see Collision Bend.

It was no trouble finding out where Manley lived; hey, I'm a private investigator, I know how to do those things.

What I didn't know was the price Manley had paid for this apartment. My estimate was upward of two million bucks—and probably half a million more for the furniture and weird abstract art on the walls. He'd not been bequeathed a piece of Northcoast Downs, but while his late uncle had made sure he'd have nothing to do with running the racetrack, he'd set things up so Manley Markham would never have to apply for food stamps.

It was mid-afternoon when I arrived, unannounced. Markham

was in wrinkled and faded designer jeans that I guessed cost him more than three hundred dollars, a white silk shirt on its second or third wearing between dry cleanings, and a pair of fuzzy slippers with no socks. His eyes were patriotic—red, white and blue—and were sunken into his cheeks like those of a movie zombie. He was shaky, disconnected, and hung over—a daily condition, as far as I could tell. Still unshaven and unshowered—his scent was like something that had died several days earlier—and obviously ignoring his comb, he was uncertain as to who I was or whether he'd ever met me before. He was already into his second or third drink of the day, but from what I knew of him and had seen on our first meeting, three drinks by mid-afternoon was a slow start.

The living room color took me aback at first. The walls framing the floor-to-ceiling windows were all painted a bright, vivid red—the vibrant, attention-getting shade now usually seen only in lipstick worn by Scarlett Johansson. I wondered whether the shocking red on the walls helped keep Manley Markham sober longer.

It took me more than five minutes to convince him that we'd talked a few days before at the Pier W bar. Finally he nodded; I feared I'd have to go through that conversation again, explaining to him who I was and that I'd worked for Glenn Gallagher, but I seemed to reach him when I asked how often he showed up at the track.

"Hmm, let's see," he said, scratching his bewhiskered chin thoughtfully as he paced the room. Apparently, unless he was sitting on a bar stool and too hammered to get up, Manley Markham never liked to stay in one spot very long. "How often? Probably about *never.*"

"You must have a permanent pass to get in because your family owns Northcoast Downs?"

His face darkened and his eyes became almost catlike before a pounce. "My *sister* owns it—and she's no family to me. We don't even talk to each other. Cunt!" Apparently that was a favorite word.

"So you never go to the track? Never hang around back with the horses?"

"I don't gamble. I don't *like* gamblers—they're tacky." He slowed down to gaze out the window at the West Side, rubbing his hand across his face as though trying to remember in what city he lived. "I don't like horses, either; they smell bad."

"Some people smell worse than horses," I said.

"That's a matter of opinion. Besides, I got other plans; I'm gonna make a shit-pot full of money. I don't need stinky horses— or racetracks or my darling sister, either."

"Going into business for yourself?"

He gave me a smirking third-grade-boy look. "Wouldn't *you* like to know?"

There are few things more irritating than a grown man in his thirties asking, *Wouldn't you like to know?* I tried not to let my annoyance show. "What kind of business, Manley? Horses?"

"Fuck horses. I tried to make a deal with Glenn Gallagher a few months ago—a deal for his horses. You know what he did? He laughed in my face! So fuck horses and fuck him." He leaned his head toward me, almost touching my forehead with his and lowering his voice to a half-whisper. "Listen, I know this guy. Big shot in the money business, y'know? He ran one of the biggest firms in town until he got squeezed out. He's ready to get going again, and I've been thinking about investing in him." He sniffed at his own superiority—he *actually* sniffed. "As long as he makes me a partner."

"You're buying into a partnership?"

He moved away, his whiskey breath leaving with him. "It happens all the time."

"Who is this big shot guy?"

Manley wagged his head from side to side, looking more like a horse than he realized. "Nobody you'd know."

"You'd be surprised how many people I know."

"Well, this particular big shot guy was a good buddy of *your* pal Glenn Gallagher."

"I know lots of Gallagher's pals."

He put his fists on his hips, feet apart. I think he'd watched Yul Brynner as the King of Siam too many times. "Merriford Wane," he announced.

"You know Merriford Wane?"

Manley held up his second and third fingers, crossed. "We're just like that."

Merriford and Manley? What a twosome! Burlesque comedy team? Divorce law firm? I tried not to think about it. "If Wane was such a good pal of Glenn Gallagher's," I said, "why didn't he hook up with him instead of you?"

"Ask *him*," Manley said, and looked at his watch—a Rolex. "Hey! The sun's over the yardarm. I like you, Whatever-the-hell-your-name-is—so have a drink."

I shook my head. "Too early for me."

"You're just a wuss!" he said. "Don't be like that." He made his way to a liquor cabinet and pulled out a bottle of high-end, single malt scotch. "Okay, then—that leaves more for me." Putting action to the word, he filled a water glass nearly to the top. *"Sláinte,"* he chanted, a Scottish Gaelic toast for good health, and guzzled about a third of it. He put the glass down on a table and gasped. "I gotta get dressed now. Gotta go somewhere."

"Like to Pier W?"

He simpered and batted his eyes at me—again his little-boy-cute look. "That's for me to know and you to find out," he said.

I didn't give a damn where he went. I headed back to my office, little more than a five-minute drive, and spent another half-hour using my software, much of which I'd purchased to help me in my business investigations, looking up where I might find Merriford Wane.

He had a big house in Bay Village—a suburb famous because it's perched right on the lake with a great view of Cleveland's downtown, and locally famous because radio personality John Lanigan lives there and mentions it almost every day. After a time I discovered Wane had recently rented an office in a building downtown, probably three blocks from where Manley Markham lived and almost literally in the shadow of the football stadium. It's a great place if you're a football nut, but not so good if you were trying to start a business catering to the very rich who had money with which to gamble.

The sky was gray and threatening by the time I arrived, and I was startled by the building. Merriford Wane had worked as a high-end financial consultant and investor at Aventura for years;

this location for his new office bespoke low rent. The building—it didn't have a name, and rightly so—looked as if it had been on West Ninth Street since Moses Cleaveland founded the city back in 1796.

An aside: They named the city after General Cleaveland, who left and went back to Connecticut almost immediately, never to return. Some thirty-five years later, the publisher of the newspaper, the *Cleaveland Advertiser*, discovered the name was too long for its masthead and dropped the first *a*. I guess no one complained, especially not Moses Cleaveland, so they put up a statue of him in Public Square to compensate for misspelling his name.

The cage elevator, which I shared with a young woman wearing leggings, a tie-dyed sweatshirt and kohl eye shadow—nobody had told her the hippie generation has been over with for forty years—huffed and puffed its way up to the sixth floor. I got off and she proceeded to rise upward. The door to the office I searched for sported an opaque half-window, light shining behind it. Nothing had been painted on it to indicate what kind of office it was, but an index card on which was carefully written M. WANE with a Sharpie permanent marker had been Scotch-taped to the door jamb.

M. Wane—I guess if Merriford were my first name, I'd hide behind an initial, too—wore a bright orange sweater over a black shirt and black slacks, possibly in seasonal anticipation of going trick-or-treating. There wasn't much furniture in the office—a desk and executive chair that had both seen a lot of use and three visitor chairs probably purchased on a sale day at Kmart.

Wane was a short man, not much over five feet, five inches, and well-tanned, considering it was a chilly fall. His dyed brown hair was combed straight back and spray-tamed. When I entered he was pacing, talking on his cell phone, but as soon as he saw me, he said, "I have to call you back," and clicked off. He advanced on me, hand outstretched. "Hey, there. I'm Merriford Wane." He waved airily at the office. "We just moved in here a few weeks ago so we haven't gotten it fixed up just yet. But we're working on that. So—what can I do you for?"

I introduced myself and gave him my business card.

"A security firm?" he said. "We'll be hedge fund managers once we get rolling—so there won't be much in this office for anyone to steal."

"I'm not looking to sell you anything."

"Good," he said. "Then maybe I can sell *you* something. Looking for a good, juicy investment?"

"I just spoke to Manley Markham," I said. "He told me about you."

"Manley? He mentioned *me?*"

"He said the two of you were going to be partners."

Wane attempted to make his face look blank and emotionless. Nice try, I thought. "We're—discussing that."

"I see. He's going to buy his way to a partnership?"

"Like I say, we're in talks. Every business needs an injection of start-up money."

"Naturally," I said, and Wane didn't miss my glance around this temporary-looking office in an old, tired building.

"Are *you* thinking about becoming an investor, too?"

"Anybody investing his own money in this enterprise is an idiot."

He took offense. "Under the circumstances, that's pretty insulting, Mr. Jacovich."

"I know, Mr. Wane, that you became rich when you ran Aventura— rich enough to buy a lakefront mansion in Bay. So you aren't investing your own money, but you're—*discussing* Manley Markham's buying his way in. I don't think what I said was insulting at all."

He came close to me—*too* close, as I dislike having my own personal space invaded. But he had to throw his head way back to look up into my eyes. "Are you working for Manley Markham? Did he send you over here to jerk me around because I've suggested a great investment for him? I won't be jerked around! He can kiss my ass if he's having *me* investigated!"

"Your precious ass is safe. Markham isn't poking into your private affairs. But I *am* working on a situation—for the estate of Glenn Gallagher."

That made Wane gulp, blink, and back away from me. "Yeah— Glenn. I'm sorry he's gone; he died too soon."

"You and he were friends."

"Oh, sure."

"I'm wondering, then, why you didn't approach *him* to invest?"

"Not likely. We were friendly competitors."

"*'Were'* is the operative word, Mr. Wane. You were let go at the company you ran—Aventura—some time ago. I think the expression these days is 'terminated.' So you weren't competing with Glenn Gallagher anymore."

Angry: "Where'd you hear *that?* That's all bull puckey! I wasn't terminated, for Christ's sake; we negotiated a settlement."

"That must have left you even more comfortable," I said, "to start your own personal business."

"With my own money? Are you out of your fucking mind?" I've heard flip-flops like this before, especially from politicians—but never within two minutes.

"In that case," I said, "it would've made sense to approach Glenn Gallagher, wouldn't it?"

"Well, it made sense on paper. Again, we had talks. But I'll be honest with you here—I didn't trust him any farther than I could throw him."

"That's harsh."

"Maybe. But how many people get rich without a little assistance from other people's dough? That's the way life works."

"He made money at harness racing, too."

"I don't know the first thing about racing," Wane said. "Never even been to the track—certainly not with him! But I'm sure he wasn't on the up-and-up there, either."

"Interesting." I nodded my head at him. "But when you were CEO of a hedge fund company like Aventura, you must have earned a big salary and huge bonuses. Does that make *you* a crook, too?"

Wane drew himself up to his full height; people ten inches shorter than I am probably shouldn't do that. "I never said *crook,* damn it! Don't put words in my mouth."

"What's the difference? Glenn Gallagher is dead now, anyway."

He took some time thinking about a devastating response, but couldn't create one on the spur of the moment. "You must have me mixed up," Merriford Wane said finally, "with someone who gives a shit."

*   *   *

Carol Watterson looked frazzled—but it *was* the end of a long day. For a CEO like her, *no* days are easy. Ready to go home, my visit discombobulated her. At least I caused her to roll her eyes.

Her fists-on-hips greeting was almost a frontal attack. "You again? I thought we finished our business. Did you think up any other bad names to call me, or are you a masochist yourself?"

I considered it. "The answers are Yes, Sort of, No, and No."

She shut her eyes for several seconds. "I was kind of hoping to get home before the eleven o'clock news."

"It's still light outside—nowhere near eleven o'clock."

"That depends on how fast you ask questions and how fast I can answer them."

"No chit-chat, then. Talk about Merriford Wane."

"Merry Merry? How did he get into all this, anyway?"

"You call him 'Merry Merry'?"

"That's what everybody calls him," she said, wearily sitting behind her desk, "but not to his face. He's hardly merry, though; he's about as funny as a root canal."

"I know," I said. "We've met."

"Why didn't you ask *him* all about himself?"

"Anybody's autobiography is a positive spin. This is your store now, Ms. Watterson. You fill me in on what got him canned here."

She shook her head. "I'm not telling tales out of school."

"School's out. You have a board of directors here. When Wane was CEO, did he see to it that some of them were appointed?"

"He couldn't force it—that's not how businesses are run. But he sure leaned on some of those names pretty heavily."

"But those same board members he appointed to Aventura eventually voted him out?" Watterson hesitated, then nodded. "May I ask why?"

She'd been leaning back in her high-backed executive chair that looked as if it had been designed for the Empress of All the Russias. Now she hunched forward over the desktop. "I'll make it as simple as I can. He was collecting our clients' profits for them and distributing them—this way." She pantomimed, "One for you, one for me, one for you, three for me. Get the idea?"

"Was it that easy to do?" I asked.

"It was and still is—but not for me and not for most honest hedge fund directors. For Merry?" She made a funny face. "I don't even *know* how much he stole. I'd have locked him away in some dungeon to starve to death on bread and water, but the Aventura board of directors was afraid of publicity that might close the doors here. They just wanted it all to go away quietly, so they booted his ass to the curb, paid off the clients he'd screwed, kicked *me* upstairs into this job, and we're all trying to forget it."

I scratched my head; everybody loves money, everybody hates bad publicity, everybody hates everybody else. It's a boring life. "He's ginning up to start his own firm," I said.

Carol Watterson shrugged. "It's a free country."

I laughed. "I thought that expression went out along with John Quincy Adams."

"It probably did. Then again, it *is* just an expression."

"He's angling for a financial boost," I said, "from Manley Markham."

"The guy who owns Northcoast Downs?"

"Not exactly. When their uncle died and left Chloe Markham the track, Manley was cut out of the loop, and he's pretty ticked off about it. But he's got *beaucoup* bucks, anyway—and apparently Merry Wane is trying to get his hands on it."

"That sounds logical. Merry Wane would steal the pennies off his dead grandmother's eyes."

"Was Wane connected with Glenn Gallagher?"

"They knew each other," Carol Watterson said. "Rivals—the same way I knew Glenn. We weren't friends, and I doubt Merry and Glenn were friends, either. I suppose they ran into each other at meetings or benefits. I could just about guarantee that Merry tried to hit him up for an investment because he does it with everybody."

"Are you familiar," I asked, "with an attorney named David Weaver?"

"Weaver? Merry Wane's lawyer?"

"Wow," I said.

"Why the 'wow'?"

"Weaver was Glenn Gallagher's lawyer, too."

"No big surprise." Watterson said. "That's the type of client Weaver goes after."

"Big money clients."

She nodded. "The best kind."

"So we can draw a line from Weaver to Merry Wane to Gallagher to Weaver."

"They knew each other, they were all out to make a buck. But were they actually connected? I don't know."

"I don't either," I said, buttoning my car coat and preparing to leave. "But then again—six degrees of separation . . . "

CHAPTER TWENTY-ONE

K.O.

Y ou ought to take the day off," K.O. told Carli, "and come with me to the track so you can get to know the horses—up close and personal."

Carli Wysocki, wrapped up in a pretty printed robe and fuzzy slippers, took another sip of her hot coffee, both hands wrapped around the red mug to ward off the October morning chill in her Beachwood apartment, and watched Kevin O'Bannion donning the clothes he'd brought with him the night before so he wouldn't have to drive all the way back to Mentor for a fresh outfit. She smiled behind her mug; if he moved in with her—as she had suggested—he wouldn't have to worry about lugging two or three sets of clothes around all the time. And neither of them would need two different toothbrushes, one for her apartment and one for his.

She pushed her hair back from her forehead. "Going with you to play with the horses would be fun—but what if I showed up at the store later this morning, smelling like a horse, to sell perfume to rich Beachwood women?"

"Horses smell good," K.O. said as he buttoned his shirt. Then he moved toward her, arms circling for an embrace. "But *you* always smell good—no matter what."

She put her palm against his chest to keep him away. "Don't start, Kevin! Then we'll have to take showers again and we'll both be late for work."

He mock-pouted. "You're strict!"

"And you're raunchy."

His look grew serious. "Not all the time, Carli. Sometimes I just like—*looking* at you. When I wake up and there you are on the pillow, or you're reading, or watching a movie. I like touching you—just holding your hand." He smiled sadly. "Or just coming up behind you and kissing the back of your neck while you're cutting up a green pepper."

"Kevin," she said, her own voice quivering a little, "you're so damn romantic!"

"Just telling the truth," he said.

She ran her teeth over her lower lip. "I know."

It grew quiet. K.O. finished dressing, walked into Carli's bathroom, and combed his hair. When he came out, Carli said, "How's your face?"

He laughed. "I was born with it, so I can't do a damn thing about it."

"No, silly, your—what is it? It's not a scar."

"Not yet—I hope. But it's not hurting much anymore. And my elbow's okay, too."

"What about the other guy?"

"The guy I beat up?" K.O. said. "Del Fiddler?"

"Is that his name? How's *he* doing?"

"I don't think he'll be racing for a while—unless he figures out how to drive a sulky with one leg in a hip-to-toe cast—or whistling through teeth that aren't there anymore."

"You beat up everybody that badly?"

"If he'd just thrown a punch at me I would've punched him back. Coming at me with a horsewhip is a different story."

"Never got hit with a whip before?"

"No. I've been hit with a leather belt, a wire coat hanger, a chair, a pillow case full of pop cans, and a soaking wet towel that hurt worse than any of the others. But not a horsewhip—until now."

Carli didn't move, clutching her coffee mug close. Then, putting it down on her dresser, she rushed to him, enveloping him with her arms and burying her face in his neck. Her squeeze would have felt like a bear hug to anyone not as tough as K.O.

"Hey," he said, kissing her hair, letting its ends tickle his nose. "Are you crying?"

"I hate it that people hurt you."

"Shh," he said. "It's over, honey. It's all over."

"No, it *isn't* over," she said, taking a ragged breath. "Somebody just hurt you. Somebody hurt you right after I first met you. People are always hurting you!"

"Listen. Except for my father—that's the rule, you know, you never hit your father—except for him, I always hurt the bastards right back, only worse. Then they never try hurting me again." He kissed her eyes gently, her eyelashes brushing his lips. He tasted the salty tears and allowed them to repose on his tongue for a while before swallowing them—he loved how she tasted, no matter where he kissed her.

"Nobody will ever hurt *you*," he said softly, his mouth on that incredibly soft patch of skin at the corner of her eye. "Nobody— *ever.*"

When K.O. arrived at Northcoast Downs half an hour later, he was surprised the security guards actually nodded at him and said "Hiya," instead of grilling him as in the past, as if he were a terrorist. That told him he'd been hanging around the track too long.

As he walked toward Glenn Gallagher's barn—what was now Walt Holman's barn—he had to lift his shoulders to keep out the nipping wind swooping down from the northwest.

It was a busy morning, as it always is backside. Many horses were already out for their morning exercise. The chill breeze didn't seem to bother them, but it crossed K.O.'s mind that they *might* not enjoy the preview of winter any more than he did. He realized racing horses were treated well, if only to keep them healthy for the competition.

Out in front of the barn, Carl Fulwood had wheeled out a barrel full of horse dung and was pushing it up the ramp of a big yellow wagon—known to all without much imagination or creativity as the shit wagon. Later in the day the wagon would be emptied at the track's communal dump, and eventually the cargo would be sold as fertilizer. There's nothing, K.O. thought, that Northcoast Downs wouldn't sell for profit.

"Hey," K.O. called out, "remember me?"

Fulwood looked up with sleepy lizard eyes, widening them in recognition. "Whaddya say?"

"I just dropped back for a bit. Guess it's because I like horses so much."

"Great. Then *you* shovel their shit."

"Sorry, got my good shoes on."

"You work for that other guy, right? The Polack guy."

"Slovenian guy."

"He was here with some spade lady cop the morning they found Gecko floating. They asked lotsa questions."

"Right. That's what they *do*. So—what's going on around here today?"

Shrug.

"Damn shamc about Gecko, though, huh?"

Another shrug.

"Did you know him well?"

"Whaddya think? I seen him every fuckin' day. Now I gotta do his jobs—like *this*." Fulwood gestured angrily with his chin at the rank accumulation in the wagon.

"You were friends, then?"

"Not friends. He was old enough to be my father, he was a drunk, and hc ran with skanky whores. No friend of mine."

"Then you didn't like him?"

"Didn't like him or not like him. He was just—here."

K.O. offered an understanding nod. "So how do you feel about him getting killed?"

"How would I feel about a guy in China who gets the clap? It got nothing to do with me."

"So," K.O. said carefully, "do you think he got killed rather than accidentally falling into the therapy pool and drowning?"

Fulwood moved down the ramp with his now-empty barrow. "I'm no rocket scientist, okay? But I'm no retard, either. I shovel this crap and I haul hay bales and I run the exercise wheel sometimes—or whatever else they tell me to do."

"Who tells you?"

Fulwood thought about that for a while. "Walt, mostly. Gallagher, sometimes—when he was still alive—but mostly Walt."

"Uh-huh."

"I just do my job an' collect my paycheck every two weeks an' mind my damn business."

"I see. And did Walt tell Gecko what to do?"

"It's Walt's barn; he's the boss."

"So—about Gecko?"

Fulwood began trundling the wheelbarrow back into the barn. "Who knows? He din't hang out at the therapy pool—that wasn't part of his job. The other thing is, though, that he was an alky."

K.O. moved quickly to keep pace with him. "So he might've fallen in?"

"He mighta."

"Did he ever go into the clubhouse with the fans who paid their way in? Did he drink at that bar?"

"Hell, no! None of us are spose'ta go there."

"The grooms and the trainers?"

"Usually not," Fulwood said. "Just the owners and their super-rich friends. An' the payin' customers for sure. Us? We're usually dirty—and smell like what I'm standin' in."

"I did see Gecko in there the night Glenn Gallagher died, though."

Carl Fulwood laughed. "People sneak in everywhere, if they can. Din't you ever sneak in to see a movie or a ballgame?"

"When I was a kid, yeah. Gecko was no kid."

Fulwood wiped sweat from his forehead with the back of his sleeve; chilly as the weather was, collecting horse poop was hard work. "He wasn't there for no drink. He couldn' afford bar drinks. He was prolly lookin' for his girlfriend."

"He had a girlfriend?"

"He had any girlfriend he could pay for. This one ho he was kinda hooked up on lives right next door to him in his motel."

Milan had described her in his notes. "Leanne?"

"Yeah."

"Did they have a fight?"

"What'd they have to fight about?" Carlby Fulwood said. "If he had fifteen extra bucks she copped his joint. Otherwise they din't much see each other—not on purpose, anyhow."

K.O. sighed. "Well, nice talking to you anyway, Carl."

"Yeah, okay—see ya."

Carl Fulwood went back inside, doing a subtle Fred Astaire dance move to avoid stepping on the two cats in the doorway, and K.O. began walking away until he noticed Jerry Nemo coming toward him from Barn Number Four, waving.

"Back again, kid?" Nemo had changed his shirt since their last meeting, but wore the same suit, the same silly hat, the same silly beard. "You're gonna turn into a horse trainer yet."

"Not this morning, though. Going for coffee?"

"I never said no to a cuppa coffee. Thanks for inviting me."

It wasn't exactly an invitation, K.O. thought, but he'd submit the dollar charge on his expense report. He fell in step beside Nemo. "Visiting that horse you wanted to sell me?"

Nemo's eyes gleamed. "You're in the market now?"

"No—just asking. Making conversation. You keep that horse in Fiddler's barn?"

Nemo smirked. "I keep him in there so's I can drop by and watch Fiddler's wife bend over to pick something up."

"Fiddler wouldn't like that."

"Right now, Fiddler can't say nothin' about it. Somebody put him in the hospital." He turned his head, staring at the fading welt on K.O.'s cheek. "It was you did it, right?"

"Fiddler and I—didn't have a meeting of the minds."

"You're some kinda tough guy, huh?"

"Exactly."

That made Nemo gulp; K.O. drove in harder. "Tell me, Mr. Nemo—do you keep all your horses in Fiddler's barn when you're trying to sell them?"

"Not always." They turned toward the kitchen. "Depends on who's got a stall they ain't using."

"Sometimes you keep your horses in Gallagher's barn? Or I should say now, Holman's barn?"

"Sometimes."

They went inside. K.O. ordered two coffees while Jerry Nemo filled his pockets with sugar packets and napkins again. As soon as they sat down, K.O. said, "I know you sometimes try to sell horses with all sorts of health problems." Nemo began to protest, but K.O. stopped him. "Don't deny it, okay?"

Nemo waved a hand before his face as though shooing away a mosquito. "You're not my customer, kiddo, so I don't give a damn what you say about me."

"I won't spread it around if that worries you." K.O. blew on his coffee to cool it. "Do trainers or grooms in those barns catch on to you? They know horse health better than you do."

K.O. watched as Jerry Nemo warred with himself. Finally he admitted, "You're no cop, so it don't matter what I say to you, right? Okay—I spose it's happened. Backside here, it's a small town. Everybody gossips—puts down everybody else; it's the American pastime."

"Did it happen to you? In Gallagher's barn?"

"I don't remember." When Jerry Nemo sipped his coffee, he made a bubbling sound as if eating hot soup.

"Was it Gecko who caught you?"

Nemo looked puzzled. "Gecko? Christ, no—he was always more than halfway out of everything, anyway."

"Who was it, then?

"It's old business, kid—and it's none a your business, either."

"It is, because there are so damn many questions around here."

"Why'n't you quit askin' 'em, then?"

"Where's the fun in that?" K.O. pushed his chair back and stood up. "Enjoy the rest of your coffee, Mr. Nemo."

Back in the barn, Carl Fulwood was nowhere to be found; neither was Jobie Dash. K.O. asked one of the other grooms he'd not been introduced to—a middle-aged woman wearing baggy overalls tucked into a pair of worn work boots, a sweatshirt pulled over *another* sweat shirt, and a rally cap with "Northbrook Downs" and the silhouette of a horse and sulky on its crown—if she knew the whereabouts of Walt Holman. She said, "He's always some-where close by. Stick around—hang out with the horses if you want." Then she lifted up one warning finger. "Don't smoke in here, though."

"I won't. I quit—when I was born."

He worked his way toward the rear of the barn, and each horse came to the door of the stall to see who was visiting. When he got to Imperion's stall he stopped, hugging the horse's sleek gray neck. "Hey, big guy—remember me? You took me for a ride the other morning. I've missed you." Imperion nuzzled K.O.s face, kissing his ear. "Wow—nice! I love you, too. We're best friends now, huh? BFFs?" He hugged Imperion tighter. "Works for me, fella."

Imperion's neck was soft to his touch and his breath smelled almost sweet. K.O. knew he was cared for well, even petted and fed carrot and apple treats by their grooms, but he couldn't shake off the feeling that all these horses were prisoners—living in their stalls twenty-three hours a day, then strapped up with leggings, bits, and blinders to be taken out once a day for exercise only so they could race successfully.

K.O. could have stayed there, hugging and petting Imperion for the rest of the day. Rodney, his cat, was very loving—when *he* felt like it and when he'd had enough, he would wander away, either to bathe himself, to stare out the window at the birds in the trees, or more than likely just go to sleep—which was the primary occupation of any cat. Horses, on the other hand, just couldn't get enough love.

Finally Walt Holman came back into the barn, his step brisk and his jacket zipped up to the chin. "Damn, boy—you lovin' up Imperion again? What are you, gay for horses?"

"*Gay*," K.O. said with a little heat, "for any animal."

"Hey, listen—quit your regular job and sign on with me so's you can be with horses twenty-four seven. I'm one groom short anyway."

"One short?"

"Well . . . " Holman unzipped his jacket a few inches. "Ain't got Gecko anymore, so the crews back here pick up the slack. You'd fit right in. You look like you got a strong back."

"I'll have to think about it. But I'm not exactly Gecko."

"I guess not. He was a fall-down drunk."

K.O. could once more smell bourbon on Holman's breath. "You've been known to toast a friend every so often, too. Right?"

"We all drink. It's a lifestyle here, backside. But Gecko, he was a heavy-hitting alcoholic, which is a different thing altogether. Before long, he woulda gotten fired anyway."

"You were going to fire him?"

"Not me. I woulda delivered the news, but it was Chloe Markham wanted him gone. Complaints about Gecko somehow found their way to her a lot, about him gossiping and getting people back here mad at each other. Since he worked for me, she let me hear about it. She hates all the people on the backside; we're a necessary nuisance—but especially the ones who take up her time. They're a real thorn in her side. And with the casino deal they're working on, she'd worry about anyone who gives this place a bad name. Guess she'd damn sure make me fire him now if she could—him falling into the therapy pool stinkin' drunk isn't good PR for what she wants seen as a wholesome family experience."

"A family experience? Gambling is the big moneymaker here."

"Sure," Walt said. "But we like gamblers to bring their kids. There's games for them—machines, I mean—and a playground area. Why would the owner of this track want kids running into Gecko staggering around with his fly open and some whore's lipstick all over his pants?"

"Why indeed?" K.O. said.

"Well, like I say, we're short-handed around here, so I got to get back to work—and get these bums around here working faster, too." Walt started away, calling over his shoulder, "Stick around and play with Imperion all you want; just don't get in anybody's way."

K.O. waved goodbye, went outside and started up his car. Not wanting to make phone calls parked in front of Holman's barn, he drove about two hundred yards away, still on track property, and sat there with the motor running; the warmth feeling good on the chilly morning. He punched out a few numbers, disappointed at listening to recorded replies, and then called Milan Jacovich.

CHAPTER TWENTY-TWO

MILAN

I talked with K.O., or rather listened to him, scratching some quick notes about his meetings on my yellow pad, hoping I'd be able to read them later. Usually I can't; I don't get paid for my penmanship. Under my desk, Booger was snoring more quietly than usual—but he would occasionally groan like a very old man whose every joint ached when he tried to get out of bed in the morning.

What was I going to do with Booger, anyway? I'd never had a dog in my life and had hardly ever been around one, especially one as peculiar-looking as he. He'd spent the night in my apartment; I was grateful he hadn't decided to sleep in my bed with me, but apparently no one told him not to pass wind once every hour, like Old Faithful. I'd taken him for a walk before I set out on my day's business, and was interested to note that he was most fascinated with the trees and fire hydrants on Cedar Road that he'd never visited before.

Booger. What the hell kind of a name is Booger? If I let him hang around for a while—just for a while, as dog care didn't come easily to me, nor did it fit my lifestyle—I'd have to come up with a better name for him. "Buck" had worked for Jack London; *Lad: A Dog* made Albert Payson Terhune famous. But those names were already taken. I toyed with the idea of finding a bookstore and purchasing a copy of *What to Name the Baby*, but dismissed it.

I turned my attention to what K.O. was telling me about *his* day.

"So you want to talk to Chloe Markham again?" I said, underlining her first name several times on my yellow pad. "What does she have to do with a minimum-wage guy like Gecko? She never goes backside at the track. I wouldn't think she'd be aware of Gecko's existence, much less wanting to fire him."

K.O. said, "I called her office, but she hasn't been there all day. Should I go to her home?"

"No. I'll see her."

"What do you want me to do for the rest of the day?"

"Find out everything possible about Chloe. Her finances, whatever history there is on her, and whatever you can dig up on her brother Manley."

"And about her boy toy, Skippy, too?"

I laughed. "It wouldn't hurt."

I clipped Booger's leash to his collar, led him downstairs to the parking lot which he gleefully anointed, and then put him in the car and headed for Chloe Markham's house.

She lived on the lakefront in Bay Village, just about as far west as one could go and still be in Cuyahoga County. I wouldn't call it a palace, exactly—but it was one hell of a big house. I found myself in a two-story atrium, staring up at the curled, sweeping stairway almost overwhelmed by a gigantic chandelier that might have come from the Palace of Versailles. I had to concede it was a beautiful house—too beautiful, I think, for someone like me to live in. I pad around my apartment in stocking feet, eat breakfast standing up as I get ready for work, drink beer and eat potato chips in front of the TV set, fall asleep on my sofa watching an old black-and-white film on TCM and wake up the next morning with a stiff back. None of that could happen in Chloe Markham's mini-mansion.

It was Skip Swain who opened the door. No ascot—too early in the day. But his shirt was blindingly white, shimmering silk with poofy sleeves and a collar that made me think of Tyrone Power. Skip's hair was sprayed solid like Conway Twitty's, and he wore too-tight leather pants like a 1970s rock star—except Skip Swain hadn't even been born in the 1970s.

I re-introduced myself to him. "We've met once before," I said. "At the track."

He didn't shake hands but left mine waving in the air in front of him. Ass-hat! "So?"

"The night Glenn Gallagher died. I was his guest."

"Oh," he said. "Oh, sure."

He *wasn't* sure. He didn't have the foggiest notion of who I was until I gave him my business card and explained why I was there—to see Chloe Markham.

He didn't like that; his faux smile cooled rapidly. "I don't recall her inviting you here."

"I just want a few minutes with her."

He glanced over his shoulder at the stairway. "She's busy."

"I'll wait."

"You can't do that," he bristled.

"Yes, I can."

He stuck out his jaw, ready for a fight. "Want me to call a cop?"

"Go ahead," I said, taking my cell phone from my pocket. "And I'll call a *Plain Dealer* reporter. He'll just *love* hearing all about a suspicious death at Northcoast Downs that Chloe Markham's boy toy tries to keep her from talking about. It might even make the front page."

That slowed him down. "Look—Chloe already spoke to one of your people and answered all his questions. She doesn't know a damn thing about Gallagher! Why come here and bother her again?"

"I have different questions."

"Ask *me*, then."

I put my cell phone back in my pocket. This would be like speaking Farsi to an Amish carpenter. "Can we sit down some-where?"

"We can talk right here," he said. I don't think he wanted me to sit on one of Chloe Markham's very expensive sofas in the living room to my right. Not only was this house too fancy for me to live in, it was apparently too fancy for me to get past the entryway.

"If you insist, Skippy," I said.

His head jerked back on his neck as if I'd slapped him hard, right across the mouth. "That's *Skip!*" he said angrily. "Better still—you call me *Mister* Swain."

"*Mister?* Seriously?" I chuckled, which rankled him even further. "Can you ever forgive me? Okay, then, *Mister* Swain. Tell me about Gecko."

"What?"

"Gecko."

"That lizard on the insurance commercials?"

"No. One of the grooms who worked backside at the track." That confused him even more. "Backside?"

"In the barns, not the clubhouse. Where the horses live."

"Well, I don't know any Gecko. I've never even been—what do you call it again? The backside? I've never been in the backside."

"Gecko," I said, "is the guy who drowned in the therapy pool."

Whatever expression he'd chosen to put on his face disappeared back to wherever it came from. "I heard about that, but I didn't know his name was Gecko. What the hell kind of a name is Gecko?"

"It's a nickname," I said. "Like Skip."

"Go fuck yourself," he said—mean.

"Okay, but I'll buy myself dinner first." I shifted from one foot to the other. "Meantime, just run along upstairs—or wherever it is you have to run along to—and tell Chloe she has a visitor."

That was worse than if I'd punched him in the nose—and I did it deliberately. There is little more demeaning to a grown man than telling him to "run along." He was too humiliated to answer; after I'd easily won the staring contest, he spun on his heel and went up the winding staircase.

Minutes later Chloe came downstairs, dressed very casually— it was her own home, after all—in simple slacks and a blouse that probably cost more than a thousand dollars. I guess when someone is born rich and then inherits even more money, arrogance is stamped right on his face like a scar.

She didn't even come down to my level, but stayed on the bottom step—posing. Apparently she wouldn't invite me any farther inside, either. "What is it," she said, "that brings you to my *home* in the middle of the morning?"

"Gecko."

She looked startled, as if I'd made a peculiar noise. "I thought your person—that young boy—was asking about Glenn Gallagher."

"He *was* asking about Glenn. And he's a quarter of a century old, by the way—and his name is Kevin O'Bannion. Hardly a *boy*, wouldn't you agree?"

She didn't like that and chose not to answer. "What's his name again? Gecko?"

"His real name was Royal Shadcoe," I said.

"Royal Shadcoe? Well, look, I'm sorry about it—obviously—somebody drowning. But I don't even know who he was."

"He was a groom in Walt Holman's barn."

She shrugged. "That means he wasn't one of my employees. He was Walt's—or, I suppose, Glenn's."

"You didn't want to fire him?"

"*Fire* him? I never even heard of him before this very minute."

Skip Swain came almost all the way downstairs and stood behind her on the next step, listening.

"Never talked to Walt about getting rid of him?"

"I don't tell anyone who to hire or who to fire. As long as they aren't selling drugs out of my racetrack, I don't give a damn who they are."

"I don't suppose you know everyone who works at the track," I said.

"I have too many employees to know all their names. And this Ginko . . . "

"Gecko."

" . . . didn't work for me, so why would I want him fired?"

"You didn't suggest to Walt that he should get rid of him?"

"No."

"You've taken up enough of our time," Skip Swain said after an attention-getting throat clear.

I looked up at him on the step. "On the fat chance that I'd be in *your* house, I might even pay attention to you. This *isn't* your house, though—so butt out."

He puffed out his chest and extended his chin. It's hard not to punch an easy target like a stuck-out chin—but I made myself not think about it. I wondered, however, whether K.O. would have been as discreet as I. "Don't fuck with me, buddy!" he mock-threatened. "I have some pretty damn important connections in this state. With one phone call I can fucking ruin you!"

I laughed. "You keep threatening to call somebody, Skippy—so *do* it. I think you had to use a shoehorn to fit your fat ass into those ultra-effete leather pants, and the tightness went to your brain."

Now Chloe was furious, too. *"Skip!"* she howled at me.

"You actually want me to skip, Ms. Markham? At my age?"

"I want you out of my home!" she said, deigning to descend from the step, march past me, and fling open the front door, wide. "Right goddamn now!" She folded her arms defensively across her chest, her way of assuring me she was no one with whom one should mess. Not very convincing—but any further conversation here would be a waste of time.

When I got to my car, Booger was as delighted to see me as if he'd been left alone for several years. He leaped, yipped, slobbered, wagged—and before I started the car, I allowed him to pee on Chloe Markham's front lawn, disappointed that was *all* he needed to do.

Driving back to my office, I thought about Chloe and Skippy— *Skip*. They both *might* have been lying through their teeth—but I doubted it. They were too enchanted with their own wealth and importance to even consider killing another human being.

Stuffing oneself into extra-tight leather pants can't be considered murder. Suicide? Yes.

Milan Security was closed up tight. All afternoon K.O. had been on the Internet and had printed out all sorts of things about Chloe and Manley Markham, left on my desk along with a cryptic note: *"See you in the morning."*

I was put off by the scrawled message. I had plans for the evening—business plans—and had hoped K.O. would be there with me. But I don't pay him that much—and he's worked overtime or given up hunks of his weekends before. Besides, he took a hard crack across the face with a horsewhip and he probably deserved an evening to himself.

So I decided to kill some time before heading out again by reading K.O.'s research. It was thorough—and damned interesting.

Chloe Markham was in her early thirties when her multimillionaire childless uncle died and bequeathed her Northcoast Downs, which he'd founded, along with enough money so that she wouldn't worry about that subject again for the rest of her life. He also arranged that much of his liquid assets remained with the track's accounts instead of hers, so Chloe wouldn't have to write out a personal check for as much as a plug nickel to keep the place decent, the horses cared for, and even the public restrooms cleaned on a regular basis. Her forthcoming deal with a major restaurant chain to turn the Downs into a full-blown casino, which would make her even *more* money, had been created and overseen by her second-in-command, Everett Valmer, who'd worked for her uncle from the beginning and had inherited a percentage of the racetrack, too. It was clearly good news for Chloe, since she obviously didn't have much of a head for business. When one has inherited beaucoup riches, one doesn't need brains.

There were pages printed from the Internet about Chloe Markham's social life as well. A state senator, an internationally known cardiac surgeon, a former suburban mayor, a local TV news investigative reporter, an award-winning Cleveland author, not one but *two* members of the Cleveland Browns football team, and of course, Skip Swain—the indolent rich kid who lived on his family's investments and profits from backstage political power— had all been photographed and reported on by the newspapers as they squired her to various parties, benefits, and high-society social events for my town's very wealthy upper-upper class. Romances, as such, were not proven, but the supposition was there each time the Cleveland *paparazzi's* photos were printed with her evening's escort peering lustfully down the front of Chloe's dazzling evening gowns. I'd even met some of them personally, in other venues, but still, it was quite a stack of print-outs K.O. had left for me to peruse.

There was one other of her high-profile dates I noticed: Victor Gaimari.

Victor, about my age, had never married, but he was very good-looking—a bit of a latter-day Cesar Romero lookalike—and in the two decades I've known him, he was always seen with the most beautiful women in Greater Cleveland, most of them rich, like Chloe. The more-than-twenty-years difference in their ages obviously hadn't bothered him—and I suppose it hadn't bothered Chloe, either, although many of *her* romantic entanglements involved much younger men than herself. I believe the attraction and fascination with Victor, who although financially well-off probably had a lot less money than Chloe Markham, was more because of *who* he is—the head of the organized Cleveland mob when he's not being a stockbroker and investment banker—than with how much he had in the bank.

Glenn Gallagher had been Victor's rival in the financial business—but Victor wasn't into murder. He was into a hell of a lot of other illegal or unethical things, carried out by his subordinates, but never murder. Like his late uncle, Giancarlo D'Allessandro, he'd accepted the fact that the mob no longer operates as Al Capone and Charlie Lucky Luciano and the Gotti family used to, but are legitimate businessmen—with some extremely *non*-legitimate pursuits they preferred not to talk about.

I started reading K.O.'s meticulous research into Chloe's brother, Manley.

He'd been kicked out of both Brown University and Dartmouth—for "conduct unbecoming." His alma mater, therefore, was the Betty Ford Clinic in California, and he fit in there so well that he'd returned twice more to dry out and swear he'd sin no more. According to K.O.'s trusty laptop, Manley's trust fund gave him two hundred thousand annually—not a royal sum, as trust funds go, but three times what I make in a year, and I have to *earn* every cent of mine.

I stopped reading for a while, wandered over to my windows and looked out on the now-choppy waters of the Cuyahoga River—which, translated, turns out to be "Crooked River River" because *cuyahoga*, in the Iroquois language, *means* "crooked river." Standing by the window sometimes gives me calmness. Mostly it's looking at downtown. It's grown a lot in my lifetime, and after a dip lasting a decade, it's fighting its way back, socially and economically. Still, it's a town built by those who couldn't speak the language, or if they did, it was with a heavy accent.

I've never been comfortable with the very rich, people like the Markhams. They're often pleasant enough, and very charitable, but their values differ from mine—and sometimes their ethics, too. My father, who barely spoke ten words of English, came to Cleveland right after World War II ended, worked fifty hours a week on the hot melting floor of a steel mill just south of downtown, and died too early. My mother, also a Ljubljana native, stayed home and cooked, washed all our clothes by hand on one of those old-fashioned washboards, and kept our little home in the St. Clair-Superior area, just a few blocks from St. Vitus Slovenian parish, cleaner than any hospital I've ever visited. We rented that little home until we could afford to buy it outright—for, I think, about twelve thousand dollars. That generation of newcomers from Eastern Europe didn't believe in going into debt; whatever it was, if they couldn't afford it, they chose to do without it.

We were the working poor—immigrants and children of immigrants, and my peers worked with their hands. Teachers, newspaper reporters, retail clerks, bank tellers, and career military, especially the enlisted ranks, and not the shimmering-gold-braid officers.

Cops—like my late, great best friend Marko Meglich. (When he turned thirty, he'd changed his first name from Marko to just plain Mark—but he hadn't done it legally; it still read 'Marko' on his driver's license and passport and credit cards—and it always bugged him when I called him Marko.)

These people, for the most part, didn't get rich, or if they did, it was through their sweat and muscle. The rest always made approximately the same annual money as I did.

Some rose to great heights, bypassing their parents as they became doctors, lawyers, financial mavens, Cleveland mayors, Ohio governors, even United States senators—but they never lost the Eastern European values with which they were raised. They were unlike the *uber*-rich, born and raised with a silver spoon in every available orifice, and who can buy everything, but value nothing.

Except *more*.

That's why I didn't Americanize my name, which many find difficult, if not impossible, to pronounce. When they bravely attempt it, they invariably say *Mee*-lan, which is the European way, or choose Mi-*lahn*, like the city in Italy.

By the time I stopped looking out the window, it was more than halfway to twilight.

I called Tobe at work, told her I'd stop off at my apartment to leave Booger there, and asked if she wanted to accompany me to Northcoast Downs again that evening.

I struck out.

"Is Proud Milan running again tonight?" she said. "If he's not, I'd just as soon sit home and paint my toenails."

"I don't know who's running. I'm not going there to watch the races."

Her tone grew more serious. "If it's business—your kind of business—I can't have any part in it. Not legally, anyway. Sorry, Milan, but Summit County isn't my venue."

Tobe couldn't see me shrug. "You're a Cleveland city cop, Tobe—but my license is from the state of Ohio. If Keith Barent is there tonight, I'll back off."

"Keith Barent *Johnson*," she said. "Milan—don't go there armed, okay?"

"The state says I can carry concealed."

"The state doesn't say bullets bounce off you, though."

"Nobody's going to shoot me."

"You don't know that."

"I'm not chasing hardened criminals," I said. "If I'm looking for a killer, he caused Glenn Gallagher, somehow, to have a heart attack—and he drowned Gecko in a pool. Nobody's shot anybody, Tobe. For a change, there were no guns involved. So—worst case scenario—tonight won't be the gunfight at the O.K. corral."

She spoke softly—sadly. "If you get home before midnight, call and let me know you're okay."

"And interfere with the glorious enhancement of your toenails?"

"Then call first thing in the morning."

"First thing in the morning, I'd rather just nudge you."

"Too bad for you, Lover Boy, because if you're out and about on business, nudging is off the table for tonight. 'Festivities' are like going to the track: if you don't bet, you don't win."

CHAPTER TWENTY-THREE

MILAN

I left Booger ensconced on the couch and left my Glock where it always lives—on the highest shelf in the closet—before I headed for the track. Hot dogs, burgers, and nachos at the track don't add up to salubrious nutrition, so I popped into an Applebee's instead—not much different, actually, but their menu is more diverse and you get to eat like a grown-up while sitting at a table with a napkin in your lap.

When I arrived at Northcoast Downs, I didn't head backside right away, but parked my car where all other customers do in a vast, sprawling lot, flashed my visitor pass at the woman taking paid admissions at the door so I could get in for nothing, and found my way into the huge downstairs area with the TV sets and betting carrels. The first race wouldn't start for another twenty minutes, but it was crowded already; many of the bettors had been there since the track had opened that morning.

I tried not to bump into gamblers walking and studying racing forms at the same time as I looked at the crowd for someone I might know. They seemed vaguely familiar from the time when I'd been there on the night Glenn Gallagher died—or maybe there's a certain look to all of them: those who never get fresh air or see sunshine or think about food, sex, politics, religion or the price of eggs—only about their next wager.

Finally I spotted John Terranova, standing in a room smaller than the one with all the carrels and staring up at a TV set that was tuned not to other racetracks all over the world, but to local

Channel 12 and the evening news. At the anchor desk was Vivian Truscott, the elegant news maven for the last twenty years, still looking blonde and regal although it now was hard to forget her being shat upon while in a jogging cart on the track.

"Hello again, John," I said to Terranova.

"Hey. You getting to be a regular here now? Turning into a gambler, are you?"

"No. Just looking around."

"For what?"

"I won't know until I find it. Are you here with Victor Gaimari?"

"No way, Milan! If Victor's out at night, it's to a fancier place than this dump."

"And always with a beautiful woman, right?"

Terranova shrugged. "He's usually got pretty good taste in coochie."

"Usually?"

"*You* know. He don't wanna get married or nothin'; he plays the field." The TV blasted a commercial from a car company on the west side; the principal player, obviously a co-owner, was shouting, gesturing madly, and acting as if he'd just slipped a screw loose. Commercials are too loud.

"Didn't he date Chloe Markham for a while?" I asked.

"Oh yeah—her. He went out with her three, maybe four times. Spent one night at her house—told me to pick him up the next morning, stop first at his place and bring him a fresh outfit. Suit, shirt, tie, stuff like that. And that was it, he never fucked her again—far as I know."

"Short, but sweet, huh?"

"Short, yeah. Sweet? I dunno about that," Terranova said. "She's a ball-buster—never even looked at me, never said 'hello' or nothin'—like I was a piece a fuckin' furniture."

"Is that why Victor stopped seeing her? Because she treated you like furniture?"

"Lissen, Milan," John Terranova said, "I dropped outa high school when I was sixteen. Victor pays me pretty good considering I never learned how to do nothin' in my whole life except drive him around, do errands for him—"

"Beat people up, too."

"Sometimes, yeah." He looked at me. "Are you still pissed off about that?"

"No, I'm not. You were just doing your job. And that was a long time ago—twenty-five years."

He scratched his head. "That long ago? Jeez! Well, I'm no kid no more, I ain't beat anyone up in so long, I can't even remember."

"That's good to hear," I said. "At your age, they might beat you up back."

He laughed. "You an' me, Milan, we're about the same age as each other, right?"

"Yes—but you're better looking than I am."

He actually reached up and patted his black-going-gray curly hair into place, then flushed, embarrassed that I'd seen him do it. "Hey, I gotta go," Terranova said, "and get a bet down on the first race."

I wished him luck and watched him scurry away, then headed out into the big room. Electricity hung in the air, a sharp, tingly edge of anticipation. It wasn't like a heavyweight championship fight or the Super Bowl about to kick off, but all the gamblers seemed excited. And just as the track announcer said, "And they're off and racing," my cell phone chirped—K.O. on the caller ID screen.

"Where are you, Milan?" he said.

"I'm at the racetrack. Where are you?"

"At my place. I'm in the bedroom, but Carli and I are having pizza."

"Nice."

"I invited Jake Foote to join us, too, if that's okay."

"You're off-duty—you can invite anyone to dinner you want."

"Uh—well, here's the other thing. Carli suggested that I move in with her. I mean into her apartment. Full time. It's not a done deal yet—but we're discussing."

"So you called me so I can wish you premature congratulations?"

His laugh didn't sound amused. "That's very nice of you." He took a moment. "I called Jake this afternoon and asked for a favor—the invitation was spur of the moment. I figure the Summit County coroner wasn't going to open up for you; she doesn't even know you. And she probably won't talk to me again, either. But she was willing to talk to Jake—about Gecko."

"Give me a second, K.O. It's noisy in here." I retraced my steps to the smaller room where I'd just spoken to Terranova, faded into a corner far from the Channel 12 newscast, and plugged my right ear with my finger so I could hear K.O. clearly in my left. "Go ahead," I said.

"According to the post-mortem report, Royal Shadcoe's death was by drowning."

"That's not exactly a news flash."

"No, the news flash is that before Mr. Shadcoe drowned, the back of his skull had been caved in by what was probably a blunt instrument."

"We have visitor passes. That makes us suspects, K.O."

"Maybe, but I don't think so. Jake put in a good word for us to the coroner."

"Us? He and I have never met."

K.O. coughed a frog out of his throat. "Well, for me, anyway. Which means that I can put it a good word for you."

"I'm touched," I said.

"So maybe the killer is wandering around there with you. Watch your ass, Milan. I'll worry about you."

"I'll worry about you, too."

"Why?"

"Because," I said, "there isn't nearly enough closet space in Carli's apartment for two people to hang everything they own."

"Unless you give me a raise, Milan, I've only got two outfits, anyway."

"Which ones?"

"This one," K.O. said. "And that one."

There was a betting window downstairs, right behind the bar that Glenn had mentioned most of the horsemen preferred because of the betting clerk, Mildred, who'd been there several years longer than forever. At that moment no one was waving money around, so I walked up to Mildred behind the counter. Well into her sixties, her eyeglasses were cat's-eye-shaped and had bright red rims, and her hair was dyed as dead black as shoe polish. Perhaps it *was* shoe polish.

I showed her my pass and bet two dollars to win on horse 6. I had no idea of the horse's name or record, and for that piddling amount I didn't give a damn whether I won. I was more interested in conversation.

"I'm not a regular here," I said, then added, "Mildred," which was on the name badge pinned to her white shirt. *Mildred* isn't a name you hear often anymore. "But I hear you're the best bet-taker at the entire track."

She shrugged. "It's okay with me, mister."

I took out a business card and handed it to her. She squinted at it through those glasses, eyebrows raised toward her hairline in surprise. Then she mispronounced both my first and last names. "A private investigator? Jeez, I never met one of you guys before." She studied me carefully, as if I were a painting at a garage sale that she was considering buying—for two dollars. "You don't look like a private eye."

"What does a private eye look like?"

"Alan Ladd," she said. Alan Ladd had been a popular tough guy film star during the 1940s and 1950s, which means that either she watched old Turner Classic Movies at home on TV or she was older than I thought.

"Alan Ladd was a lot better looking, and not nearly as tall as I am," I said.

She nodded. "That explains it."

"I was a friend of Glenn Gallagher's. You remember him?"

"What are you, *kidding* me? Sure I remember him—he only died a few days ago." Mildred clucked sadly. "A nice guy he was—always left a good tip when he won at my station. Nice presents at Christmas, too, and on my birthday—fruit baskets or something."

"Did his buddies from backside bet with you, too?"

"The other drivers and trainers? Sure. They still do."

"Pike Sullivan?"

"Yeah, on nights he doesn't drive. I don't even know if he's here tonight."

"Walt Holman bets with you?"

"All the time."

"Does he win a lot?"

She considered the question. "Walt? He's no big gambler. More than likely he breaks even. He'd stop down at the bar a couple times a night, then carry it up here and lay down his ten spot."

I nodded. "Did you know Gecko?"

Mildred's face grew sad for a moment. "Aw. Everybody knew Gecko—and kinda liked him because he never really bugged them. I don't think he ever met a stranger in his life." She looked up at whatever supreme being was hanging out near the ceiling. "He'd talk your ear off if you let him."

"About what?"

"About anything. Horses, sure—and his one or two hooker girlfriends who lived in the same building he did. But he talked about people, too—who work here. He knew who was screwing who, who was having a sexy 'do' without their husband or wife knowing about it, who had money trouble or booze trouble, or drug trouble. He knew everything—and blabbed it to anybody who'd listen." She sighed. "He's gone now, God love him."

"Yeah, that was a damn shame," I said. "How about Del Fiddler? Were you and he buddies?"

Her lips almost disappeared and she squared her shoulders. "Fiddler? Sheesh! If he came up here, I'd kick him so hard his balls would wind up under his chin."

"You don't care much for him?"

"He's a mean son of a—" She stopped, cleared her throat. "He's not a nice person. Mean to everybody, that pretty wife of his included." She shuddered. "He's mean to horses, too. I think he gets off on causing pain. If he's some kind of friend of yours, well, I'm sorry, but that's the way I feel."

"He's no friend of mine, Mildred. Do you know Chloe Markham personally? I guess she's the big boss around here. Does she bet with you?"

"She don't bet at all. She probly wouldn't recognize a horse unless he sat on her. I don't see her much unless she's tryin' to impress somebody. She don't talk to working people or even say 'hello.' She don't talk to anybody, *period*—unless it's a rich guy."

"Do you take bets from her boyfriend?"

That made Mildred laugh aloud—one staccato blast from deep in her chest. "Which one? Who can keep track of all her boyfriends, anyway? She changes 'em like I change my socks."

She made *me* laugh. Not many do, because not many Cleve-landers are funny, unless they're talking about the Browns foot-ball team. Those who *are* funny, like Bob Hope, Drew Carey, Kaye Ballard, and Tim Conway, move away from here to be funny some-place else. "Did Chloe have much to do with Glenn Gallagher?"

Mildred shrugged. "I'd say not. He was too old for her. Besides, they didn't like each other."

That made me wonder again *why* there was animosity be-tween Chloe and Gallagher. Maybe at one time there *was* a love affair that went wrong. Then I shook it off; I don't think Chloe ever perceived her sexual entanglements as "love affairs." Besides, Glenn had been hung up on Jen Taylor.

"So," I said, "the bar down here is where all the backside guys go to drink?"

She nodded. "Not a sit-down-and-booze kinda bar, though. Too noisy for a good talk. Those guys walk around carrying their drinks with 'em."

"Who's the bartender down there, Mildred?"

"There's a couple different ones. I don't know their schedule. Phyllis is one; Trenda's the other."

"Trenda?" I said. "With a T? I never heard that name before."

"Me, neither. That's 'cuz she's younger—well, younger than me, anyhow. People name their kids the funniest damn things these days." She looked at my business card again. "You here working tonight? Asking questions?"

"That's what I do."

"Well—I don't think I helped you much."

"You helped a lot, Mildred." I slipped a ten dollar bill over the counter to her.

"What's this for?"

"My personal thanks for the help." I placed my betting ticket in front of her, too. "Keep this—and if the horse wins, you collect. It's yours."

She shook her head vehemently. "I can't cash in a winning ticket; my ass'd get fired."

"Then," I said, "give it to someone who needs it."

She looked at the ticket again. "Okay—but this horse isn't gonna win."

"How do you know that?"

She turned both hands palms up and hunched her shoulders. "Dead money," she said.

I waved goodbye and headed back downstairs. The horses and drivers were out on the track now. Squinting out the window, I saw horse number six trotting easily along with the rest of the racers. He was the one I'd bet on—chestnut with a black mane and a white star on his forehead. I'd heard somewhere that many Amish were superstitious about the colors of their horses, preferring big chestnuts like this one. If stuck with a horse of an unlucky color, some might sell it at auctions frequented by buyers for the slaughterhouse—a thought that made me shudder.

I found the bar easily. Most of the crowd drank beer, but there was a relatively decent array of hard liquor, too, although I saw no single-malt scotch or expensive small-distillery bourbons. I did immediately locate a bottle of Armagnac; they stocked it just because Glenn had preferred it—a new, as-yet-unopened bottle, the plastic seal still visible at the neck.

The bartender *was* young—and I surmised what her name was even before I could read it on her badge. She wore a Northcoast Downs visor over her medium-long ponytail. She was cute and bouncy, and both her cheeks dimpled when she smiled.

"Hey, Trenda," I said.

"Hey yourself," she said, "whoever you are."

"I'm a thirsty man—which is what brought me to you." I checked out the beers on tap. No Stroh's. "Can I get a Bud?" I'm not fond of Budweiser, but I had few choices—and several questions for Trenda, though she didn't know it yet.

She gave me the beer in a waxed-paper cup. I pointed at the Armagnac bottle. "Pretty fancy for a place like this, isn't it? Armagnac? I don't think I've ever tried that."

"You want a shot?"

"Not tonight."

Trenda giggled. "I never even *heard* of it before I started working here."

The crowd noise rose as the first race began so I raised my voice. "You sell lots of Armagnac?"

She shook her head. "Nobody ever asks for it except one man

who used to own a bunch of horses—he drove them, too. But he passed away recently, poor guy."

"Glenn Gallagher?" I said carefully.

"You knew him?"

"I was here with him the night he died."

Trenda looked sad. "Aw, jeez. I miss him. I mean, times he was here, he poured himself at least four drinks every night."

My heart took a couple of double-beats. "He poured it himself?"

"Yeah. He started doing that when I was real busy here, like on weekends and holidays—and it got to be a habit. He always scooted behind the bar, went right to his bottle, poured himself a nice stiff one, and left twenty bucks underneath it every time." She fluttered her eyelids. "Nice tip."

"Wouldn't he get in trouble for coming behind the bar?"

"They just march right to the bar, grab themselves a glass and a bottle, and always pay for it." She flinched. "Anybody else might get into deep doo-doo for doing that, 'cuz there are cameras taping all over the place, including this bar."

"Are they taping me right now?"

She pointed up at an unobtrusive camera in the ceiling. "Smile," she suggested.

I *did* smile at the lens. I waved, too, and felt like a fool for doing so. Then I said, "Does Walt Holman come by and pour his own drinks, too?"

"Sure," Trenda said, "but he's a bourbon guy. He always goes for the Maker's Mark. He never leaves a big tip, either."

I drank half the beer, thanked her, and left a twenty dollar bill on the bar. That startled her. "Are you as rich as Glenn was?" she called after me.

"I'm rich," I said over my shoulder, "because I have great friends."

I headed for the clubhouse exit, hearing the crowd cheer behind me. The first race had ended, and I had no idea which horse had won. I didn't care, either—I'd given my betting ticket away.

Outside in the too-early dark, the end of October felt like the beginning of January. With no more hint of the sun, the temperature hovered in the low thirties, and the wind was blowing right through my jacket and fleece shirt. Several days from now, every kid in Greater Cleveland would be out trick-or-treating and moaning the necessity of wearing warm coats over their costumes. How many little girls would choose a princess costume over a wicked witch get-up? How many boys would be vampires or werewolves or some other monster? I couldn't remember *what* my boys, Milan Junior and Stephen, dressed up in for their Halloween days.

I walked around the southern end of the clubhouse. Even though the parking lot was more than three-quarters full, there was no one outside on foot. At the guarded entrance to backside, the sentries who knew me from my earlier trips there had left and the evening shift had taken over. The two new security guys wanted more from me than just a flash of my visitor pass, and it took me five minutes to explain who I was and who had issued the pass before they relented and let me in.

There were more horses and sulkies out now, this time piloted by professional drivers all wearing their own unique colors, ready for a serious race. The buzz from the gamblers still sitting outside to watch the contests was like inconsequential elevator music.

The person I ran into first—one not aboard a racing sulky— was Pike Sullivan. In his red-and-gold colors and puffing on a cigarette, he was heading toward the kitchen when he saw me.

"How'd you manage to get back here, sir? You should be in the nice, cozy clubhouse having a drink and losing your money—unless you were betting on me. Hey, I'm Pike Sullivan."

I'd heard about his morning exchange with K.O. Apparently his ego never stopped. "Not tonight," I said. "Did you drive in the first race?"

"Negative. I'm in the fourth and eighth races, so I'm grabbing a cup of coffee first."

"I'm an investigator," I said, giving him my business card, "just asking a few questions about the recent deaths around here."

"I met one of your other guys, too. I even took him for a jog." He nodded sagely. "Gallagher kicking the bucket and Gecko drowning in the therapy pool; there's been enough questions."

"But not nearly enough answers."

Pike glowered at me. "You're not going to ask *me* questions, are you?"

"I might."

He actually sniffed his arrogance. "I might not answer."

"Just a couple," I said. "Like, are you involved in any sort of deal with Walt Holman?"

"What kind of deal?"

"Co-owning horses. Partnerships on anything."

"I do my own thing and let everybody else do theirs. I play the stock market—when the market's good. And I bet on other sports—mostly football—but never on racing."

"Why not on racing?"

His staccato laugh cut the quiet night air. "Do I really look that dumb?"

"You never can tell," I said.

"Are you insulting me?"

"Now *you're* the one asking questions, Mr. Sullivan."

He drew his shoulders back, suggested I perform a physical impossibility on myself—not the first time I'd heard that one, either—and stomped away toward the kitchen. I patted my jacket pocket for gloves that I didn't have with me, then put my hands in my pockets and continued toward Holman's barn.

The first horse-and-driver teams were heading back to their stalls; those readying for the second race moved toward the track. When I got to Holman's barn, I stepped out of the way, fast, as a sulky rumbled by me and turned toward the bright light and the crowds. I went inside. Jobie Dash was moving into a recently vacated stall with a shovel, but he stopped and glared at me. "You're not supposed to be back here during the races," he said.

"Where's Mr. Holman?"

Jobie jerked his thumb toward the rear of the barn. I thanked him and strolled past, feeling his eyes burning a hole in my back. Holman came out of another stall and regarded me as narrowly as did Jobie.

"What are *you* doing here?" he said.

"Came by to see you."

"Why?"

"Because," I said, "you're a very rich guy now. I always like to know rich guys."

His pause was hardly detectable, save for a fast blink of his eyelids and a dry swallow. "What do you mean by that?"

"I heard all about your bequest. Impressive."

"Uh—I don't want that getting around."

"You're inheriting everything in harness racing that Glenn Gallahger owned. Why would you want to keep it quiet?"

"I—just do."

"You also want to keep it quiet how you always walk behind the bar in the clubhouse during race nights and pour your own drinks?"

Now his lips all but disappeared. "I don't do it sneaky; horse owners do it all the time." He looked around, but there was no one in the barn besides Jobie Dash. "Listen, Mr.—uh"

"Jacovich," I said.

"Right. I guess I'm more used to the kid—your partner—being here. You wanna take a walk?"

"A walk?"

He indicated the nearly empty barn with a sweeping hand. "It gets crazy in here on race nights."

It didn't look crazy to me, but I didn't comment.

"We could have a real talk along the way—if that's what you want."

"It's cold out," I said.

"Walking'll warm you up. Come on—I'll buy you a drink later."

"You'll just walk behind the bar and get me a Bud?"

"That's because I'm kinda special at this track now—just like Glenn was. So—you drink Bud?" He shook his head sadly. "Not much imagination."

"I make my living with my imagination. But there's just not much diversity in the Northcoast Downs beer locker." I lowered my voice a little. "They *do* carry Armagnac—but you know that."

"I don't drink Armagnac."

"I guess nobody drinks it around here anymore. Isn't that so?"

"I don't know. Come on," he said, taking my elbow and leading me the length of the barn again, past where Jobie Dash watched us as he shoveled horse dung into one pile in the stall. Then we stepped out into the cool, bracing wind of night.

CHAPTER TWENTY-FOUR

K.O.

Jake Foote looked every bit like what he was—a plainclothes cop with the Painesville police department for more than thirty years. Foote worked hard at his job, at knocking over criminals, and making the world a better place to live. A bit over six feet, iron-gray hair in a buzz-cut with a trimmed mustache to go with it, dark-blue eyes, a solid build weighing only about ten pounds more than it should, and size 12½ feet encased in shiny black cowboy boots, he wasn't a cop anyone would mess with. One look at the flattened knuckles of his right hand was a good suggestion to surrender and go quietly. He didn't look that fearsome, however, munching down an early-evening pepperoni, sausage, green pepper, and onion pizza slice in K.O.'s small, cozy living room, washing it down with a Sam Adams, and regarding Carli Wysocki, cuddled up next to K.O., with avuncular admiration.

She was in her usual outfit when not selling expensive cosmetics in Beachwood—jeans and a sweater. Her short, dark hair always looked as though she combed it with her fingers, which made her look that much more adorable to K.O. Jake Foote, however, studied her carefully, the way longtime cops studied everything.

Finally he said, "You're a one-of-a-kind lady, Carli. Do you know that?

"Why? Because I did such a great job ordering pizza over the phone?"

"Because I never knew K.O. to go out more than twice with any woman in his whole life."

"You don't *know* about my whole life, Jake," K.O. protested. He was on the rump-sprung sofa with Carli, Rodney draped across the back of it, his body close to K.O.'s head, his contented purring audible clear across the room.

"That's what *you* think, buddy—unless you went desert-nutso over in Afghanistan and fell in love with the beautiful daughter of one of those war lords. But I guarantee none of them were even close to being as pretty as Carli."

K.O. toasted his thanks with a bottle of beer, and Carli tried not to blush. "You want me to leave the room so you can talk about me, Sergeant?"

"I've got no trouble doing it in front of you. K.O.'s one of my guys—somebody I keep track of ever since I met him nearly ten years ago."

"You arrested him."

Jake looked at K.O. approvingly. "You told her all about your past?"

"I said I was the illegitimate son of the king of Belgium," K.O. said, "but she wouldn't buy it—so I just told her the truth."

"You've always been a lousy liar," Jake said. "You should quit that altogether." He patted his lips with a paper napkin. "So you two are thinking about cohabiting, huh?"

"Thinking about it," K.O. said.

"I've got two bedrooms in my place," Carli said, "and I only sleep in one. Kevin can use the other one as his office. There's a pretty big closet in there for him, too."

Jake nodded. "Every private eye wanna-be needs his own office. How long have you two been dating, anyway?"

K.O. said, "Three months. *Almost* three months."

Jake sighed. "I guess that's plenty long enough—if you really have feelings for each other."

K.O. and Carli traded looks; Carli smiled, but K.O. was deadly serious. "That's pretty obvious."

"So why don't you just get married?"

There ensued absolute silence in the room, as if someone had loudly passed gas in church. Both young people were busy memorizing their shoes. Finally Jake offered, "Did I say something wrong?"

Carli said quietly, "We're not quite ready for that, yet."

K.O. didn't say anything.

"Sorry I shot my mouth off," Jake said. "I've been divorced way longer than I was married. Don't pay any attention to advice about marriage from me."

"It's okay, sergeant," Carli said. "I won't be a cosmetics clerk all my life. I want to get into public relations—maybe on the political side of it. I've got my degree in communications, and I've submitted a lot of applications. The economy's still shaky, so lots of locals aren't doing that much hiring. But I wouldn't want to get married until I had a good, solid career."

"Where'd you get your degree, Carli?"

"Kent State."

K.O. turned his head away and murmured, "Just like Milan."

"Sounds good," Jake Foote said. "Not much P.R. job activity in Lake County—but something in Cleveland'll happen for you pretty soon," and he crossed his fingers, "with any luck. Meantime, if K.O. wants to live with you, I'll kick in my pick-up truck to help him move."

Jake left half an hour later. Carli carried the empty beer bottles into the kitchen and put them in the garbage while K.O. demolished the large, now-empty pizza box. Neither spoke for a while until K.O. rinsed his hands in the kitchen sink.

"I didn't know you were a college graduate," he said sullenly, "until just this minute."

Carli shrugged. "I thought I'd mentioned it. We've only been together a few months, Kevin. We haven't shared with each other every single thing that happened in our lives up until five seconds ago."

"I didn't go to college."

"I know."

"I went right from juvie into the military—and they had my ass in Iraq before I could turn around. After that, they sent me directly to Afghanistan. I couldn't have gone to college if I wanted to." Pain throbbed at him behind his eyes. "You're about ten times smarter than I am."

"That's not even partly true! I know geology and calculus better than you—which I'll never use again in my life. But you're a really sharp, smart man. You've got street smarts."

He waved away the thought, went back into the living room and slumped down on the sofa again. Rodney awoke from his nap—cats spend three-quarters of the time napping—and crawled down over K.O.'s shoulder to nestle in his lap, rewarding him with a loud, mellow purr and begging for a scratch under his chin. "What street smarts? I'm just Milan's errand boy."

"He doesn't send you on errands. You learn from him every day; you even tell me so." Carli emerged from the kitchen and sat down next to K.O., reaching over and tickling Rodney's neck. "You can't do that kind of job on your own unless you learn. Milan's being very patient with you, and you're every bit as smart as he is in a lot of ways. You helped him a lot—just today."

"How you figure that?"

Carli dropped her hand from tickling Rodney and placed it on K.O.'s thigh. "Think about it, Kevin. Milan wanted the results of that Gecko guy's post-mortem, and he couldn't get it from the Summit County Sheriff's office. Neither could Tobe because they didn't like her. So Milan gave up on it—but *you? You* called Jake Foote and asked *him* to get the autopsy report. And he got it—which proves it was murder! You passed it along to Milan, and he's probably at the racetrack right now looking into it further. That makes you pretty damn smart."

K.O. sulked, unwilling to admit it. "Well, *you're* smarter than me. You learned more than I'll ever know if I live to be a hundred." He ran his free hand through his hair, but he didn't tamp it down as he wanted to—he made it more messy. "Why do you stick with me? You got a whole future ahead of you. I'll just slow you down."

"You won't slow me down, silly! Think about it for a minute. All the time we've been together—have I been the one who's in charge?"

"Not exactly—"

"'Not exactly' is right. We decide on things together. Nobody bosses the other one around; I couldn't live that way if we did."

K.O. just stroked Rodney gently; the cat closed his eyes in enjoyment and peace.

Carli moved closer to him. "What's upsetting you?"

"I guess," K.O. said, "I'm weirded out that you never told me about going to college before." He looked down at Rodney, not really seeing him at all. "All those smart college guys you must've dated . . ."

She frowned. "That sounds slutty."

"I didn't mean it like that."

"It sounded like it. I've been with you—solidly and faithfully—since the moment we met, which ought to tell you something. I asked you to move in with me, and not because I wanted you to pay half my apartment rent, but because I wanted to be with you all the time."

"When Jake suggested we get married, you said we weren't ready for that."

"Well, we're *not* ready for marriage. I don't know about you, but I believe those vows about 'til death us do part. However—we *are* ready to take it to the next level—at least *I'm* ready." Her wan smile didn't cheer K.O. very much. "And by the way, we aren't ready because you haven't asked me. That's the man's job. I'm a pretty modern gal, but I'm not into Sadie Hawkins Day."

"Who's Sadie Hawkins?"

"You've got Google on your laptop; look it up."

K.O. threw his hands up in frustration. "See what I mean? I'm stupid."

She dropped her head for a moment. Then she stood up. "Right. If you find out who Sadie Hawkins is, you'll be the smartest guy in the world. So I'll go on home and give you time to bone up on it."

She kissed him atop his head—hardly passionate. Then she bent lower and kissed Rodney goodnight as well.

After she had shrugged on her jacket and the door had closed behind her, K.O. sat there for several minutes. He *did* feel stupid; mortified. Why hadn't she told him before that she was a college grad; that she wanted more from her life than being a store clerk; that she knew all about the high-flying business of publicity, promotion, public relations?

Then again, when *should* she have told him? The day they'd
met at the cosmetics shop where she worked? When he'd first
asked her for a date? Their first meal together? The first time
they made love? The ninth time? The seventeenth? He stood up,
nearly dumping Rodney onto the floor, and stalked around his
apartment for a while, rubbing his eyes, shaking his head, wondering whether it were physically possible to kick himself in the
ass.

CHAPTER TWENTY-FIVE

MILAN

There was a nearly full moon hovering over Northcoast Downs, appearing like a tease and then disappearing again as it danced in and out between the lightweight clouds. In the area outside the barns, there was plenty of illumination. But the further away we got, the darker it became. Darkness was spooky, some claim, although the last time I thought anything was spooky, it was at a movie theater and actress Linda Blair was turning her head around one hundred eighty degrees and spitting up pea soup.

Walt Holman had assured me the walk would warm me up, but he was taking unhurried, deliberate steps beside me, and I slowed to his pace, which didn't generate much inner heat.

"You're not driving a race tonight?" I said.

"Nope. I wasn't 'up' to climbing into my colors. I'm too busy with other things right now. Not that I'm too old, mind you—active drivers in their seventies race at this park all the time. It's not like playing basketball, y' know. It don't matter if the knees go."

"Too busy because now you own an entire barn full of racing horses."

Holman nodded his head slowly. "That's why you're here, right? About the horses?"

"Among other things."

"*My* horses."

"They are now, aren't they?"

"Damn right. I *co*-owned horses with Glenn. Now I own all of them, outright—and all of his other horses, too."

"He was generous to you, Walt. In his will."

"I guess he was. God rest his soul."

"I'm not so sure," I said, "Glenn's soul is resting. I think his soul is pissed off to the max."

"Why?"

"Because somebody helped him cross that Rainbow Bridge before he was ready to."

Holman's sound was more of a snort. "That Rainbow Bridge business, that's just about animals. When pets die before you do, they're supposed to wait for you at the Rainbow Bridge." He wiped his mouth with the back of his hand. "I don't believe in any of that. When you die, you die. There's no Rainbow Bridge." He reached inside his jacket and pulled out a small silver flask. "Drink?"

I shook my head. He unscrewed the top, put the flask to his lips, and threw his head back. It was a long drink, and when he came up for air I could see that his face had grown red, even in the darkness.

"I'm not religious either, Walt. But Glenn's soul is stalking around up there—or down there, wherever he is—because somebody killed him."

He shook his head almost violently from side to side, as if he'd heard something obscene. "Nobody killed him. He had a heart attack. You *know* it was; he kicked off right in front of you."

"It *looked* like a heart attack."

"You're no doctor," he scoffed.

"No—but I'm a puzzle-solver."

"Crossword puzzles?"

"No. I like the jigsaw puzzles better."

Holman rubbed his hands together as we walked. "Never got into puzzles—all those little pieces."

"There's nothing as exciting as those little pieces finally fitting together to make the whole picture."

He veered a little bit to his right so we were walking away from the crowded stands and the horses entering and exiting the track, leaving the well-lighted area and heading in the direction of the exercise wheel, now deserted.

"I'm thinking," Walt Holman said, "you came here tonight to bust me or something."

I didn't answer; just waited for him to talk when he felt like it. He ran his hand over his face, brushing away cobwebs that weren't there. "You never got rich being a private dick, did you?"

"It's a living."

"Do a lot of Slovaks do what you do?"

I sighed. "It amazes me that so many people from Cleveland don't know the difference between Slovaks and Slovenians."

"I'm not a Clevelander," Holman said. "Not by birth, anyway. I grew up in Kentucky. But I know what you're saying. My training other people's horses, *that's* not getting rich."

"Glenn was rich."

"He was a jealous motherfucker, too. He didn't like anybody else being rich. He hated Chloe Markham—never said a good word about her because she inherited this whole place, which made her richer than him. Now she'll turn it into a Vegas-style casino and make even *more* money."

"Are you saying Chloe Markham killed Gallagher?"

"You're the detective," Holman said, "not me."

"I wonder how she did that—cause him to have a fatal heart attack."

"Maybe she just hollered 'Boo!' Or maybe she slipped into the kitchen of the clubhouse when nobody was looking and poisoned his filet mignon."

"Or maybe," I said, "she slipped something into his drink at the bar."

The bones at each side of his lower jaw jumped beneath his skin. "Interesting. Those little jigsaw pieces fitting together, eh?"

"Not quite."

"Why not?"

"What would Chloe be doing behind the bar?"

"She owns this track," Holman said. "She can go anywhere she wants."

"Not behind the bar. Trenda would have remembered that because Chloe's never even talked to her. She'd know whether Chloe marched her ass behind the bar, opened Gallagher's favorite bottle of Armagnac, and slipped something into it."

We'd arrived just outside the exercise wheel, and Holman stopped. The bourbon on his breath made me almost dizzy. "Poison? He didn't die of poison."

"No—from a massive overdose of digitalis."

He was two steps behind me, and I must have surprised him because I heard his quick intake of breath.

"I doubt Chloe Markham knows anything about digitalis," I continued. "But you're a horse trainer, Walt. You know what digitalis can do to a horse—and to a human being. An overdose for someone with a heart condition who takes digitalis regularly can kill him. Like *that!*" And I snapped my fingers.

He said, "You can't just get digitalis off the shelf at Drug Mart. You need a prescription."

"Not if you can steal it. You hang around Dr. Sheila McHale's truck when she comes around every morning—she doesn't count her medications every day like a regular hospital does. What would it take for you to pocket a little bit until you had enough to pour into Gallagher's bottle of Armagnac? Nobody else wants Armagnac at the track; hardly anybody knows what it *is*. But you walk behind the bar several times an evening to pour your bourbon and nobody notices that, so who could tell if you were doping Gallagher's drink of choice?"

"Why would I do that?"

"To inherit all his racetrack holdings—maybe at least a million bucks for you."

"How the hell would I know about that? I didn't think he'd leave me anything at all, except maybe the six horses I co-owned with him."

"Maybe you don't know about your bank account, either. It was checked today. I don't have the exact amount in my head, but it's written down in my office. A big, *big* deposit from about two weeks ago—more than you've ever had before in your life. You also said you'd buy me a drink at the bar, but you've got a flask in your pocket; you weren't planning on visiting the bar at all tonight."

"Keeping track of me, eh? Well, go fuck yourself," he said.

"There's more, though, Walt. There's Gecko. He wasn't the smartest guy in the world, and he was drunk most of the time when he wasn't getting serviced by his skanky hooker girlfriend—but he was sober enough mornings to notice you palming digitalis from the vet's truck. The poor bastard was always a few sandwiches short of a picnic, so when Gallagher died, he confronted you with it instead of telling a cop—and you put him off for a while, hoping he'd forget about it."

"Like elephants," Holman said, "fat, sloppy drunks never forget, either."

"Then," I said, "when he showed up blotto in the middle of the night, you crushed in the back of his head with something—maybe a shovel your guys use to clean out the horses' stalls—and then you tossed him into the therapy pool and held him down until he stopped breathing." I waited for him to answer, but he didn't. I said, "How'm I doing so far, Walt?"

"Just dandy," Walt Holman said. Then, faster than I dreamed he'd be, his leathery fist struck me as hard as I've ever been hit, just below my left ear.

I staggered forward a few steps, trying to keep my balance—but the strength of the punch combined with the surprise didn't help me a bit. I went down on my hands and knees, and when I raised my head, he hit me again, even harder.

Pain clouded my thinking. My vision started to go dark as when a light bulb—the old-fashioned kind—would flicker and announce it was ready to go out. As I felt myself falling forward into unconsciousness, my last thought—the only one I remember—was "Damn! *Another* concussion!"

CHAPTER TWENTY-SIX

K.O.

K.O. had finished washing the dishes, stacking them in the drainer rather than drying them and putting them away; drying was a waste of time, anyway. Besides, he wasn't expecting more company who might look askance at drying dishes before he'd be able to put them away the next morning.

Was he ever going to have company again?

He'd blown it; he knew he'd done so. He'd learned many things in his short life, but keeping his mouth shut when he should wasn't one of them. It had shaken him down to his toes to learn that Carli Wysocki was a college graduate and had her heart set on a sophisticated job in public relations, while he had only gotten through high school correspondence courses in juvenile detention.

Damn! he thought. Carli didn't make him feel stupid—the perception of stupidity was his alone and he felt helpless to do anything about it. So he'd switched the guilt from himself onto the woman he loved—and now here he was, at eight o'clock in the evening, washing dishes by himself and wishing he could invent a time machine that would immediately transport him back to five o'clock before that conversation had occurred.

His eye found the calendar tacked up on the face of one of his kitchen cabinets. It was almost Halloween—time for the rug rats to circulate the neighborhood with implied revenge for the lack of ransom. He almost smiled. That's what "trick-or-treat" used to be; a threat. I'll trick you unless you give me a treat.

When his phone rang—he'd never programmed it to sound like

some rock band or Beethoven; it was just the ring of a phone—he stumbled over himself to answer it, needing to locate it first. He didn't own a land line because he hardly knew anyone who would call him at home; the few people in his life, like Milan and Jake Foote and Suzanne Davis, always rang his cell—and when he was home he didn't have a specific place where he kept it.

His hand hovered over the phone still in the pocket of his jacket. Was it Carli? Was she calling to patch things up? The horror of this might be a bye-bye-and-come-get-your-toothbrush-and-the-extra-pair-of-underwear-you-left-in-my-top-dresser-drawer call. He could barely breathe because of the sudden tightness in his gut. Was that TV commercial of an elephant sitting on someone's chest real life?

"K.O.," he said when he lifted the phone to his ear.

"Hey—glad I caught you. It's Cullen Gallagher."

"Oh." Disappointed, naturally—and puzzled.

"I tried calling your office even though I know you aren't there evenings. I rang Milan on his cell a few times, but didn't get an answer. So you're next on the list."

"What can I do for you, Cullen? It's after hours."

"You remember my telling you that a few years ago my father gave me a copy of his will but that I'd never read it? Never opened it? Well—I *did* open it. Just tonight. I'd almost forgotten that he'd given it to me, but I found it—and opened it. It's nowhere near the same will that got read to me."

"How do you mean?"

"In the will I have, he left twenty-four percent more of his investment firm to Jen Taylor. He left the other fifty-one percent to me."

"Wow."

"The horses he co-owned with Holman? He left all those horses to him, but the rest of the horses he owned then, or if he acquired more in the future—he left those to me, too. And he left me the house."

"I see."

"You know what else?"

"It's too late in the day for guessing, Cullen."

"The power of attorney? The control of everything that he

owned when he died? Well, he named *me* power of attorney. Not David Weaver. *Me.*"

"That gives you a hell of a lot of power. When," K.O. wanted to know, "was this will dated?"

He heard paper rustling on the other end. "The ninth day of June, 2010."

K.O. reached for a pen and pad. "And the date on the will Weaver read?"

More rustling. "The seventeenth of November, 2011."

"Things can happen in a short space of time like that—and people have been known to change their wills. It seems like your father changed his."

"Why would he do that to his own son? We always got along pretty well—not really close, but other than my mother, whom I don't see more than once a year, if that, he was the only family I had."

"I understand."

"*You* understand? You don't understand a goddamn thing."

"I understand he changed his will and kind of left you on the outside."

"Yes—but *why*?"

"Your voice is up there where only dogs can hear it," K.O. said. "Take a nice deep breath. Loosen up the muscles in your neck and shoulders. Just relax—and think it over. You'd know better than anyone why your dad might have changed his will."

"That's the thing. There was no reason to. We'd never had a fight or an argument or anything. Maybe about politics—I *teach* political science—but there wasn't any real problem between us."

K.O. mulled that over. "Not enough, I wouldn't think, to make him change his will."

Cullen Gallagher's voice became a whine. "How can we find out why?"

"That'd take an incredible amount of research and investigation—with no guarantee we'd ever find an answer."

"I'll pay for it."

"I'm just an employee. I don't make decisions like that. It'd be up to Milan."

"That's why I called him in the first place! Jesus, who ignores their cell phone? Is he working on another case, too?"

"Not that I know about."

"Is there another number where I can reach him?"

K.O. would have jumped out the window before he passed out Tobe Blaine's phone number. "I'd try to find him for you, Cullen, but there's not much anyone can do about your father's last will and testament at nine o'clock at night. He'll be in touch with you first thing in the morning."

Cullen's sigh roared through the telephone like a typhoon. "I'm sorry I bothered you," he said at last. "You have no idea how upset I am about this."

K.O. considered the millions of Glenn Gallagher's estate at stake. "Yes, I do," he said.

After the hang-up, he thought about that will some more. Then he opened another beer and punched out Milan's cell number. He got the pleasant automated response and the instruction to leave a message. He didn't; there would be no point.

Milan had told him—several times—that he hated the idea of cell phones, but times had blown right past him in changing so he'd been forced to carry one. He still didn't like it—but why would he actually not answer it?

Sipping his beer, he reluctantly called Tobe—reluctant because Milan might actually *be* there, and the two of them might be—otherwise engaged? He shook his head in frustration; why did *he* get all the hard stuff to do?

"No, he's not here," Tobe told him. "We don't spend every evening together, K.O. We both have lives. So I'm all by myself, listening to music on my iPad and reading a book."

"Do you have any idea where Milan went tonight?"

"He doesn't always check in with me before he does something," Tobe said, "but he did say he was planning to drop by the racetrack again. I'm a Cleveland cop; I can't go out there storming around and asking people questions. The racetrack isn't my bailiwick."

K.O. scratched *bailiwick* on his pad so he could look it up later and discover its definition. In the meantime, Tobe's tone changed; it wasn't worrisome, exactly, but it was a far cry from being light-hearted. "That's not like him."

"He always answers his phone. It could be business. It could be his kids. It could be an emergency."

Nervously K.O. nibbled on a loose piece of skin at the side of his thumb, realizing that had always been a habit of his—like Milan's habit from childhood of doodling on his yellow pad a gallows and an empty rope. He took his hand away from his mouth, almost angry. "Are you going over there now to see if you can find him, Tobe?"

"I want to—but I really can't. I have rules."

"Well," K.O. said, pushing the beer bottle away from himself and looking around to see where he'd tossed his jacket, "I don't."

CHAPTER TWENTY-SEVEN

MILAN

E ven before the thumping pain in my head announced itself to me while my eyes were still closed, I noticed the smells, the strongest one being horse and dirt, in which my face now rested. It reminded me where I was; whatever concussion I'd suffered had momentarily wiped from my mind Northcoast Downs and all that went with it. In the distance the crowd mumbled; there was no race at that moment so everyone was discussing their loss on the last one or their pick on the next one. I could have exploded and no one would have noticed.

The stink of rubber, too—strong, irritating, making my nose tingle, mixed in with horse scent. Only half conscious, I tried to put the two smells together so I could figure out where I was.

I smelled something else, and tasted it as well. Alcohol. Residue of whiskey loitered in my mouth, as well as saturated my shirt and jacket.

Not much of a drinker of hard stuff, it took me a while to recognize it as some sort of bourbon. I smelled of it, but I guess I didn't enjoy drinking it.

Strange thoughts when you're transitioning from stone-cold unconscious to waking up slowly and painfully. I tried to focus my eyes, but they weren't quite working. Whatever I saw seemed as though it were on an old-time TV screen where the pictures looked double and out-of-focus. When I raised my head and looked around, I realized I was in a horse-sized compartment of the exercise wheel, on the far side of the carousel-like contraption where no one was likely to see me, especially since there were no lights around, and only a sixty-watt bulb inside the hut where the controls are. Horses trotted around in this thing every day to get a bit warmed up—the rubber smell was the ground-up tires mixed in with dirt to go easy on horses' hooves.

It was nighttime. The horses competing in the current races wouldn't be here, and the ones not scheduled were resting. I sneaked a peek at my wristwatch; again, I couldn't see it very well, but it looked to me as if it were somewhere around a quarter past nine.

It took a few moments more to realize who dumped me in here; Walt Holman had knocked me cold in the first place, and almost as big as me, he was able to haul me around wherever he wanted. He knew I'd spotted him for killing Glenn Gallagher and probably for drowning Gecko, too, and he wanted to be rid of me, get me out of his way before I turned him over to the police. But I didn't comprehend why he didn't finish me off when he had the chance, why he'd "stored" me someplace where no one might find me until morning.

I managed to raise myself up on my hands and knees, squeezing my eyes shut and then opening them again in hope that I'd stop seeing double anymore. No such luck.

I reached over to the wooden side railing with one hand and hauled myself to my feet, but I was not yet in shape to do much besides stand there, swaying, unable to make my feet move. Some tiny person with an enormous sledgehammer was hiding inside my head and playing a tympani roll behind my eyes. Dizziness stole away my breath, and I hung my head low on my chest until I got myself together. I'd suffered a concussion—I couldn't count how many others I'd suffered in my lifetime.

I don't know how long I stood there clutching the side of the enclosure—probably less than a minute, but my perception of time passing seemed much longer. The race-watchers were making noise now, sounding as if it were coming from an old radio that had been locked in the bottom of a closet beneath a stack of blankets—far away and indistinct.

Finally I dared a look around. I had no idea how to get out

of there. I'd never even seen the exercise wheel before; I'd only heard about it from K.O.

Then some machinery kicked on, but I couldn't discern what it was. The sides of the enclosure seemed to come alive. Dizzy again, I stood planted there until something hard hit me in the back and shoulders from behind and knocked me flat on my face again.

The exercise wheel was moving!

Within a few seconds another slab of rubber passed over me, and I knew that if I tried to rise I'd be clobbered again by the metal separation of the compartments. The second jolt made things more clear. Someone was inside the little shed from which the exercise wheel was operated—and had turned it on. Part of the steel enclosure passed over me, then disappeared, and another took its place. The wheel turned faster; any horse inside would be forced into a canter. I flattened myself against the earth, my nose burrowing into the dirt as the machine whirled over me. If I raised my head even slightly, the damn thing would knock my brains out.

The heavy rubber clawing across my back every few seconds was rubbing me raw. I couldn't just lie there forever. Before the unseen operator in the shed kicked it up to maximum speed, I had to take a desperate chance.

I jumped to my feet, head pounding, and started running as fast as I could. I made it about eight steps before I got slammed again across the shoulders and fell on my face.

Lying there being flogged by the rubber sheets, I realized I couldn't possibly stand up and run fast enough to outpace the exercise wheel. It was for racehorses who move at a breathtaking pace—not for a sixty-year-old man with a brand-new concussion.

I've been in many tight spots during my career and had managed to fight my way out of all of them. But I never had to battle a huge machine before, especially one knocking hell out of me. I just couldn't lie there all night being raked over by sheets of stiff rubber; I had to get out of there.

It took me about a minute to come up with a plan, and it was a lousy one—but under the circumstances, it was just about all I had.

I wriggled my body around, absorbing more blows, until I

was facing backward instead of frontward, which didn't help my health at all, as now the rubber was striking my head instead of my back. It had been installed so if a horse wasn't moving quickly enough for its exercise, it wouldn't be hurt by the rubber. Then again, I'm a lot smaller than a horse.

I took another thirty seconds to get my breath under control, and then, timing it as well as I could, I raised myself up and grabbed hold of the oncoming rubber sheet. Hanging on for dear life, I had no choice but to let it drag me along with it, scraping my heels along the ground, even ripping off both my shoes as I took at least two full circle trips around the wheel.

Finally I was able to claw my way up, so I hung by my hands on the metal wall of the compartment. After a few more turns I pulled myself higher so my feet were encountering metal, too; now I was on an amusement park ride, holding on for dear life— but there was nothing amusing about it.

Whirling around the wheel, I had a better chance of scoping out the situation, and from my lofty viewpoint, it didn't look good. There was no way of getting out of my twenty-by-ten compartment while it was moving. There was a wide opening between the top of the wooden sides and the roof of the wheel enclosure, but I couldn't move nearly fast enough to haul my aging and now-sore and bruised bones out.

As I whizzed by the shed I craned my neck, trying to see who was inside, who was torturing me, but the wheel raced too swiftly, probably at around thirty miles an hour, so all I could see—or at least *thought* I saw—were two figures, little more than silhouettes. I couldn't recognize them.

Every muscle in my body ached and throbbed. I didn't have much time left to remain hanging onto the back wall of the compartment before weakness would overtake me; I'd let go, fall, and be crushed, if not beheaded, by the fast-moving steel fence-wall I clutched—rubber-covered or not.

You read in books that when a person is dying, his whole life flashes before his eyes. It's not true at all. It's a corny faux-literary conceit. Near to letting go, I wasn't watching a speeded-up movie of my life. I just felt frustrated, stupid, and sorely lacking a better plan. I shouldn't have come backside alone at Northcoast Downs to confront Walt Holman. I should have brought K.O. with me or even gotten in touch with the Summit County Sheriff's Department on the off-chance Deputy Keith Johnson—Keith *Barent* Johnson—wouldn't laugh in my face and slam the phone down in my ear.

I should have brought my 9 mm Glock with me, too.

Just when I was ready to give up the ghost—under those circumstances a very disturbing cliché, by the way—the noise of the machine changed, and I felt the wheel slowing down. I waited until it stopped completely before I released my shaking hands from the metal fence and dropped heavily to the ground. The fall knocked the wind out of me—whatever was left—and I allowed myself as long as it took to slowly fill up my lungs again. Then, awkwardly scrabbling for a handhold on the wooden side of the enclosure, I hauled myself to my feet.

I'd wound up on the far side of the wheel, remote from the control shack. But eventually I saw a figure walk out and into the darkness. Finally, he caught sight of me.

"Hey," he called. "You all right?"

I tried to yell back, but I couldn't. Instead I answered with a weak wave.

"Climb out through the top there," he hollered again, returning my wave. "You'll be okay now."

I leaned back against the wood, closing my eyes until the pain in my head subsided. It didn't. Clambering up the side of the enclosure and squeezing my large body out through an opening ten feet above the ground seemed an impossible task. When I walked back around to the shack, the first thing I saw was Walt Holman, sitting silently on the floor just below the control panel, bleeding from two broken teeth in the front of his mouth.

Jobie Dash met me halfway and was supporting me as I staggered. I looked from him to Holman and then back again.

"Nice going," I said.

"You, too. I thought you'd be a goner before I got the wheel turned off. What you did in there—man, that was almost impossible."

What would *anyone* do when challenged by the impossible? Just what I did.

I went to sleep.

CHAPTER TWENTY-EIGHT

MILAN

The hospital didn't release me with a smile; when you're an overnight "guest" there and you're sick, they actually enjoy being in control. K.O. had arrived first thing in the morning with clothes he'd picked up from my apartment—even shoes, which most people would have forgotten. He'd also fed and taken Booger for an early-morning walk, cruising Devonshire Boulevard where the historical old Alcazar Hotel stands. K.O. is such an animal lover that, if he hadn't had Rodney as his roommate, he would have taken care of Booger, whether I'd asked him to or not. I'd been ruminating about how much actual work keeping a dog might entail—and about permanently sharing my home and hearth with a creature named Booger.

I'd informed my night nurse, who was funny and pleasant and never forgot to plump my pillow even when she was sticking a thermometer in my ear, and who was a lot more fun than the overworked and curt day nurse, that I was checking out whether they liked it or not. We negotiated; she couldn't find my personal doctor, but eventually tracked down another one who spoke with a heavy accent I couldn't identify. We finally agreed that if I signed a form that gives me full responsibility for myself from the moment I stepped outside the hospital, he'd let me go—but he insisted that I wait to be trundled downstairs in a wheelchair. The way I was feeling at that moment, the wheelchair ride sounded like heaven.

My protégé talked to me as I squeezed my pain-wracked body

into my clothes. Just bending over to pull on my socks was a particular torture to the small of my back—but I'd have chosen a quick death over asking anyone to help me put on my own socks. Pride, you know.

K.O. was lugging around a ton of his own self-inflicted injured pride, and he wanted me to know about it.

"You can't depend on me, man," he said. "I screwed up, major league! I left you in the lurch last night and you nearly got killed."

"You didn't leave me anywhere, K.O. I can't expect you to figure out where I am every minute of my life by reading tea leaves or something."

He looked confused. "Tea leaves? I thought all tea comes in little bags."

"I'll explain to you about tea some other time."

"Better explain it to Jobie Dash instead. It was him who saved you, Milan—not me—and all he does for a living is shovel horse shit. Even Jobie's smarter than I am. You and Carli have a truckload of degrees between you, but I barely got out of high school—and *that* school was behind bars!"

I was sitting on the bed, one shoe on my foot and the other in my hand, wondering if the pulled muscles in my lower back would torture me again if I attempted to force my foot into that shoe. This wasn't the conversation I'd planned, as K.O. and I had a few more things to do to close out the Gallagher-Gecko case.

Still—one dare not ignore sudden opportunities that might never arise again. So . . .

"K.O.," I said, "I've never had a full-time employee in my life until you came along. If you weren't smart, I'd have said goodbye to you after our first case. You remember that one? The one where you saved my life out on the sand bar in Conneaut? Yeah—*that* one. So I hardly think you're stupid—but I *do* think right now you're being a dumb ass. There's a difference. And as for Carli—if she didn't think you were a terrific guy, she wouldn't hang around with you for ten minutes. Don't you know how crazy she is about you? She looks at you like you're a Greek god."

K.O. blushed in spite of himself. "I'm not exactly a Greek god, Milan."

"I don't think so, either, but Carli does—whatever that means

with you twenty-somethings today. Get real, K.O. or get left behind—in love, in business, and in life."

"But . . ."

"You want college? Good, start slow. Enroll in a class that in-
terests you and helps your career—even the career you're dream-
ing about. You don't necessarily need a four-year degree unless
you really want one."

He shook his head almost violently. "Going to college costs a
fortune."

"I can kick in a few bucks at the start. If you like it, maybe I can
pull some strings and get you a partial scholarship. And college
loans."

"I'll be dead before I can pay off college loans."

"You might make a damn good living and you can pay those
off, easy. Or maybe you'll win big on the Ohio lottery."

"In a horse's ass!" K.O. said.

I couldn't repress a shudder. "Under the circumstances," I said,
memory kicking back about twelve hours, "let's not talk about
horses' asses."

The autumn sun glowed by the time I left the hospital. K.O.
drove me directly to Summit County Sheriff's Headquarters.
Deputy Johnson was there, and he began our conversation by
talking tough—until I congratulated him for making a major
homicide pinch all by himself and getting Walt Holman behind
bars. I knew he wouldn't parse that too closely—and I was right;
he loved the idea of having his name all over that bust, and he
suddenly became my best friend. He offered us coffee, and when
I declined—and there wasn't a teabag in the entire building—he
ordered one of his less-experienced deputies to run across the
street to the coffee shop and get me a large orange juice.

Holman, in the meantime, was wailing like a banshee to get
out of his holding cell; I heard him from all the way downstairs
in the lock-up. Since landing in custody, he'd been demanding
the right to place his one phone call, which he finally made to his
lawyer at ten o'clock that morning.

I was delighted to find that out. The previous evening's concussion might have temporarily scrambled my brains, but the
name of Holman's lawyer reminded me what I needed to do next.

*   *   *

We picked up Tobe at the Justice Center downtown. I'd called her half an hour earlier and she agreed to join us; I didn't know how she got away with leaving her job whenever she felt like it. Maybe she had an understanding with Lieutenant Florence McHargue, her immediate supervisor, but I had no idea what it was. McHargue and I have known each other a dozen years, locking horns more than once. I wondered how she felt about my relationship with Tobe—*her* cop. It doesn't bother *me* a nickel's worth, nor Tobe, either. Not much bothers her; that's what makes her a good cop.

Arriving in Solon, I wasn't sure if the woman whose desk was closest to the front door of the building was a receptionist or not; she wasn't the high-style type one notices at front desks in high-end law firms downtown. She was decked out in a long-sleeved, faded denim shirt and a pair of cargo pants I'm certain she'd worn that morning for pulling weeds in her garden.

But this, after all, was Solon.

In any event, she looked up from what she was doing—a Sudoko puzzle?—but said nothing as we marched past her—perhaps because Tobe flashed her badge. Garden clothes or no, she knew a cop when she saw one.

Weaver's face, when we sidled into his cubicle, expressed his wish that he were senior partner at a top-rung firm in Tower City and that someone would have backed us away as soon as we stepped off the elevator. Not that anyone could back off Tobe Blaine; when she wanted to go someplace, there was little anyone could do to stop her.

"You need an appointment, Jacovich," Weaver said. "And who are these people, anyway?"

Tobe showed her buzzer and introduced herself. "This is all the appointment I need, Mr. Weaver."

Weaver fiddled nervously with papers on his desk. "Homicide, eh? Well, you're in the wrong neighborhood—nobody's killed anyone."

"Not necessarily," K.O. said.

Weaver gave him the stink-eye. "Who the hell are you?"

"My associate," I said. "Mr. O'Bannion."

The lawyer didn't want to shake hands and neither did K.O. He turned on Tobe instead. "You're with the Cleveland Police Department, Sergeant. You have no jurisdiction here."

"Thank God you're a lawyer, Mr. Weaver, so you can tell me all the legalities of what I've been doing for the last twenty years."

Defiantly, he placed fists on hips—hardly resembling Errol Flynn's patented pose as Robin Hood. "All right then, state your business."

"Are you aware," I said, "that Glenn Gallagher gave Cullen a copy of his will a few years ago?"

Weaver looked shocked but soldiered on. "I had no idea."

"That will's very different from the one you read to Glenn's heirs."

He cleared his throat but only halfway. He covered his mouth with his fist and coughed out the rest of it. "People change their wills all the time. Glenn did—and, naturally, I helped him."

"Naturally—giving yourself the power of attorney, which puts you in control of just about everything Glenn Gallagher ever owned."

"That's the way he wanted it. I just wrote down what he told me."

"Why, then, since he gave Cullen a copy of his earlier will, didn't he give him this one, too?"

"I have no idea what he did or didn't do. It was none of my business."

"That's interesting," K.O. said. "No idea of what he did, but you got to look at all his bank accounts first, even before he had the chance."

"That's the way he wanted it,"

"You know what I think?" said Tobe. "Or do you want to guess?"

"I want to call my lawyer."

"You *are* a lawyer, Mr. Weaver," I said, "but if you holler loud enough, every other lawyer in the office will come running."

Tobe pointed a red-nailed finger at him the way she might aim a weapon at a shooting range. "You dicked around with Gallagher's will so you got most of it yourself. Not *all* of it—that'd raise questions. You set aside a small pittance for Glenn's son."

"Two hundred G's," K.O. mumbled.

"And the rest *you* control. Nobody else can touch a dime of it—except Walt Holman." Tobe advanced toward Weaver, who backed up until his shoulders rubbed against the side of his cubicle. "What he inherited—in *your* version of the will—is worth about a million bucks."

"A payment," I said, "for Holman to find a way to kill off Glenn Gallagher and make it look like a heart attack."

"That's a goddamn lie!" Weaver roared. His face, already pale, turned a few shades grayer as he realized everyone in the building had heard him. Then he added more softly, "I wasn't anywhere near Northcoast Downs."

"You didn't have to be. You knew about Glenn's heart condition and that he took digitalis. So you figured out how to get your hands on all his millions, didn't you? You promised Holman that if he stole some digitalis from Dr. Bunny McHale's truck and quietly slipped enough into his Armagnac behind the bar to kill him if he had three or four drinks of it, you'd make sure he got all of Gallagher's harness racing holdings—and you got the rest."

"And Gallagher *always* had three or four drinks," K.O. said. "You and Holman both knew that."

"And on that particular night," I said, "he was drinking more than usual because he wanted to talk to me about something else. And that something else was you, wasn't it, counselor?"

K.O. bored in this time, raising his voice loud enough to further shatter Weaver's composure. It's hard to shake up a lawyer, but K.O. managed. "Holman screwed up, though, didn't he? Because Gecko—what was his real name again, Milan?"

"Royal Shadcoe."

"Yeah, Royal Shadcoe. He watched Holman boost that digitalis—and during one of his few moments of relative sobriety, he confronted Holman with it. So Holman had to get rid of him, too, the only way he knew how. He waited until Gecko was swacked again, like he was every night, and he crushed in the back of his skull, threw him in the therapy pool, and held him under."

"You can't prove that!"

"Sure we can," Tobe said easily. "The med examiner found finger marks on the back of Gecko's neck. Maybe whatever lawyer comes running in here when you holler for him can demand that you get to see the post mortem report, too. But it won't matter because Holman already confessed to Milan—just before he tried to kill *him*." She snapped her fingers. "Oh, damn it! I forgot—he confessed to the Summit County sheriff, too."

Weaver's telephone rang—too loudly. Half the office had overheard our entire conversation. His face had gone from gray to as white as a marshmallow, and he stared at the instrument as if it were a blood-spattered, recently sated vulture that had flapped into his office and perched on the edge of his desk. "That's probably Holman now," I observed. "He only gets one phone call, and he's been bitching all night to ring you up to come in and lawyer for him."

"Don't bother answering," Tobe said. "You're under arrest—for committing fraud and forgery on Gallagher Investment Management, Inc. And by the way, that's located right in Cleveland—which *is* my jurisdiction. As far as double murder . . . we can nail you as an accomplice to that—easy-peasey."

"Easy-peasey?" I said.

"That's Raleigh talk," Tobe explained. She stepped closer to David Weaver and took a pair of handcuffs from her belt and jangled them in front of his nose. "Time's up, Mr. Weaver, and I have things to do. Are you ready to turn around and put your hands behind your back? Or will I have to hurt you?"

EPILOGUE

MILAN

Tobe and I decided to celebrate Halloween night together. We'd talked before about what costumes we'd choose for the occasion and finally decided we'd dress as Adam and Eve—*before* the much-talked-about apple incident and, ergo, before fig leaves. It was eleven o'clock—the kidlets dressed up as pirates and princesses and monsters and superheroes had gone home—and we were in my bed, drinking our celebratory champagne and discussing how well the Cullen Gallagher case had turned out.

The Summit County district attorney was licking her chops in anticipation of Walt Holman's trial for double murder. He was sixty-one years old; if he were convicted of both homicides—highly likely, since he repeated his confession to just about everyone who'd listen—his future looked dim and he would probably die in prison.

He'd been sitting in the sheriff's basement, howling for an attorney. David Weaver, however, would not be defending him in court, as he'd asked. The state of Ohio clamped down on his license almost at once. Weaver was being charged with fraud and forgery in Cuyahoga County—to which he'd also confessed and tried to throw himself upon the mercy of the court—and in Summit County for "conspiracy to commit murder." He hadn't admitted to *that* felony but Holman had told the D.A. all about it, so Weaver's future looked bleak. He was currently out on bond for one-tenth of a million and a half—almost all the money he had in the world, mostly stolen from Gallagher's firm. If he leaves the state, a bounty hunter would be sent after him—and bounty hunters never miss a trick or else *they* have to pay the courts the remaining ninety percent. He knows that—and since his own bank accounts have been frozen, he'll stick around Northeast Ohio as long as the courts want him to.

When it all shakes out—things like that take time as courts are even slower than the United States Congress—Glenn Gallagher's "new will" will be nullified, his original one will be deemed valid, and Cullen Gallagher will receive everything to which he was entitled, meaning he'll be an exceptionally rich man. He's planning on moving into his father's beautiful home and selling all the Gallagher horses *and* the Gallagher-Holman horses and getting out of the harness racing business once and for all. Jen Taylor, who already owned a quarter of Gallagher Investment Management Inc., would now own 49 percent of it to Cullen's 51 percent. The charities Glenn had supported—most of them animal sanctuaries—which were omitted from Weaver's forged document will once again be smiling.

Gallagher's last will and testament didn't bequeath me a damn thing—but Cullen paid up my contract and has promised Milan Security another ten thousand dollars as a bonus as soon as Weaver and Holman are locked securely away. Half of that goes to K.O. I hope he'll spend some on college studies.

Dr. Sheila McHale—"Bunny"—had her license suspended, along with her husband's. She's done nothing wrong—as far as I know—but her negligence and her husband's, allowing medications to be stolen from their truck, was inexcusable and the veterinary licensing board will be addressing that. In the meantime the McHales are volunteering at Happy Trails, the animal rescue center in Ravenna to which Glenn Gallagher had left a chunk of money, taking care of rescued horses, cows, ponies, pigs, geese, and fighting roosters.

Chloe Markham and Everett Valmer haven't put the deal together that will turn Northcoast Downs into a "racino," although Valmer works on it every day. Apparently Skip Swain is now out of Chloe's life; I'm sure he's been replaced, but no one has told me by whom. Chloe never dumps one boyfriend until she has another one warming up in the bullpen. And Skip—well, he lives on daddy's dole, so he'll wind up in someone else's bed, doing what he does best.

Manley Markham will probably drink himself either into a mandatory rehab or into the Markham mausoleum in Lake View Cemetery.

Jobie Dash, Carl Fulwood, Trenda the bartender, and Mildred the betting clerk will probably stay on at Northcoast Downs; they love their jobs, although for different reasons. Pike Sullivan will keep driving as long as he can, if only to support the women he refers to as his three wives. Jerry Nemo will always hang around the track—or another track somewhere else—trying to sell a lame or half-blind horse to the next sucker who comes along. As far as Leanne, Gecko's neighbor/hooker—I don't think she had any definite plans.

Their problem might be if Chloe *does* turn her track into something bigger and more wonderful, in which case she might abandon harness racing altogether in Greater Cleveland. That will mean all her low-level employees will drift away to other tracks and other cities, possibly because they love horses and don't want to be too far from any of them.

Del and Wanda Fiddler didn't even wait around for a disaster to happen. They just didn't show up for work one day. When someone at the track had checked, they'd packed up and moved out of their apartment nearby. Nobody knows where they've gone, but most know *why:* Del Fiddler's knee won't ever again work well. Maybe he can get it fixed, maybe not. He *can* get his jaw wired and his broken or missing teeth replaced, but it'll cost a bundle. As for Wanda, she'll be missed by the dozens of men to whom she cheerfully exposes her enhanced breasts on request—but not for very long.

Inept CPA Paul Darrie, Dr. Howard Lichtig, CEO Carol Watterson, and the strange "Merry Merry" Wane have already disappeared from my consciousness. That's the trouble with being a private investigator—many interviews and searches wind up as an exercise in futility.

Tobe and I weren't worrying about that on Halloween night; we were having too much of a good time. We each finished off what was left in our champagne glasses. "Our next drink," I said, "should be a toast to K.O. and Carli, who are moving in together this weekend." As I refilled, I said, "Think it's the beginning of their 'forever'?"

"Who knows? I sure don't."

I took great care with my next question. "Have you ever lived with someone?"

Tobe shook her head. "College roommates. But that doesn't count, does it? So the answer is no."

"Ever think about it?"

She leaned up on one elbow. "Are you hitting on me?"

"I already hit on you. We're in bed together and we're naked— or aren't you paying attention?"

"I meant hitting on me to move in with you—or you move in with me."

"I've thought about it—since K.O. and Carli are doing it."

"First of all," Tobe said, "there's a city rule: Cleveland Police Department officers have to live in Cleveland. You live in Cleveland Heights, Milan—different mayor, different P.D., different taxes—the works. So I couldn't move in here if I wanted to—not and keep my job, too. And you've seen my apartment; it's on the near west side, it's nice, but it's too small for more than one person. So if we *did* move in together, we'd have to find a new place."

"Well," I said . . .

"I just moved into mine. I'm liking it. And you—you've lived here for how long, now?"

"For about a third of my life."

"So there you go." I started to say something, but she put a hand on my lips. "You've lived alone for a long time—and I've been alone my entire life. I don't even know if I'd adjust to a roommate."

"Is that what we'd be? Roommates?"

"Roommates with privileges. I wouldn't dream of giving up the privileges, Milan." She threw an arm around my neck and nuzzled in my shoulder. "But I'm single, always been single, in my late forties, and not ready to change. We'd shoot each other after two weeks. We both need our alone time."

"Why shoot each other? Do I aggravate you?"

"Sometimes. And I know I irritate you sometimes, too. That's what people do with each other when they're close—all people."

"Name one thing I do that aggravates you," I said.

"Too many to mention in one evening. Maybe I'll write a book about it." She nibbled on my earlobe and then moved her mouth down to kiss my neck.

Very nice—until she lifted her head up and sniffed the air.

"My God!" she said.

"What?"

"Now *that* irritates me! And you've never done it before. You know how sensitive my nose is! Hyperosmia, remember?" She glared at me. "Gross! Men usually don't fart in bed with a woman unless they've been married a hell of a long time."

"I didn't do anything!"

"Trust me, I can smell it."

"So can I," I said. "But it wasn't me. We have another room-mate, now."

"We *do?*" Tobe's forehead crinkled, then she leaned over and looked over the edge of the bed onto the floor. "Oh, yeah. Hey, there, Booger—what's up?"

The dog lay on the floor at her side of the bed. When their eyes met, his tail thumped happily against the carpet. She took a deep breath and held it while she leaned down and scratched Booger behind one ear. Then, looking at me, she exhaled and fanned her hand in front of her face. "Phew! He needs a walk."

"I took him out two hours ago," I said. "He can wait."

"He'll gas us to death in the meantime." She pulled the covers up around her neck. "What are you going to do with him, any-way? Take him to a shelter?"

"Who'd adopt him?" I said. "Look at him. They'd euthanize him within days. I can't let that happen."

"Now you sound like K.O."

"I've always loved animals, but I've never taken care of one before. And I'm sure as hell not going to send Booger off to a certain death."

"So you're going to keep him?"

"Unless I can palm him off on somebody, I don't have any other choice."

Booger managed to stand up on his hind legs and put his front paws on the edge of the bed, his tongue lolling out of the side of his mouth; he knew we were talking about him. Tobe stroked his head and neck again. "Poor old guy. He's no puppy, Milan."

I reached across Tobe and petted his neck myself. "I don't know how I'm going to live with a creature named Booger. Suppose he gets out by accident and I have to go looking for him. Imagine me walking down Cedar Road calling out 'Here, Booger.'"

Tobe laughed. "Change his name, then."

"He already knows what his name is."

"Give him a new name and say it a lot, like whenever you feed him or walk him—or just when you talk to him. It'll be nice having someone to talk to, even if he only farts back at you. Come up with something more creative."

"You're a smart detective. Why don't you name him?"

"Okay," she said slowly, "How about this one? Herbie."

"After Booger, anything would be an improvement. But Herbie?"

"It's a cop thing. A while back, a Lorain cop named Ric Broz found a pit bull—completely emaciated and badly injured—left to die in the front yard of an abandoned house. Whatever horrible had been done to that dog, he weighed a third of what he should, and his head was swollen so badly that both his eyes were shut. The cop took him to the shelter, and visited him every day while he was recuperating. He turned out to be very sweet and loving—pit bulls are, until they're trained not to be. The cop named the dog Herbie."

"Nice story," I said.

"Yeah, but then they found out Herbie had incurable brain cancer. So the cop took him home and treated him like king for as long as he had left—until he died in his arms." She shook her head. "Why not rename Booger Herbie—and make sure the rest of his life is better than the first part?"

I looked over at the dog's rather silly-looking face. "Hey, Herbie," I said. He still had his front paws on the bed, and he was smiling—actually smiling, and his tail was madly beating out a Buddy Rich tempo.

"I think he likes it," I said.

"Hoo-wah! That calls for more champagne!" She took the bottle from the nightstand and refilled our glasses. "Here's to Herbie, then. Welcome to *our* world."

We clinked glasses and drank. Then I rolled over toward Tobe. "I think," I said, "this calls for another celebration."

She put her champagne down and opened her arms for me. "I thought you'd never ask," she said.

This might have been one of our longer celebrations. Herbie, formerly Booger, padded around to my side of the bed, stretched out, and went to sleep.

And Herbie, it turned out, had more tact than I could ever have imagined possible for him. He didn't peek once!

AFTERWORD FROM DAN KENNEDY

It was a great privilege and great fun introducing Les Roberts, Milan, Tobe, K.O. and Carli to a sport I've loved my entire life, harness racing. I own horses competing in several states but most of them race here in Ohio, and I drive professionally myself in about two hundred races a year, almost entirely at Northfield Park in Northfield, Ohio. It's fair to say I'm a bona fide insider. As such, there are six things I'd like you to know:

First, most of the folks at tracks—the trainers, grooms or care-takers, and drivers—are honest, salt-of-the-earth, hard-working people with diverse backgrounds. Some have little education, some have M.B.A.s. Some are "track rats," while others have homes in the communities surrounding the tracks, and their spouses have civilian jobs, their kids attend your kids' schools, they worship next to you in your church. Such ordinary people are no fun to write about or read about. We do have our fair share of oddball and eccentric and distinctive characters, no more or less I think than in any other occupation or even large office, but none of the characters featured here are real. They're all fictional. There has also been some fictional license taken with the physical layout of a racetrack, its backside, its grandstand, and clubhouse, and its operations so every detail is not correct, but overall Les has given you the flavor of it all perfectly.

Second, there is *some* evil in every business and *some* cheating in every sport. The evil in ours is the people who do not care about their horses and do not treat them well. This is rare, it is frowned upon, it usually leads to being ostracized from a track's backside community, if not actually having their licenses sus-pended or revoked or being expelled and prohibited from racing. The cheating in our sport, as in most, centers around doping or fixing of outcomes. Neither is frequent. Neither is tolerated. Every racetrack, as well as every state racing commission, is zealous in preventing both kinds of cheating, and in punishing it if detected. I doubt there is any more of this—and there is quite possibly less—than goes on in professional football, basketball, baseball, cycling, even the Olympics. This book didn't bring in cheating or doping, but I am often asked about it. The fixed race is mostly a thing of fiction or a figment of the imagination of a disgruntled bettor. There is considerable anti-doping testing to safeguard the horses' health and to protect the integrity of the sport for all of us competing in it and for the bettors.

Third, the horses themselves have jobs, just as you and I do, and I do not think that is a bad thing at all. They are noble equine athletes. Conditioned since childhood to be competitive performers, most actually want to race, have intelligence about what they do, and know when they have done well. They do not have to be forced to race. Most also want to go out for their daily exercise, and many nicker to lobby to be first out of the barn in the morning. They are, in a sense, as K.O. put it, prisoners—but they also have, by and large, pretty good lives. A standardbred, the breed of harness racing, is a stronger, more durable horse than are thoroughbreds. Our horses will race as often as weekly, year-round here in Ohio, usually with several week- to two-week-long vacations a year, out to pastures. At the track, they get varied exercise, jogging on the track, walking or jogging on the exercise wheel in which Milan found himself, or turned loose to play and run about as they please in turn-out corrals. They are well fed and well cared for. We do not keep them up all hours of the night smoking, drinking, and playing poker, nor eating junk food! Virtually all the people working with them intimately genuinely love them and are good friends to them. The pay for these jobs is low, so it is a labor of love for most. For an owner like me, having the stable of twenty to twenty-five of them that I do is, I think, akin to a much wealthier man's owning of a pro sports team. My athletes are equine, not human, but the thrill and pride are comparable.

Fourth, these horses also get good retirements. Not always. There are economic pressures on owners—and most owners are not rich people, but are schoolteachers, police officers, small business owners, and farmers who love the sport. But increasingly, owners are choosing to place their horses in good second careers and retirement homes, notably through the non-profit adoption organizations our industry supports, like New Vocations. I urge you to visit www.HorseAdoptions.com. You'll be fascinated by all the different new vocations retired racehorses fulfill. By the way, they make outstanding pleasure-riding and trail-riding horses, so if you're in the market for one, please consider adopting one of ours.

Fifth, harness racing delivers very significant, positive economic impact to the communities in which racetracks are located and to the state as a whole. Its roots are agricultural, and it supports a great deal of farming, as well as our county fair network in Ohio. For many, the breeding farm, the growing of hay, the harness racing operation itself is a multi-generational family business. Blacksmiths and veterinarians are employed. Many young people have summer vacation and weekend jobs around these horses, and learn a work ethic and respect for animals in this environment. A racetrack is very different from a casino. Much of its money stays in its community and in its state, and it supports a great diversity of employment and farm and property ownership, all part of the local and state tax bases. It is all about people and their horses, not cold, robotic machines.

Finally, harness racing is an iconic born-in-America sport with a rich tradition, and it is a great entertainment product. An evening with family or friends at the races is a novel and exciting replacement for yet another dinner 'n' movie. Try it. You may find yourself fascinated by the horses, the people, the pageantry, the competition. It's accessible: you can stand right at the rail, nearly close enough to touch the horses as they go by, or you can relax over dinner in the glass-enclosed clubhouse. You don't need to be a diehard gambler or know the in's and out's of handicapping to enjoy racing, or to go in with friends and wager a few dollars, choosing by the horse's name, as Milan did, or color, or the look he gives you in the post parade. However, it's also no more difficult to learn to read the racing program than it is to learn to play a card game. For more information, please visit the United States

Trotting Association's Web site at www.USTA.com, or check out our sport's magazine, *Hoof Beats*, on Facebook, at facebook.com/hoofbeatsmagzine. If you're a Clevelander like Les, Milan and friends, and me, check out NorthfieldPark the track where I race. We race year 'round, regardless of the weather. If you're ever in the Goshen, New York, area, visit The Harness Racing Museum and Hall of Fame.

If you enjoyed Milan's latest adventure with harness racing as its background, I hope it will inspire an interest in our sport.

ACKNOWLEDGMENTS

This novel, it shouldn't surprise you, is fiction. I didn't violate fact, but I did twist it around a bit so it would fit. However, the story about Officer Ric Broz and Herbie the Pit Bull is absolutely true.

I couldn't possibly have written this book without the help, support, and contributions of Dan S. Kennedy, who has *forgotten* more than I'll ever know about harness racing. I thank him, too, for my many trips to the track, taking notes, teaching me what things are like there, front and back—and being able to actually play with and feed carrots to those beautiful, loving horses.

My thanks to Bari Rubin and Trudy Brandenburg, both of whom frittered away their youths working as grooms at harness racing tracks, and filled me in more about what happens backside where the customers are never invited.

My appreciation, as always, to Dr. Milan Yakovich and to Diana Yakovich Montagino.

And as always, to Holly Albin, who's the real reason I bother waking up each morning.

—Les Roberts

ABOUT LES ROBERTS

Les Roberts is the author of 17 mystery novels featuring Cleveland detective Milan Jacovich, as well as 11 other books. The past president of both the Private Eye Writers of America and the American Crime Writer's League, he came to mystery writing after a 24-year career in Hollywood. He was the first producer and head writer of the *Hollywood Squares* and wrote for *The Andy Griffith Show*, *The Jackie Gleason Show*, and *The Man from U.N.C.L.E.*, among others. He has been a professional actor, a singer, a jazz musician, a teacher, and a film critic. In 2003 he received the Sherwood Anderson Literary Award. A native of Chicago, he now lives in Northeast Ohio.

ABOUT DAN KENNEDY

Dan is predominately a strategic business and marketing advisor, consultant, professional speaker, and author of more than twenty business books (www.NoBSBooks.com). He was born, raised, and lives in the Cleveland area, and local businesspeople may well have seen him speak at large seminar events held in Gund Arena. Once, he also competed in a chariot race down Euclid Avenue, announced by John Lanigan. His love of harness racing began in his youth.